When Wallflowers Die

When Wallflowers Die

A Phoebe Siegel Mystery

Sandra West Prowell

Walker and Company
New York

First published in the United States of America in 1996
by Walker Publishing Company, Inc.

Published simultaneously in Canada by Thomas Allen & Son Canada, Limited, Markham, Ontario

ISBN 0-8027-3254-2

Printed in the United States of America

*This one's for
Bruce,
who wisely married a
Wallflower.
He kept me in a warm place
on the sunny side of the house
and watched me bloom.
We won't talk about the fertilizer.*

When Wallflowers Die

1

Memories slumber in dark recesses. We bury them in the coffins of our minds and think of them no more until a sound, a smell, a word resurrects them and uncovers them to the light. They live again. Embarrassment turns to laughter, grief to solace. But murder? Murder remembered tortures and haunts and bruises the soul. It lives a parallel life to disconnected events and people that somehow pick up the stench.

No one knew what Ellen Dahl Maitland, the lone heiress of one of the largest fortunes in Montana, was thinking in the early-morning hours of June 1, back in 1968, but they pieced together some of what she did. Ellen hadn't gone to bed as early as she usually did, but instead curled up in a chair with a copy of Rosemary's Baby *she had checked out of Parmly Library two days before. She read well past midnight. At some point in the wee hours of the morning she placed a brass owl bookmark ten pages from the end, walked upstairs, drew a bath, and soaked there for the next two hours.*

Sometime after that, she sat down on the stool in front of her mahogany dressing table and pulled a pair of black-net nylons up her legs and attached them to the snaps hanging from her black garter belt. She was not wearing panties. A long-sleeved bolero jacket of see-through red nylon completed the ensemble. Last, she donned a full-length London Fog raincoat. There was no rain in the forecast.

Ellen left the house around five-thirty A.M., *spoke briefly with the paperboy, backed her 1968 red MG out of the garage, and drove off. Her whereabouts until two-twenty that afternoon are undeter-*

*mined, but it was then that she showed up at the Bunk House Motel,
a sleazy pay-and-lay off I-90 and Twenty-seventh Street South. In
what passed for an office, and supposedly checking in alone, she
placed twenty-one dollars on the counter; a room was hers for three
hours. The clerk, Gummy, remembered her recoiling as she breathed
in the scent of stale booze and cigarettes. In his statement he de-
scribed her as a classy bitch. He asked no questions. Curiosity was
not a job requirement.*

At three P.M. on that day in June, I was unwillingly dropped off at a
friend's house a couple of blocks east of South Park. Dressed in a
poufy, blue satin implement of medieval torture known as a party
dress, I joined a group of my preadolescent peers in Tiffany Barber's
backyard to celebrate her birthday.

I'd been bought off: Wear the dress, attend the party, and when
the party ended my father would pick me up, take me home to
change clothes, and then head to the banks of the Yellowstone River
for a couple of hours of fishing. Just the two of us. Those times were
rare and I cherished them. The lives of cops encroach on their lives
as husbands and fathers, wives and mothers.

By four o'clock I had weathered the ceremonious ripping-open-
of-the-packages as the blond, sausage-curled, porcine-faced Tiffany
sneered at each present and tossed it casually aside, gorged myself
on bad cake and melting ice cream, and fended off a kiss-attack
from Jimmy Canero with a well-placed kick to the crotch. I mean, I
really had a crush on this guy and had to let him know. I'm sure he
thought of that as he writhed on the ground.

Everyone was full of anticipation. The piñata that hung from a
cottonwood limb was begging to be destroyed. Mrs. Barber called
us together and laid down the law: sticks could only be swung overhead. Anyone violating this rule would be disarmed. With blindfolds
in place, sticks clutched in a two-handed grip, we went to work.

*The image of Ellen Dahl Maitland's assailant must have been mir-
rored in her eyes just before the first blow from an undetermined
weapon fell across her face with a rage strong enough to fracture*

her right orbital socket and explode her eye. Carpenters working on the roof at the opposite end of the motel from where Ellen's face and skull were being rendered to a mass of bone fragments, torn tissue, and blood, heard nothing, saw nothing. The sounds of their Skil saws and hammers drowned out whatever screams there might have been.

We peaked in a frenzy within seconds. One after another our blows made contact with a hollow *thwack*. I took my best shot at the piñata, lodging my stick inside it. My hand vibrated as someone else brought their weapon down on mine. The stinging sensation it caused coursed through my palm. I tugged at my stick, trying to free it, and lifted the blindfold just as the donkey erupted, spilling its contents onto the ground. The deed was done.

The injuries had been too numerous and too savage and too anatomically traumatic to leave any semblance of her plain, haunting beauty. Ellen Maitland's face was obliterated, the damage so thorough it was impossible to determine the weapon or the number of blows she had received.

By five P.M. the party was breaking up. I'd been sitting curbside for what seemed like a long time when sirens cut through the still summer air one block west and shrieked south toward the Interstate. A half hour later my mother showed up. The only explanation I got was that Dad had been called into work.

It was a strange week at my house. We saw very little of my dad. There were hushed late-night conversations between him and Mother as she brought his saved dinner from the oven and sat with him while he ate. I remember catching her crying one afternoon and asking her what was wrong. She mumbled something into her handkerchief and waved me away with her hand. I was just young enough and selfish enough to resent anything that took my father's attention away from me and brought my mother to tears.

It wasn't a hard week to remember. Five days after Ellen Maitland died in a love-for-sale motel, Sirhan Sirhan shot and killed

Bobby Kennedy at the Ambassador in L.A. The front page of *The Billings Gazette* dedicated itself to national mourning and relegated a local tragedy to the back of the paper.

Now, twenty-seven years past that June day, on a biting winter's night, my telephone rang, and as soon as I answered it, Ellen Maitland reached out from the grave and put a stranglehold on my life.

The call came at the same time I was anticipating that my clogged sinuses were going to blow off the front of my face. I'd had my shot of NyQuil and was bundled on the couch watching the sing-along version of *Grease,* doing my best to sing along.

"Ms. Siegel?"

"Speaking."

"This is Bob Maitland."

"Okay."

There was a pause. "Do you know who I am?"

"Of course, Mr. Maitland . . ."

"Bob, please."

"I know who you are, Bob." Who the hell didn't know who he was; the golden boy of the state Republicans, and only the most popular political figure in Montana since Mike Mansfield. Rumor had it that he was about to announce his run for governor. "What can I do for you?"

"We need to talk. I had a conversation with a friend of yours, Maggie Mason. She encouraged me to call you."

"Okay."

"Are you all right? You sound a little . . ."

"If I sound like I'm dying, Bob," I said and emphasized his name, "that's because I *am* dying. I have a combination of Ebola and hantavirus and probably don't have more than a few hours to live."

I could hear him chuckle. "Bad stuff. I had it a while back. It took me a long time to shake it."

"That's comforting. What's on your mind?"

"Maggie said you're about the best investigator around. Are you up for a little business?"

"Depends on what it is."

"I see no problem with that. Would it be possible to meet at my home?"

"Why not? Let's make it before noon."

"Eleven tomorrow morning?"

"Sure. Directions?" I wrote them down as he gave them. "Great. Can you give me an idea of what this is about? I should tell you up-front that I don't do child-custody cases, bedroom windows, personal injury, or—"

"My wife was murdered twenty-seven years ago. It remains unsolved."

"After twenty-seven years?"

"The book is never closed on a murder case."

"I'm aware of that. Where's law enforcement in all this?"

"After this much time, who's interested? Those initially involved stayed with it for a long, long time. Some retired, some just gave up. Now and then on the anniversary of her murder or if some hotshot journalist does an article on unsolved crimes in the state, something'll show up in the paper. That could change."

"How so?" I tilted my head to the left to see if I could give my right sinus some relief. It didn't work.

"Can I be frank with you?"

I was silent. As soon as prospective clients say words to that effect, I know I'll get partial truths.

"I was questioned at length, and, to some, I'm still a suspect. I was never charged, but many people read guilt into the fact that I had retained an attorney. Now I find myself with the same problem I had back then."

"Which is?"

"Let's just say there are some creative conversations taking place among my political enemies. The potential spins that could be created . . . well, they're overpowering."

"Sounds like it."

"In a nutshell, they have every intention of digging this up if and when I announce my candidacy for governor. But let's save it until tomorrow. You sound like you could use a good night's sleep. Eleven, then?"

"I'll be there."

I hung up and immediately dialed Maggie Mason.

"Maggie," I said after she answered. "Bob Maitland called."

"Oh good, I was hoping he would. You sound like shit."

"I feel like shit. Tell me about this guy."

"Bobby?"

"You call him Bobby? Just how well do you know him and in what sense?"

"Let's see, I know he has a mole on his ass and his two most favorite words are 'oh baby' said in rapid succession. Bobby and I had a thing a few years back. No big deal. He's one of the good guys. We need him, Phoebe. We need him as governor. I'm behind him all the way, and you know I loathe those political pricks. Besides, maybe I'll write a kiss-and-tell book and make my fortune."

"Don't hold back." I blew my nose and immediately went into a coughing spasm. "You are one sick woman, Mason."

"Me? Listen to you. God, are you taking anything for that?"

"If it can be swallowed or inhaled it's sitting right in front of me. Tell me more."

"Do you remember the murder? It happened in 'sixty-eight."

"No, I don't. Fill me in."

"I know nothing. Wait, I take that back, I've heard fragments. Something to the effect that he had been married and was widowed early on, but nothing substantial. We dated for seven or eight months, and it wasn't until near the end of that time that he told me about her. I was shocked to find out she was Rosella Dahl's daughter."

"Ellen Dahl Maitland, daughter of the dragon lady. Damn, I do remember that."

"Dragon lady? What the hell are you talking about? Are you running a fever or something?"

"Dahl's House. That Gothic structure down on Division Street. The trip when I was a kid running around town on Halloween was to make a stop at Dahl's House. It was a spooky place. Complete with its own crone."

"You're regressing, Siegel. I'd really like to stay on here and relive your childhood with you, but I've got a brief to finish. Hear Bob out and let me know how it goes. I owe you one."

"If I live to see the sun come up, I'll do what I can."

"If I were you, I'd get to bed. You really do sound like hell."

"You realize this virus is virulent enough to travel through phone wires? Now you're infected. They're breeding inside you as we speak."

"At least someone's getting a little. Good night, Phoebe."

The line went dead.

The NyQuil was taking effect. I stretched out on the couch and pulled the blankets I had piled on top of me up under my chin. The amber glow from the fireplace licked the walls and shadow-danced around the room. Memories teased the fringes of my consciousness. I remembered the day: Tiffany Barber and Jimmy Canero, the piñata, and how we bludgeoned it over and over again. Our frenzy abated, we turned and walked away. So, apparently, had Ellen Maitland's killer.

2

"**P**hoebe. Phoebe, honey."
Someone's hand rested on my shoulder, pushing it gently up and down on the couch.
"Wake up. You had us worried."

"Am I dead?" My tongue was stuck to the roof of my mouth.

Another voice drifted in. "Oh, for Christ's sake. You've only got a head cold. How bad can it be?"

I struggled to open my eyes. Out-of-focus images floated around me. My mother placed her hand on my forehead.

"She does feel warm, Kehly."

"Look what she's got on. Flannel pajamas, a sweater, and fifty pounds of blankets. Who wouldn't be?" Kehly looked down at me and shook her head. "Get up, Fee. Mom's been calling you all morning. She was convinced we'd find you in a coma on the floor."

"Your compassion is overwhelming. What time is it?"

"Nine o'clock."

"Shit." I pulled myself to a sitting position and rested my head in my hands. "I've got a meeting with someone at eleven." I lifted my head and looked at my inquisitors. "How the hell do you two figure that nine o'clock is *all morning*?"

Neither of them answered.

"Get up now and take a shower. While I pick up around here, Kehly can fix you something to eat."

"I don't think so. She's more than capable of cooking for herself."

"Aren't you whining in an octave higher than usual? I don't want any breakfast, Mom. I'll grab some orange juice."

"See? She's just a today kind of independent woman. Let's go."
Kehly started to leave the room.

"Just hold on there," Mom said as she glared at her youngest
daughter. "I said I'd tidy up, and I will. You know how much better
you feel in a clean house."

"Clean house? Neither of us will live that long, Mother."

"God, I'm glad you stopped by, Kehly. I'm feeling better already."
I stood and headed for the stairs. "I'm going to take that shower
now."

"God, if I had a camera I could make a fortune off just one picture." Kehly leaned against the doorjamb and laughed.

I didn't. Anyone who's had a Montana cold knows they can pinpoint the exact time the first symptoms appeared and invaded every
nook and cranny of their body, and when death was imminent. I've
never done illness well. I take it personally; it becomes me against
them. This time I was losing the battle.

Three days on my back, sleeping sporadically and channel surfing
through the infomercials in the middle of the night, did little for my
attitude. When I wrote down the one-eight-hundred numbers for
hair add-ons and a painted plate portraying Elvis as Jesus, I knew I
was terminal. So I turned to over-the-counter drugs that kept my
mouth dry and the pain to a minimum.

I avoided the mirror in the bathroom as I peeled off the sweaty
nightgown and sweater and got into the shower. The jetting hot
water pulsating on my body wasn't as good as sex but damn close.
The knots in my muscles slowly untied and slipped down the drain.
The steam was doing wonders for my sinuses. I stayed in until the
water temperature cooled.

By the time I got dressed and downstairs again, coffee had been
made, dishes had been done. A plate of buttered toast and a tall
glass of orange juice was waiting for me.

"You didn't have to do this, Mom."

"Of course I did. I didn't come out in this weather for my health."
She dried another plate, one of several in the drainer, and turned
back to her work. "What's this meeting you have?"

"A prospective client." I sat down and started eating a piece of
toast.

"And who might that be?"

"You know I can't talk about that."

"Remember the ground rules, Phoebe." Kehly leaned against the counter, folded her arms over her chest, and stared me down. "You don't know me. We are not in any way, shape, or form related to each other. You got that?"

One isolated incident a couple of years back when I was working a case, and she couldn't let go of it. Granted, she could have died, but instead of kicking a rock off the path and going on, she gathers the damn things up and carries them with her. I suspect that is why she has become the self-help queen of Billings; she needs to carry the weight. It keeps her in a constant state of penance.

"How's the weather?" I broke the stare and looked toward my mother. "Still snowing?"

"Nope. It's let up for a while. But Lord, is it brisk."

"Then it must be below zero." I looked at Kehly and raised my eyebrows.

"Five below, to be exact, and there's more snow in the forecast. I guess you could say it's brisk out. Yeah. Brisk is good."

Kehly and I smiled at each other. There are numerous techniques people use to survive a Montana winter. Our mother's was to admit to nothing more formidable than brisk when it came to temperature. Windchill meant nothing to her. Only brisk counted.

Raising the glass of orange juice to my mouth, I watched her over the rim as she took all of the flatware out of the utensil drawer and began sorting it. A twinge of sadness twisted inside me. She had no one to take care of anymore; only her own clothes to launder and fold, meals cooked for one. It bothered me.

"Hey, Kehly. Now that Rudy is history, why don't you consider moving home?"

"Pardon me?"

"Move in with Mom. You could save some money, and—"

"Rudy is not history, Phoebe. Our living situation has just changed. We're in transition. I have intimacy problems I'm dealing with, so we've joined an intimacy group."

"Let me get this straight. You guys still have a thing, but you're not living together."

"I don't think this is appropriate—" Kehly said as she nodded her head sideways toward her mother.

Not oblivious, but unwilling to admit that Kehly would live with a man out of wedlock, Mother started humming.

Kehly, visibly pissed, said, "Why don't you move home?"

"My inner child doesn't want to."

"Who was it you said you were meeting, dear?" Mother asked in an obvious attempt to intervene.

"I didn't."

Kehly reached for the receiver on the kitchen wall before the phone finished ringing the first time and said hello.

"No, this is her sister. Who's calling?"

She was quiet for about thirty seconds. "Hold on, I'll see if she's taking calls."

I shook my head and stood up. She smirked, covered the mouth-piece with her hand. "It's soon-to-be governor Bob Maitland. He wants to meet you here at eleven instead of at his house."

"Give me the damn phone." I grabbed it from her and stretched the cord around the doorjamb into the living room.

"Mr. Maitland?"

"How are you feeling?" he asked. "You sounded a little rough last night."

"Better, thanks. What's up?"

"This may sound somewhat trivial, but it may be a better idea if we meet somewhere other than my home. I've been wrestling with this issue all night. If the press got hold of my meeting with you— well, I'm not ready for that yet."

"Yet? Maybe we should establish some ground rules. I won't work under the scrutiny of the press."

"You have my word that I'll do everything within my power to prevent that from arising."

I looked around the edge of the doorjamb and saw my mother and sister listening to the conversation in dead silence. When they saw me, both turned and busied themselves at the counter.

"I'll see you here around eleven. Do you know where I live?"

"Maggie said you were in the old banker's house down by the river."

"That was one of its least illustrious phases, but yes, that's where I am."

"See you in a while."

I hung up the phone and leaned against the wall. "Are you my secretary or something, Kehly?"

"Just trying to help the sick and infirm."

"Like hell. Don't do that again. Okay?"

"Fine. I'm out of here. Come on, Mom."

"Oh, quit it, you two. We need to help Phoebe pick this place up. Look at it, and she has Mr. Maitland coming over shortly."

"Mom, my work is confidential. I don't need this all over your neighborhood network."

She turned, a pained expression on her face. She didn't have to say a thing.

"I'm sorry, Mother. I feel like hell. That goes for you too, Kehly. I really do appreciate you guys coming over. Okay?"

No one said anything for a minute. Then Kehly opened her arms wide and grinned at me.

"Group hug?" She asked with her eyes stretched wide and a malicious grin on her face.

"Don't push." I tried not to laugh.

"Honey, do you know who Mr. Maitland is?"

"Yes, Mother. I do."

"Poor man. Poor, poor man. And Mrs. Dahl—" She hesitated and crossed herself. "She and Rose, both losing children like that."

"Rose? Rose who?" Kehly asked. "What children?"

"Rose Kennedy. Don't you remember? Her son Bobby was killed a few days after Mrs. Dahl's daughter was murdered." She dried her hands on a dish towel and sat down at the table across from me. "You were too young, Kehly. Mrs. Dahl's daughter was married to Mr. Maitland, and someone murdered her. That was back in nineteen sixty-eight. I'll never forget it. Two good, strong Catholic mothers burying their children. We held vigils for them both at the church."

"God, Mom, you sound like you were on a first-name basis with Bobby Kennedy's mother."

"I held her in high esteem, Kehly. Just like I did Mrs. Dahl."

"Then you knew Mrs. Dahl?" I asked.

"Me? Lord, no. But I knew her companion, Grace Driscoll. Grace and I are still members of the Foresters. We prepared many a luncheon for funerals, she and I did. Oh yes, I heard firsthand how Mrs. Dahl suffered. I heard firsthand about a lot of things."

"Daddy was on the force then, wasn't he?"

"Yes. He was. But he was only involved in the investigation for the first week or so. There was something else, something that came up, and he was pulled off it." She looked toward the ceiling. "They were so shorthanded back then, honey, they pulled them off cases and handed them other ones quicker than they could catch their breath. But I think it was because they knew who did it, although your father was never sure. Let me think about it some more."

"It doesn't matter. Forget it."

"Well, it matters to me. This sounds like good stuff. Why does Maitland need a private investigator?"

"I don't know, Kehly. I haven't talked to him yet."

"When will you be talking to him?" Mother asked.

I wrinkled my forehead and looked at her.

"You're right. You're right. I just wish to God you would get a real job."

"Like mine." Kehly elbowed me in the shoulder.

"I worried about your father and your brothers constantly. With the exception of Michael, that is."

"And they say nothing's forever," I mumbled into the glass of orange juice.

"What was that, dear?"

"Nothing. Listen, he's going to show up in a while, and it would be better if, uh—"

"I understand. Say no more. Will you come by later?"

"Sure, Mom. Thanks, both of you."

I walked them to the door and opened it. The arctic air blasted me in the face.

"Stay off the NyQuil, Fee. You could get into the habit."

"When I start pouring it over ice, I'll worry."

                    *   *   *

It had been a year since I caved in, decided to cruise the information highway, and went out and bought myself a computer. For the first six months I was nothing more than roadkill. Then I got the hang of it and hooked up with some information brokers nationwide. Anything from a shoe size to an in-depth background check on any residence and seven of the neighbors was available. The wave of the future had rolled in. Privacy in the United States was fast becoming obsolete. In most instances same-day reports were available over the modem or through the fax. Separation had fewer degrees than a Montana winter.

I debated running a check on Maitland but decided to wait until after I had talked with him. For all I knew, this guy was some grief freak, or worse. Maggie wasn't the best judge of men, particularly ones she let into her life. But in any initial interview I needed to be open. No amount of technology will ever replace your gut instincts.

3

*P*olitics in Montana is a simple concept and has been since the days the vigilantes ruled; throw some shit, see what sticks, and follow the smell with the tenacity of a bloodhound. A rope thrown over a limb with a noose on the end may be a thing of the past, but it's still a threat on the lips of the Freemen, self-styled guardians of the Great Plains. Now, instead of a .45 on the hip, those who want to rule shoot off their mouths. In many ways, it's just as deadly.

Old King Coal still rules the eastern part of the state, while the legendary copper kings of Butte, gone but not forgotten, left a legacy of two-fisted politicking that has yet to die. The political seat of Montana is in the west, where a sheepman's son became senator and the son of an immigrant who spoke broken English moved into the governor's mansion.

Our politicians, if nothing else, are stories in themselves. Two in our illustrious past, both governors, left their own historical footprints on Montana's soil. The first territorial governor was stabbed and thrown off a steamboat in Fort Benton, never to be seen again. No one looked too hard, too long, to determine why or who. Another, admittedly in a testosterone storm, was snared in a bust on a cathouse in New Orleans. No big deal. But when he proclaimed publicly, "You can't arrest me, I'm the governor of Montana," the sun set on his political future.

I don't like politics, nor do I like politicians. Law enforcement has a sharp, cynical edge honed on broken promises and a lack of vision—hindsight and foresight and everything in between—from the state legislature. The face of law enforcement in the state is changing, and not for the better. Violent crimes take precedence. The rest—rubber checks, white-collar crime, and negligent fathers on the run from child-support payments—are shoved to the bottom of the list. Victims of petty vandalism and stolen bikes can scrap any thought of the benevolent boys in blue showing up at their doors. It's as close to being a thing of the past as you can get.

Hence, Maitland. The great hope of law enforcement. I'd watched him interviewed on television a few times and was duly impressed with his call for stiffer laws and more cops on the street, but I don't jump on anyone's bandwagon. I'm just not a team player.

I watched him through the curtains as he pulled up the driveway and got out of his car. When I opened the door, he looked up. He was a good-looking silver-haired guy with a big media smile that flashed a set of too-white teeth.

"I've got some things in the car I want you to have," he yelled through the whiteness of his breath that hung on the cold air.

I held the door open as he walked in, a stack of folders piled in a box cradled in his arms. His leather-gloved right hand found its way out from under the box. I shook it.

"It's good to meet you, Phoebe. Where can I put these?"

"Follow me. My office is this way." I led him down the hall toward what had once been the library.

All I could think of was the mole on his ass and Maggie.

He placed the boxes on the floor, removed his coat, and sat down in the chair in front of my desk. I seated myself behind it.

"You've done a lot with this place. New porch?"

"As a matter of fact, it is. I had it built last year. You seem to know this house."

"I was interested in it the last time it was on the market. I didn't realize you were the one that jumped on it first. I've got some pictures you might be interested in that my mother-in-law gave me. I believe they were taken during the construction. Interested?"

"Definitely. I've got the original deed but not much else."

"I've always been interested in these old places. You're living in history every day. It must be nice."

"I like it." I wasn't very good at I like your shirt, do you like mine? "So what can I do for you, Bob?"

He sighed, resituated himself in the chair, and looked down at the floor. "This is tougher than I thought it would be. Where do I start?"

"Any place you're comfortable."

"I've decided to announce my candidacy, and I've got excess baggage that needs to be cleared up, or at least neutralized."

"Twenty-seven years is a real stretch."

"Yes, it is."

"Why don't you go back twenty-seven years and give me some background?"

"I was young. Ambitious. Just out of law school in Missoula and ended up down here, at the Dahl law firm." He shook his head and looked toward the window. "God, I was so sure of myself. What a break. Old man Dahl had been dead a long time, but the firm was thriving. They were looking for a younger man that could pull in business from people born in this century. I jumped at it."

"Sounds like a dream come true."

"For a poor kid off the south side of Helena? You bet it was. I just didn't know what came with the job."

I stood. "Would you like some coffee?"

"Sure. That would be great."

"Follow me."

In the kitchen I took two cups from the cupboard, filled them with coffee, and handed him one.

"You really keep this place up. Must be hard with something this big."

Little did he know. "It's tough, but I stay on top of it." We walked back to the office.

"What came with the job?"

"Ellen. The daughter. I was there for a month and started getting invitations to dinner from Rosella Dahl. It was strange as hell. Just the old lady and me." He sipped his coffee and sat the cup on the desk. "I've got to let this cool awhile. Bad stomach." He patted his abdomen and continued. "Have you ever been inside Dahl's House?"

"No. I haven't."

"There's no word to describe it. The first time I stepped through those doors, I was so overwhelmed I couldn't speak. It didn't help that Rosella watched my every reaction like a hawk watches a rabbit. I was in awe of my surroundings, and more so, I was in awe of her. Six months later I was married to Ellen."

"Short engagement."

"Too short. Christ, what a mistake. Disastrous for both of us."

"And the marriage stayed intact until—"

"I'm not sure it was ever intact, but we stayed together until Ellen's murder."

"How long had you been married?"

"It would have been two years that coming September." He stood and walked to the window. "Two years," he repeated softly.

He turned, leaned against the sill, his hands in his pockets, and shook his head. "Twenty-seven years gives you a lot of time to think and to come to terms with your life. It's not always pleasant."

"How did you find out something had happened to her?"

"Two officers came to the house around seven, seven-thirty that night. I'd been at the office finishing up some prep work for a case I had that started the next morning. It was probably six-thirty when I got home. I was upstairs in our apartment." He stopped and placed his hand in front of him in the air. "It's not really an apartment, but that's how they always referred to the second-floor area. There are several oversize bedrooms that open onto a larger main room. One of the bedrooms was ours."

He walked to the chair and sat down again. A tiredness washed over his face.

"Get back to the detectives."

"I heard Grace, one of Rosella's employees, screaming my name. I thought something had happened to Rosella. She'd been out of sorts that past week, and I really thought that was why Grace sounded so hysterical. When I got downstairs there were two plainclothes detectives. Ellen's MG had been found parked on a side street a couple of blocks from the Bunk House Motel."

"That's all?" I had instinctively pulled a pad in front of me and started jotting some notes for myself.

"You really don't need to take notes, I have—"

"This is for my own reference. What happened next?"

"They said they had found a body, a woman's body, at the Bunk House. The first thought that hit me was that someone stole the MG. They asked me if my wife was at home."

"And she wasn't."

"No. I was so shook I looked at Grace, and she said Ellen hadn't been home all day. That's when they asked me to come with them and take a look at this woman."

"Did you go with them?"

"Yes. But not before I called a friend of mine, an attorney."

I tapped the pencil on the table and watched him.

"Go ahead and ask. Why did I think I needed an attorney? Instinct. Fear. Who the hell knows? Like I said, I've had twenty-seven years to come to terms with all of this. It was a dumb, highly incriminating move."

He was right. "Who was this attorney?"

"Dave Gordon."

"Judge Dave Gordon?" I asked incredulously. Gordon was a district judge known for having a bad attitude, no heart, and cow crap, often odiferous, on the cowboy boots he wore under his robe in the courtroom.

"One and the same. There was a bunch of us that hung out in those days, plotting our futures and sowing our oats. Dave wanted to make enough money with the firm he was with to open and fund a freebie law clinic. He ended up on the bench and raising cattle on the side. Funny how life takes you in other directions."

"Why don't you keep going."

"Dave came to the house immediately. We followed the detectives in Dave's car. There was a crowd: the paper, a couple of TV stations, everybody pushing toward that room. They prepared me before they took me in"—Maitland stood and walked back to the window—"but nothing anyone could have said would have prepared me for what I saw. I didn't recognize her. There was no face."

I didn't push. He appeared genuinely disturbed by the memory. When he turned toward me, he had tears in his eyes.

"Her face was unrecognizable. Then I saw the raincoat on the bed, and I knew it was her. One of the detectives stepped past me and raised her left hand. That wedding ring looked as big as a house. It was all I could see. I don't remember much after that."

"You said there was a suspect."

"There was a crew working at the motel that whole day. Something to do with the roof. They brought them all in for questioning, but there was this young guy who had taken a late lunch break. Said he had an appointment, but it didn't check out."

Maitland paced back and forth from the window to the front of my desk, where he would stop for a moment, look at me intensely, and then continue pacing.

"Was there an arrest?"

"They didn't really have anything to hold him on. Finally, that Friday, they picked him up for outstanding traffic tickets and figured he'd have to sit it out for the weekend. He bonded out that night and didn't make his court appearance Monday morning. He was gone. The guy disappeared like he never existed. They had no leads as to his whereabouts, and they hit a wall with his family. Someone came up with the bright idea that he was probably dead because he saw the real killer leaving the motel. That's when the DA's office focused on me. When all was said and done, there wasn't enough to hold me over for trial. That's how they left it."

I watched him for a long time as he stood, his back to me, and stared out the window. Neither of us spoke. Only when I started tapping my pencil on the desk again did he turn.

"That leaves one big question." I leaned back in my chair and watched his face.

"Ask it."

"What was there, Bob? Why you?"

A twitch, barely discernible, contracted the muscle beneath his right eye. For a long time he said nothing. "This isn't about me. It's about Joey Marino. I want you to find him, or at the very least find out if he's dead or alive." He said each word precisely, slowly. "What information I have is in those files. I'll open every door I can for you."

I continued staring at him. The energy in the room changed. I wasn't sure I liked it.

"Joey Marino," he repeated. "That's who you're after. Not me. Him. Are you interested or not?"

Good question. "Let me look over this stuff, and I'll let you know in a couple of days."

"Fair enough," he said as he visibly relaxed.

For some reason, I didn't.

4

I'd been selective about the cases I was willing to commit to. When you rub up against or jump into the middle of someone else's life, you end up dealing with the sludge of human misery. Some of it sticks. Investigators get dirty. To maintain a balance you have to protect yourself, keep your edge, form no opinions until you have all the facts. Problem was, I was already forming an opinion about Bob Maitland. One little statement threw me, turned me off. He had referred to his wife, murdered wife, as *"Ellen, the daughter."*

I picked up the box he had brought in with him and piled the folders on my desk as I mulled it over. Why, after this long, could the memory of Ellen Dahl Maitland bring tears to his eyes but miss the mark on what came from between his lips?

I opened the first file and looked into the face of a younger Bob Maitland, his face frozen in grief, his lips formed in a silent *no* that screamed off the page. Disembodied hands, product of a poor crop job, clutched both of Maitland's shoulders as he strained forward. The headline read:

ELLEN DAHL MAITLAND FOUND BRUTALLY SLAIN IN SOUTHSIDE MOTEL

It was enough to start the most pious of tongues wagging with speculation. The Dahl name placed in a headline with a southside motel was scandal at its best. The meat of the article was lean on details; her body was found, identified by Maitland, no further details available, and Rosella Dahl was in seclusion.

Other photos, neatly clipped and dated in pen, showed the motel, the Dahl mansion, the chief of police fending off the press in front of the courthouse, the victim. I had no idea what the murder statistics were back in 1968, but this particular murder must have rocked the state. I scanned my memory for what I knew of the Dahl family and found very little. The house was another story.

Everyone in town knew it had been designed by the same architect that designed the Dakota apartment building and the Plaza Hotel in New York City. Any Billings tour guide knew the name Henry James Hardenbergh. It was a small sidebar in Montana's history that spoke of better days and separated the old money from the new. I opened the next file. A full-page spread, folded neatly in quarters, gave a history of the Dahl family.

Willard Dahl, a rounder with an eye for the women, won the house in a poker game shortly after it was built. A cattleman who never spent a night on the plains, he lived long enough to spawn a son, Willard II, and leave a widow in the driver's seat of the Dahl fortune. Willard II was sent out of state to schools in the East, came home an attorney with a proper Bostonian wife on his arm, and laid claim to the family legacy. The Dahl law firm was founded. When Willard III was but a babe in arms, Willard II decided to blow a clot in his brain and become the most celebrated coitus interruptus in Billings's brothel history. The press must have loved it. Willard III eventually found his way into the arms of an inferior (his mother refused to attend the wedding) by the name of Rosella Moore. He moved his new bride into Dahl's House the same day Mother Dahl moved into the carriage house.

There were more moves to come. Willard moved into the great beyond, victim of a gun-cleaning accident; there was some speculation that had he not been trying to clean the barrel of a loaded twelve-gauge shotgun with his tongue, he would have lived to see his daughter Ellen grow to womanhood. Oddly, Mother Dahl moved from the carriage house back into the big house the day of Willard's funeral. It ended there.

The article went on to list the acts of charity with which Rosella anointed the less fortunate on every major holiday. She furnished three different parks in Billings with play equipment, set up several different scholarships for promising but indigent high school students through the years, and refused to give interviews. Mother Dahl eventually died of natural causes and moved permanently out of the house.

I moved on to the next file. Staring up at me, captured for an eternity in an eight-by-ten black-and-white photo, was Ellen Dahl Maitland. It took me off guard. Her lackluster eyes focused on mine. She was hauntingly plain, with features that were unremarkable in every sense of the word. Her straight, obviously dark, long hair framed her face. Her bangs were cut straight across and hung low enough to conceal her eyebrows. She wasn't homely, she wasn't pretty. She just *was*. She wasn't smiling, nor was she frowning. She just *was*. It was the look of the vanquished, the look of someone who long ago bowed before life and said, "Do with me what you will," and life had taken her up on it.

Now she *wasn't*. But she had me. It may have been the only time she had anyone.

You can't get along without friends in this business. They're not the type of friends who will bring a bad tuna casserole to a potluck, and you end up choking it down anyway. These are get-it-done friends, favor friends: a fence who works out of his garage, a cop with a soft spot, or a snitch like Dougie who keeps his ear to the asphalt so he can pick up a couple of bucks to support his habit.

The information doesn't have a price tag, but the habits do, and that's what you pay for. Dougie is a slimeball, but he's cheap. For the price of a double feature at the local porno movie house, where he can sit down front with his fly open, Dougie will tell you anything. Dougie's real worth is that he's pushing the seventy-year mark, and fifty of those years he's made it his business to know everything about anything, and who was involved. In his younger years he pimped a few girls and sold a little dope. When the sixties rolled in, Dougie's bankroll rolled out. Sex was there for the asking, and everyone and his brother was sharing, not selling, pot. Dougie, because of the geographics, would have known about the Maitland murder. When it was in business, the Bunk House would have been on his turf. I made a mental note to locate him at some point.

Right now, though, I needed more than newspaper clippings on the murders. I needed it all. That the book had been open on this one for nearly thirty years intrigued me. How did Ellen Maitland get from the best house in town to the Bunk House? What had happened? Who had happened?

I picked up the phone and dialed. It rang twice before someone answered.

"Kyle?"

"Hey. I thought you were sick."

"I am. Any traditional remedies you might know of?"

"Sweating."

"Forget it, I tried that. Remember?"

"There are other ways to sweat, Phoebe." I could hear him yawning.

"You don't sound up to it."

"There you go. Always teasing."

"I meant—"

"Uh-huh. Sure."

Kyle Old Wolf, Deputy Sheriff Kyle Old Wolf, without much effort, turned me into a giddy twelve-year-old schoolgirl. I hated it. Sort of. We'd known each other, without really knowing each other, for a good number of years. After my relationship with a local attorney had ended, I swore I wouldn't jump into another one—relationship, that is—and I hadn't. But Kyle? Kyle was a different story. To be around him put me off guard. We ended up spending a lot of platonic time together over the past year, and had even gone so far as to share a box of hot buttered popcorn at a movie.

The closest we had come to an intimate relationship was during that movie. Kyle had leaned over to whisper something to me, his lips grazed my ear, and the warmth from his breath paralyzed me with sensations that ran the length of my body and tied my stomach in a knot. I stuffed my mouth full of popcorn and hoped I wouldn't choke to death.

"Are you on shift today?"

"I just came off."

"God, I'm sorry, Kyle. I thought you were on days."

"I am. I'm just covering for someone. What's up?"

"When you have time, I need to talk to you."

"Concerning?"

"Bob Maitland. Know him?"

"Yeah, I know him. Stay away from him. Why?"

"We'll talk. Are you up for dinner tonight?"

"Sure, why not. I've got to go in at eleven. You're cooking?"

"Are you really feeling that brave, Kyle?"

"You're right. Call the Windmill and see if you can get us in around seven."

"Six? I hate eating that late."

"Fine."

"Go back to sleep. I'll meet you there."

He grunted something and hung up.

I propped Ellen's picture in front of my computer monitor and stared at her for a moment. Whatever medicinal powers my early-morning shower had on my Montana cold were fading. I opened my desk drawer, pulled out a bottle of DayQuil from my stash, uncapped it, and took a couple of gulps.

"Here's to you, Ellen," I said and raised the bottle in a toast. "You're going to have to talk to me."

5

My brother Michael is one of the most handsome, most virile, most sensually charismatic men I have ever known. I don't say that because he's my brother, I say that because he's a priest, and it doesn't wear well on priests. I once caught him in a clinch with his high school sweetheart in the church basement. No big deal, except that it was a year ago and he's been a priest for eight. We had not spoken of it since. The choice wasn't his, it was mine.

When I saw his car parked in front of my mother's house, I damn near didn't park and go in. There was definitely an ecclesiastical crisis coming, and the fallout was something I wanted to avoid. There's a special promised place in heaven for Irish mothers whose sons become priests. It's not written anywhere, it's just truth. I'm not sure what's promised an Irish mother whose son becomes a rabbi like my brother Aaron chose to do, but I'm sure it too is special. She was equally proud of both. Michael was God's gift to her. Aaron was her gift to God in atonement for falling in love with a Jewish man, and in turn for what that man, my father, gave up. My mother was covered in both directions, but nothing had the potential to collapse her life more than just the thought of Michael turning his collar in for Cara Menendez.

When I walked into the kitchen and saw both Michael and Cara sitting at my mother's table, I sucked in all the air in the house and didn't let it out again until my mother turned and smiled.

"Phoebe, look who's here—Cara."

Both Michael and Cara paled. I knew I could have some fun with this.

"Well, what do you know. Cara. How long have you been in town?"

"Awhile." She stood, walked toward me, kissed me on the cheek, and whispered in my ear, "Please, Phoebe. Don't say anything. Okay?"

Like what, Cara? That you're fucking my brother? Puh-leeze. "It's just like I saw you, uh—last year or so. Boy, does time fly. How long has it been?" *Since you've had illicit love with my brother.* I looked at Michael when I asked.

"It's been too long, Phoebe. I've missed you."

"Well, I've missed you, too." *You vow-breaking slut.* "Just pop into town for a visit?"

"I've moved back permanently. I'm hoping to get some freelance work and set up my own business."

"Something to do with design?"

"Of course. It's all I know. But I do have a couple of other ideas, if that doesn't work out."

"Where are you staying?"

"With my parents. They sold their house a couple of years ago and moved into an apartment, so we're pretty crowded. The yard work just got to be too much for them."

"I told Cara she could move into one of the bedrooms here. Don't you think that would be a good idea, Phoebe?"

My mouth dropped open, but I couldn't speak.

"I appreciate the offer, but I'm sure that I haven't exhausted every possibility. I'm kind of a stickler. I need one that will serve the purpose."

"Oh." There were so many things I wanted to say, but I opted for polite. "Good luck, Cara. If I can do anything to help, you know I'll be glad to."

"How's sleuthing, little sister? Didn't Roger coin the phrase 'Queen of Cloak'?"

I ignored Michael's stab at steering things onto safer ground. He knew what I wasn't saying and how much I wanted to say it.

"Michael told me you were doing investigative work. It must be fascinating." Cara continued to smile at me.

"Not usually."

"Fee isn't exactly a team player. She's better off working for herself. Alone. Right?"

"I'll tell you what, Michael, you've got God covered, and I handle the godless. I find them less hypocritical."

The room fell silent.

"Well, well, well." Always the peacemaker, Mother looked nervously from Michael to me. "Coffee, anyone?"

"No thanks, Mom. We can't stay much longer. I heard you've been sick, Fee."

"That's an understatement, but I'll get through it. What's new with you, Michael?"

"Same old, same old."

"And how's your flock?"

"Intact. Are you still seeing Kyle?"

"Why?"

"Oh, I don't know. Could it be possible that I'm interested in your life? Why so defensive?"

"I'm sorry, Michael." And on some level I was. "Human contact is probably not the smartest thing for me right now. I really feel like shit. Yes, I see Kyle when our schedules cooperate."

"She just feels out of sorts. I'm sure seeing Cara has helped tremendously. I know I've often wondered what Cara was up to. Haven't you, Phoebe?"

Sadly, I knew the answer to that one. "I've asked myself that very thing for the last year, Mom. 'I wonder what that Cara is up to?' "

"I think we better get you home," Michael said as he reached for the jacket hanging on the back of his chair. His cheeks were flushed. "Cara's been working with the girls' volleyball team at the church, and they had one heck of a workout this afternoon."

"It really brought back some memories," Cara said. "It's good to be home."

"It's good to have you home, honey." My mother stood and embraced her. "Please come back over. My children get so busy with their own lives I hardly see them. With the exception of Michael, of course. Lord only knows how full his plate is."

"I'll be back. I promise." Cara turned toward me. "Phoebe, I'd love to have lunch with you soon. Can you squeeze me in?"

"I don't do—"

"She'd love it. Wouldn't you, Fee?" Michael's words hung like an unanswered prayer.

"Just love it," I said, finally.

"Good. I'll make sure I give Cara your phone number, and she can call you."

"See you later, Mother." Michael kissed her on the cheek.

"Don't you forget that I've got lots of room over here, Cara," Mother said and turned to Michael. "Now, you take her right home. You know how those old biddies wag their tongues. All they need to see is you out alone with this beautiful young lady, and—" Mother started giggling.

I did the same, only louder. "How ridiculous. Boy. That would be a stretch. Michael and Cara?"

I'd gone too far. I looked at Michael, and the pleading, helpless look on his face silenced me.

"I'll see you later, Fee. I mean it, I really hope you get it together."

They left. I read once that you shouldn't sleep downwind from a victory, the smell will get to you. Whoever wrote that had me in mind.

"That Cara just gets prettier. Don't you think so?"

"She's beautiful, Mother." I took a cookie from the plate on the table, sat down, and took a bite. "I wish to hell I could taste something."

"She came real close to being your sister-in-law, you know."

"Real close. How long were they here?"

"About an hour. Michael wanted to surprise me."

"He always did have the best surprises. Come on and sit down. You look tired."

"Do you think Michael misses not having married and raised a family?" She stood at the back-door window and stared out into the yard.

"I don't know. I always thought he'd make a better husband than most men. He's a lot like Daddy was, he loves kids. Who knows?"

"I know," she said triumphantly as she came to the table and sat down across from me. "It's a calling. He didn't choose it, God spoke to him. Who could question it?"

We had to talk about something else; I didn't know how much longer I could keep my mouth shut. So I got back to business. "I'd like to meet your friend Mrs. Driscoll, Mom. Does she still work for that Dahl woman?"

"Lord, Grace will be there until one of them dies. Mrs. Dahl and the Foresters are all she has."

"Ya know, Mother, after all these years, every time you've mentioned the Foresters I've had visions of all these ladies from the church heading to the woods to do battle with an infestation of Japanese pine beetles."

No one laughs better than my mother.

"Why didn't you ask?"

"I don't know. To be honest, I just thought of it as your thing."

She reached out and placed her hand on the side of my face. "It's hard to think of you and the others as grown up. I still want to be your mother—"

"You *are* my mother. What's up with you?"

"Nothing. Nothing's up. I just miss having my kids home. That's all."

She moved her hand, got up, and turned toward the sink. "Now, why do you want to meet Grace Driscoll?"

"I want to talk to her about Ellen Maitland. Do you think she'd talk to me?"

"I don't know. All I can do is ask. She is very loyal to Rosella Dahl, Phoebe. And I can tell you right now that she has no use for that Mr. Maitland."

"Why didn't you say that this morning? I thought he had your vote."

"He does. But that has nothing to do with what I know about his personal life. I've read all that stuff about President Kennedy and his indiscretions. It didn't make him any less of a president."

"Are you saying that Mr. Maitland committed some indiscretions?"

"He's a man, Phoebe. What do you think? Besides, Grace was against that marriage. She couldn't for the life of her understand why Rosella supported it." She leaned across the table and whispered. "Grace told me the banns were posted a couple of weeks after that man walked through the front door for the first time."

"Maybe the families knew each other. There could have been some history there, Mother."

"Not according to Grace. She caught him one time, you know." She sat straighter in her chair in indignation.

"Grace?"

"Uh-huh."

"Caught him in what?"

"Mangy Detroit."

"Why would they have been in Detroit?"

"They weren't in Detroit, for God's sake, they were *doing* Mangy Detroit. And—before the wedding, I might add."

"I'm not getting it, Mom."

"Rosella and Ellen had gone to Minneapolis to find a wedding gown, and while they were gone, it was Grace's job to stay on top of the caterers and the RSVPs. The normal stuff she always did. And one morning she let herself into the house, expecting no one to be there, and she heard laughing coming from one of the apartments upstairs."

"Okay, go on."

"I'm not sure I should even be telling this, Phoebe. Grace—"

"Grace will never know, Mother. You have my word."

"Well, Grace went upstairs, and sure enough, there they were. All three of them. Mr. Maitland, another young man, and this, this—"

I leaned forward. "Go on."

"A young woman. All three of them drunk as skunks, naked as newborn babies, and in Rosella's bed of all things."

"What did she do?" *After she bit through her tongue.*

"What could she do? She tiptoed back downstairs and slammed the back door real hard a few times. When she couldn't hear any more giggling, she went to her office and started in on her work."

"I take it she never told anyone."

"Of course not."

"Just you."

"Well, I think Mrs. Clawsen was with us, and maybe Lydia, Lydia Robinson. Now that I think of it, I know Lydia was there, because she was the one that told us they call that Mangy Detroit."

"They call *what* Mangy—God, whatever—?"

"Those kind of romps. Three people. For God's sake, Phoebe, I'm not going to spell it out for you."

I looked at her frustration and wondered if I should reread Margaret Mead. Then the synapses fired, and it hit me with a megavolt of discovery. Ménage à trois. Jesus. She looked so puzzled at my lack of understanding.

If I had moved a muscle, taken a breath, or blinked I would have lost it. I knew my mouth was open. The picture of three women, one being my mother, sitting around aghast at Grace's story was too much for me.

"Are you all right, honey?"

"Fine, Mother. It's a bladder thing. I have to, uh—" I stood, tightened my butt muscles, and walked, geisha style, to the bathroom.

When I came back my mother was just coming down from upstairs.

"I turned your bed down, Phoebe, and I don't want an argument."

"I can go home and go to—"

"Go on up and crawl in or you won't get one more shred of information out of me, and I won't talk to Grace."

"You drive a hard bargain, Mother, but I've got things to do."

"It'll wait. You look terrible, and you weren't all that nice to your brother and Cara. You need some good rest without breathing in all those hairballs from that cat."

"Stud? He doesn't have hairballs."

"Well, your house smells like cat," she said, grabbing me by the shoulders and pointing me upstairs. "Get going."

"What brought Stud up?"

"If you have allergies and have a cat it can wear down your immune system. That could be what's wrong with you. You laying on that couch breathing in all that cat hair and dander—don't you know what happens to it? It gets trapped in all those little hairs in your nose—no wonder you're sick."

"God, Mother. Enough. I'm going."

"Besides, you know I don't approve of animals in the house. Particularly cats." Her voice drifted up the stairs behind me. "Did you know that allergies can affect your moods?"

"Wake me up by five," I called back down the stairs. "I'm meeting someone for dinner."

I slipped off my shoes and my Levi's and crawled into bed. The thought of Cara occupying it at some point in the future pissed me off, but then again, who knows, it could just be the hairballs trapped inside my nose.

Life was stacking up. I would contact Dougie tomorrow and see how good his memory really was, give my brother a call and apologize for being such a bitch, and if I wasn't feeling better, hit the emergency room and see if they could save my life. I had approximately thirty-six hours in which to give Bob "Mangy Detroit" Maitland my answer about whether I would take him on. As the sirens of sleep called to me, I snuggled under the comforters and pushed my head into the down pillow. Or was it Ellen Maitland's voice, so long silenced, given sound again?

6

The Windmill is tucked between two beer distributors, Fred Briggs's and Intermountain, on First Avenue South. It's cramped, short on decor, and dimly lit, but you can't beat the prices or the food. It takes a steak knife to pare down bite-size pieces of their specialty: barbecued shrimp the size of a toddler's fist.

I walked through the front door thirty minutes late and saw Kyle sitting in the horseshoe-shaped booth in the far corner. I walked over and slid in opposite him.

"If I thought my body would bend, I'd lie down," I said as I unwrapped the muffler that wound around my head and neck.

"Why so late?" Kyle moved closer in the booth. "Here, let me hang your coat up."

"Don't come any closer. I'm still toxic." I slipped off my coat and put it on the bench between us. "I'm late because I slipped into a coma at my mother's house. God, I hate this shit."

"You'll live. Trust me."

"Have you ordered?"

"Yeah, I did."

"Shrimp?"

"Shrimp for you. Ribs for me."

"I won't be able to taste anything, but what the hell."

Kyle signaled to the waitress and pointed toward his coffee cup and mine. "You're up for coffee, aren't you?"

"Always. Did you get some sleep?"

"Some. I've been curious about Maitland. What's going on?"

"How well do you know him?"

"Not that well personally. By word of mouth? It's a judgment call."

"Where did that 'stay away from him' come from?"

"He's a media hound. I'm not saying the guy isn't sincere, but he has a good-old-boy group that he hangs with that plays the press for all it's worth. I don't think it's any secret that he's got his eye on the state capitol."

The waitress returned with a carafe of coffee and filled our cups.

"Thanks," Kyle said as he looked up at her and smiled.

"That still doesn't answer my question. It's pretty obvious that you don't like the guy."

"He smiles too much. He's too smooth."

"He's a politician, for Christ's sake. Couldn't you come up with something like he picks his nose in public or kicks puppies?"

"I can get close enough. How about he's squeezed all the mileage he can out of his dead wife?"

"You know about that?"

"Who doesn't? He's like clockwork, or so the guys tell me down at the City. He drops in, inquires about the case, wants to know who's on it, and then goes into his spiel about tougher laws, more support for law enforcement, more pay for cops, added personnel—"

"I get the picture, Kyle."

"The list goes on. He's an opportunist, Phoebe. Stay away from him."

"I don't know that I can do that."

"It's easy. Say no to whatever it is he wants."

The waitress walked up with a long paper bib for Kyle.

"This is for you," she said as she reached around his neck and tied the strings. Visibly blushing, she smoothed the paper bib down the front of his chest.

Kyle has that effect on women, and it's unnerving if you happen to be the woman with him at the moment. Even when you know the guy, it's hard to get past his uncommon good looks. His lips slide easily over his teeth into a smile that doesn't lie, and his eyes, usually clueless as to what he is thinking, can melt you when emotion breaks through. Happy or sad, they wrap you in their warm obsidian darkness.

Kyle stood and looked down at me. "I've got to use the little room. I'll be back."

"Wearing that bib? Some of those cowboys in the bar are liable to give you a bad time."

"I don't think so. Don't die on me, okay?"

I was sick, and I was vulnerable. Not a good position to be in. At least not for me. I watched him walk down the short hall and toward the rest rooms. He didn't have that lumbering walk that most big men have. All legs, narrow hips, and broad shoulders, he was light on his feet and stood tall with an undefinable pride. It wasn't easy for Native American men in Montana, although things were slowly changing. He was still the only Indian on either the Billings PD or the Sheriff's Department, but even the most hardcore rednecks reluctantly respected him.

We'd been moving toward a relationship for the past year. Even packing a lot of excess baggage, I found myself lusting.

By the time he returned, dinner had been served.

"How's the shrimp?"

"Probably as succulent as ever. Too bad I can't taste it."

"Consider it sustenance."

"Kyle, how do they handle old case files at the PD?"

"I couldn't tell you for sure, but probably the same way we do it at the County: They're stored in the files, and when we get a rookie we turn him loose on them."

"Fresh perspective?"

"You bet. I've seen them pick up on things that people have missed over the years. And it's good training. These guys are thorough. They need to show some competency, and everyone dreams of busting some old homicide. Is that what Maitland's after?"

"Yeah. It is. Do you know anything about this whole thing, Kyle?"

"Just that it happened. But like I said, I'd stay out of it."

"Like I said, I'm not sure I can."

"Why doesn't that surprise me?" He picked up his coffee cup and took a drink. "Root around a little bit more. If I were you, I'd find some old-timer from back then and see what he remembers."

"I intend to."

"You know what happens, Phoebe. Every once in a while you get one that sticks. Something about certain cases just bores a hole in your head and moves in."

"I know. Ellen Maitland did that to me this afternoon."

"The dead wife?"

"Yeah. He brought a box of files over, and there was this one picture of her—I can't get it out of my mind. It's not so much Maitland himself, Kyle, it's her."

"She's been dead for years, Phoebe. The chances of you finding—"

"I know, I know. There was a guy, young guy, that they had in custody briefly. He vanished. Poof. No trace of him in twenty-seven years."

"How old?"

"Probably nineteen, twenty. Someplace around there."

"From here?"

"As far as I know. I guess that's what bothers me. A kid that age would have one helluva time cutting off family for that long unless—"

"Unless he's dead."

"You got it."

Kyle looked at his watch. "I've got to get going. Feeling any better?"

"Do I look any better?"

"Not a lot. You sound pretty plugged."

"It's the hairballs that are lodged in my sinuses."

"The what?"

"Never mind. It's a long story." I stood and reached for my jacket on the bench. "Thanks for dinner."

"Anytime. Next time I'll cook for you. Go home, Phoebe. Get some rest."

"That's all I've been doing. Keep in touch, okay?"

"A word of advice?"

"Why not?"

"If you go for this Maitland thing, don't work it in a vacuum. That's not Maitland's style, but it's yours. I don't think it'd be wise."

"How so?" He was right, it was my style. The fewer people involved, the less shit you had to deal with.

"Just a gut feeling. I can't back it up." He leaned down and kissed me on the forehead.

"Chicken."

"It's not the germs. It's the barbecue sauce."

"Shit." I picked up the cloth napkin, dipped it in my glass of water, and wiped my mouth off. "Hey, Kyle?"

"Yeah?"

"Take off the bib."

The wind was blowing out of the north by the time we reached our vehicles. It didn't take much to know the windchill was into negative double digits. Snow pelted my face. My sinuses ached in protest. I pulled the choke out on my '49 Chevy truck and hoped it would start. It did. Grudgingly. The wipers moved over the windshield, creating a fan-shaped pattern big enough to see out of. I pressed my foot down on the gas with the gear still in neutral, hoping to shoot some warmth into the heater. It didn't happen. I drove out of the lot behind Kyle and followed him east on First Avenue South until we hit Twenty-seventh Street. He turned left, and I turned right and headed toward the Yellowstone.

Traffic was light until I crossed over the Interstate and turned left on the frontage road. Then it became nonexistent. Snow glided across the road in front of me, carried on the back of a low-crawling ground blizzard. There was a wall of white that threw the beams from the headlights back at me and jerked visibility down to zero. I slowed, knowing I was getting near the drive that led up to the house. My mailbox came into view.

In Montana, when you pull into the middle of the road to make a right-hand turn, it's called a farmer's hook, and that's what I did to avoid the drift building around the base of the mailbox. Without warning, a massive plume of snow jetted toward me as a car sped backward out of my driveway. My wipers groaned under the added weight.

I instinctively pulled sharply toward the mailbox and threw my right arm up in front of my face, preparing for what I thought was an inevitable collision. Lowering my arm, I saw nothing but white on the windshield. The wiper motor whined, struggling momentarily as the blades moved slowly to the left side of the glass. I leaned forward, trying to get a make on the car and what its next move was. Whoever was behind the wheel punched the lights on bright, blinding me. The car's motor gunned.

My only thought at that second was that I was going to be rammed, head-on. I threw myself to the passenger side of the cab and tried to open the door. The truck had come up alongside the mailbox, and there was no way I was going to get out on that side. Again, the screeching whine of an engine revving cut through the silent, white night. The headlights moved toward me in one blinding flash. I braced myself.

A great wake of snow swirled over the truck as the car bypassed me and roared down the road. I opened the driver's door and jumped out, trying to see at least the taillights of the fleeing car. A spray of snow and exhaust blasted me in the face. Two bloodred lights, shaped like arched eyebrows, were visible only for a second, but that second gave me a lead on the make. There was no doubt: a Chevy sedan, '59 or '60, and it didn't ring a bell.

I didn't count how many times I put the truck in reverse and then first, trying to rock it loose from the drift. Before I pulled up in front of the house, I parked and got out, looking for footprints on the drive and on the porch. There were none. But there were two distinct tire tracks, rapidly being erased by the wind. Whoever it was had not gotten out of the car. It could have been something as simple as a couple of parked kids trying to generate a little heat, although I doubted it. Hedonist though I may be, there's a limit on my taste for passion out of doors.

I opened the door to every girl's dream, an impatient Stud. He twisted between my legs in his usual figure eight as I took off my coat, pulled the shoes off my frozen feet, and rubbed my hands together. Something was different. I stood still and looked around. There was no sound, no movement, only the air flowing in and out of my nose. That was it. Air flow. I had no idea an adrenaline rush could be so beneficial. My sinuses had cleared up.

After feeding the cat and getting into a pair of sweatpants and a T-shirt, I walked into my office and turned on the banker's lamp on my desk. The muted light glowing through the green shade cast a shimmering haze throughout the room. I sat down and pushed play on my answering machine. There were three harried call-me-back-as-soon-as-you-get-home messages from my mother, one cryptic re-member-me-when-all-those-jobs-open-up-in-Helena, and one that simply said in a female voice I did not recognize, "I'll call back." There were four hang-ups interspersed between, but that was noth-ing new.

I leaned back in my chair with my hands clasped behind my head and looked into Ellen Maitland's face in the photo. The phone rang.

"Phoebe?"

"Yes, Mother."

"That answering machine is the rudest thing in the world. I'm not going to talk to it anymore."

"I was about to call you. I just walked in the door a few min-utes—"

"Did you know it's all over the news?"

"What's all over the news?"

"They had Mr. Maitland on Channel Eight. He said he had hired the best private investigator in town. You."

"He what?" I sat up and slammed my hand down on the desk so hard it stung.

"He said he had the best. Phoebe Siegel."

"So much for the *private*. Damn him."

"I just thought you'd like to know. How are you feeling, honey?"

"Better."

"And dinner? How was that?"

"I couldn't taste much, but it was fine. Thanks, Mom. I've got to get off here."

"You sound upset. Maybe I shouldn't have told you."

"I would have found out anyway. I'll talk to you tomorrow."

"Good night, sweetheart. Sleep tight."

I hung up. All I could think of was what a son of a bitch Maitland was. Kyle had been right. I took the files out of the box and turned on my copier.

7

*I*t was past midnight when I finished copying all the papers and news clippings that Maitland had left with me. I owed him one. A big one. I just hadn't figured out how to pay it off yet. Looking at the stack of papers, I couldn't figure out why I even duplicated them. There was no way I would work a case for Bob Maitland, potential political icon or not. Blocking Ellen Maitland from my mind proved impossible. I could work the case on my own, but to what purpose. It all added up to a file with no leads that had been milked by him for twenty-seven years.

The wind had picked up and was howling through the eaves of the house. The fire I had built in the fireplace earlier was burning down, so I chucked in another log, turned out all the lights in the house, and sat down on the couch. I was so angry I felt half sick at my stomach. I'd been had, and now it was a matter of pride.

I stared at the phone on the stand beside the couch. My father loved quoting Benjamin Disraeli. One of his favorites was, "The fool wonders, the wise man asks." Everything in me was telling me to pick up the phone, call the creep, and ask him what the hell he thought he was pulling. Did I look stupid, or was it just an assumption? I decided against calling. Everything could wait until morning. Or so I thought.

The adrenaline rush had long subsided. I hurt everywhere, and the sinuses were again throbbing against my cheekbones and forehead. Watching the luminous face of the digital clock on the mantel, I waited for the Tylenol and NyQuil I had taken to kick in. I had it figured down to forty-six minutes. There were fifteen minutes left before the pain in the simple act of blinking would subside. With any luck I'd lose the anger in sleep.

At first I couldn't figure out if the noise I heard was the doorbell or the phone. Whichever, it pulled me out of a deep comfortable slumber and stopped before I could pinpoint it. The house was silent. My mind was in a NyQuil pause I didn't feel like fighting. I turned on my side just as the noise, now obviously the phone, rang out again. It was enough to bring me up to a sitting position on the couch. I don't remember saying hello, I think I just held the receiver to my ear.

"Hello? Siegel?"

"Kyle?"

No one responded.

"Who is this?" I asked.

"This is, uh . . . someone you don't know."

I squinted and looked at the clock. "This is a hell of an hour for someone I don't know to call."

"Don't hang up! I—I gotta talk to ya. It's, uh . . . I heard that lawyer on television tonight. It ain't like I haven't been trying to call. I have."

"I checked my messages. You weren't on there. Call me when the sun comes up."

"It might . . ." His voice was low and raspy. Urgent. "I did call ya, Siegel. I just didn't leave no messages."

"What lawyer are you talking about? Wait . . . let's back up. I need a name, your name, or I'm off here."

He was silent. I stood, picked up the phone, and carried it with me into the kitchen. Placing it on the counter, I cradled the receiver between my ear and my shoulder and turned on the water.

"Okay, fella. It's your call. I'm—"

"Look, Siegel. My name ain't going to mean a thing to you. The information I got will."

"Name first." I filled a glass with water and took a drink, hoping it would unstick my teeth from my cheeks.

"Fuck. Chillman, man. My name is Chillman."

"Chillman what?"

"My damn name is Frank. You want the whole fuckin' thing? Franklin Edward Chillman."

"All right, Mr. Chillman. By my clock it's three-ten A.M. By three-twenty I damn well better be back to sleep. What's on your mind?"

"That Maitland dude? Are you working for him?"

"I can't answer that. Cut to the chase, Mr. Chillman. You've got about seven minutes left."

"That woman, his wife? The one that was murdered?"

"Ellen?"

"Yeah, that's her. You got any ideas on who did her?"

"Do you?"

"Damn straight. Interested?"

I dragged the phone back into the living room and turned the lamp on before I sat down. "You're down to four minutes."

"Okay, okay. If you ain't working for Maitland, I want to hire you myself. I can't pay much, but I got a car I can sell, and I got information."

"Now you're down to three and a half minutes."

"There was another murder."

"Tonight?"

"Hell no, not tonight. Right after that Maitland woman got it. Twenty-four hours later. Only nobody gave a shit."

"How do you know about this, Mr. Chillman?"

"I know because I . . . the second person killed, she was my sister."

"And your sister's name?" I rummaged around on the coffee table and found a pen but no paper. The carton the NyQuil came in would have to do. I tore it open.

"Chili. Her real name was Rita, Rita Chillman, but everybody called her Chili."

"You said nobody gave a shit. Did anyone know about it?"

"Hell, yes. The pigs knew. The fuckin' paper knew. It just ain't no big deal if some white trash gets taken out."

"Nice way to talk about your sister."

"She'd been givin' it up since she was fourteen. Probably before then, for all I know. But she was a damn good person, and she didn't . . ." He choked up. "Shit. She didn't deserve what she got."

"Giving it up. You mean she worked the streets?"

"Early on she did. Had some pimp that beat her up and tore her down. But she got away from scum and went legit."

"She got off the street?"

"You might say that. She went to work for Big Dorothy and life got better for her. Got better for my whole family. Then she got mixed up with . . ."

"With?"

"I ain't ready to let that go yet. Chili died the same reason that rich bitch did, and by the same fuckin' hands."

"What in the hell are you talking about?" I was now paying attention.

"I got it all, Siegel. All you need to rip it wide open."

"Where are you, Frank?"

"I been staying in the country. Out at the end of Grand."

Locally, out at the end of Grand Avenue means following Grand Avenue west out of Billings and could be just about any place between Billings and Livingston, which is about one hundred and twenty miles away.

"Where in the country?"

"Do we have a deal, Siegel?"

"I need more. Look, it's late. Why don't you come to my house in the morning, and we can both lay our cards on the table?"

"This won't wait. I already made some calls, and shit will be coming down."

"Calls? Calls to whom, for Christ's sake?"

"You can be here in forty minutes. The roads are a little thick, but you can get through."

"Let me get this straight. You want me to meet you in the country at this hour? In this weather? On some vague information? How the hell do I even know you're who you say you are?"

"I'm no fool, Siegel."

"You can damn well bet I'm not either, Chillman."

"I'll give you this. I just did six months in Alpha house. You know it?"

"Sure. The prerelease center down on First Avenue. Did you just—"

"Yeah, I did time. Hard time. My PO is Janet Sloane. I'll call her and have her call you. She'll tell you Frank Chillman ain't no nutcase. Deal?"

"Call her at this hour? That'll be interesting."

I knew Janet, and I liked and respected her. She looked like Alice in Wonderland, but word among the good-old-boy network was that she was so tough that she filed her nails on her beard. They hadn't scored with her.

"She said call her, any time of the day or night. Is it a deal, Siegel?"

"One more question?"

"Shoot."

"What do you know about Joey Marino?"

"The chump they tried to frame? Hell, he's probably dead after this long. I know who killed 'im. I got it all. You hear this?"

I heard paper rustling. "I hear it."

"That's my insurance, Siegel. It's all in there."

"Okay. She calls within the next five minutes and I'll be there. But where is there?"

He sounded as excited as a kid as he blurted out directions. I wrote them down on the inside of the NyQuil box and turned on the television to the Weather Channel. Twenty-three degrees below zero coupled with a full moon and my pissy disposition made any-thing possible, including decisions coming from my gut and not from a rational thought process.

Three minutes had passed, and the phone hadn't rung. My drugged mind was pulling me back down, talking to me through the pillow, taunting me with comfort and sleep. Just as I was ready to give in, the phone rang. Against my better judgment, I answered it.

"You sure keep weird hours, Phoebe. Have I done something to offend you lately, or was it in one of my past lives?"

"Janet. What can I say?"

"You can tell me what the hell is going on."

"He's your boy. You tell me."

She sighed. "Hold on and let me light a cigarette."

"They'll kill ya, Janet."

"Not as fast as these goddamn phone calls in the middle of the night will." I could hear the click of a lighter and seconds later an exhale. "Okay. Why am I calling you?"

"What?"

"All Frank asked me to do was call you and tell you he's not a whacko."

"With a clear conscience can you tell me he's not?"

She laughed and said, "Sure. With a clear conscience. Frank's tendency is, uh, how to put this? He obsesses about incidents in his life, but he's a smart guy. He's going to take a little time, but I think he's got a chance of making it."

"Huh."

"He didn't say, but I can bet this is about his sister. Right?"

"Do you know anything about that situation?"

"Not much. I usually try to steer him away from it. I'll tell you what, why don't you get ahold of me tomorrow, and I'll fill the blank spaces. But now? I'm going back to sleep, and you should do the same."

"Right. What time tomorrow?"

"I don't know—I don't want to get up and find my book. Seems to me that I've got a couple of presentence gigs in court. Let's say after lunch, one-thirty?"

"Sounds good. I'll be there. Janet?"

"Yeah?"

"Is there a chance this guy could flip out and, uh . . . be a problem?"

"Is he dangerous? There're no guarantees. You know that. My best guess is that he's not. But then again—"

"Oh shit."

"Ya know, Phoebe, everyone loved Ted Bundy." She laughed. "Seriously, out of most of the yahoos on my caseload, Frank would be at the bottom of the list."

"Thanks, Janet."

I hung up and considered my options. There was an urgency in Frank Chillman's voice that told me he had something. What that something was I didn't know. To go or not to go. Was there any question?

Dressing for the occasion, I pulled on three pairs of sweatpants, two pairs of socks under my Sorrels, a T-shirt, two sweaters, and a knit Cat-in-the-Hat cap. The cap, a Christmas present from Kehly, was supposed to get me in touch with my inner child. Admittedly, I caught myself reciting *Green Eggs and Ham* once, but what the hell. Call it a weak moment.

As I took my parka out of the closet my hand hit the shoulder holster hanging from the hook. I had Smith Brothers cough drops; did I need Smith & Wesson under my arm? Lifting it from the hook, I walked to my oak dresser and got the clip out of the back of the top drawer, pushed it in, and put the 10mm on the bed while I strapped the belt on. I had to open it two holes to allow for the bulky sweaters. It was stupid enough to go out in the middle of the night. But without a weapon? No way. I pulled on the parka, went back downstairs, found the NyQuil box with the directions written on it, and walked out the front door.

Winter in Montana is a challenge on many levels, with vehicles right at the top. When it drops way below zero, we plug them in: Without the luxury of a garage, head bolt heaters are a necessity up here, particularly when your truck of choice is a '49 Chevy that longs to live in Arizona. The truck has a six-volt electrical system in a twelve-volt world, so it needs all the help it can get under arctic conditions to get the engine to turn over.

I'd been through a lot with the Chevy, and even with all the draw-backs and the ability to buy another vehicle, I couldn't let go. Once it got going, it plowed through the snow like a Panzer tank, and more important, there wasn't a time I got in it when I didn't feel closer to my brother Ben.

I pulled the thirty-foot cord loose from the plug hanging out the front grille, coiled it near the house, and walked back to the truck. It turned over and caught on the second try. I left it in neutral, got back out, and brushed off the windshield with my arm. After sitting for a couple of minutes just to give the beast a chance to heat up, I shifted into second and stepped on the gas. The one thing you don't do is park where you can't pull forward. I'd made that mistake a few days before and ended up driving down the road in reverse until the transmission warmed up and I could shift the damn thing.

I pulled out of the driveway and pointed the truck toward town. Armed with an inner tube filled with sand in the bed, I had all the traction I needed. The city was dead. There wasn't another vehicle on the road when I pulled onto Twenty-seventh Street South and headed north. I wanted pavement under the tires for as long as possible. Anyone starting from the center of Billings is fifteen, twenty minutes max from the country in any direction. I opted to follow Grand out of the city for as long as I could and tacked another half hour onto that twenty-minute max.

By the time I stopped at the four-way light on Shiloh Road, the lights of the city were fading in the rearview mirror. The inside of the cab was not warm enough to melt the thin rope of frost that lined the top of the windshield. One small wave of heat was coming up from the defrost slot and gave me a narrow wedge to see through. Haloed yard lights strained under the frigid temperatures. The distance between the lights widened until all that was left was uninterrupted night. A great sense of loneliness and apprehension spread through me.

8

G rand Avenue ran out of road at Eighty-eighth Street. Only in Montana could you see a green-flagged pole coming out of the ground in the middle of nowhere, just to let you know where you are; the city fathers were obviously planning for the future. I turned south for a quarter of a mile and then west on Tripp. Pushing in the clutch and pressing on the brake pedal, I came to a stop when I could go no farther. Buffalo Trail Road stretched silently to my right and to my left.

At the end of Tripp there's a monument rising on the west side of Buffalo Trail. It sits there like an oversize headstone, commemorating a battle that took place in the deep of winter in another time as a band of Chief Joseph's Nez Percé were making a run for the Sweet Grass Hills in the north. For the great chief's flight toward freedom it was the beginning of the end. Some say the anguish, the desperation, and the death of that battle are soaked into the ground and tilled under what is now plowed farmland. The thought sobered me. I was getting spooked.

I fumbled around on the seat until I found the NyQuil box. According to Frank's directions, I was on track. Even in the cab of the truck I could see my breath white on the air. Plumes of snow as fine as diamond dust traced across the blanketed fields under the phosphorescent light of the moon. There was a stillness, a dead calm, that pressed down on the ground even as veils of white slid from the sandstone cliffs to the north and disappeared into the night. The snowscape seemed alive, in constant shimmering motion.

The heaviness of the cold pushed the exhaust down toward the roadbed. The ground wind caught it and snaked it under the truck.

I could smell it as it seeped into the cab. One more look at the directions, and then I shifted into second, let out the clutch, and turned right onto Buffalo Trail.

Frank had said there would be a small hill, and after cresting that I would drop down and cross a bridge. Just past that I was to turn left on Canyon Creek Road and follow the canyon. It was small and narrow and twisting. Cliffs cradled the road on my right, and a ridge to my left in the distance looked eerie and jagged with the ebony silhouettes of Bull Pine.

I rounded a curve, going about fifteen miles per hour, and saw a house to my left. The windows were dark. Smoke from the chimney, unable to break through the weight of the cold, succumbed, crawling down the sides of the chimney and over the roof. A large black dog appeared out of nowhere, snarling and barking and scaring the shit out of me. His eyes glinted red in my headlights. He paced me a short way. After a few yards he gave up and disappeared. The road straightened out.

I watched for a cabin in a stand of cottonwood trees that would be on my left. It was there, and also dark. I was getting closer and still had not seen another vehicle. The sane people were at home, warm, sleeping. I crossed another bridge and checked my odometer. Frank had said the place he was staying at was half a mile beyond this bridge and off the road a ways.

I slowed down as much as possible without killing the engine. Leaning forward, I rubbed my gloved hand on the windshield, thinking I had seen the dim glow of a yard light. Whatever it was, it disappeared. If I hit a steep incline, I would know I had gone too far and should backtrack the length of half a city block. Sure as hell, I found myself at the bottom of a road that curved steeply up and out of sight. I shifted into reverse and tried backing up. The rear fishtailed to the right and slipped into a rut buried under the snow. Instead of slamming on the brakes, I tried to steer into the backward slide and only made matters worse. When I finally came to a stop I knew damn well I was stuck. I shifted into neutral, pulled on the emergency brake, and got out.

The rear end of the truck was a good two feet into a snowbank. The engine choked and then died as I frantically tried to dig a trench down to the exhaust pipe with my hands.

"Don't panic," I said out loud. My own voice shocked me in the stillness. "You can't be that far past his place. Christ. Now I'm talking to myself."

I got back into the truck and turned the lights and the starter off. The inside of my nose burned with every frigid breath. I wrapped the long tail of my Cat Hat around my face and pulled the hood up on the parka.

"Here goes nothing." I started walking down the road.

I hadn't gone a hundred feet when I stopped and threw the hood back off my head. Music? I pushed the edge of the cap up and off my ears and listened. My face was stinging, and I made the near-fatal mistake of letting the tail of the knit cap fall from my face. My lips, wet from the moisture of my breath, felt freeze-dried within seconds. Straining, I couldn't hear a damn thing. I walked on.

The snow was well above my Sorrels and made it impossible to pick up my pace. I could see rectangular panes of light and the outline of a house. Stumbling toward what I thought was the road leading to it, I stepped onto a plain of white snow and fell down an embankment. There's not a lot of pain involved in falling into a cushion of snow, but it sure as hell scares the crap out of you. I floundered and tried to find solid ground that would put me back onto the road. It was a struggle that was full of words I didn't know I knew.

By the time I crawled back up on the road I was really pissed. My face ached from the melting snow caked on it. A dull throb gripped my forehead as I brushed off. My hands stopped. This time there was no mistake. The sound of music floated through the cold. It was definitely coming from the house. As I neared, I thought I saw a shadow move by one of the windows, so I called out.

"Frank! Hey! I hope you've got heat in there."

No one answered.

"Frank! Frank Chillman! I'm fucking freezing to death out here!"

My lips were so stiff, my words didn't sound right. Still, no one answered. I came around the corner of the house, stepped up onto a porch that ran the entire front, and heard something that stopped me dead in my tracks. It was a summer sound, and it didn't make sense: the gentle slap, slap of a thin-framed screen door, swaying in a gentle breeze.

"Frank?" I called out again. "Are you in there?"

I craned my neck forward. The door was standing wide open. I pushed my back up against the front of the house, pulled off my gloves, and put them in my parka pockets.

"You okay in there?" As quietly as possible I started pulling the zipper open on the front of the coat. It seemed fifty feet long. "You really should tell me if you're in there, Frank."

The zipper parted. I slid my right hand up toward the holster, unsnapped it, and pulled out the 10mm. My fingers were already stiff. Both of my hands tightened around the grip as I moved it up toward my face and breathed on my hands. The thumb on my right hand automatically released the safety on the left side of the gun.

I inched toward the front door. The music stopped. The news started. A radio. Pushing my head back against the wall, I raised the gun, breathed on my hands again.

"I'm coming in, Frank."

I pushed away from the wall so fast, I shocked myself and took a squat stance in front of the open door. It was a shotgun house: the kind that you can look straight through to the back entrance. The back screen was swinging gently, intermittently hitting the jamb. A small drift of snow had slunk through the front door onto the linoleum. It crunched under my feet as I edged in.

It was a huge room, sparsely furnished. The kitchen was beyond a wide arch, through which an acrid odor spilled into the living room. A door to my right stood ominously closed. In three steps I was in front of it. I moved to the left side and again pressed myself up against the wall. The house reeked of fuel oil burning in the two space heaters I could see. They were no match for the subzero temperatures that had invaded the house.

"Frank?"

Nothing. I stood quietly, listened, and stiffened when I heard a soft keening. It stopped and then came again in shrill staccato bursts. Reaching over, I grabbed the knob with my left hand, turned it, threw the door wide open, and stormed into the room. Light from the living room spilled past me, throwing my shadow in front of me.

Something moved on the floor at my feet. I took a step back and tried to find a light switch. There was none. A cord hung from the middle of the ceiling weighted by a canning jar ring. It glistened in the dull light. Cautiously, I moved forward, reached for the cord, and pulled it. A bare bulb strained to light the room.

There was a stack of rumpled blankets on a bed, and that was it. Oddly, makeshift shelves in a doorless closet held stacks of neatly folded and sorted clothing. Odder still was the pup that sat at my feet in the middle of a puddle of urine, looking up at me.

"I know the feeling. I could do the same thing right now," I said in a whisper.

I backed out of the room. The pup followed, running in and out of my legs, raking my pants with his front paws. It wasn't helping. I coaxed him back into the bedroom and closed the door. He immediately started scratching on the bare wood floor. As I moved into the kitchen, the pup's whine intensified to a full-fledged bark.

There was a chrome dinette set in the kitchen with a lemon-yellow surface and two chairs with cotton hanging from tears on the backrests. A refrigerator older than I was towered in one corner. A cast-iron frying pan sizzled on an electric stove. I walked over and turned the burner off under a pan full of what looked like fried potatoes and onions. They weren't burned, but they weren't far from it either. The side of the coffeepot on the back burner was hot.

Wherever he was, he hadn't been gone long. There had not been any other vehicles on the road, so if he left, he left on foot, and I couldn't buy that. It didn't take a genius to figure out that something was wrong with the whole scene. A shiver coursed through my body, and it wasn't entirely caused by the biting cold. I edged out the back screen. There were no footprints leading away from the door. I glanced behind me. How could there be? My own prints were being erased as soon as I lifted my feet.

I was facing into the wind. Cascades of fine-grained snow were blowing from the roofs of two large structures that loomed up in the night a hundred feet or so behind the house. As I neared, the snow pelted my face with the sting of a thousand shards of glass. I started toward them, holding the 10mm with both hands up and to the right of my body. My eyes narrowed as I fought to see through the cloak of white.

The wind died down as if some giant hand had grabbed it from behind and cast it aside. The air vibrated around me in shimmering glints of cold that hung in the air. I stopped and looked down the drifted corridor between the two buildings. In the monochromatic night, from the blackest black to the whitest white, a pulsating red glow spilled across the snow. There was no sound, no movement, just the throb of crimson matching the drumming of my own heart. I listened, frozen in a feeling of impending doom. My muscles tensed as I struggled forward in the snow. My hands felt nothing, not even the grip of the pistol.

When I reached the end of the corridor between the buildings I stopped and leaned up against the side of the one on my left. The source of the metronome-steady flashing was just around the edge of the building. Taking a deep breath, I tried exhaling on my hands to bring feeling back into them. The cold seared my throat. I stepped around the building with my hands straight out in front of me and stopped dead in my tracks.

The same arched taillights that I had seen on the back of the car that had sped past me from my drive blinked on and off in front of me, reflecting off the barrel of my gun. No sound. No movement. Just the red strobe of the taillights. I walked toward the driver's side of the car.

"Frank? Hey! If you're in the car, let me know."

I moved closer, waiting for an answer. Still nothing. Holding the gun in my right hand, I reached for the door handle of the car and depressed the button with my thumb. It was as stiff as my hand was numb. I pulled to wrench it open. It gave an inch but no more. I pulled again, and then again with what I had left. The door gave, but more slowly than I had anticipated. Stepping back, I watched in horror as the weight of the door slowly pulled it open. For what seemed an eternity, the left side of a man's head followed the opening door. Everything moved in slow motion as the head tore loose from the window, releasing the body that followed it to tumble sideways from the car.

"Shit!" Words came from my throat over my tongue and against my teeth as my frozen lips tried to come together. "Oh God! God!"

What had been the left side of the man's head stayed on the window. Frozen pink froth and tissue clung to the glass in a frozen mass.

Dead eyes stared up from a frostbitten face, hanging out of the car, upside down. I knew that the body, clothed in nothing but a white T-shirt and Levi's, was Frank Chillman. The surreal light refracting off the snow pulsed, bathing him in a dead red glow.

I stumbled backward, dropping my gun. My first thought was that whoever did this was still here. Lurking somewhere in the shadows. I crawled through the snow, digging for the pistol, ignoring the pain in my hands. Touching something hard, I grabbed under the coldness and clasped my hand around the grip. I turned over to a sitting position and crab-crawled backward. My breath came in short bursts. The rear wall of the building stopped me. Pressing up against it, I felt my back ache as I willed myself to slide through it and disappear inside.

I brought my knees up to my chest, my arms hanging limp over them. The weight of the 10mm doubled, tripled, in my right hand. I sat there and stared, transfixed, at the garish scene. There was no noise, just the night that quivered in the bitter cold, overpowering horror, and death. I blinked only when a plaintive howl from the house split the silence.

Minutes passed like hours as I waited for the deputies to arrive. I had called 911 only after I knew I would sound coherent. When you're treading onto the big boys' playground, it's best if you maintain a facade of rock-solid guts. That's why I puked away from the house before I made the call.

They had been on the scene at least two hours when a persimmon-colored sunrise started breaking over the eastern horizon, pushing light blue shadows over the hills. I sat in Kyle's Chevy Blazer with the pup, wrapped in a blanket, nestled sound asleep on the seat beside me. What had been lethally still last night was now a flurry of county detectives and the coroner. The area looked obscenely giftwrapped in the bright yellow scene-of-the-crime tape strung everywhere. Three detectives, two on one end and one on the other, carried the bright blue body bag past me and shoved it unceremoniously into the rear of another Blazer. I turned away and looked back only when someone tapped on the driver's-side window.

Pete Jackson grinned at me. I leaned over the pup and pressed the electric switch that brought the window down.

"Hey, Siegel, you hear about the new safe house for women they're opening up in town?"

"No, Pete. What about it?"

"It's called Tempura House, for lightly battered women."

He spit a stream of brown down toward the ground and laughed so hard he started choking.

"You're a pig, Jackson."

"What the hell happened to your sense of humor?"

"It's there. It just doesn't respond to bullshit."

"A little gallows humor keeps us sane, Siegel."

"I'll let you in on something: It isn't working," I said and looked away.

He said nothing for a moment and then reached in through the window and placed his hand on my shoulder.

"This was a rough one. I was only trying to lighten things up."

I looked at him as he moved his hand from my shoulder to the pup's head and gently stroked it. Pete was one helluva detective. He played things by the book but meted out his own form of compassionate street justice that usually involved young offenders. There was one problem. Pete was a prick. A chauvinist prick. Off duty, he drove a black Dodge truck with a bumper sticker that said, "You can borrow my truck, my dog, and maybe my wife. But my gun? NEVER!!"

"Did you know this guy?"

"No."

"There were some papers, uh . . . under the guy's feet, Siegel. Kinda messy and frozen to the mat, but we took the mat out. I should be able to get a better look at them when it thaws. You sure you didn't know this guy?"

"Watch my lips, Pete. N-O, no. I did not know him."

"As far as I can make out, there's a car title that's signed off and notarized. Your name is written on a piece of paper that's paperclipped to it."

"I told you, he called me. That's it."

"What the hell were you doing out here alone in the first place? It's colder than a witch's tit."

"Dammit, Pete!"

"Sorry, Siegel. You aren't one of those feminazis, are you?"

"Oh, God—"

"They want you in the house, Jackson—Clint Beemer specifically asked for you," Kyle said as he walked up to the Blazer.

Pete walked off without another word.

"Good thing you came along when you did, Kyle. I was getting ready to shoot him."

Kyle laughed and said, "Pete's a good old boy. He means well. Don't let him get to you."

"Boy is the key word here, Kyle."

"How's the coffee feel?"

"Life-giving."

"You're going to have to give him a statement, you know."

"I figured as much. Are they through?"

"They brought Chillman out."

"I saw that."

"Hell, his head must have frozen to that window. Looks like a .45 to me, Phoebe. Probably a hollow point to do that much damage."

"I talked to him an hour and a half before I got out here. Shit."

"He was on parole. The coroner found Janet Sloane's card in his wallet."

"I know."

"Anything else you know?"

"Just what I already told you. He called and said he had some information for me. He wanted to hire me."

"Listen, Fred Jenkins rode up here with me. He's offered to drive your truck back. What do you think?"

"I think he's a fool. We are talking minimal heat output at best."

"Is it okay?"

"Sure. Did they get it out of the snowbank?"

"They did. Let me tell them I'm heading back. Wait here."

"I have no plans."

I looked toward the Blazer that held the body of Frank Chillman. He didn't have any plans either.

9

There wasn't enough energy left in me to feel sick. I had passed exhaustion hours before. Pete Jackson had at least slipped into his kinder alter ego and had not pushed me during the statement.

"You're sure that's all?" he asked as he prodded me gently.

"That's it. I had one conversation with him. Like I told you, I think he was at my house, parked in the driveway, when I came home last night. I recognized the taillights."

"You don't have any idea about what he wanted to hire you for?"

"Something about his sister being murdered years ago—damn, Pete. We've been through this, and I'm hanging on by a fucking thread here."

"I talked with Janet Sloane. She's blown away by this. Said Chillman had a chance. He'd done okay at Alpha and was supposed to start work next week."

"I know nothing about a job. He didn't mention that."

"Okay. Then I guess we're through. I may have you back in, Siegel, so stay available. Oh, Janet wants you to stop by her office."

"Not right now. I've got to get some sleep."

"Give her a call and let her know, or she won't think I gave you the message. I don't want her on my back."

"Will do. I'm outta here. Pete?"

"Yeah?"

"What about the pup? What's going to happen to it?"

"What pup? The only pup I know about is the new one Wolf has. He had it in here a while ago. Nice-looking German shepherd."

"Kyle—"

"I haven't seen any stray, Siegel. If I did, I'd have to take it down to the pound." He leaned back in his office chair with his hands clasped behind his head and grinned at me. "Wolf ran *his* pup back home. Got a message for him?"

"I'll catch him later. Thanks, Pete."

My truck was parked in the city lot. I crawled in, oblivious to the cold. Exhaustion held my body and my mind captive. My eyes were so heavy, I cracked the window to let some cold hit my face, hoping it would prod me into staying awake long enough to make it home. The air was clear and crisp. Steam rose from the pavement as car exhaust melted the snow that had fallen and drifted the night before.

I came through the front door of my house at nine-thirty to the sound of the phone ringing. Walking into my office, I reached down for the base of the phone and turned the ringer off. I shed my boots and clothing, not giving a damn where they fell, as I followed the same annoying ringing into the living room and silenced that phone also. Sleep couldn't wait. Everything else could. The comfort of the couch swallowed me up as I pulled the blankets up to my shoulders. Stud jumped on the couch, sniffed around, and started one of his low growls. I knew I smelled like pup. He hated canines, but then again, he hated just about everything.

We went through our usual ritual, which involved me pushing him down and him jumping right back up and kneading through the blankets with his stiletto claws.

"If you're hungry, go kill a mouse," I said and pushed him down one final time.

I watched him out of one eye as he strutted back and forth between the couch and the coffee table, snapping his tail with the efficiency of a bullwhip. He was pissed. Not a good thing. I listened to him knock everything off the coffee table. It took a while for him to shove the phone to the edge and over. The last thing I heard before I fell asleep was some distant voice saying, "If you want to make a call, please hang up and dial again." I hung up all right, on everything around me, particularly the last six hours.

By two that afternoon I was on my way back into town. Two television stations and the newspaper had left numerous messages on the machine. Frank Chillman, virtually unknown in life, was a lead story in death. Funny how life works. I wondered what he would have thought. I'd made an appointment to meet with Janet Sloane at Scooterz Pub off Twenty-seventh Street and Third. Scooterz caters to the downtown crowd and had become my place to conduct business when I didn't want to do it at home. The cop shop is close by, so it naturally draws the kind of crowd I'm comfortable hanging with.

The gods smiled and opened up a parking spot right in front of Barjon Books. I dropped some change in the meter and entered Scooterz, ordered my usual, a double mocha, and sat down at a table. Janet walked in before I even had the seat warm.

"I don't goddamn believe it. What the hell happened?" She pulled off her coat and hung it over the back of her chair. "Shit. What a way to start a day. You okay?"

"I'm fine. Janet—"

"Don't get emotional on me, Phoebe. I don't think I could take it."

How the hell do you keep emotion out of something like this? I sat in silence and sipped the latte.

"God, life sucks sometimes. Do you know what the success rate is in this business? Zilch. Fucking zilch. You get one that you know has a chance, and you end up getting too damn involved." She reached into her purse, pulled out a Kleenex, and wiped her eyes before tears spilled down her cheeks. "I mean, I just can't do emotion right now. I just have to deal with it."

"Do you want to order anything?" I asked.

"Not right now. Later. Ya know, for as much of a bitch as everyone thinks I am, I get hooked once in a while. On a personal level. Know what I mean?"

"Sure, Janet. It happens."

Janet had the habit of punctuating statements by leaning forward and bobbing her head up and down like one of those spring-action animals you see in the back window of tacky cars. She was hurting, and I felt for her, but I needed information.

"Janet, if you have anything that can help me, I'd appreciate it if you'd tell me."

"Dead is dead. What can I add?"

"I want to know about Frank. Way back. Do you have anything on that?"

"Just from the psych workups and what he and I talked about. I told you he could be obsessive. The shrink he saw in Deer Lodge assessed him the same way. He couldn't get off this thing with his sister."

"You knew she was a hooker?"

"I did. I'm not sure Frank ever accepted that. He felt she made the best move in her life when she started working for Big Dorothy."

I laughed out loud. "The madam from Manhattan. They're a fading breed."

"Nonexistent. Hell, she had this city by the balls for decades."

"So I've heard. Is she around?"

"Far as I know."

"What was the obsession? The bottom line with his sister?"

"I couldn't get into his juvey files, but from what I heard firsthand from him and from what he told the shrink, she supported the family. The mother cleaned office buildings at night when she could. The family was tight, believe it or not. His sister died when he was thirteen years old, and it was downhill from there. The mother couldn't pull it together after the daughter died."

"So what happened?"

"It gets worse. Two years later the mother dies, and the kids—"

"Kids?"

"Frank had a younger sister. All three kids had different fathers, by the way. Anyhow, the kids went into foster care. They were split up. That didn't bode well for Frank. He stayed in trouble, bouncing from home to home."

"Christ."

"They finally found an older couple that lived south of here on a farm. Frank thrived. Frank was smart, he tested out with an IQ of one forty-four. When he turned eighteen he was no longer a ward of the state, so the state cut him loose. He stayed on the farm with, Christ, what was their name . . . I don't remember. Anyway, things were going fine. Then the old guy drops dead, the wife is distraught, and the couple's kids move in on a lucrative situation. They put the woman in a rest home and sell the place."

"Let me guess the rest. Frank is cut out of everything."

"You got it."

"He had a few run-ins with the law. Nothing major, mostly driving under the influence, which back then they let slide, and outstanding tickets."

"That put him in prison?"

"No. He was sliding down a one-way chute to nowhere. He got caught inside an attorney's office, ransacking the place."

"Do you know whose office it was?"

"Not off the top of my head. But he got ten years."

"First offense?"

"Yup. There was always something odd about his file."

"What do you mean, Janet?"

"Every damn time he came up for parole it was denied. He served his sentence almost to the end. I think he had eighteen months to go."

"I take it he had problems inside."

"Model prisoner. Doesn't that strike you as just a little off center?"

"Particularly when no one serves a full sentence in this state. Not even back then. Janet, I need to see what you have on Frank."

"I can't do that."

"You can. I think you really believed in this guy. It's not too late to do something for him."

"He's dead, for Christ's sake. What's to be done?"

"At least get the name of the attorney. Okay?"

"That I can do. I don't have to say that it puts my butt—"

"You don't have to say it. Where's the sister, the younger one?"

"Living here. Divorced, a couple of kids. She's okay. I like her. She even offered to have Frank live with her, but he refused."

"Does she know what happened yet?"

"Yeah. I went over there as soon as I heard this morning and told her. She was his only living relative."

"The father?"

"Who the hell knows? I don't know how she's going to handle burying him by herself. I mean financially. You know what she did? As soon as she was old enough, she drove to Deer Lodge twice a month to see Frank."

"They stayed in touch?"

"Through it all."

"Who is she, Janet?" I took a pen and small notebook out of my jacket pocket.

"Simon. Becky Simon. She lives on the west end off Rehberg on Dover Drive. Ten-ten Dover. She's a teacher at one of the elementary schools out there."

"Thanks, Janet." I wrote the address down and a note to myself to contact one of the funeral homes. "Off the subject, what do you know about Bob Maitland?"

"Ooh. Nothing at all. Ask me what I'd like to know about him." She blushed. "He's sure a good-looking son of a gun. I don't know of a single woman in town who doesn't dream a little dream about Maitland. Why do you ask? I thought you were, uh—"

"I am. Sort of. You think he's on the up-and-up?"

"From what I can tell. Want me to put my ear to the ground?"

"No. It's no big deal. I better get out of here. I really want to stop by and see Frank's sister."

"Why do I get the feeling that you're into this deeper than you'll admit?"

"Don't ask, Janet. I don't have any answers right now. Don't forget that name for me. My machine is on if I'm not home."

"Great. Phoebe? I always have thought that it was odd as hell that Frank didn't get paroled before now. I always wanted to dig on that one, but my caseload is out of sight. I just never got around to it. Keep that in mind."

"I will. Catch you later."

After dropping another couple of dimes in the parking meter, I headed for the courthouse. Walking in through the doors that faced Third Avenue, I squeezed through a crowd trying to get to the elevator. The detective division of the Sheriff's Department was on the second floor, and one flight of stairs seemed like an unnecessary walk. There was a camera crew set up, a couple of faces from the *Gazette* that I recognized, and a voice that sounded vaguely familiar from within the crowd.

"We not only need a break in the weather," the faceless voice said. The crowd responded with laughter. "We also need a break from the archaic laws that seem to favor the criminal and not the citizen. I've had firsthand experience with violent crime. You all know that. My wife, Ellen, was senselessly slaughtered over a quarter of a century ago, and the man responsible has not, to this very day, been brought to justice."

Maitland. I tried backing up toward the doors, but found myself blocked by a woman who must have weighed three hundred pounds.

"Excuse me," I said in a whisper. "I'd like to get through."

"Isn't he just wonderful? I live alone, and Lord knows I'm scared all the time. A woman my age shouldn't live in constant fear. Don't you agree?"

"Right. Now excuse me, please." There was no getting around her.

"Hush up now." She looked down at me over her double chins. The words sprayed from her mouth. I wiped my forehead off and hushed up. The last thing I needed was to draw attention to my presence.

"Is that why you've hired an investigator? To reopen your wife's case?" someone asked from the front.

"Not just any investigator. The best."

"I've got to get out of here. You're going to have to excuse me." My voice was just loud enough to turn the heads of the *Gazette* people whom I recognized.

"Hey! Let's hear from her. She's right back here."

I felt like someone hit me with an electric bull prod. This time, the entire crowd turned around and scanned everyone standing near the back. I could hear Maitland.

"She's where? Move aside, move aside. Let her come on over here. Where are you, Phoebe?"

Moses couldn't have parted the sea any better. There we were, Maitland and me, staring each other down across the marble floor. Hands pushed me forward until I was standing next to him. He put his arm around my shoulder.

"How did you hear about it?"

Questions were coming fast and furious.

"Where do you start on a murder that happened that long ago?"

"Is this just a slick way to get the spotlight on your upcoming political race?"

"Hold on. Hold on. Let's take a breath here. As Phoebe informed me on our first meeting, the 'private' in private investigator means just that. Let's not put her on the spot." Maitland held his hands up; the crowd quieted down.

This guy was unbelievable.

I heard the bell on the elevator and turned toward it just as Maggie Mason stepped out, briefcase in hand. She stopped, grinned at me, walked to the edge of the crowd, and gave me a thumbs-up sign.

"It's your choice, Phoebe. If you don't want to comment, they'll understand." Maitland leaned down and whispered. "Give me a hand here."

I glanced at Maggie one more time and then straight at the crowd.

"I have no agreement with Mr. Maitland and do not consider him my client."

"Are you just ironing out some wrinkles before—"

A cacophony of voices rose. Maitland stiffened beside me. I saw him lean down, say something to someone on the other side of him. I also saw that person step away and disappear.

"What are you saying, Miss Siegel?"

"I'm saying that I do not now, nor do I intend to, represent Mr. Maitland."

Maitland, without moving his lips, teeth together, media smile smeared across his face, said under his breath, "You'll regret this."

"Do you have any interest at all in this case?" someone asked from my left.

Out of the corner of my eye I saw the guy that had been standing on Maitland's left whispering something to one of the media people. I tried to watch him as he moved through the crowd and disappeared again.

"Do I have an interest?" I asked back.

"Are you investigating this case or not?"

They could smell blood. Aggression laced their questions.

"I am. But not for Mr. Maitland."

"Then who?" They seemed to ask in unison.

"Frank Chillman and Ellen Dahl Maitland."

They moved forward in a unified wave.

"What's the connection between the two?"

"Isn't that the guy that bought it last night sometime?"

"Does this mean you won't endorse Maitland?"

"Who the hell is Frank Chillman?"

I was caught in a rapid gunfire of questions coming from all directions. A voice boomed from my left. Heads turned toward the sound. The crowd fell silent.

"What was that?" a woman from Channel Eight asked.

"My question was directed to Ms. Siegel. Weren't you involved in the death of your husband three years ago, and wasn't he a Billings police officer? And aren't you now involved in the death of Frank Chillman last night? Doesn't sound like a good track record."

Again the crowd moved as one and turned toward the reporter. I couldn't talk. I just stared at him and hoped my mouth wasn't hanging open. Involuntarily my muscles tensed as I tried to work my way through the crowd. Someone grabbed my arm and held on. I tried to throw it off.

"It's me, Phoebe. Maggie. Come this way."

I obeyed and let her lead me toward the elevator. She frantically pushed the button. I stared at the doors, hoping to hell they opened soon.

"Is that true, Ms. Siegel?"

"Were you charged?"

"Under what circumstances?"

The doors slid open. The voices behind me blended into a dull roar as I stepped into the elevator and pushed myself into a corner. Maggie held the crowd at bay and punched a floor number. The doors slid closed.

"Fuck. The son of a bitch."

"Don't blame his mother," Maggie said and laughed uncomfortably. "God, I am so sorry. What the hell is going on?"

"The bastard!" I screamed as the doors slid open. Three older women stood and stared at me in disbelief.

"PMS," Maggie said, looked at them, and shrugged. "It's that time of the month."

They acknowledged concern and shuffled aside as we stepped out. I looked back and saw them peeking around the doors of the elevator. I followed Maggie down the hall and through the door

she opened ahead of me into the law library. I paced back and
forth.

"He sent one of his fucking flunkies to set that up. I saw him,
Maggie. Damn! So help me, the little prick isn't going to get away
with this. I'll nail his balls to the wall."

"Does this mean you don't find him attractive?"

All I could do was look at her.

10

Dover Road cut through one of the numerous new subdivisions that were stretching like tentacles in every direction on the fringe of Billings. Walled off, fenced off, or by the intentional cloning of the structures, they were cloistered minicommunities in which everything was determinedly cute: kids, porch lights, new midsize cars sporting the most popular fashion colors parked in driveways off the mazes of cul-de-sacs. All of this enabled the inhabitants to live cute little lives. Only the numbers on the house separated Becky Simon from the rest. I pulled up in front. Sure enough, it was cute. Too cute to associate it with the grieving that was more than likely taking place inside.

I parked the truck, got out, and walked up to the front door. It took three pushes on the doorbell before she opened the door.

"Yes?" Her voice was as soft as she was gentle looking.

"Are you Becky Simon?"

"Yes, I am."

"My name is Phoebe Siegel. I just left Janet Sloane—"

"My brother Frank contacted you, didn't he?" She stepped back from the door. "Jeez. I don't know where my head is. Come on in. It's freezing."

"Thanks." I stepped into the house. It was immaculate, even with the scattering of toys across the living room floor. "I know this is a bad time, Becky, but I need to talk to you about Frank."

"Don't worry about it. Let's sit in the dining room. I'm more comfortable in there. Coffee?" I followed as she crossed the living room picking up toys as she went. "Watch your step. My kids, ya know, they, uh . . ."

Becky stopped, leaned down, picked up a stuffed white polar bear that lay at her feet, and held it up to her face. I could hear a muffled sob.

"God, I'm so sorry. It's just that it's so hard to believe he's gone. He bought this for Max, my six-year-old. Max carries it with him everywhere he goes." She raised one hand and wiped the tears on her cheeks with the tips of her fingers. "I really didn't mean to—"

"Maybe it would be better if I came back tomorrow or some other day." Christ, I felt like one of those hard-ass reporters who would stick a microphone in someone's face and ask, "How do you feel seeing your father, son, brother, or husband, bloated, being pulled from the river?"

"Today or tomorrow, it's not going to get better for a long, long time. Sit down. Please."

I walked to a high-backed chair and started to sit.

"Damn! Wait!" She moved quickly toward me. "Don't sit there."

Grief is one thing; this was slightly irrational. I moved aside as Becky stepped around me and picked up a piece of jelly-covered toast from the seat of the chair.

"You wouldn't want this on your rear." She walked back into the kitchen and placed the toast on the counter. "Sorry I yelled. Like I said, it was a tough morning. Go ahead and sit down. Did I ask you if you wanted coffee?"

"Sure."

"Do you take anything in it?"

"No. Black."

Becky Simon had to stand on tiptoe to get a cup from the shelf in the cupboard. Even the weight of the carafe as she poured coffee into the cup appeared ponderous in her small hand. She carried the cup to the table, set it down in front of me, and then filled her own.

"I've been sitting here just staring since Janet left. I don't know how I got the kids ready for school, and then sure enough, I forgot Allison's lunch and had to run it up to her."

"I'm not very good at knowing the right thing to say, Becky. I didn't really know Frank."

"I did," she said, smiling broadly, and for a fleeting second the agonized look left her brown eyes and was replaced with a twinkle. "You would have liked him. He was rough on the edges but, God

. . . he was so loving. Particularly with the kids. He was great with them."

There's two sides to every coin. This one was intriguing. It wasn't exactly the profile of the tough-talking ex-con who had called me in the middle of the night and ended up dead with his brains frozen to a car window.

"I'm sure he was."

"All we had was each other, you know. He had it so tough, and I had it so easy. Jesus, it just doesn't make sense that we stayed so close."

"You were in foster care. Right?"

"I suppose technically that's what it was, but it was the only home I knew. I don't remember my mother or my sister Rita. Just through Frank. I wasn't bounced around from foster home to foster home, if that's what you're asking.

"I think I was ten when they finally let Frank see me. He was eight years older than me, and I barely remembered him. Little things come back now and then. Maybe they're memories, I don't know. All I do know is that Frank was my brother, and I loved him." Tears welled up in her eyes again. "I wish I wouldn't do this."

"This is never easy, Becky, but I would like to ask you some questions."

"You and everyone else."

"Have the police been out here?"

"A Detective Jackson called. He'll be out later today. I told him I just couldn't handle anything right now. I'm not sure he liked being put off, but he was at least nice about it."

"I know Pete Jackson. He's good at what he does."

She ran her hand through her chestnut brown hair from her forehead back. When she stopped, the weight of her thick tresses fell back into place and framed her doll-like face. There was a subtle ethnicity about her: the dark eyes fringed with thick black lashes and the deep olive complexion.

"Frank told me he was going to hire you. Does he owe you any money or anything? I don't have much, but—"

"Frank and I worked it out, Becky. There's no money owed. Janet tells me you're divorced."

"Isn't everyone?" She smiled halfheartedly. "Going on four years.

The last thing I wanted to do in life was turn my children into latch-key kids. My daughter is in third grade, and Max is in first. We moved into this house last year, and we love it. The kids—" She stopped, stared at me with those deep-set eyes, and smiled sadly. "You're not here to talk about my kids or my house or my divorce. You're here about Frank. What do you need to know?"

"When did you last talk to him, Becky?"

"Last night. We had one of the best conversations we'd ever had. But it had been going like that lately. Really good talks. A lot about the past. A lot about the future. He thought he had one, you know?"

"Pardon me?"

"A future. He thought he had a future."

"He told you he was going to hire me. Did he tell you why?"

"Yes. It was in regards to Rita, but I've heard about Rita for years. His letters were full of her. Don't be so quick to dismiss his suspicions." She wrinkled her forehead and leaned toward me. "Frank was a very intelligent man. He made mistakes, I know that. But he was good where it counts: in his heart."

"I'm not challenging that at all. You say you don't remember your sister?"

"No one ever told me anything about Rita until I was about thirteen. My parents, foster parents, same thing—well, they didn't really want me to have a past, just a wonderful future. Looking back, we did a lot of pretending." She drank what was left of her coffee and stood. "But they couldn't protect me from everything. Would you like some more coffee?"

"Why not? I've been living on caffeine and cold medicine."

"You've got it, huh? It took me weeks to get rid of it. It seemed like the kids were sick every other week last fall. What are you taking?"

"NyQuil and son of NyQuil. Whatever that stuff is you take during the day."

"It gets better and then it gets worse," Becky said as she filled my cup.

"Thanks, on both counts. What do you mean, they couldn't protect you from everything?"

"When I was about thirteen, maybe fourteen, I was invited to a sleep-over at this girl's house. There were five or six of us all camped out in sleeping bags in the basement, and for some reason I had to go upstairs, probably to use the bathroom, and I overheard her parents. They were talking about me."

I couldn't see the significance in any of this but listened anyway. She was going through a hard time. If reminiscing helped, why not?

"At first I thought they were arguing, so I sat down on the top stair and waited for a chance to sneak to the bathroom. I mean, I didn't want to embarrass them or myself. Then my name came up."

"In what context?"

"He, the father, wanted me out of the house."

"Why in the hell—excuse me, Becky—why would he have a problem with you being there?"

"He was telling his wife that my sister was a whore and my brother was no good. It was the first time I had heard anything about Rita. Up until then her name had never been mentioned to me."

"What did you do?"

"I walked up to them, told them I wanted to call my parents and have them come pick me up. They both looked so shocked. She, the wife, walked over and put her arm around my shoulder and tried to reassure me that would not be necessary."

"Did you leave?"

"Yes. I called my father and he came immediately."

"Did you tell them what had happened? They must have wondered what was up."

"You bet I did. I felt pretty betrayed. Like everyone knew but me. Thank God my best friend, Tina, left with me. I mean, it was so odd. After all these years I still feel the humiliation, like it happened this morning. Now, as an adult, it just makes me angry as heck."

"Did you ever see the daughter after that?"

"I had to go through school with her. And ya know? She never talked to me again. It was like I didn't exist."

"We've all got those nasty memories from school. They hurt. Even if I can't remember names from back then, I definitely remember the feelings."

"I'll never forget her name. It was Diana. Diana . . . let's see . . .

darn it." Becky grinned. "Diana something. Guess I'm not as good as I thought I was."

"No matter. What happened to her?"

"She's been married three times and in and out of rehab centers for drug and alcohol abuse. And she accomplished all of that without my influence. I know it sounds horrid, but I do take some delight in that fact."

I laughed and agreed with her.

"Becky, Frank felt that there was a connection between your sister's death and another death that occurred at the same time. Did he talk about that?"

"Yes. He did. He said that it was a big cover-up and that no one really cared much about Rita's death. I pretty much substantiated that on my own."

"How so?"

"Remember the sleep-over? After that my friend and I got really curious. We went down to the library and pored over the newspaper articles. That's when I first found out about the other woman that had been killed. The papers were plastered with column after column about Ellen Maitland. There were two"—Becky held up two fingers—"two mentions of Rita. The first was when her body was found. The second was about her working as a prostitute for that madam. I guess her obituary would count as three."

"Hmm. Realizing that this is already a tough situation for you, Becky, I just don't know how to ask what I need to ask."

"Just do it. I need some closure on many things that Frank and I talked about. We had plans, Frank and I. But he had to follow this thing with Rita to some conclusion."

"Do you know of anyone who he felt threatened by? Anyone who would want him dead?"

Becky ran her hand through her hair again and became pensive. "I thought he was excitable last night, on edge or something. He was scared. What I was hearing in his voice was fear."

"Fear of what?"

"He'd made contact with someone he had been trying to see. I don't know if it was on the phone or in person, or what. But he had some kind of contact with this person. I tried to get him to tell me who it was, but he thought it would be better if I didn't know. He worried about me and the kids constantly."

"He may have had good reason."

Her eyes widened. I could hear her suck in her breath.

"We could be in danger—my kids . . ."

"I didn't mean it that way." I was lying, and she knew it.

"You meant it exactly that way. For God's sake, if I have to take precautions, please tell me."

I could hear the hysteria rising in her voice. "Frank was murdered. My bet is that he was onto something, and because of that something, he died. It's hard to tell who knows you even exist, Becky. You had separate lives up until recently. Most of your contact with Frank was corresponding with him in prison."

"That's true. But I never hid Frank. He was my brother."

"Let me put it this way. All those years ago at that sleep-over, Deanna's parents—"

"Diana."

"Diana's parent's apparently knew about both Frank and Rita. I take it that the connection between the both of them and you was common knowledge back then. I'm hoping that his poking around and resurrecting all of this wouldn't be linked to you, but who knows?"

"So I have to be careful."

"I would suggest that. Make sure you know who you're talking to. Don't give any interviews, and watch what you put in the obituary."

"I don't understand. He has to have an obituary. I'm the only family he had."

"I'm not saying don't put anything in. Use your maiden name or simply put he is survived by a sister."

"That's so—"

"Necessary. Trust me on this."

"I have some things that Frank asked me to put into my safety deposit box. He told me that they were copies of some very important papers, and that if anything should happen to him I was to give them to you."

"They're where?" I had figured that when Frank died, any information he had died with him.

"The copies are in my safety deposit box. There's also an audiotape. He gave it to me a couple of days ago. I've never looked in the envelope because Frank asked me not to."

"He sure took a lot for granted," I mumbled under my breath.

"Pardon me?"

"I was just thinking out loud. He was so sure I would take this case. Why?"

"All he ever told me was that he thought you were a good person. I wish I could give you a better reason than that, but I can't."

"You said the *copies,* like you know where the originals are. Do you?"

"They were with Frank. He told me he had several copies of the tape, and that the papers were hidden out at that place where he was staying."

My mind flashed on the crime scene. Nothing had appeared ransacked, only recently and eerily abandoned. By now the detectives had gone over the place with the proverbial fine-tooth comb.

"How soon can you get down and pull those papers out of your safety deposit box?"

"Tomorrow. In the morning. There's no way I can do it today. I've got—"

"Tomorrow will be fine, Becky. We need some time to have a talk about the conversations you and your brother had. We'll work that out tomorrow." I pulled one of my cards out of my jacket pocket and handed it to her. "Call me when you get them. In fact, if you want someone to go down with you, I'd be glad to."

"I'd like that." She took the card, read it, and placed it on the table between us. "Here you've been sitting all this time with your jacket on. I'm sorry—you must be sweltering."

"As a matter of fact, I'm freezing. Have been for a week. It's been a long night, and I think I need to give you some space." I stood and walked toward the front door.

"Do you think I should be fearful?" Becky asked as she followed me. "I don't want to overreact or anything, but—"

"I think you'll be fine. Just keep the obit short, like we talked about. And I would hold off talking to any of the media."

"I can't imagine why they would be interested."

"They'll be interested, Becky. Trust me."

"Diana Gordon."

"Pardon me?"

"The sleep-over. Remember? Her name was Diana Gordon. Her father was an attorney." Becky tapped her forehead with her fingertips.

I searched my own memory banks. Maitland's buddy back when was an attorney named Gordon. "Do you remember his first name?"

"Don, Dan . . . uh, David. That's it. David. He's a judge now. Judge David Gordon. Do you know him?"

"Not personally, but I've heard his name." I didn't tell her how recently.

How the hell did Dave Gordon, wanna-be defender of the indigent, have knowledge of the Chillman family and then use that knowledge so cruelly against a young girl?

She opened the door, and I stepped out onto the porch. The cold swept in so quickly it formed a sheet of vapor between us. I reached up to pull the jacket collar up around my neck. The blast of cold brought a deep throbbing pain to my sinuses.

"It seems so sad to think about burying Frank in this weather." Becky's voice was barely above a whisper.

"I know what you mean." I looked across the street, down a couple of houses, and could see two men standing inside a house under construction. "They couldn't pay me enough to work outside in this—"

It happened fast, yet all motion slowed down. I saw the glint like a shaft of lightning that flashed and was gone. Turning back toward Becky, I saw her smiling, saw her mouth form words I couldn't hear. My hands pushed out and hit her in the chest. She fell backward. There was no sound, just an imploding in my head, and I was falling, twisting down toward the snow that was swelling toward me. There was no pain. No time to think. A lifetime passed as I settled full-length onto the porch, snow mushrooming up around my face. A penetrating cold drove against my cheek. Tiny ice prisms formed microscopic crystals in front of my eyes and fascinated me with the geometric detail. Then they were dying, melting from the breath that came in loud swooshing sounds from deep inside my mind. My eyes closed to a red-black veil and then opened in time to see the seeping crimson of my own blood as it dyed the snow around my head.

11

I was climbing up out of a dense fog on a greased ladder. Two, three rungs at a time, and then the sense of falling. Climb again and fall. The throbbing in my head pumped voices to the edge of my consciousness. A blinding light slammed my eyes shut. I shook my head back and forth, rolling the pain from one side to the other.

"Phoebe? Come on, now. Open your eyes. The bad stuff is behind you. Only good girls get a Barney sticker."

I was dead and about to be stamped with the sign of the Antichrist: Barney. No last rites, and I hadn't been to confession in ten years. Not a good scenario for everlasting peace. Then again, maybe I wasn't dead. There was no Zelda screaming, "Go toward the light, Phoebe. Go toward the light."

I opened my eyes in time to catch another blinding beam.

"Get that fucking light out of my eyes." My voice echoed inside my head. I wasn't sure I was speaking or just thinking.

"That's what I like. Spunk. Good old-fashioned spunk."

People were giggling. I tried to open my eyes and concentrate on bringing the blurred images leaning over me into focus.

"Hi there," he said, his face a couple of feet from mine. He was good-looking, hazel-eyed, young, and he was twirling a Barney sucker in front of my face.

I squinted and opened my eyes again.

"How many of these do you see?" he asked and started humming the "Jeopardy" theme.

"Thirty-six."

"Good answer. That's exactly how many I'm holding."

"Does this work with all the girls?" I tried to sit up.

"Take that a little slow."

He slid an arm under me and helped me to a sitting position. Someone else swung my legs over the edge of the gurney. I could feel cool air on my butt and on my back.

"We're all through with you. How do you feel?"

"You're the doctor. How the hell do you think I feel?"

"Are you allergic to anything?" By this time he had his clipboard and was taking notes.

"Pain."

"Pardon me?"

"I'm allergic to pain." I touched the left side of my head. The skin was numb. The skin was bare. "What the hell happened to my hair?"

"We had to shave a small area. Don't worry about it. Chances are it'll grow back."

"This isn't a damn horse race. Chances are? Chances are? What the fuck does that mean?"

"It means that the amount of scarring that takes place will determine whether the hair grows back. I guess I'd be glad to be alive. You came close. Do you remember what happened?"

"Vaguely. I saw a flash. Several flashes."

Without looking up from the clipboard, he said, "Anything after the first flash was my flashlight. But I mean it, you're damn lucky."

"The woman that was with me. Is she—"

"She's fine. You hit her hard enough in the chest that her breasts were coming out her back, but other than that—"

"Where the hell did they ever find you?" I hated it, but I had to laugh and it hurt. I held both sides of my head with my hands. "Can I get out of here?"

"Like that?"

I reached behind me and tried to close the back of the gown. "I don't dress or undress in front of strangers."

He looked at me with a knowing smile. "Trust me, we are not strangers."

"You? You undressed me?"

"Let's just say I was at the scene. Your clothes are over there. By the way, are you really a PI?"

"Really."

"Seems a little hazardous. I don't want you doing anything for a couple of days."

"Right. Can I go now?"

"I'm not kidding. I want you to take it easy. Do you have a regular family physician?"

"No."

"Then come back up here in, say . . . four days. We'll take another look at it. I used a big enough dose of Novocain to clean it up and get a good look at what damage was done, but it's going to take on a life of its own when that numbness leaves. I don't want to give you anything strong, no narcotics, but I do want to give you something to take the edge off."

"Great. Now can I get the hell out of here?"

"If you feel steady enough on your feet. I'll have the nurse bring in a prescription for you. Take care of yourself."

He walked over, patted me on the shoulder, and left.

"Can I see her?" I recognized Pete Jackson's deep voice coming from somewhere outside the curtain that blocked me off from the rest of the sick and injured.

"Sure, go on in. The doctor wants to write her a prescription, and then we're through with her."

A large hand came around the curtain, pushing it to one side just as I reached behind me and tried to close the gaping gown.

"Hey, Siegel."

"Jesus, Jackson."

"No, Pete Jackson. Deputy Jackson to you, sweetie. How ya doin'?"

"How do I look like I'm doing, Pete?"

"Not that bad, considering."

"Considering what?"

"Considering that the side of your head is shaved. Is that one of those punk cuts?" He shifted the toothpick in his mouth from one side to the other and tried not to smile.

"Shit." My hand went up to the side of my head. I touched the shaven part and winced with pain. "Does it look that bad?"

"Hell, it'll grow back, Siegel. You're lucky you're alive."

That was the second time I'd heard that in the past several minutes. And they were right, of course. I was lucky. Even if I wasn't shaking on the outside, my guts were quivering like Jell-O. The bullet had grazed the left side of my head just above my ear, tearing the skin off as it went. The rest of my hair felt matted and stiff.

"Becky, how is she?"

"Shook as hell but damn lucky too. You're fast on your feet. I'm impressed. Up to answering some questions?"

"Shoot."

"Bad choice of words." He again shifted the toothpick as he walked over and pulled a stool on rollers nearer to the bed. "How much do you remember?"

I opened my mouth just as the nurse peeked around the corner.

"Is there someone I can call for you, Ms. Siegel?"

"Yes, as a matter of fact there is. Maggie Mason. Don't play this up too much, but tell her I need a ride to my truck."

"I can take you to your truck." Pete looked offended.

"No, Pete. I'd have to put up with your bad jokes," I said and smiled at him. I gave the nurse Maggie's phone number. "You were asking?"

"What keyed you in that there was a shooter? You had to be aware of something, or you wouldn't have pushed Becky Simon back into the house."

"It was so damn fast, Pete. I've been sitting here trying to make sense out of what happened myself. There were these guys on the north side of the block, down a couple of lots in one of those houses that are under construction. Hell, you know how cold it is out, and I guess it struck me odd that they would be working on it."

Pete had reached into his pocket and pulled out a tablet, prepared to take notes. He pinched the bridge of his nose with his fingers and said nothing.

"You're getting this down, right?" I asked.

"Those guys you saw? They were working. They'd gone out there to check on some rolls of Tyvek. Apparently someone ripped them off a week or so back, and they wanted to make sure they were down in the basement."

"I saw the flash, Pete. It came from that house."

"The flash you saw from that house was the sun hitting off some Blue Board."

"What the hell is that?"

"It's a Styrofoam sheeting they use on the outside of these new houses. It's backed with a foil, and they were also moving sheets of that down to the basement. The sun must have caught it just right."

"Pete—"

"The angle of where the bullet entered the siding on the house tells me it came from farther up."

"Farther up where? I know what I saw."

"You know what you think you saw. That whole area is under construction. The way we see it is that it came from a block up. Each street sits up higher than the one below it. Kinda terraced? We also think the hit was for Mrs. Simon. You saved her life, Siegel."

"You've checked these guys out?"

"Oh, yeah. Talked to the contractor they're employed with and confirmed he knew they were out there. They brought you in, by the way."

"Really."

"They heard the shot, looked across the street, and saw one woman flying backward into the house and another, you, taking a nosedive off the porch. They busted their asses over there."

"You got the bullet?"

"Sure did. It's a Nosler eighty-grain."

"A reload?"

"Yup. Not exactly something your imported hit man, oops— sorry, Siegel, hit person—"

"Knock it off, Pete."

"Well now, I don't want to piss you off," Pete said and smiled at me. "I'm just trying to lighten the situation. Like I was saying, it's not a professional hit, but a hit all the same."

"I can't help you with anything, Pete. If you've checked these guys out, then I saw nothing."

"It isn't much of a stretch to figure out this is connected to the Chillman thing last night."

I shrugged.

"Siegel, you know the drill."

"Jackson." I sighed, mimicking him. "What are you talking about?"

"Don't go stepping on any toes on this one."

"And whose toes are we talking about here?"

"We've got two investigations going on, and we don't want any interference. Private dicks and real dicks—"

"Why, Pete, are you talking dirty to me?"

He blushed and shifted the toothpick again. "I'm being serious here. The whole damn department knows you were at Chillman's last night. They—"

"We—"

"Okay. *We* don't want you getting in the way. Not saying you're not good at your job, Siegel, it's just that we can handle it."

"So handle it and don't worry your pretty little head about me, Jackson." He was really pissing me off.

The nurse came back with two slips of paper in her hand.

"This one is for pain. And this is what you need to do to take care of the wound. Wait a day to wash your hair or have someone help you with it. We don't want that site to get wet. There's always a chance for infection."

"Can I go now?"

"As soon as I get this guy out of here," she said, smiling toward Pete. "Would you step out, Deputy, so she can get dressed?"

"Sure. Siegel, I might drop by your house later."

"Call first, Pete. I may be on drugs."

"By the way, your friend is in the waiting room," the nurse said as she pulled the curtain aside and motioned Pete out. "I'll tell her you'll be right out."

I stepped down onto the stool beside the gurney, got dressed, and prepared myself to meet the barrage of questions I knew would be coming.

Maggie took me to the truck. Becky Simon's garage door was open and minus a car. I couldn't imagine what was going through her mind. Her brother dead one minute, and her own life on the line the next. I had only myself to worry about. She had two little kids. Tough break.

Maggie also insisted on following me to the pharmacy and forced me to sit in the truck while she went in and filled the prescription. By the time we walked through the front door of my house, Maggie had apparently exhausted herself. She took her boots and coat off and walked straight into the kitchen.

"Want me to make some coffee?" I could hear her rinsing out the carafe for the coffeemaker. "On second thought, maybe caffeine isn't the way to go. How about tea? Are you up for tea?"

"No, probably not, and no."

"What?"

"I don't want anything, maybe some water." I sat down at the table and rested my head in my hands. "And I thought my sinuses were pain in the purest form."

"Does it hurt?"

"Yeah, Maggie. It hurts. I guess I could compare it to trepanning with a chain saw. When you get through over there, I want you to sit down."

"Phoebe, I don't want to get in the middle between you and Bob Maitland—"

"You're already in the middle, whether you like it or not. You saw the bullshit antics he pulled down at the courthouse. I think—no, I *know*—he's capable of a helluva lot more."

"I don't agree with you, Phoebe." Maggie turned to face me. Her green eyes snapped. "If you two have had a falling-out, then so be it. But we don't know if he planted that bit of news on one of those reporters, do we?"

"I know. I saw him talk to one of his little weasels and watched him as he pushed through that throng and whispered in that guy's ear. Shit. Why the hell would I lie about that?"

"I'm not saying you're lying. I'm just saying that I didn't see the same thing you did. I've known Bob since I've been in Billings. We had a relationship at one time—"

"Maggie, for God's sake, listen to yourself. Simply because you fucked this guy, does that mean he's—"

"That was not only unnecessary, it was damn mean-spirited, Phoebe. Just damn—"

"I'm sorry. Shit, it's been a rough twenty-four hours. Come on and sit down. Just hear me out, okay?"

She eyed me suspiciously as she leaned against the counter. We'd also known each other a long time. She had a mind like a steel bear trap, with loyalties just as strong. I respected Maggie, and I needed her right now, if for nothing else, then as a sounding board.

"I'll listen. No guarantees, but I will listen." She walked to the table, pulled out a chair, and sat down opposite me. "Well? Let's have it."

"Maggie, I think he may have killed his wife."

"Oh, for Christ's sake, Phoebe. Are you sure you're not having some residual problems from that gunshot wound? Bob would never, I would stake my own life on it, I . . . I . . ."

"Maggie, you said you would hear me out. That's all I ask."

"This is absurd, but go ahead. I said I'd listen."

"When Maitland first came over here, he was as charismatic as everyone said he would be. The perfect politician. Call it intuition, call it whatever you like, but something isn't right with that guy. He referred to his dead wife as 'the daughter,' and something about that spooked me. The deal at the courthouse was premeditated, Maggie. He had information on me involving the death of my ex-husband before he even contacted me, just in case he needed it."

"I suggested you, Phoebe. It was me," she said and thumped her index finger into her chest.

"Think back, Maggie. How did my name come up?"

"We were talking—"

"About what?"

"Just a minute here, I'm trying to remember. I think he called me and told me he was looking for a good private investigator. I had talked about you—"

"Right there. You had talked about me before. Did he know we were friends?"

"Yes. But—"

"So when he told you he was looking for a PI, who do you suppose he figured you'd suggest?"

"Oh, Phoebe, that's off the wall."

"He knew damned well you'd suggest me. He was loaded for bear, Maggie. He prepared for any fallout, no matter what direction it came from. When Frank Chillman first called me, I thought he was some kook. But he wasn't, Maggie, and now he's dead. He told me that there was another murder around the time that Ellen Maitland was killed: a young woman by the name of Rita Chillman, Frank's sister. He was just a kid when it all came down, but he dedicated his sorry existence to gathering information about his sister's murder."

"Obsessive."

"Probably. But just because you're paranoid, doesn't mean someone isn't out to get you."

"You read the poster in my office. Right?"

"Right. He told his sister, Becky Simon—"

"She's Frank Chillman's sister? Jeez."

"Yes, she is, and she could have had her head blown off this afternoon. Why? Because she has the information, or at least copies of it, that Frank was going to give to me. Coincidence? I don't think so."

"Have you seen the material yet?"

"No, but she was going to get it out of her safety deposit box tomorrow morning. God only knows she's probably left the state by now. Hell, Maggie, she has two little kids."

"This still doesn't prove to me that Bob is involved."

"Does the name Dave Gordon ring a bell?"

"Oh, come now, you know it does. I'm an attorney. Remember? Who the hell doesn't know Judge Gordon?"

"Do you know also that Gordon and Maitland were boozing buddies at the time Maitland met Ellen Dahl? And through the short-lived marriage, I might add."

"There's some kind of bad blood between Gordon and Bob, Phoebe. Has been for years. No one quite knows why—"

"I don't buy that. Somebody knows the history between those two. And furthermore, Dave Gordon had knowledge of the Chillman family, to the point that he didn't want his daughter mingling with Becky Simon, née Chillman, a long time ago. Hell, Becky was thirteen years old, in foster care, leading a decent life. Where would Gordon come up with that if there isn't some nexus here?"

Maggie was silent. At some point she had moved her chair back from the table and folded her arms across her chest. Her eyes were narrow, troubled.

"I'm not getting through to you, am I? You're closing up on me, Maggie. Don't do it."

"Interesting facts, Phoebe, but scattered. When did you say you'd be getting that information?"

"I'll find out. I'll call her. I told her I'd go with her to pick it up. She's probably scared out of her mind about now."

"You get the info, and I'll come back over and we'll go through it. On the off chance that you're onto something, what did you want me to do, Phoebe?"

"I need someone to know what's going on. It's down to that. Plus, I might need some favors."

"That makes me nervous as hell. What kind of favors?"

"You're already close to Maitland."

"He saw me pull you into the elevator. He's not stupid."

"That's what I'm counting on."

"You want me to spy on Maitland?"

"Look, we'll go over this information, and between us, if you are convinced, we'll come up with something."

"Ya know, Siegel, Dashiell Hammett married a girl from my hometown."

"From Butte? I didn't know that."

"Are you sure you know your parentage? I thought perhaps you could be related to—"

"Get serious."

"Get the information. We'll talk."

"Will you be at home?"

"Yeah, I will. Are you going to be all right here by yourself?"

"I've got Stud, remember? And if that doesn't work, I can always infect them with this fucking cold."

"Viruses? Yeah, that'd be good. I've got to get out of here, Phoebe. Call me."

I followed Maggie to the door. She put her coat and boots on and left without saying another word. She was in a helluva position. Maggie had fierce loyalties, and Maitland had been important to her for whatever time it was they had been together. She was one of the strongest women I had ever known, and against staggering odds she had managed to build one of the most respected law careers in the state.

Looking through the glass in the front door, I watched her as she got into her car and just sat there for a minute, her elbows on top of the steering wheel, her head resting on her hands. I wondered just how fresh her relationship with Maitland was. Had it really ended, in her mind? Maybe not. I watched her back out of the drive, the exhaust from her car curling up and disappearing in the frigid air.

I walked into my office and sat down in the chair behind my desk. Ellen Dahl Maitland's picture was still propped against my monitor. I picked it up and laid it on the desk in front of me.

"You've gotta talk to me. Give me something to go on." Again, I was pulled into those sad eyes. "Talk about a strange trio: me, you, and Frank Chillman. Who would've thought? Your husband is going to give me a rough time—in fact, it's already started—but I've got this feeling that you know about rough times, Ellen. I don't even know where that's coming from. Give me a hand here, okay?"

A chill ran down my spine. Maybe she was answering me. I'd become comfortable talking to the dead. It was one of the legacies handed down from dearly departed Aunt Zelda. Cemeteries turned out to be a place I hung out. I didn't do strangers in the cemetery, just family. The Siegels weren't short on family in Mountain View Cemetery. I wanted to believe, like Zelda did, that they heard every word we spoke and if necessary could respond on some level, instruct us, comfort us.

There had been an instructor at the FBI Academy that taught crime scene investigation. His favorite reminder was that the living will lie, the dead won't. He elaborated by telling us to listen not only to the dead but to everything at the scene. "If you've got ears and eyes," he said, "you'll hear them screaming and see the answers spread right out in front of you." Maybe not as strongly and for a different set of reasons, but Zelda and this instructor seemed to agree.

I shivered and looked toward the front door to see if I had left it open. I hadn't. Ellen Maitland wanted to be heard. I put the picture down, reached for the phone book, and looked up Rosella Dahl. It was time.

12

Rosella Dahl had an answering machine. I don't know if I was disappointed or relieved, but it did give me a take on her voice: deep, authoritative, and cold. I left my name and number, and hoped. The receiver was barely in the cradle before the phone started ringing.

"Jesus, Mary, and Joseph," the voice shrieked.

"Mother?"

"I can't take it, Phoebe. I just can't take it like I used to. To hear something like that on the news—"

"Shit. Mom, I'm sorry. I didn't think it—"

"You didn't think? You—didn't—think. That's the problem."

"Mom—"

"Don't *Mom* me, Phoebe Zelda. Don't you dare. Do you have any idea what it's like to hear that your own daughter has been shot? Does the daughter call?"

"Mom, wait a—"

"No. She doesn't call. Now we come to the question, why didn't she call? So? Why didn't you call?"

"I was a little busy, Mother."

"Too busy for your own mother? I nearly died, Phoebe. I just . . . I just . . ." She burst into tears, wrenching sobs.

"Calm down. Jeez. I'm fine, Mom. I wasn't really shot, it was a nick, just a graze."

"It was a bullet," she said as she continued to cry.

"I should have called. It never entered my mind that the news would pick this up so fast. You're right. You never should have heard it like you did, and I apologize."

She sniffled. "You don't know what this puts me through. There are other jobs out there. Jobs that are more suitable—"

"Don't start, Mother. Please. I said I was sorry, and I am."

"It's dangerous. Too secretive. Isn't it enough I buried your brother? Isn't it enough that your own sister was put in jeopardy? Isn't it—"

"You know, Mother, this could be a two-way street. You haven't even asked how I am. I'd think you'd want to know that."

Even her silence was guilt-ridden. "Of course I would. How are you?"

"I'm fine. I've got a little bit of a headache, but other than that I'm fine."

"Now, what happened at the courthouse, Phoebe?"

"I was hoping you wouldn't see that."

"Well, I did. Mr. Maitland wasn't that happy about the events. He even suggested that you were unstable, Phoebe."

"He what?" I sat up straight in the chair. "That son of a bitch. That prick."

She gasped and sputtered. "You're talking to your mother."

Before I could apologize, again, for my verbal transgressions, an urgent knocking rattled the glass on the front door.

"What's that banging?" she asked.

"Someone's at the door, Mom, I have to go. I'll come by tomorrow."

"We're not through talking, young lady."

"Right. I gotta go. Tomorrow. Okay?"

"Good night, Phoebe."

I hung up the phone, walked to the door, and looked through the curtain. Becky Simon was standing there, her face expressionless when she saw me. I opened the door.

"You should have called me, Becky. Come on in."

"I can't. The kids are in the car. We're staying at my mom and dad's tonight. I just wasn't comfortable staying at home."

"I understand. Are you okay?"

"I will be. I need to know my kids are safe. I'm here to give you this." She handed me two large manila envelopes. "I haven't looked in these. I don't want to know what Frank thought. It'll be better for me if I don't know."

"Thanks, Becky. I really didn't expect these until tomorrow."

"I wanted it out of the way. If the sheriff's detective asks me if I have any information, I can say no. Is that a lie? I don't want to lie."

"Well . . ."

The horn on her car blared. We both jumped.

"I've got to go. The kids are tired. How's your head?"

"Intact. Are you doing okay, really?"

"No. I'm not." Tears welled up in her eyes. "I can't believe all of this is happening in my life."

"We still need to talk, Becky. Call me. Please."

"I will. But not for a couple of days. I still have to talk to Detective Jackson. We did get a chance briefly today, but he has more questions. That's why I thought I'd get those out of the way. I almost didn't make it to the bank on time."

"I appreciate it."

The horn blared again. "Well, good-bye." She turned and walked down the stairs, stopped and looked back at me. "I saw what happened at the courthouse. I'm sorry this has all come into your life. If I could change it, I would."

"It didn't just come into my life, Becky, it's a choice on my part. Don't worry about it. Good night."

She got into the car and backed out of the driveway. I liked Becky Simon, the kind of person she was. In a way she was as much a victim as her brother. In some ways, even more so. She had the rest of her life to live with the shit that was inevitably going to come down. All I could hope for was that she had a rest of her life, and that it added up to many, many years.

I was freezing. The cold had surged into the house, and even as I closed the door, I could feel it all around me. The wound on my head was trying to get my attention, but the weight of the manila envelopes I held won. After I made sure the door was locked, I turned out the lights and headed upstairs. I'd been on the couch for the past week. But that night I'd share my bed with Frank Chillman, and since I wasn't that hot on the idea, I figured I might as well be in a comfort zone.

Old houses have personalities of their own. Some nights they breathe, usually loudly enough to stand the hairs up on your head.

Creaks and groans are the expanding and contracting of the walls and floors; the old furnace downstairs has a song of its own that it sings in the middle of the night; pings and bangs pass for footsteps on squeaky floorboards or stairs. But I had adjusted. Or so I thought.

I turned on the stairs once and looked toward the front door, thinking I heard something coming from the front porch. I didn't hear it again. Stud followed me, more obediently than usual, up the rest of the stairs and into the bedroom. I undressed, pulled on a sleep shirt, and crawled into bed. Stud took his usual place at my feet, stretched, and fell immediately asleep.

Only the lamp by the bedside was on. There was a wheezing sound as the wind wound through the eaves. A cottonwood bowed under a gust just long enough to scrape a branch across the window on the south side of the room.

I propped myself up against the oak headboard, opened the manila envelope marked number one, and pulled out a sheaf of papers. On top was an envelope with my name written on it. I opened it and pulled out a folded piece of notebook paper. The handwriting was worse than my own, and that was a stretch, but it was readable. The first line said, "If you are reading this I am dead." I lowered the letter and looked toward the window. I wanted the night sounds, both outside and inside the house, to stop. He was dead all right, but seeing the words scrawled in his own handwriting gave them a ghostly voice that drew me back to the night before and the deadly landscape of Frank Chillman's murder. I tried to block the sounds and continued reading.

At some point exhaustion pulled me into sleep. I woke to sun spilling into the southern window of the bedroom, the sound of melting snow dripping from the roof, and the persistent ringing of the phone. I reached for the receiver and mumbled something that was supposed to be "Hello." My own voice came back at me—*You have reached 555-0464. You know what to do*—and on top of that another voice on the other end of the line was saying, "Hello, are you there? Phoebe?"

"Kyle?"

"Phoebe, I've been trying to call you all morning. Where the hell have you been?"

"In a coma. Let me turn this thing off."

"What?"

"I was sleeping, Kyle. Nice to finally hear from you."

"I had to take a prisoner down to Cheyenne."

"That's a creative excuse."

"Stop. I didn't get back until this morning. Pete Jackson got hold of me at the motel last night and told me what happened."

"Well, isn't that just special of Pete?" My conversation with him had left me a little embittered.

"I thought it damn nice. What's the matter? You and Pete have a run-in?"

"What would ever give you that idea?"

"I tried to call but kept getting that damn machine. How're you doing?"

"As well as can be expected—considering."

"Would you get serious here? I damn near threw up after I got off the phone with Pete."

"You could have left a message on the machine telling me you were going out of town."

"I did. Have you picked up your messages?"

I had to think on that for a minute.

"Well, did you?"

"No. Sorry. Why didn't Pete say something to me?"

"I think he had his hands full. I'm coming over."

I dangled my feet over the edge of the bed and stood up. Dragging the phone behind me, I walked to my dresser and looked into the mirror. What looked back at me was not familiar.

"Wait awhile. I've got to take a bath."

Kyle was silent for a moment before he said, "I could wash your back?" And then he laughed.

"And leave out my front?"

"What am I going to do with you, Phoebe?"

"Between the two of us, we could probably come up with something."

"I'll be there in an hour."

"See ya then. Kyle?"

"Yeah?"

"How's the pup?"

"Pete picked him up at my place last night and took him home. The pup shit all over Pete's house. His wife is home steam cleaning as we speak."

"Jesus," I said and couldn't help laughing. It gave me some sick sense of satisfaction.

"I'll see you soon." Kyle hung up.

There's nothing more horrifying than looking into a mirror and seeing the side of your head shaved. It is not attractive. The term *malpractice* crossed my mind. To follow the hospital's advice and not get that side of my head wet proved impossible in the shower. I watched as the blood that had matted in my hair rinsed down over my body and into the drain. It was only then that I realized how close I had come to ending up like Frank.

By the time I finished, got dressed, gathered up the papers that were now strewn all over the bed, and went downstairs, my mind was once again full of Frank Chillman. I had read and reread all the material and looked at the family photos Frank had placed in the second manila envelope. They belonged with Becky Simon.

Other than Frank putting his memories of his sister Rita down on paper, two things intrigued me. The first was a set of newspaper clippings about Joey Marino, the suspected killer of Ellen Maitland, and how he had been held overnight in jail on outstanding warrants for vehicle violations. Bonded out the next morning, which was a Saturday, he disappeared, never to be seen again. Nothing was missing with him, just the clothes on his back.

There were three or four short articles, pleas to the community—"Have you seen this man?"—and a larger one, complete with a picture of Marino. He was a good-looking kid twenty-seven years ago, rather benign. Not what I expected. It was obvious that the picture had been blown up from a group shot, because I could see an extra shoulder on either side of him. My guess that he had been part of a baseball team didn't come through some brilliant deduction. The shirt he was wearing and what was available as far as sports in the area gave it away.

The second item of note was the tape. I brought a small recorder out of my office and into the kitchen. I was waiting for the coffee-maker to finish and just putting the tape in the recorder when I looked up and saw Kyle at the back door. My mind was a million miles away, and seeing his face put me through the roof.

"Little jumpy?" he asked as I let him in.

"I don't know what would give you that idea, Kyle. That's how I get around the house: leaping three feet at a time. Why the back door?"

"It's sloppy out there. Thirty-four sunny degrees. I didn't want to track up your house."

"That's damn considerate." I walked over to him, slid my arms under his and around his back. It felt good to lean against him and hear the rhythm of his heartbeat.

Kyle leaned down and nuzzled his face in my neck, kissing it softly. "What brought this on?"

"Are you complaining?"

"Nope. I like it." His breath felt warm, reassuring, against my cheek as he spoke. "I'm just worried you have, uh . . . some kind of brain damage. I mean, I don't want it to heal and have this go away."

I tried to pull away. He held me tighter.

"Why do you say shit like that?"

"Just a humor check, Phoebe. Nothing more." He stepped back from me and lifted his hands in the air in mock surrender. "Making sure everything is intact."

I loved his smile, the way it reached his eyes. But he scared the hell out of me. Or maybe what I was beginning to feel for him scared the hell out of me. It was a good moment. I'd need the memory of that sooner than I knew.

"Coffee?" I asked.

"Sure. What's this?" He tapped his finger on the recorder. "Nine Inch Nails?"

"Their greatest hits."

"I figured with that punk hairdo you would need some tunes to go with it."

I sat a cup of coffee down in front of him. "I was impressed that you hadn't mentioned the missing hair."

"Hair? Missing?"

"Forget it." I sat down across from him. "I'm sure Jackson briefed you on what came down yesterday."

"That he did."

"Kyle, I'm onto something here, and—"

"Don't, Phoebe. I don't want to hear anything."

"I just want to bounce some things off you."

"The last time we 'bounced some things' around I almost got nailed for withholding evidence. On this one, Phoebe, I just can't—"

"I wasn't asking for help, I just wanted to . . . the hell with it. You're right. It sets you up."

"Guess who I ran into this morning?"

"Literally? Did you turn someone into a bow tie for the front of the county's Blazer?"

Every emotion played itself out in Kyle's eyes. I had learned to watch them as a mood barometer. He had turned from playful to serious.

I slid my hand down my face, wiping my smile off, and tried like hell to look serious. "Who did you run into?" I asked and sipped my coffee.

"Christ, you're impossible," Kyle said and shook his head. "Nick Spano."

"God, I haven't seen him for years. I wasn't even sure he was still around. How is he?"

"Good. He's good. He, uh . . . it'd be a good idea to get in touch with him."

"His wife died when I was at the academy in Virginia. My mother wrote me about it. Talk about an old warrior. He and my father made dicks at the same time."

"So I heard. At length."

"What's he doing? Just hanging around?"

"Still with the department."

"No. I don't believe it. Nick? Hell, Kyle, he's got to be—"

"—ornery as hell."

"That wasn't what I was going to say."

"He wanted me to give you a message, Phoebe."

"Yeah? What?"

Kyle reached into his jacket pocket and pulled out a piece of paper. "This is his home phone number. He wants you to call him as soon as possible. Or you can get hold of him at the department."

"You know what I remember? The sharkskin suits he wore. The way he combed his hair straight back and always talked like everything was a secret he was whispering in your ear."

"Call him."

"I don't have time, Kyle. Will you tell him I said hello?"

"Make time. Call him."

"Is he dying or something?"

"It would be worth your while to call him," he said as he wrinkled his forehead and nodded his head.

I looked behind me and then at him. "Am I missing something here?"

"Oh, for Christ's sake, Phoebe. Just call the guy."

"Why the urgency? What's going on, Kyle?"

He looked at me like he was gauging something. "Shit."

"Well? What?"

"Nick was on both cases. The Maitland woman and Rita Chillman. It was his obsession. He saw you on television in the middle of that Maitland mess and then he heard about Frank Chillman. Nick's getting up there in years, Phoebe. Some of the guys think he's losing it. I'm not so sure of that."

"Why the hell didn't you just say this in the first place?"

"Word's already out. No leaks. Everybody and his brother knows I'm seeing you, Phoebe, and—"

"And they're giving you a rough time. Fuck, I'm sorry, Kyle."

"They're not giving me anything. Pete? He's okay. We talked about it, and he said he talked to you."

"He did. I didn't like it."

"Give him a break. He's worried I'll take the shit on this if anything gets out. Maitland's been all over the place."

"Why doesn't that surprise me? Thanks for the Nick thing. I'll call him."

"I thought the guy was going to throw a clot. After the years he put in, I don't think being an evidence officer is much of a challenge. I've got to get out of here."

Kyle stood, walked around the table. His lips brushed the top of my head.

"Will you be by later?"

"Yeah. I'll call first. Stay out of trouble."

"You know me—"

"That's why I said it. Try, anyway."

He walked out the back door, and I walked to the front of the house so I could get another look at him. Things were escalating between us. Neither of us could do much except joke about it. I hated thinking he'd catch shit at the Sheriff's Department because of his involvement with me and the supposed pillow talk between us. Little did they know that nothing was going on. We'd never had a talk with our heads on pillows, but I could dream, couldn't I? Kehly's theory was that if a man and a woman talk about it, even if they are joking, it's going to happen. For once I wanted my kid sister to be right.

13

I hadn't heard Nick's voice in years. The whisper was still there, a little more mysterious maybe, but still there. I questioned my father about it once when I was a kid, and he told me that Nick was the best detective he'd ever seen because of that whisper. He said that it made people feel important, blocked everything else out except Nick and who he was talking to. Nice technique, but to me it signaled definite control issues.

No one answered at Nick's home, so I ended up calling him at work. In the first seconds of our conversation I thought he was standoffish, confused as to why I was calling. Uncomfortable, I wondered if Kyle knew what the hell he was talking about until the whispered voice dropped an octave and Nick asked if I could meet him within the next thirty minutes. I agreed. He picked the place: Elmer's Pancake House, out on Central.

Before I left the house I checked the machine for messages. There were two from Kyle from the day before, just like he said there would be. Kehly took up at least a quarter of the tape, letting me know in no uncertain terms what I had done to Mother. Maggie was brief: Call her. My brother Michael was another story. I listened to his message a couple of times and wondered if the shakiness in his voice was anger or fear. Totally out of character, he wanted to stop by around nine this evening. There was nothing from Rosella Dahl. I started to dial the rectory where Michael lived and thought better of it: One crisis at a time was about all I could handle. He'd have to wait.

* * *

Billings on a good day is all sky, usually the bluest of blue, and light traffic. This was a good day. The streets were a soupy mess of exhaust-grayed slush that erupted over the windshield each time a car passed me. It was a small price to pay, coming out of a hard winter. Steam rose from the exposed pavement and was quickly devoured by the sun that beat down over the city. I stopped for the light on Lewis and Twenty-fourth Street West and glanced at the guy in the Cherokee Jeep next to me. He smiled and tipped his index finger toward me. Funny how a veritable heat wave can impact a Montanan's personality. We have a love-hate romance going on with the weather out here. It's a jealous lover that can be unpredictably harsh: a dominatrix that whips us with polar winds and bitter cold, beating us into submission only to soothe us, tempt us with promises of spring. A gravel-voiced radio jock seductively announced the temperature. Thirty-nine degrees. First beautiful day in some time and me forced to wear a cap.

By the time I walked through the doors at Elmer's, Nick was on his second cup of coffee and waiting for a refill. He had seated himself at a corner table in the farthest recess of the restaurant. I tried to remember when I had seen him last but couldn't pull it in. As far as I could tell, he hadn't changed that much. A gentleman from the old school, Nick stood as I approached the table, walked around, and pulled out a chair for me.

"Hey, Nick," I said as I sat down. "You really shouldn't, uh . . . get a woman used to things that don't happen anymore."

"Well, if they don't happen, they should. Just can't break old habits, Phoebe. How've you been doing?"

"Fine. Just fine. And you?"

"Older, a few more wrinkles. How's your mother?"

"She's doing great. I'd like to see her get out more, but her thing has always been her home. You should drop by and say hello. She'd enjoy that, Nick."

"I just might do that one of these days. Everyone else? They're doing okay?"

"Great. All of us."

A plump, dark-eyed waitress with her hair pulled neatly into a bun and a name tag labeling her a Glenda approached the table.

"Are you ready to order now?" She stood poised, pencil and pad in her hand.

"Yeah. I'm ready." Nick looked up and smiled. He had a way of looking at people, never moving his eyes from theirs. He could make the guiltless feel guilty. "I'll have three eggs, hash browns, sausage, uh—"

"Toast? Whole wheat or white?"

"White, please. But I want four slices. Does that come with jam? Jelly?"

"Sure does." Glenda turned and looked at me.

"Coffee. Black. Nothing else."

"Excuse me." Nick raised his hand, catching her attention and mine. "Slap on another side of sausage and a side of hash browns and a large milk to my order. Okay?"

"It's okay with me, fella, but I'm not too sure about your arteries." She turned to me again and smiled. "And you're just speedin' today. Right?"

"Today and every day."

"Sure I can't get you a cinnamon roll or something?"

I could feel my butt spread and spill over the sides of the chair just listening to Nick order. "I'm sure. I'll just sit here and fan the smell from his food over to me."

Glenda turned and walked away.

"Jesus, Nick. You really should drop in on my mother. She'd love to feed you." His eyes told me he hadn't heard a word I said.

"Rumor has it you're up to your eyeballs in a couple of areas."

"You know rumors, Nick. You just can't always count on them."

"Aren't you interested in what those rumors are?"

"Not particularly."

"Good. Then I'm going to cut to the chase. I'd like to help on this one."

"Nick—"

"Now, wait a minute before you protest too much," he said as he raised his hand to silence me. "This has nothing to do with how competent I think you are, Phoebe. Maybe 'help' is the wrong word. I've kept my eye on you since you came home. You do good work. A little, uh . . . let's just say you step outside the line now and then.

That Cutter Gage thing was damn good. You did right by your brother. Me? I never bought into that bullshit in the first place. I guess what I'm trying to say is that I know you can handle anything that comes up, so don't take offense."

"Nick, I'm not taking—"

"You gotta understand one thing. Ellen Maitland has been boring a hole in my chest for years. Your dad's also, for that matter. To this day I've never seen anything that compares to the Maitland murder."

"That bad?"

"Worse. A lot of things came down during that one. Strange happenings. There were two of them, you know. Two dead women, and dammit, those two were connected—"

"Rita Chillman and Ellen?"

"You got it. Some goddamn—excuse the language . . ."

"It's okay, Nick."

"Always that invisible thread that tied those two together. We could just never see the damn thing. But you mark my words, that thread exists."

"What about the Marino kid? Did he do Ellen Maitland?"

"I wrestled with that one. I knew old man Marino, Joey's father, my whole life. Eleven kids in that family. How do they say it? It's a Catholic thing."

I snickered. That it was.

"I watched Joey Marino grow up, for Christ's sake. I've always been hard-pressed to buy the killer thing with him, but he sure as hell had strikes against him."

"Which were?"

"The crew he was working with didn't know where he was during the time Maitland must have been killed, and he himself was vague as hell about that one. Said he had an appointment but couldn't ever come up with anything that would hold water. Fact was, he refused to cooperate on every level."

"What about the crime scene? I can't believe the old something left, something taken didn't apply."

"There was nothing at the motel. Just Ellen Maitland, beaten so badly her bottom jaw was shoved up into the roof of her mouth, and that wasn't the worst of it."

"Here's breakfast, lunch, and dinner for you, sir," Glenda said as she set three different plates down in front of Nick and then placed a carafe and cup in front of me. With her hands on her hips she smiled and said, "And here's your coffee, sweetie. Anything else I can get either of you?"

"No, nothing. This will be fine, sweet cheeks." Nick looked up from his mounds of food and smiled. Glenda, on the other hand, looked puzzled for an instant. Then she smiled and waved her hand out in front of her. "Oh, I get it. You're one of those, uh . . . one of those . . . let me think about this."

"Right, I'm one of those. It'll come to you, Glenda. Just take your time." I looked back at Nick. "You were going to say?"

Glenda moved on, glancing back once as she serviced another table, a confused, questioning look still on her face.

Nick burst into laughter. "What the hell is 'one of those'?"

"I don't have the slightest idea."

"Where was I?" Nick tapped his right temple with his index finger. "Anyway, it was one of the most thorough investigations I've seen. We went over that motel room so many times I felt like I lived there. And I swear to you we checked each and every blade of grass down at Josephine Lake. Even had divers down. Nothing."

"That's where they found Rita Chillman?"

"Uh-huh. Sad one. All dressed up and not going anywhere."

"What do you mean, Nick, all dressed up?"

"I'd seen Rita, Chili, whatever you want to call her, around town all the time once she hit the streets. You could spot her in a minute. Always dressed in red patent leather. Beautiful kid too. Eyes like a doe. She wore those red skirts so short her fanny was hanging out."

"Cheap advertising."

"Damnedest thing. The day they found her she was wearing a nice suit. Gray, as I recall. She looked like a secretary in that thing. I had a tough time believing it was Chili, dead, laying out there all alone like that. She'd been out there for a couple of days in some tall grass back in some rose thickets. Saddest damn thing I'd ever seen,

Phoebe, except for Ellen Maitland. So there we were with two cases on our hands: a lady dressed like a whore and a whore dressed like a lady. Both dead, and it's been hanging like some stink over me all these years. I don't like it."

"Let's get back to your invisible thread . . ."

"When someone blew Frank Chillman's brains out and took a shot at you, that thread was out there again. Something has stirred that dragon that's been hiding for twenty-seven years. You know dragons, Phoebe. I don't want to see you get burned."

"Let me worry about that."

"I can't do that. Your father was one of the best men I've ever known. Hell, Phoebe, you think I wouldn't be letting him down if I didn't look out for you?"

"I don't think I need to be looked out for, Nick. I don't want you to be offended, but . . . I'll tell you what, let's look at this as a sharing process."

Nick, elbows on the table, hands folded under his chin, smiled at me but said nothing for a moment. His eyes sparkled. Here he was, the old warrior, sitting across from someone he more than likely considered Ben Siegel's girl. It could work for me or against me.

"Well, what do you say? Can you live with that? I need an answer, Nick. I don't want you wasting your time, or—"

"—yours."

"Yeah. Or mine."

"You've got an attitude like your dad had, Phoebe. It takes me back. What's kept you out of the department?"

"What?"

"What's kept you off the force?"

"Are we changing tracks here or something?"

"You want a sharing thing. Right?"

"Sounds good. Yeah, that's what I want."

"Then, if we're going into a partnership—"

"I don't remember saying anything about a partnership, Nick."

"That's what I'm calling it. And if we're going to be partners, don't you think I have a right to know a little about what makes you tick?"

"Jesus, Nick."

"Why a PI?"

"Why not?"

"Why not a cop?"

"I work better by myself." He was making me uncomfortable.

"Hell, you probably could have gone right into dicks, Phoebe."

"Is this some test?"

"No. No test. Just curious."

"Look, you wanted me to get in touch with you. So, here I am." My voice was rising. "If it's all right with you, we can do some bonding later, but for right now I'd really appreciate it, Nick, if we could get back on track."

He looked around the room and then back at me but said nothing.

"I'm sorry, Nick. Shit." I felt like an ass. "I'm a little tense."

"Don't worry about it. I've probably been in Evidence too long. Out of the mainstream. When my juices start flowing I get pushy."

"Nick, there's no other way to ask this, so I'll just ask it. How far do you want to go on this?"

"The distance, or I wouldn't be here. I'm outta the department for good here in the next few months, and I'd feel better knowing I helped close the door on this one. It's the one and only big hole in an otherwise damn good record. Understand?"

"I understand."

He reached across the table and extended his hand. "How about it?"

"You've got a deal." I reached back and shook his hand. "I'm not easy to work with. You asked me why a PI instead of a cop?"

"It doesn't matter. Like you said, we'll do a little, what did you call it? Bonding? Well, I call it a shit session, and we'll have one down the road."

"A shit session?" I laughed.

"That's what your old man called it. We burned a lot of midnight oil, Ben and I. That's when we'd have our shit sessions. I knew him better than I knew my own brother. Liked him better, too." There was a waver in his husky, whispered voice. "I miss him."

I reached out and patted his hand. "Me too, Nick. Me too. I think he'd approve of this. I think I approve right along with him."

"Then let's get down to business." Nick placed his hand on top of mine and grinned. "We've got a lot to talk about."

"Hey, your food's getting cold. Better eat up."

"Ah, hell, Phoebe. I don't eat this shit. I'm fighting a cholesterol problem. Just makes me feel good to order it. It's worth the five or six bucks to know I'm in control."

"Makes sense to me, Nick."

"Now, that's a step in the right direction. We're already understanding each other. What do you want to know?"

"I want your take on where Bob Maitland figures in all this."

"Maitland's an asshole. A phony. Dumb as a rock and dangerous as hell."

"You think he killed his wife?"

"Yeah. I do. At least, I did—"

"You're waffling."

"I'd put my money on Maitland. Something about him always gave me the willies. For a while I thought we had him, but it was a blowout. When they pulled us, me and your dad, off the Maitland case and gave us the Chillman kid, we tried like hell to connect him with Chili and couldn't do it. After they picked up Joey Marino we tried to tie Joey to Chili, and it just wasn't there. We knew the two murders were somehow connected, although no one else bought it. Just me and your dad. And I'll tell you something else, your old man had instincts second to none. Then Joey jumped and flat fell off the earth."

"Never to be seen again."

"Right."

"Hmm. Is there a possibility that the Marino kid saw something that day at the motel and ended up dead?"

"Maybe. There isn't one single person connected to the case who wouldn't agree with the he's-dead theory. It's hung in there for a long time. The take was he killed himself out of remorse or that he did see something and the real killer took him out. To me that's just a damn excuse for closing the lid. You know how these cases go. People stop talking. It's old news. They lose their pull after a while. The trail just dries up."

"Maitland has done everything he can to keep it alive. Why?"

"He works it, and it works for him. He's got the department around his little finger. Tougher laws, tougher judges, more money for the cops, you name it and he's for it." Nick raised his hand and signaled to the ever-hovering Glenda. "Could we get some more coffee over here?"

"Be right there," she answered.

"Like clockwork," Nick said as he continued. "He resurrects his wife and something ends up in the news. I've watched that son of a bitch for over twenty years, and he's good. Real good."

"Why didn't you go after him?"

"I tried. We were a good nine months into both cases when some stories made the rounds in town about some kinky sex shit some young attorneys were involved in with a few of Big Dorothy's girls. Maitland's name came up."

"Did it go anywhere?"

"I thought it was going somewhere. I spent so much time with Big Dorothy my wife was beginning to wonder what the hell I was up to. And then poof, Dorothy up and disappears. Clears out."

"Did you try to find her?"

"Sure. Your dad and I flew to New Orleans on a tip that she had started up another house. We found her, all right. She still wasn't talking. I'll tell you one thing, her circumstances had improved."

"How so, Nick?"

"Hell, she was down in the French Quarter in some big house that must have set her back a fortune. Sure beat the hell out of the cribs she had up here."

"Maybe she saved her money."

"Or . . ."

"Someone wanted her out of town and paid her big bucks to do it."

"You got it. But who? Again, my money is on Maitland."

"There's a hook here, Nick. Why would Maitland kill the goose that laid the golden egg? What did he have with Ellen Maitland dead?"

"I think that golden egg, as you call it, was laid before he even agreed to marry her. Maitland is as stupid as a fox."

Glenda approached the table, filled our cups, and looked down at the plates full of food in front of Nick. "Is there something wrong with your breakfast?"

Nick placed his hand above the plates, palm open. "It's great. Everything's perfect."

"You haven't touched a thing. Can I stick that in the microwave for you?"

"No. You can't. I want it cold. Okay?"

"Whatever." Glenda raised her eyebrows and walked away.

"I go through this every time I go out for breakfast."

"Oh? I wonder why?" I was starting to really like this guy. "What about Big Dorothy? You had no luck at all?"

"None. She came back to town about six years ago."

"Have you talked to her?"

"Once. For about twenty seconds. You've got to realize that Dorothy holds the dirt on some of Billings's biggest names. All it took was one call, and I was told to back off. That I wasn't on that case anymore, and that she'd sue the city for harassment. She's clean. Living in a retirement home out here on the west end."

"A nursing home?"

"No. It's connected to one, but she's in her own apartment. They're pricey."

"So she's still got money. I'm going to assume she's not listed under Big Dorothy."

Nick laughed. "Nope. She's going by Dorothy Valentine."

"Don't."

"Really. That's her given name. Her friends call her Dot."

"I guess I have to pay a visit to Dot."

"She's connected, Phoebe. All she has to do is pick up her phone."

"She might be connected, but I'm always up to a challenge. Do you think she knows anything, or am I going to be wasting my time?"

"Hell, she's got to be in her mid-seventies, close to eighty years old, and lived hard. But she knows something. You bet she does. In fact, I'd go so far as to say she might be the key to the whole damn thing."

"Then it's worth a try. What's the name of this place, and where is it?"

"I don't know what kind of shape she's in, and in her prime she was a handful."

"I can handle it, Nick."

"Then go for it. It's called the Estates. It's that spread-out bunch of buildings on the corner of Shiloh and Grand Avenue just west of the Yegen golf course. You can't miss it. It's pretty lush."

"Nick, I need access to—"

"Don't ask. I know what you need, and I'll make sure they get to you."

"I feel funny having you put your butt on the line like this."

"It's my butt and my line. I feel fifteen years younger just thinking about getting back in the harness. I'll be in touch. Soon. How late is too late at night to call?"

"I've got a machine, and I'm usually up late. Makes no difference."

"It's going to be better if I contact you from now on."

"Understood. If I'm not around, just leave a time when you'll call back, and if I can, I'll be there. Nick?"

"Yeah?"

"Are the Marinos still in town?"

"The old man, Louis, died a couple of years back, but his wife is still around. It's in the phone book under Louis's name."

"I'm outta here. I'll be talking to you."

"Are you going out to the Estates?"

"I've got to make a quick trip to Laurel first. That should take about forty minutes out and back, and then I'll drop in on Dot."

"Good luck." Nick dropped a five-dollar bill on the table, stood, and followed me toward the front doors. "Still driving the truck?" he asked as he held the door open for me to walk out.

"Yeah. I am."

"That's good. Real good."

"This winter has been a little tougher on it than most, but it's hanging in there."

"Aren't we all?"

He had that wistful look that men get, older men, when they think time is running out on them. They always want to talk, and talk fast like they won't get everything said that they need to say. Standing in that parking lot, shoulder to shoulder with Nick Spano, an all-too-familiar sense of grief tap-danced across my chest. I missed my dad, and I missed my brother Ben. At that moment, if there had been a way to raise them from the dead and breathe my own life into them, I would have done it. No matter what the price. I wanted them both there. But they weren't, and I wasn't sure I could ever accept that. Not totally. I sighed deeply and looked toward Nick.

"I enjoyed this, Nick. I really did."

"Me too. You've become quite a woman."

"I'd say you have also, but . . ."

"Always the mouth," he said as he laughed. "Later?"

"Later."

It took me twenty minutes to hit the city limits of Laurel, booming metropolis, home of Montana Rail Link, with a population of around seven thousand. A mostly German community that housed German POWs on the city's outskirts during World War II, it's a clean little city that boasts a lot of community pride. I needed a service that most Laurelians despised, and that was a phone booth I could call long distance from, to Billings. Although it was part of Yellowstone County, and although you could call Pryor toll-free even when it was forty miles away, the fine citizens from Laurel got it stuck to them by good old U.S. West. But what was new?

I pulled into Ricky's IGA and parked in front of the phone booth, got out of the truck, and paged through the directory. When I found what I was looking for I lifted the receiver and punched the zero.

"I'm calling collect, 406-555-3274. My name is Joey, Joey Marino."

"Joy?"

"No. Joe, it's short for Josephine."

"Sorry, you just didn't sound like a—"

"Happens all the time."

It was a long shot, but all I could do was hope. The line went dead while she made the connection. Finally the operator came back on.

"Go ahead, your party is connected."

"Joey, honey. Why are you calling collect? Is something wrong? Are the kids okay? Joey? Hello? Are you there?"

I hung up. The panic in her voice was obvious, and I did the obligatory Catholic guilt. But one thing was for sure, there was a damn good chance that Joey Marino was alive somewhere. It was time to find out where that somewhere was.

14

On my way back to Billings I had time to think about the conversation I had had with Nick. I wanted, needed, all the information he had or could get his hands on, but I knew I wouldn't tell him about my phone call to Mrs. Marino. He wouldn't have liked it. Nick was putting his ass on the line for me, but more important there was a payoff for him: resolution and closure, and he'd retire from the Billings PD with an atomic bang. What was one little bit of information? No big deal. Hell, it could be wishful thinking on my part. There could be a grandson named Joey. For that matter, there could be a nephew. Could be anybody. My gut told me I was right on, but why build up Nick's expectations on the slim chance I was calling it wrong? That little internal conversation made me feel better. If nothing else, I was getting damn good at justifying my choices.

Funny what a bullet alongside the head can do. My instincts were turned on high, my mind was tracking at five hundred miles an hour, and my sinuses were clear. What more could a girl ask? One thing: a lucid audience with the legendary madam, Dorothy Valentine.

The Estates was a sprawling complex of one-story buildings that stretched from the corner of Grand and Shiloh on the north and from Broadwater Avenue on the south. Nothing gave it away to be a nursing home. Condos? Maybe. But a home for the elderly? No way. The brass plaque embedded in the redbrick wall to the left of the driveway stated simply:

THE ESTATES
THE NEXT STEP

The next step to what? Was that what they were calling *it* now? The next step? Sobering, but clever.

Steam rose from paths that webbed from the main complex to several smaller units that stood alone. It took a lot of money to have heated walks in this part of the country, but then again everything about the place shouted money. I'd driven by the Estates before and figured they were just another wave of the condos that had been cropping up on every viable edge of Billings. Real estate in Billings means big bucks. Apparently "the next step" did too.

Even under winter's last gasp, the landscaping was nothing short of spectacular. When I got out of the truck and started walking toward the entrance, I could see two ice-covered ponds flanked by benches and picnic tables that were tucked under redwood arbors.

The view was picture-perfect. To the north, sandstone cliffs that formed the northern rim of the Yellowstone Valley stretched from east to west as far as the eye could see. Two massive mountain ranges on the southern horizon, the Pryors and the Beartooths, were dwarfed under Montana's Big Sky. South Hills, barren and draped in purple shadows, stood on the far side of the river. Quite a sight from the Estates. Not bad digs.

I pushed the doorbell. Cathedral chimes echoed on the other side of the door. A polyester-clad woman, apparently proud of her teeth, came to the door with a smile so wide it looked painful.

"Hi there," she said as she smiled and stepped aside for me to enter. "Looks like we're in for a change in the weather."

"You know what they say?"

"What was that?"

"The weather—if you don't like it, wait a minute and it'll change?"

"Oh, right. I guess I have heard that." The wound and shave job on the side of my head seemed to hold a special fascination for her. She didn't ask, and I didn't offer. "Are you here to visit someone?"

"Dorothy Valentine. Is she up to—"

"Would you mind waiting just a moment? I left someone on hold on the phone. Have a seat right over there, and I'll be right back."

"Okay. Over here?" I looked around the foyer.

"Yes. Just have a seat for one teeny minute, and we'll be right back."

"Okay." I swear she thought of reaching out and patting me on the head for being obedient. My eyebrows dropping down on my eyelids must have dissuaded her.

"Right back, then." She sang more than said it and disappeared around a corner.

Music wafted through the mauve, gray, and plum decor of the room from unseen speakers. Frank Sinatra singing "I Did It My Way" took me a little by surprise, but hey, what's the harm in a little reflection when you're waiting for the next step? The deep-green and maroon overstuffed couches and chairs were occupied by a variety of conscious, semiconscious, and snoring people, both male and female. I didn't know hair came in so many shades of silver and white.

I shivered, realizing how out of touch I was with the senior citizenry of the world. There they were, scattered among the finery, the crystal chandeliers, the ornate gold frames that housed baroque paintings of children and angels, and Frank's swooning voice, like some afterthought. The luxury couldn't hide the fact that they were all waiting to die. It was a feet-first place, and that's how they'd leave. It was chillingly the ghost of my hopefully distant future, a future that I thus far had refused to acknowledge.

I sat down on a footstool at the front of a chair, looked around, and noticed two gentlemen sitting across from each other, a checkerboard between them. Considering their ages, I was impressed that they were doing something that took a fair amount of concentration. I watched. Then I watched some more. Nothing happened. I stood and walked over to where they sat.

"Who's winning?"

Not only did they not respond but when I looked down at the board, there were no checkers.

"Shit," I mumbled under my breath and started to back up until something edged the calves of my legs. Turning, I saw a small, impish-looking silver-haired woman tipping sideways, her hands clutching the top rail of her walker.

"Oh God, I'm so sorry," I gasped as I reached out and steadied the walker, knocking my cap off in the process.

"It happens all the time. It's these darned carpets. You just can't hear a person coming up to you. I've tried to tell them, but what do I know? Been on this earth some eighty-eight years and worked for almost sixty-five of those, but what do I know?"

I smiled. There was fire in her eyes as she shook her bony fist in the air in front of her. My kind of woman.

"Are you sure you're okay?"

She eyed me with a silent intensity. "What happened to your head?"

"I got shot." What the hell. I had a feeling that she had earned the truth.

"Lucky you didn't lose an ear. Who shot you?"

"To tell you the truth, I don't know," I said, replacing my cap.

"Hmm. Coulda killed ya."

"Sure could have."

"Don't bother those boys playing checkers. Beverly, he's the one on the right, has been known to pitch a fit once in a while. Helluva thing to name a man, Beverly. Isn't it?"

"It's not a name I'd pick, but—"

"He coulda grown up to be a sissy. Makes you wonder why some people have kids."

"They don't have any checkers."

"Can't have 'em. They stick the darn things in their mouths. Beverly choked one day, had to have that Heimlich maneuver done on him. He spit it halfway across the room. Never saw anything like it. Who're you?"

"My name is Phoebe. Who are you?" I stuck my hand out and was surprised at the strength of her grip.

"Ida Steffanich. You from around here?"

"My whole life."

"Who're you here to see?"

"Dorothy Valentine."

"Dot, huh. What do ya want with her?"

"I—"

"Come on, Ida. I'll take care of this lady. Why don't we go down to the dining room and get some juice?"

"All three of us?"

"No. You."

"Then why the heck do you always say we? Are *we* feeling okay? Have *our* bowels moved? What do *we* have planned for today?"

I pushed my tongue hard against the inside of my cheek to keep from laughing and finally had to turn around and walk away. What a woman. I should be so lucky at that age.

"I'm so sorry I made you wait like that."

I turned and looked in the face of the woman who had allowed me entrance.

"No problem."

"I'm Barbra Cushing. I'm the receptionist and head greeter." She waved both her hands up and fanned them by her shoulders, displaying her three-inch nails. "So—greetings." The singsong voice was nerve-grating. "Now, which of our residents are you here to visit?"

"Dorothy Valentine. Where can I find her?"

"We like to keep the residents active. It helps with their—" She tapped her temple with her finger and whispered, "If you know what I mean."

I looked over her shoulder at the checkerless checker game. "Right."

"Dot should be over at the recreation hall about this time," she said as she checked her watch, looked up, and pasted some pout on her face. "I'll point you in the right direction, but I won't be able to take you all the way because no one would be up here to get the buzzer or the phone."

Barbra placed her hand on my elbow and steered me down a hall past a beauty shop where a plump bleached blond worked on another head of silver hair, a large library with no one in it, and a canteen with round tables and ice cream chairs, most of which were occupied.

We followed the hall through a glass-enclosed walkway until we came to a locked door. Barbra reached into her pocket and removed a large ring of keys.

"I wouldn't normally have anyone cut through here, but it's the shortest route. Is that all right with you?"

"Whatever works."

The door opened to the outdoors.

"Just follow the path and stay to the right. There'll be another door, and if you ring the buzzer one of the gals will let you in. Someone should be able to direct you to Dorothy."

"Is she able to—does she understand, uh—what shape is she in?

You know, uh—" I tried the language she seemed to prefer and tapped my temple with my index finger.

"Dorothy? Dorothy Valentine?" She burst into laughter that immobilized her. Her face flushed as she gasped for breath. "I'm sorry. I . . . I thought you were aware of her, uh . . . you don't know her?"

"Yes, I know her. I just haven't seen her for a while."

Fighting for breath, she continued to laugh and closed the door. I was alone between two buildings, with a preconceived idea of what I was going to find with Dorothy Valentine and prepared for the worst. At the top of the scale I would find someone as spunky as Ida. At the bottom? Beverly, the near-sissy. What I got was more than I had bargained for.

I rang the buzzer. The door opened. A swell of boogie-woogie rode a pulsating bass that filled a room full of gyrating men and women. Pick a color and it was there, drooping on or clinging to the myriad of bodies. Flailing arms swung up from their sides, clapped over their heads and dropped back to their hips. Whether they were standing, bracing themselves on walkers, or sitting in wheelchairs, there was movement and whooping and hollering.

"Are you looking for someone?" a young man yelled as he closed the door behind me.

"Dorothy Valentine," I yelled back.

He shrugged, cupped his hand by his ear, and leaned closer. I took a deep breath and yelled her name louder just as the music stopped. Everyone turned to where we were standing.

"Great timing," he said as he smiled. "Dot's probably not wound down yet."

"She's in good enough shape—I mean, she's exercising?"

"You might say that," he said without losing the smile. "Can you hang for a minute?"

"Sure." He intrigued me. I never could figure out how anyone could maintain one of those widespread smiles and talk at the same time.

"Does she know you're coming?" Still, the smile.

"No. Is that a problem?"

"It's cool with me, but it might not be with Dot. Let's find out." He disappeared into the throng.

The kaleidoscope of colors was blinding. From hot pink Lycra to royal purple to neon yellow, sweatsuits and stretch pants, leggings and leotards draped the rotund and the frail. Paintbox-colored headbands adorned the silver-haired exercisers. Maybe this was the next step, stretch halos and all.

I looked around the room and tried to guess which was the infamous Dot. With any luck at all she would be upright, lucid, and willing to talk. But then again . . .

A hand rested on my shoulder. I turned. Standing in front of me was the most magnificent example of female aging I had ever seen. I took a step backward. I guessed her at five feet nine as I craned my neck to look up into her face. Her makeup, if she wore any, was flawless. Her skin was taut and practically wrinkle-free. Her eyes were bluer than any I had ever seen and betrayed a generous smile with a trace of distrust.

"Did we have an appointment I've forgotten?" She blotted her face with a towel, hung it around her neck, and reached out with her right hand. "I'm Dorothy. And you are—?"

"Phoebe Siegel, and no, we didn't have an appointment." I reached back and shook her hand. "Is this a bad time?"

"Depends on what you want." She placed her hands on her hips and bent from side to side. "I've got to work the kinks out. They give me one helluva workout."

I didn't reply. Exercise in my mind was a form of self-abuse, and never let it be said I abuse myself.

"So . . . what is it you want to see me about?"

"Rita Chillman."

I watched her face for a reaction. She took one corner of the towel around her neck and blotted her forehead while she continued to watch my face. "Rick?" she yelled, never moving her eyes from mine. "Come on over here, will ya?"

"Yeah, Dot?" Rick appeared instantly at her side.

"Wrap it up for me. Ten minutes of stretches. You know the drill."

"Sure thing."

"I'm taking—" Dorothy extended her hand palm up toward me. "Phoebe Siegel."

"Phoebe Siegel to my place. I doubt that I'll be long."

She turned away from me without a word and started walking toward the door I had come in. I followed her, like an intimidated schoolgirl, out the door and down a branching path that led away from the complex. We rounded a corner and came up to a compound of stand-alone patio homes surrounded by a tall wrought-iron fence. The gate was locked. She reached inside the front of her tight-fitting Lycra top, pulled out a key on the end of a chain that encircled her neck, and leaned forward to fit one of two keys into the keyhole and open the gate.

She stepped aside to let me pass. The silence was screaming at me. There was a presence with this woman, an energy, that had caught me by surprise, and I wasn't liking it. Without acknowledgment, she took a left and followed a path that led to a one-story house set off from the others. She stepped up onto a wide porch, reached again inside her shirt, and withdrew the keys, unlocked the front door, and waved me past her and inside.

The house, like its occupant, was near-perfect gorgeous and looked as if someone named Stevie who loved track lighting had decorated the place. Dorothy walked to a white leather couch, sat down, put her Reebocked feet up on the glass-topped coffee table in front of it, and watched me as I stood by the front door.

"Are you going to sit down?"

I needed to get in control of the situation. Act professional. The only thing I wasn't doing was shuffling my feet. "I should have called—" I walked to a wing chair across the coffee table from her. "If this is a bad time I could—"

"Let's cut to the chase, honey. What are you here for?"

"I told you. I'd like to talk with you about Rita Chillman."

"Chili?" She closed her eyes and massaged the bridge of her nose. When she opened them and looked at me she was smiling. "Chili has been dead for twenty-seven years. Try something else."

"I have nothing else."

She studied me. Her arms were spread across the back of the couch, feet still propped on the coffee table. I felt myself shifting sideways in the chair and looking everywhere but at her.

"Then we don't have anything to talk about, do we?"

"I—"

"You're Benny Siegel's girl."

"Excuse me?"

"Through the eyes. Uh-huh. It's the eyes. Always thinking. Always a step ahead, or trying to be."

Dorothy tapped her thumbnail against her front teeth and kept staring directly at me.

"You knew my father?"

"Oh yes. I knew Benny well. Very well."

It was the smug, insinuating look on her face that pissed me off. "What the hell do you mean by that? Let's define *well* here."

"Cool down, sweetie. And sit down."

I wasn't aware that I was standing, looking down at her. Her words were ringing in my ears: *Well . . . very well.* All I could see in front of me was this chic, gorgeous creature who just happened to be the legendary madam of Billings, if not the whole damn state of Montana, and she "knew" my father. *Well? Very well?* My face was flushed, and my nails were digging into the palms of my hands. So much for controlling the situation and professionalism. I sat down.

Dorothy looked at her watch and then at me. "You've got fifteen minutes to pique my curiosity and tell me why you're here, or—" She hitched her thumb toward the door. "By the way, I saw you on the news, taking on Bobby Maitland. I'm going to assume that you're not here on his behalf."

"Would that make a difference?"

"Yes. It would."

"Nick Spano thought you might, uh . . . enlighten me."

"Enlighten you?" She smiled. "With what? The meaning of life?"

"Chili did work for you. Right?"

"How is Nicky? Hell, I haven't seen him since your father's funeral."

"You were at my father's funeral? Oh, shit." The weight of my chin tripled as it fell down toward my chest. "You—wait. Just hold on a minute." I held both of my hands up toward her. "I'm not here, Ms. Valentine—"

"Dot."

"Whatever. You've made it clear that I have just fifteen minutes,

and I'm sure as hell not going to use those minutes catching you up
on Nicky Spano." My brain cramped as I thought of my father being
called Benny Siegel.

She said nothing for a minute, just sat there and smiled at me,
moving her head up and down, tapping that damn inch-long red
thumbnail on her Hollywood teeth.

"Frank Chillman was murdered this week."

"So I heard."

"He has a sister still living in Billings. I was at her house yesterday, and someone took a shot at either her or me."

"Is that the crease on the side of your head?"

After the Nicky-Benny bullshit, I decided to use one of her tactics
and ignore the question. "Frank had contacted me and wanted to
hire me. He said he had information that tied Chili's murder in with
Ellen Maitland's. You probably didn't know Ellen—"

"No," she said softly. The thumbnail stopped tapping. "I didn't
know Ellen. What did he tell you?"

"Not a helluva lot. Some rambling things on paper, but enough
to convince me that he was onto something."

"I heard on the news that he'd done some time."

"Yeah, he had. More than his share. Someone put a lot of pres-
sure on the right people to keep him there."

"Humor me for a minute. What happened between you and
Bobby?"

"Bobby?" This woman had a way with Ys. "You mean Maitland?
I don't think I can—"

"Let me set the scenario. He approached you about finding out
who murdered his wife."

I said nothing.

"When you found out that he may just have ulterior motives,
you bunched it, pissed him off, and he set you up for a little public
humiliation. Am I right so far?"

"I—"

"How about a drink? Do you have a preference?"

She stood and walked to a black-lacquered cabinet with silver
teardrop pulls and opened both doors. A fully stocked bar slid out

on terraced shelves. The cut crystal decanters caught the sunlight flashing through the windows and mirrored shafts of light.

"No, thank you." I watched as she poured herself a hefty glassful from one of the decanters and wondered if she still entertained privately.

She walked back to the couch with the glass in her hand, sat down, and took a drink. Her eyes never left my face as she lifted the glass toward the ceiling. "Vodka, the elixir of life. Sure you won't imbibe with me?"

"Couldn't be surer."

She took a longer drink, leaned back into the couch, and put her feet on top of the coffee table.

"Bobby Maitland is not someone to toy with. I'd stay as far away from him as you can. You came back at him, and he isn't going to look upon that kindly."

"Are you telling me I should be afraid of Maitland?"

"A little fear can be a healthy thing now and again."

"Will you talk to me about Rita Chillman?"

Dot finished off the vodka in her glass, swished it around in her mouth before she swallowed, and started tapping her teeth again with her thumbnail. She was reading me.

"Well?"

"What do you want to know about Chili?"

"Who killed her?"

She threw her head back and laughed. "Just like your old man. Cut to the quick. I gotta give it to ya. Who do you think killed her?"

"I thought I got to ask the questions. Maitland?"

"Why would Maitland kill her? How do you know he even knew her?"

"I don't. But you do. She worked for you."

"Chili . . ." Dot leaned her back, closed her eyes, and rubbed her forehead. "God, that was so long ago. Chili was one of my best girls. I took her off the streets after she got beat up one night, and I made an honest woman of her. She was no bigger than a minute. No one touched her after she came to me. No one dared."

"Someone dared."

She stood and walked back to the bar. The glass held more this time. In one sip she emptied it a third of the way and sat back down. "Chili was soft, naive. Or so I thought. Come to find out the little bitch had balls. Steel ones. Chili was as shrewd as they come." Dot became silent. Her eyes closed. When they opened, she sat straight up, drank what was left in the glass, and set it down on the coffee table. "Ya know, I had dreams. Lots of them. And then"—she snapped her fingers—"like that, they were gone. And why, you ask?"

I just sat there and looked at her, not knowing how to handle the shift.

"Ask me, goddammit! You wanted to ask me questions, ask me!"

"Okay, I'll play. What happened to your dreams, Dot?"

"Chili is what happened. She found my dreams and crawled into them. Destroyed them."

"I'm not following you. How—"

"I want you to get out of here. Now."

"Look, Dot—"

"We're not through talking. I owe that much to your old man. But not now. I've got to think. So go on. Get out."

"I can stick around for a while. Do you want another drink?" I reached for the glass she had placed on the table.

She reached out and knocked the glass off the table. "I'm not some candy-assed rah-rah girl you can run a hustle on. I said we'd talk later, so get the hell out before I change my mind."

I got out. I wondered what memories the vodka had awakened in Dorothy Valentine's mind. Or perhaps they never slept; maybe they just waited for the vodka to give them voice. Now all I could hope was that the voice she fought to suppress would start screaming.

15

Billings has always been a house divided, north to south. The early rumblings of the Great Northern Railroad, now Montana Rail Link, locally referred to as MRL, had not dropped a decibel over the years. Whistles still screeched through the day and the night like lonesome sirens calling the indigent to points east and west. Some made it. Some didn't. But those whisky-breathed, unshaven riders-of-rail knew their place. They seldom if ever strayed north. That was WASP land, and they knew it. But to the south houses still rattled under the megaton weight of the cars rolling by. And to the south, old women were still good for an occasional handout.

This was Dougie's neighborhood. He never strayed unless it was his winter trip to St. Vincent's for his yearly bout of pneumonia. Dougie the snitch, and that was the nicest thing anyone could say about him, was an information powermonger. He had a brain that held the names, faces, dates, and times of every sleazy happening that had occurred since he had taken up residence. Some say he came from a wealthy mainline family back east and had enjoyed a classical education. Others would tell a sadder tale: that Dougie was the spawn of a five-dollar-a-trick hooker from somewhere up north who turned him out when she caught him watching. Dougie never confirmed or denied either story. He liked to be talked about, wondered about. And in his own way, he turned his own tricks. He sold information for twenty bucks a pop and prided himself on never being wrong. The cops loved the information and hated Dougie.

So that's who I kept my eye out for as I sat waiting for MRL to pass. The ground under my truck quaked as the massive flatbeds stacked with new cars headed for the Laurel train yards. The noise sped past me and faded on down the tracks. The bell on the cross arms dinged as they began to rise. I looked both ways before crossing. You just never know.

After leaving Dorothy Valentine, I had opted to take Shiloh Road down to King and connect up with the Interstate. The old Chevy needed to blow a little carbon out of its guts, and I needed to get off the pockmarked city streets that were a killer on my suspension. Winter not only tested the survival skills of Big Sky residents but also revealed the piss-poor patch jobs that were laid down on the streets the summer and fall before. Besides, the truck never got a chance to really run wide open, to fifty miles per hour, that is. But what the hell.

All the way up Twenty-seventh Street I kept my eye out for Dougie but didn't see him. I turned right on Montana and pulled into a parking place in front of the St. Vincent DePaul store, a place I frequented. It was the Catholic answer to helping the poor. The middle class, the upper middle class, and the upper upper uppers came in droves to deposit their castoffs. The store turned a buck off their tax write-offs, and everyone benefited.

I was dropping some change into the parking meter when I heard a familiar voice behind me.

"Hey, girlfriend! What are you doing out and about?"

I turned. "Gin? I don't believe it. What's happened to you?" And I couldn't believe it. In front of me stood one half of my favorite twin hookers, Gin and Tonic. Only this wasn't the Gin I had last seen.

"Ya like it?" She turned in a full circle, modeling the burgundy two-piece suit she was wearing.

"You look great." And she did. Her hair hung in tiny rows of braids that reached down to her shoulders. Her makeup was perfect. Gin looked as if she was on a lunch break from a bank or some other uptown job. "I don't believe it."

"I was that bad?" She scowled as she pitched one of her hips out and placed her hand on it. The furrows in her forehead were still as intimidating as I remembered them.

She and her twin, Tonic, had helped bust a case I worked on

eighteen months before. I liked them; they were up-front about who they were. You don't find that in most people.

"Never bad, Gin. Just—uh, just . . ."

"Forget it," she said and waved her hand. "I know I look good. Eight bucks. I call that a real deal. Of course, I tell everyone that I did me some shoppin' at Paul's Petite Shop."

"Good one. Where's Tonic? Is she with you?"

"She's off to see Mama. Been in bad health. Couldn't afford for both of us to go."

"You should have gotten hold of me, Gin. I would have been glad to help you both out."

"We figured when you were through with that Monday Brown thing you were through with us too. You were straight with us. Ya know, you brought fucking—" She covered her mouth with her hand. "Damn, I'm trying to quit saying that so I can get me a respectable job."

"It'd probably help," I answered and grinned at her. "You were saying I brought you—"

"Mojo, honey. Where I'm from you either have it bad or you have it good. And as soon as you came into the picture our mojo got good, girl. Real good."

"Well, that's great. At least I hope so."

"It's a sure thing. Ask me what I've been doing for the last eighteen months."

"What have you been doing, Gin?"

"Well, it came down like this. We got busted a couple of weeks after all those stories came out in the paper about that German dude and all. But this attorney? Maggie Mason? She came down and bailed us out. She said that we had a friend who wanted to help set us up and change our lives. And before we knew it, we had us an apartment, and—"

"And?"

"Guess. Go ahead. Try and guess."

"I wouldn't have the slightest idea, Gin. Why don't you go ahead and tell me? I'm looking for someone down here, and if I don't get going I'm—"

She watched me intently, a trace of a smile on her lips.

"Sure you don't know?"

"I'm sure. Come on."

"School, honey. We went to school at the Lincoln Center, and this one you are not going to believe. We graduated. It's only a GED, but we did it. Both of us."

"Never say *only* a GED. Not everyone has one of those."

At six feet tall, Gin was an imposing figure of a woman. Her head bobbed with every word, accentuating whatever it was she was saying. That hip of hers, and her hand on it, gave drama to every word. Gin was a body-talker from her forehead down to her feet. I loved it.

"I'm proud of you. Both of you. What's next?"

"I gotta find me a job that is worthy of my new skills."

"Which are?"

"Computers, girl. I've been told that I was a natural. We have this career consultant that we meet with, and she says that I am the brightest thing she has come on in a while. I even got me a computer in my apartment now."

"Any prospects?"

"Not a fuckin'—damn. There I go again. You know I don't understand the big deal about that word. It's not like I'm going to be answering a phone and say"—Gin closed her right hand, extended her thumb and little finger, and held the hand up by her ear—" 'I'm sorry, Mr. so-and-so isn't fucking in right now, and I don't have any fucking idea of where he is.' I mean, does that even make any sense?"

"I'm sure you'll do great. You made my day. I gotta run. I'm looking for Dougie. Have you seen him, Gin?"

"That little maggot snitch? You've got to be kidding. I don't hang with no lowlifes anymore. Try the theater. I'm sure he's in there getting off."

"Thanks. And again, you look great, and I'm really proud of what you two have done. Don't lose it."

I turned to walk toward the only X-rated theater in town.

"Hey! Can we do lunch someday?"

I looked back at her and started laughing. Do lunch? "Sure. Get in touch in a couple of weeks, and we'll get together."

"Bye!"

I waved backward over my head. The twins were a good investment, and I was feeling good about it. It had been an easy thing to do after I had read about them being busted in the *Gazette*. I contacted Maggie, and within a week everything was set up. There were stipulations: no drugs, no booze, no tricks. It was a contractual thing, and they proved me right without any knowledge that I had been behind it. I mean, what the hell, all of Zelda's money sat in a Puerto Rican bank account just accumulating interest. Zelda would have liked what I did. It sure beat the hell out of pork bellies.

Dougie wasn't that hard to find. Between snaps of her gum, the bouffant blond in the ticket cage with the Walkman headphones covering her ears told me the movie would be over in five or ten minutes.

"Want to catch the end of it?" she asked with no expression, just dull detached eyes and the constant snapping.

"I'll catch the late one. I hate to come in on the end of a movie."

"Cool. Isn't that what they call a pun?"

"Excuse me?"

"You know, *come* in on the end of a movie?"

"Did you get this through Job Service?"

"Sure did. Are you looking for work?"

I smiled and walked out. It never fails to amaze me how a state agency can match up a person with the right job on any level. Our government at work.

Dougie walked out of the door with a glazed look and beads of sweat glistening on his upper lip. He didn't see me. I cringed, reached out, and grabbed his jacket sleeve.

"Slow down."

"What the—ah hell, it's you. I figured you'd come lookin' for me. What's on your mind, Siegel?"

"You sound like you already know, Dougie. You tell me."

"Want a cup of coffee?"

"Why not. What's close?"

"The Sheraton parking garage." Dougie started walking north on Twenty-seventh Street.

"What's in the parking garage?" I asked as I walked beside him.

"A friend with a full thermos."

"Jesus."

Sure as hell, he had a friend, and that friend had a full thermos out of which he filled two Styrofoam cups with the foulest mixture I had ever tasted. While I was trying to uncurl the tip of my tongue, Dougie started in.

"You've been on the news a lot, Siegel. You think that's good for business?"

"Probably not," I answered as I followed him up to the second level.

He picked an empty parking stall and walked to a retaining wall that overlooked the traffic below.

"Welcome to my office. You get used to the exhaust fumes after a while. Me? I don't mind them at all. It's a cheap high. I hear you're looking back in time, Siegel. Any ideas?"

"That's what I'm here for, Dougie. Can you give me anything?"

"She asks, Can you give me anything, Dougie? Are you kidding? I remember the whole thing like it was yesterday."

"I knew I could count on you, Dougie." He held his hand out. The tips were cut off the wool glove, exposing his dirty little fingers. I reached into my pocket, pulled out a couple of twenties, and handed him one. He took it, pocketed it, and held his hand out again.

"Oh no. Not until I hear what you have. Your going rate has always been twenty. Has it gone up?"

"On Maitland? You bet it's gone up, and it's a one-timer."

In Dougie-ese, that meant that we'd only have one conversation about it. That bothered me. "What's the big deal?"

"What's the big deal, she asks."

"There's only two of us here, Dougie." This repeating everything was an irritation second only to his habitual nose-picking. "Talk to *me*."

"Maitland. Right?"

"Right."

"Bad one, that one. Down at the cribs. They say she hung around that place for a long, long time."

"That's a new one on me. I didn't know she—"

"After she was dead, for Christ's sake. You could feel it. It became a real deal to take a trick into that room and run the story down on him. I tried it once. Couldn't get it up. Gave me the creeps."

"What did you hear? Any speculations?"

"A couple. What do you think?"

I held out my hand. "That'll cost *you*."

"I was sitting in the Western and saw you on TV. You don't want to fuck around with Maitland. He's a sick man."

"How so?" For a moment I forgot myself and sipped the coffee. "God, this is horrible shit."

Dougie took the cup from my hand, dumped the coffee over the edge of the wall, and handed the cup back to me.

"What the hell are you doing?"

"You don't like it, then it's gone. It was free, you know. You shouldn't be such a snob, Siegel."

"Back to Maitland. Do you know him?"

"I've seen him around. In the early days he and his boys used to come down here on the weekends and clear the streets of all the ladies."

"He what?"

"Five, six, maybe seven of them at a time. He and his cronies would party hard with these ladies. That's how he hooked up with Chili."

"Maitland? Maitland and Rita Chillman? You've got to be kidding." But he wasn't.

"Hell, Siegel. He was going to marry her. Then this thing came up with his wife, and sure as hell Chili, she showed up dead too. Nice gal, that one. Took real good care of her family. I heard the brother bought it. Damn shame. He was just a little shaver when Chili was on the streets. She kept that whole family dressed real nice, and everyone said she never missed Mass. Ain't that a kicker?"

I handed him the other twenty bucks. "I need more. Lots more."

"Make it fifty, give me a chance to shake some stuff loose from my mind, and I'll make this a two-timer."

"You got a deal." I dug back into my pocket and pulled out a ten-dollar bill. "Just remember I'm one of those radical consumers. I want my money's worth."

"Have I ever failed you? My rep's at stake here."

"Dougie, I need to know something. Did Maitland—"

"Maybe. Maybe he did. I can't give you a straight answer on that one, Siegel. It's in him. That's for sure. But why the hell would he cut himself out of all that money?"

"Seems like he didn't."

"Yeah. You might want to take a closer look at that."

"Does he still come down here?"

"Nope. I'd hear if he did. But there was something else, something I can't put my finger on—"

"You've cleaned me out. My pockets are empty."

"That ain't what I'm saying, dammit. I just can't call it to mind. There is someone you should talk to, though. Someone that I think knows exactly what came down."

"Who?"

"Dot Valentine. Good woman. Real good woman. Left town after all that shit happened, but she's back now. Has been for a while. I hear tell she's living the good life in a place called the Estates."

"Really." There was no good reason he had to know I'd already been there.

"And the old lady, Mrs. Dahl. And—"

"And who?"

"The judge."

"What judge?"

"The judge that was Maitland's sidekick when he was hanging around down here. Seems to me they split the sheets after this all came down. You just might want to look him up."

"You don't know his name?"

"It'll come to me. Hell, I've been sick. Bad lungs, bad prostate. Can't piss. Docs want to shove a roter rooter up my you-know-what and chew that thing out. Hell, I'd rather be dead."

"I wouldn't wait on something like that. It can only get worse."

"I've got to get on down to a buddy's for a friendly game of chess. Ten bucks a game." He held up the money I had just given him and waved it in the air. "Thanks for bankrolling it for me, Siegel. Money well spent."

"We've got a second time coming, Dougie. Don't forget that."

"Me? Like I said, my reputation is on the line. Give me a couple of days. I usually do the four o'clock movies. Meet me afterward, two days from now. See you around, Siegel."

"Two days," I answered. He walked off, but not before he shoved his index finger up his nose. At least he was consistent.

I leaned over the edge of the retaining wall and looked down at the traffic, only to see a cop looking up at me. I couldn't hear what she was saying, but the woman beside him was pointing in my direction and talking rapidly. Her hair looked a little flat on top. Wet.

The cop motioned for me to come down. I looked at the Styrofoam cup I still held in my hand. It was fully visible to the crowd that was now gathering on the street. Did I need this? No. That damn Dougie appeared at the crosswalk, looked up at me, smiled, and shrugged. I headed down the ramp.

It hadn't helped that the cop turned out to be one I didn't know. The woman was two steps away from hysterical and demanded that I be arrested for something. Anything. The cop seemed bent on impressing the citizen with his macho prowess and reamed me out, threatening to haul me in. I ingratiated myself and told him that it had been an accident, that the cup had been bumped. They both seemed to buy it, reluctantly. By the time I crawled into my truck, only to find a ticket on my windshield, I was not in a good mood. That didn't deter me from driving down to the "cribs," as Dougie referred to them. I needed to step into the room, and maybe, with any luck at all, Ellen Maitland would still be hanging around.

16

Whatever warmth the sun offered that day was fading. Snowmelt still dripped from the top of buildings, and cars kicked up exhaust-tinted sprays as they headed home in five o'clock traffic. Traffic stayed heavy until I turned left off Twenty-seventh Street onto Erie and wound my way around the Warbonnet Inn. New had given way to old, and if anything was really left of the Bunk House Motel it was now overshadowed and hidden behind the Warbonnet.

The side streets were already glazing over. I turned the heater on in the truck when I felt a chill crawl over my body. I slowed down when I saw a guy trying to jump-start a pickup truck in front of a house. The truck, nose to nose with a dated Chevy Impala, groaned as the guy inside cranked the key. When he saw me pull alongside him, he got out and walked over. I rolled the window down and leaned out.

"Tough time to have a battery go bad. Can I help?"

"Nah. I've got it." He cupped his hands, breathed into them, and then rubbed them together. "Lookin' for somebody?"

"Something. Where did the Bunk House used to stand?"

"The old cribs?"

"Yeah. Isn't it around here?"

"Follow this road on down and take a right where it says No Trespassing." He grinned as he said it.

"Anybody around down there to enforce that?"

"Just the old guy that lives in that shack behind it, and he's usually so drunk he wouldn't know the place burned down."

"Thanks." I started to roll the window back up.

"What're you looking for at that creepy fucking place? We used to party over there when I was a kid."

"Just curious."

"Helluva night to get curious about that place."

"Thanks. Hope you get your truck running."

"You got quite a rig. Ever think of selling it?"

"Never."

"You just don't see many of 'em on the road. Take it easy."

He hit the top of the cab with his hand as I pulled away and drove toward the cribs. They were just what he said: creepy. The light was fading fast, and my breath steamed in front of me. I pulled up alongside what obviously had been the office and turned the truck off. I sat for a minute and watched the headlights fall the length of the building, accentuating the boards haphazardly nailed across most of the windows. The beams created misted shadows that hung in the dull light. There was no glass left, no doors, just yawning black holes for the snow and the cold and the memories to flow in and out of.

I pushed in the knob and cut the headlights, reached under the front seat, grabbed a flashlight, and got out of the truck. The motel was L-shaped, with a dilapidated roof that stretched out over the weathered boardwalk, half of which was on the ground. Drifts of snow cuddled the sides of the building as if to embrace it. Protect it.

Beyond the motel I saw a shack that looked like nothing more than a lean-to, with a faint light glowing out through a single window. Smoke rose from the metal pipe that stuck up from the roof. The smoke was the only movement around. I stepped forward and onto the porch. A board creaked under my weight. Only a faint light of the day hung in the air around me as I walked down the porch. I was aware only of the gaping windows and doors to my right and the swishing sound of traffic on the Interstate that came in surges like the pulsating of a human heart. Maybe it was my own heart.

For a crib to be this far away from where the action would have been seemed senseless. But then again, tucked where it was, who would give it a second thought? And on slow days it probably had picked up a few unaware tourists or truckers looking for a place to crash.

I was walking the same path the little kid had followed when he discovered Ellen's body. Had the killer come this way also? I was nearing the end, feeling the end, of the rooms. Within steps, I stood in front of the last door. There was a single board nailed at an angle across it; it lifted off easily. I stepped into the darkness and turned on the flashlight. The walls that hadn't succumbed to decay down to the lathe dripped with strips of faded wallpaper. I stepped over the refuse on the floor and heard glass crunch under my feet. I looked down and saw the distorted features of my face reflected in the shards. A gust of wind came from behind me and shuffled some trash papers around my feet. It was an eerie, haunting sound.

There's a technique that some agents and investigators come by easily. It's called profiling. And although it's considered an art and not a science, when it works, it really works. These blessed or cursed individuals, depending on how you look at it, have the capability of putting themselves into the crime scene and into the victim's and killer's minds. I'd never experienced anything like that at the academy, and every time someone spoke of their own real or imagined experience I felt just a little envious. That was about to change.

The room wasn't much over nine feet by twelve, not counting the bathroom, which now consisted of a couple of pipes coming up out of the floor, or the doorless closet that had become a catchall for whatever the elements and trespassers chose to place there. I tried to picture the room the way it might have looked back then. It sure as hell wouldn't have held much more than a double bed, a dresser, and maybe a straight-backed chair, with little room left to turn around.

Another frigid breeze swept through the door and window and fanned the hanging shreds of wallpaper. They flapped bizarrely, like birds pinned against the wall. Again the strewn floor came to life, and then all fell silent. Thank God for the cold, or the garbage stench would have been unbearable. Then it happened. I turned quickly and shined my flashlight through the front door. There had been no movement, no discernible sound, just a feeling that someone had entered. No one was there. I took a step backward, catching the heel of my shoe on the uneven floorboards. The force sent me sprawling against the back wall. The flashlight flew out of my hand and landed a short distance away from me, the beam directed at my face. My head crashed against the solid barrier. I slid down the wall onto my butt and reached up to cradle my head. The light was blinding for just a moment, and then it went out.

The darkness of the room, the chill, doubled. I sat there until my eyes adjusted, took a deep breath, and tried to stand. I couldn't. There's no other way to describe it: resignation and an overwhelming sadness. The cold disappeared, the dark remained. With my back up against the wall, I stared through the darkness with the same dead stare that Ellen must have met her killer with. There was no fear, just a soulful acceptance that covered my body with the heaviness of a wet wool coat.

In that moment I knew Ellen knew her killer. It wasn't a stranger off the roof that took her life, it was someone from her life. Someone who hated her enough to obliterate her face after they felled her. Someone whose mere presence struck her dumb. A paralyzing terror surged through my mind, but it wasn't Ellen's; she had none. It was my own as a figure formed in the blackness of the doorway.

"What the hell are you doing in there?"

The silhouette's hand, raised high into the air, held a club, a board, something that could do me bodily harm. Still, I was never so glad to hear a voice in my life. I stood, picked up the flashlight, and held it defensively in my hand.

"Uh, I thought I saw some kids in here. Thought I better check it out."

"Yeah?" The voice was gruff, disbelieving. "Come on out where I can see ya."

"Then put the board down," I answered, mustering up my toughest tone. The arm went down and he stepped back. I stepped through the door and found myself standing practically toe to toe with him.

"Sorry you thought someone was, uh, was trespassing. I've got ID if you want to see it."

"Ain't been nobody down here all winter. It's the summer that brings 'em in. Little bastards don't like the cold."

"Yeah. Well, I can understand that. And it's getting colder."

"You didn't take nothing outta there, did you?"

"I don't know how long it's been since you've been inside, but I sure as hell didn't take anything. What's to take, for Christ's sake?"

"The toilet is gone. The damn sink walked out last fall. How the hell do I know you aren't the one who boosted them?"

"Trust me." I turned and started walking toward my truck.

"You won't be driving that outta here, sweetie. I flattened the tires."

"You *what*?" I turned to face him. "Say that again."

"I let the air out. How the hell did I know what you were doing down here? You could have been one of those bangers coming down here to burn me out."

"Do I look like a goddamn gang-banger? Jesus!" I walked back toward the truck. The tires were flat, all right. Flat as hell.

"Hey! This is posted property. I ain't the one breaking the law here. It's you, lady. I coulda called the cops."

"Who the fuck do you think you are?"

"The fuckin' caretaker of these premises, that's who. Who the hell do you think *you* are, lady? You got no right to come on this here property. Can't you read the damn signs—"

His voice faded behind me as I followed my tire tracks back out of the driveway. I had to find a phone. With any luck at all, the guy I had talked to jumping his truck would still be around. God smiled. His truck was running, but he was still under the hood tinkering with something. I used his phone to call Triple A.

It took an hour for them to show up. Apparently they were used to coming down and pulling cars away from the ruins of the Bunk House, but I was their first private investigator. It took another two hours for them to fill the tires: They'd empty one tank, leave for a refill of air, and return. I waited with my truck. It gave me a good view of the shack and the jerk that lived inside. Like clockwork, he peeked out of his lone window every ten or fifteen minutes with this shit-eating grin on his face. If I hadn't been a controlled person, a calm person, I would have shot him.

It was a little past eight-thirty when I pulled into my driveway. Stud was sitting in my office window, looking irritated. It was long past his dinnertime.

*   *   *

The cold I thought had left with the gunshot wound was building up again. My sinuses were throbbing, and the chill in the air wasn't helping. I was bothered by the experience I had at the Bunk House. It wasn't as sharp or as clear as some of the profiling experiences I had heard of, but it left a knowing, something in my gut, that told me it was truth: Ellen had known her assailant and accepted what was brutally to come. That pretty much put the Marino kid on the back burner as far as suspects. But he knew something. He was the key. And until I found him, I doubted that I could start to put the names and the faces into the puzzle to make a complete picture.

I fed Stud, changed into a pair of sweatpants and a football jersey, and walked into my office just in time to answer the phone.

"Hello."

"It's me."

"Me who?"

"Your brother. Who else? How are you?"

"Oh God, Michael. I forgot all about you. You wanted to talk—"

"Not wanted—I *need* to talk to you. Phoebe, I know this probably is a bad time after what you've just been through, but please don't cancel."

I felt like shit, and I wasn't in the mood.

"Are you there?"

"Of course I'm here. I answered the phone, didn't I?"

"You weren't talking, Fee. I thought maybe you'd hung up."

"Would I do that?"

"You've done that. I'm on my way."

"It'll cost you."

He laughed. "Why doesn't that surprise me? What's the deal?"

"I need Kleenex and NyQuil."

"Hitting the NyQuil again, huh?"

"I'm sick, or haven't you heard?"

"I'll stop and get your stuff. You drive a hard bargain. I'll be there in twenty minutes."

"I'll be waiting, brother dear," I replied and hung up.

I regretted my semiestrangement from Michael. He was a good

man, a little sanctimonious and the family darling, and that in itself
was irritating. He was used to hearing confessions. I wasn't, and I
figured that's what he wanted to do: confess to what I already knew.

I checked for messages. Three from my mother, one from my sister, and one from Kyle telling me he would be by a little after ten
with something that would make me feel better. I could only hope.
The last message took me so much by surprise that I replayed it three
times and didn't erase it. Mrs. Marino, Joey Marino's mother. I was
shocked. She said she would be up until midnight, waiting for my
call. Now the guilt really set in. Did she surmise that I was the one
who called her and hung up, faking a collect call from her son?
There was no way.

I dialed her number. It rang five times before she picked up.

"Mrs. Marino? This is Phoebe Siegel. I just got your message.
What can I do for you?"

"I saw your name in the paper. You're working for that young
man that was murdered. Mr. Chillman?"

"Yes, I am."

"Miss Siegel, my son was a suspect, the only suspect in the Maitland murder. Nick Spano dropped by tonight—"

"Really?" Seemed as though Nick and I were on the same wave-
length after all.

"His feeling was that we should talk. I would feel more comfortable if we didn't talk over the phone."

"I agree. Just give me a time."

"Tonight?"

It was tough to pass up, but I had to. "Tonight wouldn't be good
for me. Unless this is the only time that—"

"No, tomorrow would be fine. Would you like to come to my
home? If you came around noon we could have a bite to eat."

"Food isn't necessary, Mrs. Marino. I probably couldn't taste it
anyway. But thanks for the offer. I appreciate it."

"You do sound a little stuffed up."

"I'm just fighting some bug. Noon would be fine. I'll see you
then."

"Good-bye, and I'll see you tomorrow."

I hung up just as I heard footsteps on the front porch. I walked to the door, checked that it was Michael, and let him in. He kissed me on the cheek and patted the good side of my head.

"You are now infected with a life-form that can do for you what it has done for me."

"Cute. Where should I put this stuff?"

"I'll take it." I walked into the kitchen with Michael behind me. I took the Kleenex and the NyQuil out of the sack and set them on the table. "Am I going to be happy after this talk, Michael, or will I be pissed off?"

"Don't build dragons, Phoebe. You want to sit in here?"

"No. The living room. Maybe you could start a fire."

"Be glad to, little sis. Still feeling under the weather?"

"Yes, Michael. I am. Nothing has changed in the last twenty minutes."

He was making small talk. This was going to be big stuff. I settled down on my sickbed, the couch, and pulled a blanket up over my legs. Stud jumped up on the back of the couch and started his menacing growl as he watched Michael bunch up newspaper and put it in the fireplace. After he topped the paper off with some small pine pieces, he placed a log in and struck a match. The fire caught and gave a wonderful glow to the living room. It was misleading.

Michael sat down in my one and only overstuffed chair and took a deep breath.

"I like your Pearl Harbor decor."

"Pearl Harbor?" I queried.

"The brown mohair furniture, isn't that the time period?"

"Yeah. I just never thought of it as Pearl Harbor. But I guess you're right."

"I'm leaving the priesthood, Phoebe."

"I'd rather talk about Pearl Harbor, Michael." The only thing missing was the sound of planes heading for the coast of my mind.

17

There's history between Michael and me, and it seems that we add to it every time we are in each other's company. I love him, I just can't get along with him. And now he sat across from me, gazing into the fire like a man who had been stripped of his strength. That's one thing Michael was never short on: strength. At least, that's what I had always thought.

Families are tough propositions. Through some greater wisdom, many different personalities are thrown together, and then the real test begins. During the hard times when my sister, Kehly, was fighting a drug problem, my family became involved with the dynamics that created her problem. It wasn't something I participated in. That labeled me quickly, according to those who did partake in the unraveling of the Dysfunctional Siegels. Me? I always thought we were pretty normal, and by today's standards I guess we are. But through it all, Michael was the rock, the blessed, the priest. Looking at him now, I thought about how we had all fed off his goodness. For me, it was someone to do battle with, someone to blame for my brother Ben's death. He was a worthy foe whom I secretly respected for his commitment to the Church. The further I grew away from religion, the bigger Michael grew in my eyes. He was the sacrifice to keep the rest of us out of hell. Whoever heard of a family member of a priest going to hell? I sure as hell haven't. Not in Billings, anyway. I mean, not on my block at least.

"Michael, maybe you can do that thing the priest did in *The Thornbirds*. Father Ralph? Remember him? I mean, he pulled it off for years. They had a damn stable relationship, don't you think?"

Michael turned toward me. Even through the incredible sadness in his eyes, he managed a smile.

"Where did you come up with that? I'm not Father Ralph, Fee. I'm just me, Michael, and I need my sister right now. No flip. No judgments. No solutions. Just listen. Okay?"

"I was only trying to—"

"Please, Fee," he said as he reached out and held my foot.

"My God, I've been healed. That ingrown toenail I've had all my life? It's gone. I've been healed!"

"This was a bad idea. I thought—" He stood and looked down at me.

"Okay. Okay." I held up my arms in mock surrender. "Sit down and lay it on me. I've got to tell you right up-front, I don't know if I can handle this, Michael."

"That makes two of us."

"This isn't some snap decision, is it? Cara hasn't been back that long. It's that glow that wears off after a while. You two haven't even been around each other for years."

Michael looked at me with that don't-count-on-that look.

"So this isn't a new thing. Am I right?"

"You're right."

"Oh God, Michael. Who else have you talked to? Don't they have specialists, like doctors do?"

"You mean, like an exorcist or something?"

"Not yet. No, we don't need to call in the big guns yet, Michael. But I'm not ruling that out. Let's get back to the real problem. You're going to shake up a lot of people, Michael. Not the least of which will be Mama."

"You think I haven't thought of that? I just can't go on living the lie. Mama deserves something better, Fee. Agree?"

"It'll kill her."

"That's an exaggeration."

"Maybe not. You've always been her Michael the Priest. The transformation to her Michael the Fornicator isn't going to sit well."

"Is that what you feel? That all this is just fornicating? Some base animal drive that I can't control? Hell, Fee." He shook his head in disgust. "I'm in love with Cara. Don't make it sound like something unclean."

"Let's get real here. You took those vows, Michael. You. Not Mama, not me, not anyone else. You. And now you want to throw them away for some—"

"Don't go too far. Just don't go too far."

His eyes snapped. He was right, that would be going too far. "I don't have a damn thing against Cara, Michael. But this is going to start a tidal wave that even you won't be able to part and make go away."

"Are you ready to listen, Fee?"

"Go for it. But don't ask me to go along with this. Okay?"

"When I was in seminary, they told us we needed to love, L-O-V-E everyone. And I did, Fee. The other guys at the seminary, I loved them—"

"Mama will never be able to deal with that one, Michael."

"You know damn well what I mean. No flip, remember?"

"I'm just trying to get you to lighten up."

"They never taught us how to stop loving, Phoebe, and for the life of me I cannot stop loving her. I don't want to stop. We want to get married. We want a family. We want—"

"Michael, take a leave of absence. What do they call that? A sabbatical or something?"

"That's not an option. It would be dishonest. I don't have any intention of going back."

"Have you thought about how this is going to affect Cara? God, Michael, we're talking worse than Hester Prynne here."

"Who?"

"Hester—never mind. Do you really think that people aren't going to look at her as the woman that defrocked Michael Siegel? Not the least of which will be Mama. She cares about Cara, Michael. How the hell do you think she's going to feel about her when this hits the stands?"

"That's why I need you to help me make her understand."

"*Moi?* You're kidding. Right?"

Michael picked up the poker and stabbed at the logs. Sparks

erupted as the updraft pulled them up the chimney. He continued to stare at the fire as the flames crawled over glowing embers and licked at the logs. He seemed to find some solace in the fire. All I could think of was Dante's *Inferno*.

The muffled ringing of the phone broke through our silence.

"Damn. Where is it?" I threw the blanket back and started following the cord. I yanked it and reeled in the phone from under a couple of pillows on the floor. The displaced receiver stretched out behind it. I grabbed it, dropped it, and picked it up again.

"Hello?"

"It's Nick."

"Hey."

"Can you talk?"

"Not really. But you can."

"That information you wanted to take a look at? It's in your woodbox."

"Do you think that was wise, Nick?" I was incredulous.

"Unless someone is going through your woodbox periodically, I figured it was the best place."

I grimaced. Michael looked at me with raised eyebrows. I shook my head and tried to give him one of my it's-no-big-deal looks. He turned back to the fire.

"I dropped in on Joey Marino's mother earlier."

"I know. I heard from her."

"She had some kinda strange call today. It got her upset."

"Did she say what it was about?" Innocence doesn't come any better than when there's a priest in the house.

"Nope. Wouldn't even tell me what the caller said."

I was right. She knew someone was looking for Joey, or she would have given details about the call.

"Did you set up a time to get together?"

"I did. Look, Nick, I've got someone with me. Can I call you back?"

"No need, Phoebe. Ellen Maitland had a best friend. They grew up together. Seems that when Ellen married Maitland he put the clamps on the relationship so the two of them snuck off to see each other. She's real spooked at talking about Ellen. I don't know where that's coming from, but I think you'd get further with her than I did."

"What's her name?"

"Joanne Mullins. She works down at the Greyhound bus depot. Afternoons, I think. I caught her at home, getting ready for work. That was around two or so this afternoon."

"Address?"

"She lives down at Blain's Mobile Home Court. The street and number are in with the things I left. Damnedest thing. She just fell through the cracks when everyone latched on to Marino."

"Thanks, Nick. I'll pull that stuff out and get in touch with you tomorrow."

"Night."

"Good night, Nick."

I hung up the phone.

"Michael, I've got to do something here for a minute. Sit tight?"

"Sure."

I walked into the kitchen, opened the back door, and walked down the stairs to the woodbox. It gave me the creeps to open the damn thing in the daylight. At night, it really freaked me out. I referred to it as the Arachnae Motel. Creepy crawling multilegged little things with fangs were probably lining up, waiting to jump on my hand.

I thought better of it and walked back up to the back door. "Michael!"

"What?" He yelled back and soon appeared in the kitchen.

"I've got to get some things out of the woodbox. Could you give me a hand?"

"You've got enough wood stacked in the living room."

"It's not wood. A friend left some files in there."

"Then take them out," he said and laughed.

"Come on, Michael. Please?"

"You still haven't grown out of that yet, have you?"

"What?"

Michael walked down the steps and over to the woodbox. "It would help if you had a light out here, ya know."

"But you have the Great Light guiding you. Who needs a bulb?"

He lifted the lid on the box, reached in, and pulled out a bulky manila envelope. "Is this it?"

"Must be."

Without warning the envelope flew toward me. "Oh no!" he screamed. "They're all over it." He brushed at his arms frantically.

I jumped straight up and batted the envelope back to Michael. It fell at his feet and split open.

"Phoebe, help me." He walked toward me with outstretched arms.

"Touch me, and I swear you're dead, Michael. I mean it." I stepped backward.

"They're gone. Just like that they're gone." He raised his arms in the air.

"You are possessed. It's the exorcist, Michael. I'm calling the exorcist."

We both bent down at the same time to pick up the scattered contents of the envelope. The light from the kitchen spilled down the stairs and onto the pile. Michael froze, picked up an eight-by-ten photo, and held it up toward the dull light.

"Holy Mary Mother of God, what is this, Phoebe?"

I reached for the photo, took it from his hand, and looked at it. There was only one thing it could be: a crime scene photo of Ellen Maitland, slumped against the wall of the motel room, her skull and face bludgeoned beyond recognition.

"Why in God's name would anyone leave you something like this? I think I'm going to be sick."

I scooped the pile together. "Let's go back in."

"What's this about, Phoebe?"

"It's about my job, Michael. I'm sorry you had to see that. I'm also sorry I can't talk about it and explain it away."

"I'm not sure you could, Phoebe. No wonder Mama and Kehly worry like they do. You get shot, you've got people leaving sick pictures in your woodbox, what's next?"

"I don't know. I could stand to lose a few pounds. Maybe that's next."

"You're hopeless."

"No, just under the same restraints you are. You've got the sanctity of the confessional, and I've got confidentiality with my clients."

I took the material into my office and closed the door. When I returned to the living room, Michael was putting his coat on.

"Where're you going?"

"Home. We'll do this another night."

"Michael—" I pleaded.

"I've never seen anything like that. I've got to go."

"Promise me something," I said as I followed him to the front door.

"What?"

"Don't say anything to Mama until we talk."

"Do you really think I would ever tell her what I just saw?"

"That's not what I'm talking about, Michael. I mean about you and . . ."

"I think I'm more than capable of making decisions where my mother is concerned."

"My mother? Try *our* mother."

"Good night, Phoebe" was all he said as he walked out and closed the door behind him.

"Good night, John Boy. Shit."

We had created another page of history.

18

It was past midnight by the time I finished looking through the material Nick had gathered. The crime scene photos were as grisly as any I had ever seen. To expect Michael to be anything but repulsed was ridiculous.

There were numerous statements, as well as the photos. They ranged from Rosella Dahl herself to Maitland and down to the paperboy who had seen Ellen leave the house that morning. Nothing had any substance. Lots of investigators' notes, including those of my father. He had a weird way of initialing things that could have been misinterpreted as "bullshit." I touched the initials, knowing they were his. It sounds silly, but I kind of had the feeling that he was helping Nick and me. I guess any type of delusion works when you're up against some high walls.

All I needed was a boost to get over them. Dorothy Valentine really nagged in the back of my mind. She had said something. Something that, looking back, seemed a little too familiar for someone who knew nothing about the case. She had said, "No, I never knew Ellen." It was one of those statements that, when you go back over a conversation you had with someone, just keeps popping to the front. I was grabbing for anything, and I knew it.

According to the coroner's report, there was only one probable defensive wound on Ellen Maitland. The anterior portion of her right forearm was bruised badly enough that the skin had split. That was the least of her wounds; she could have gotten it defending herself, or it may have been a blow once she was down. Both collarbones were shattered. Either injury could have put her on the floor. But it was the compression fractures of her skull that killed her. The blunt-force trauma was so severe that portions of her skull were embedded deep inside her brain. Large sections of hair, still attached to her skull, were hanging down. The orbital sockets were decimated; not even the globes of the eyes remained intact. The nose was gone, the sinuses crushed, and one ear had been torn completely away from the side of her head.

Ellen knew whoever went after her with whatever instrument. When the face is demolished, it means that the killer and the victim probably have some kind of tie. The ferocity with which she had been attacked shook me up. This was not some tap-tap-you're-dead deal. You could see the hate, feel it. She was wearing this strange little getup that you'd expect to see on a stripper after she had peeled down to the nitty-gritty. It didn't wear well with Ellen. I propped her picture up and compared the docile, quiet beauty with the macabre crime scene photos. Michael was right. It was enough to make you sick.

The straps that passed for a black lace bra had been broken during the attack. One breast, covered in blood, was exposed. One leg was still covered with a black nylon; the other looked as if someone had dug their nails in her upper thigh and ripped the nylon down to Ellen's ankle. Intermittent scratches followed the contour of her leg. Why that, after the damage that had already been inflicted?

I found the crime scene photos of Rita Chillman. Less dramatic. She was dressed in a snappy two-piece suit; a white blouse with a ruffled collar peeked from under the jacket. She was on her back, hair neatly done, eyelids barely open. One shoe was missing from her left foot but could be seen in the photo not far from the body. One small bullet hole was visible just above her left eyebrow, near the bridge of her nose. A stream of blood had trickled down her face, following her nose line and on down over her lips and chin. A small part of the ruffled blouse was soaked where the rivulet disappeared underneath her jacket. Her head rested in a pool of blood. The exit wound was where the real damage had been done.

Frank Chillman had been shot in the head. Ellen Maitland's head had been destroyed. And Rita Chillman, dressed for her elopement, had also taken a bullet to the head. Not to mention that someone had tried to permanently part my hair. I reached up and touched the side of my head. They had probably accomplished it.

The notes that Nick included were in semichronological order. Whenever someone thought they had spotted Joey Marino, they called Maitland. They were probably hungering for the reward money he had put up. Maitland in turn would give the information to the cops, who would record the outcome of their investigation. Joey was spotted hopping a train in the Laurel train yard and dressed like a woman at the airport getting on a plane for Chicago. That wasn't nearly as good as the woman who called Maitland every year to report that she had seen him with the Shrine Circus doing an aerial act. Even that petered out. You could see by the dates how the interest waned. One thing that struck me as curious was that Maitland had requested that the outfit that Ellen had been murdered in be returned to him. His request was denied.

There were newspaper clippings, attributed to different bylines, that brought a little attention to the case by trying to resurrect the unsolved murder of the two local women. But not once, anywhere, did I see mention that anyone suspected the two murders of being linked.

My father had a reputation for being one of the most thorough investigators on the force. The Nick and Ben Show, as they were fondly referred to, never left a stone unturned. Joanne Mullins— how the hell did they miss that one? Had Joanne gone underground after Ellen's murder? And if they were such good friends, why didn't she come forth? What did she know that was never brought out? Nothing? Something?

I wrote her address down on my Nancy Drew things-to-do notepad. No lie. It exists. Kehly had found it for me, and it was the right size to fit in my pocket so I used the hell out of it. I just tried never to let a potential client or anyone I was taking a deposition from see it. But what the hell, I'd caught a local right-wing Christian minister in his Power Ranger underwear in a motel room washing a hooker's feet while she rotated her index fingers in his ears. His congregation had taken up a collection to pay me to follow up on some rumors from the choirmaster. They got their money's worth and then some. I guess a Nancy Drew notebook wasn't so bad.

The fire was burning down in the fireplace when I got around to closing up my office and turning all the lights out. Kyle hadn't shown up yet, so I didn't expect him to come by. I checked that I had locked both the front and back doors. I had. I poured myself another shot of NyQuil, slipped out of my sweatpants, and lay down on the couch. Only the last glow of the dying embers remained. They quivered in their red-white hotness, hanging on to whatever life they had left. Stud snuggled down in the crook of my legs as I turned on my side and pulled the blanket up under my chin. What a day. From Nick, to Dorothy Valentine, to Gin, to Dougie, to Michael, all of the faces and conversations rolled over the top of each other and melted into one undecipherable voice. As the voice faded, so did I. The last thing I remembered was the purring of the cat against my legs, and wishing that someone were there to hold me.

It came softly at first. A hazy sound from inside me. A tapping and then a muffled hollow sound, louder now, attempting to rouse me from the most comfortable deep sleep I had ever had.

"Go away," I mumbled and pulled the blanket up over my head.

The sound grew clearer and more persistent. I turned over on my back, pulled the cover off my face, and listened. Someone was knocking at the door, and they weren't going to go away. I looked toward a window and saw the faint beginnings of daylight. The metronome drip of water from the roof told me the temperature had come up in the night.

The knocking continued. I threw the blanket off, rolling the cat to the bottom end of the couch, and got up.

"I'm coming. Cool it. Okay?"

I staggered toward the front door and looked out of the curtains. No one was there.

"Shit."

I started back for the couch. There was a God. Whoever it was had left. I had just sat down when the knocking started again. This time it sounded like someone at the back door. I stood again and followed the sound. Some people jump up out of bed ready to do battle with the day. Not me. I need time. Caffeine. Quiet. There are sleep wrinkles, and then there are sleep wrinkles. I happen to have them so bad my face looks like a topical map of the Georgia backwoods. Not a pretty sight.

I tried to close one eye and give my other eye a better chance of opening. Through the glass of the back door, I saw Kyle holding a McDonald's bag in the air.

"Can I come in if I have food?"

"No." I leaned against the doorjamb and rubbed my face. "You're a day late, and I'm not hungry."

"Sausage McMuffins with cheese."

"You really are cruel, you know. My favorite food." I opened the door and let him in.

"You're easy, Siegel. You better take a look at that."

"When I can see, I'll take a look at that," I said and sat down at the table.

"Where's the coffee?"

"In the cupboard. There should be coffee in the pot. Pour me a cup and heat it up in the microwave."

"From yesterday?"

"No. Last week. I like it with some age on it."

"I'll make a pot."

"Please, Kyle. Just heat up what's left, and then you can make whatever your heart desires."

"You must have a lead-lined stomach."

"What happened to you last night?"

"Miss me?"

I didn't turn to watch him go through the cupboards looking for the coffee beans. "Come to think of it, no. I didn't."

"What the hell is this? Chocolate chips?"

"Where?" I turned.

He was holding the basket for the coffeepot. "Here."

I grasped the side and looked down into the basket. "I would think that a detective could figure out that those are coffee beans."

"Whole?"

"Semi. The grinder fitzed out, so I put them in a Ziploc baggie and slammed them in the drawer a few times."

"And this?" He flicked the white paper hanging over the side of the basket.

"A paper towel. I ran out of filters."

"You know you shouldn't be living on your own, don't you?"

"Kyle—"

"What did you eat last night?"

"I didn't. I got wrapped up in some other things. You never did answer me. What happened last night that deprived me of your company?"

"It got busy."

"How busy?"

Kyle opened the refrigerator and poured a glass of juice that he promptly set down in front of me. "I really don't want any slammed-bean coffee. This will have to do. Unless you're serious about heating that, uh . . . that stuff up in the microwave."

"That would be very kind of you, Kyle."

"You got it. I'm not touching it."

"What is the problem with telling me what the hell kept you so busy?"

"Just the regular crap. Somebody rolled a couple of cowboys in from Fort Smith. The roads had patches of black ice until the temperature started coming up around three this morning. You'd think people would learn how to drive on that shit, or at least just stay home."

"Sounds exciting."

"And this might interest you. Remember that little guy that hangs on the south side, Dougie the Snitch?"

"Uh-huh." I was half awake.

"Somebody beat the hell out of him last night. Some cabbie called it in. Found him lying down behind Colburns School Supply, half on and half off the tracks. Poor old fellow must have drug himself onto them trying to get some help. He's just damn lucky a train didn't—"

"Wait a minute. Dougie? What did you say?"

"Douglas Cooper. Dougie the Snitch. You know the one. Dirty little guy that has a thing for his nose?"

"Is he all right?"

"They don't think he's going to make it. We tried to get a statement from him last night, but they wouldn't let us talk to him. They've got him in intensive care. Punctured lung, thought he had a ruptured spleen, and a fractured pelvis."

"I don't believe it. I was just with him yesterday in the parking garage."

"What the hell were you doing in the parking garage with Dougie?"

"What everybody who has a clandestine meeting with Dougie does. Buying some information."

I hated it when Kyle turned cop. His eyes changed, along with his whole facial expression. He straightened up and leaned against the counter.

"Maybe we better talk. What kind of information were you buying?"

"Like I can tell you that."

"I think you better. We thought it was some random shakedown. Someone who didn't know he didn't have a pot to piss in."

"He had fifty bucks. My fifty bucks."

"Must have been serious information. I thought the going rate was twenty."

"Look, Kyle, he told me to get back with him tomorrow. He told me he had an appointment with a friend for a game of chess."

"That's it?"

"That's it."

"What parking garage?"

"The one across from the Sheraton."

"The Sheraton, huh? What time?"

"I don't know. Sometime before five. I met him coming out of Studio One. I guess he uses the parking garage as his office or some damn thing. He left around five. I know that because traffic was picking up."

"Wait a minute. You weren't the one that poured the coffee down on that woman's head, were you? Second story?"

"You should know better. Actually, Dougie poured it over the edge and left. How the hell was I supposed to know that he hit someone?"

Kyle leaned back and laughed. "I heard the dispatcher send a car out. Christ. I don't believe it."

"Kyle, can you get me in to see him?"

"I don't know. Does this have anything to do with Maitland and that mess?"

"It might. God, it might. I've got to see him."

"I'll see what I can do. You're not related to Dougie by any chance, are you?"

"What the hell are you talking about?"

"A relative? They were looking for relatives."

"You know, Kyle, I always thought there was something Siegelish about him. In fact, seems to me I heard somewhere that he was an eighth cousin, twice removed."

"That's good enough for me."

I walked over, stood on my tiptoes, and kissed him. It was quick and spontaneous until he put his hand under my chin and tilted it up. There was this moment, this incredible moment when the walls and the floors all disappeared. The muscles in my stomach tightened as he moved his mouth down toward mine. With his index finger, he traced the moisture just inside my parted lips. My arms wrapped around the hardness of his back as I pushed myself into him. I was dissolving, responding to the wetness shared between us as he kissed me, ran his tongue along the roof of my mouth. I wanted to crawl inside of him, pull him inside of me.

And then it stopped. Kyle cradled my head against his chest. I could hear his heartbeat, feel the heaviness of his breathing. He nuzzled his face in my hair.

"I wouldn't do that if I were you. Faces have gotten lost in there."

"Do you know how long I've wanted to do that?"

"Lose your face?" I could hardly catch my breath to talk. His breath was hot on my scalp.

"Just pick you up and . . ."

I backed up and put my hands on his chest. "You missed one helluva night last night, Wolf."

He laughed. "I did, huh?"

"You did. I want you to freeze this moment in your mind, because we need to take up where we left off."

"How about now—" He reached for me as I backed away.

"I've got to go to the hospital, Kyle. It's important."

"This isn't?" He smiled.

"This is. Like I said, we will—"

"Take up where we left off."

"Right. Damn. There's nothing sexier than a guy who finishes your sentences for you." I raised my eyebrows and turned to walk away. "I'm going to get dressed. I'll be down in a minute."

I was nearly to the stairs when it sounded as if Kyle was throwing up. "What happened?"

"Christ. I should know better than to drink any liquids over here unless they come out of the tap or I uncap the bottle."

The microwave was open. Kyle held the cup of slammed-bean coffee. What wasn't in the cup was down the front of his shirt.

"Look at this," he wailed as he attempted to brush off the coffee. "Now I'm all wet."

"Me too."

I watched as his mind caught up with my mouth. He looked at me and smiled. "I must be out of my mind."

"That's going to make it all the more interesting."

19

I had been sitting in the waiting room outside intensive care for an hour. The pink lady with the silver hair had the personality of a radical Gray Panther. No one can tell me that the elderly don't have power. This one had a stare that would put a sumo warrior on his knees. The eighth-cousin-twice-removed routine didn't work.

"I've heard them all, dearie. Come up with an okay from the attending physician and you'll get in to see Mr. Cooper. Our first concern is for the patient."

"And how do you suggest I get an okay from the attending physician?"

"Well, I suggest that you sit right here and hope that he comes down the hall."

"That creates another problem."

"What might that be?"

"How the hell—" She bristled and took the pencil from behind her ear. I couldn't be sure that she wouldn't throw that thing like a dart. "How will I recognize him?"

"If I'm not distracted, I'd be delighted to point him out to you."

"I'd appreciate that."

"Now take a seat, please. You're blocking other people from asking questions."

Obediently I walked over to a chair and sat. The choice of magazines was nothing short of abysmal: several back issues of *Catholic Digest*, *Runner* magazine, a couple of scholastic books, and a shredded cloth alphabet book, the unshreddable kind.

Every time I stood to stretch or walk down the hall, the panther in pink followed my every move. I decided the best thing to do was make friends with her. I sauntered back into the waiting room and over to the television. Every little old lady loved game shows. I reached up to change the station.

"Did we miss 'The Price Is Right'?"

She was up and out of her chair before my fingers touched the knob.

"Stop that. Stop that now. I have to ask you not to touch that. I retain control of the remote. Just tell me what station you want it on, and I'll change it."

"I was going to put it on a station for you, but that looks a little out of the question."

"Perhaps I haven't made myself clear. This is a waiting room. People normally come in here to wait. Perhaps you'd like to walk down to the cafeteria and have a bite to eat. You'll find it very pleasant."

Sounded good to me. "Which way is the cafeteria?"

"Straight down the hall and to the left."

"If, on the off chance that the, uh—"

"Attending physician."

"Right. If he should come by, would you tell him that I have to see Mr. Cooper? It is urgent that I speak with him."

"And your name?"

"Phoebe Siegel."

She placed the glasses that hung around her neck on a faux-pearl chain up on the bridge of her nose and carefully wrote my name down. "I'll let the doctor know you've inquired."

"No. You'll let the doctor know I need to get in to see Mr. Cooper."

The cafeteria was all but empty. I headed straight for the coffee cups and filled one from the machine. It was surprisingly good. Picking a table with a view, I sat down and looked out over a parking lot. Kyle had opted to crash at my house. I mean, after all, he had just gotten off work. The thought of him tightened muscles I didn't remember I had. I was lusting. Big time.

"Aren't you—"

I looked up. I knew I knew the face, but I couldn't put a name on it.

"And you're—"

"The doctor that treated you in the emergency room. Or have you gone into amnesia?"

"I'm not that lucky. I remember it all. How are you doing?"

"Great. And you?"

"Okay." I reached up and patted the side of my head.

He leaned down and inspected the wound. "God, I'm good."

"I'd have to agree."

"Mind if I sit down?"

"Be my guest."

He sat down across from me at the table. "So, how's business?"

"Good. It's good. And you?"

"Same old, same old."

"Do you work Emergency all the time?"

"That's my specialty. So, tell me something about this, uh, private investigator thing."

"What about it?"

"I don't know. It's intriguing. Sounds a helluva lot more exciting than holding an emesis basin for someone as they throw up. Or giving a kid a shot that you know is going to hurt like hell."

"How did you know what—"

"It was on your chart. Your friend filled in all the information. Let's face it, I've also got your address and your phone number."

"I know they are in good hands." I watched him over the top of my cup as I drank. What the hell. I may as well give it a try. "Hey, Doc. I suppose it would be asking too much to ask you for a little favor."

He looked slightly put off. "Like what?"

"I need to see a friend. They brought him in sometime during the night. He was beaten up pretty bad. Think you could swing it for me?"

"Who's the friend?"

"His name is Dougie—Douglas Cooper."

"So you're the eighth cousin twice removed who's been giving Betty a bad time."

I sat my cup down on the table. "Me, giving *her* a bad time? I'm surprised she has a human name. Betty. God, that sounds banal."

"Betty's one of my favorites. Runs a tight ship."

"That's an understatement. Come on. Can you get me in?"

He watched for a couple of minutes before answering.

"Well?" I asked.

"He's in pretty rough shape. He's going into surgery later this morning. They mashed his insides up pretty good."

"They?"

"He said *they* jumped him from behind and dragged him into the alley."

"He's talking?"

"Hard to understand, but yeah, he manages to get a few words out. Is it that important that you see him now, or can you wait until tomorrow?"

"Tomorrow might be too late. Not only for me, but what if he doesn't come out of surgery?"

"There's a possibility of that. We get this guy in a couple of times each winter. He's been losing ground this past year. Dougie the Snitch. What a character."

"You know—"

"Hell yes, I know. He never made any bones about it. He'd do three-, maybe four-week stints up here. If I needed to know anything, Dougie was who I went to. Of course, for me it came free. You?"

"I'm afraid I contributed to his income."

"Come on and I'll take you down."

"I owe you one."

"Dinner?"

"Dinner? You and me?"

"Won't be as painful as your head wound."

"I don't know—"

"I've got references."

"I'll tell you what. Give me thirty minutes with Dougie, and you're on."

"Fifteen."

"Fifteen and we go to lunch."

"Lunch it is, then. Didn't Betty tell you that our first concern—"

"Is to the patient. I'll take fifteen."

For the life of me, I couldn't remember the doctor's name. I also didn't remember how good-looking he was: tall, constantly smiling, just a hint of gray in his brown hair. The fact that he had his hair pulled back in a ponytail only added to his charm. Not your average doc.

We entered the intensive care unit the back way and thankfully avoided Betty. The nurses' station was in the center, surrounded by individual rooms stacked full of some unnerving-looking electronic equipment. There was a camaraderie going on between the people in scrubs who were standing around the center station that seemed out of place. After all, these were critical patients. Maybe the medical personnel survived by the same kind of gallows humor that cops used.

The doctor steered me toward one of the rooms and entered before me. It was hard to tell it was Dougie in the bed. He looked small and frail. His entire face was swollen, and he had a tube that disappeared into his nose. Even under the sheet his stomach looked grossly swollen. There wasn't much of a resemblance to the Dougie who had ushered me into his parking-garage office.

"How ya doing, buddy? Need anything for pain?" Dougie's eyes opened, rolled back for a second, and closed again. "He's doing some heavy drugs. You may not get a lot out of him, but come on over and try."

"Dougie, it's Phoebe. This is a helluva way to get out of our meeting . . ."

He tried to open his eyes again as he turned his head toward the sound of my voice. He tried to raise his left hand but couldn't get it more than a couple of inches off the bed. I reached out and held it.

"In spite of everything, he really does look better than I've ever seen him look. Who shaved him and cleaned him up?"

"We had to. He was pretty ripe." The doctor whispered. "Can't take them into surgery unless they're at least halfway disinfected. I'm going to get out of here and give you some privacy. Five. No longer."

I nodded. "Dougie, it's me. Phoebe. Can you hear me at all?" He squeezed my hand and attempted to nod.

Crooking his index finger, he signaled me to come closer to him. I leaned down. His voice was barely above a raspy whisper.

"I can't understand what you're saying."

He tried again. "Paper."

"You want paper? Is that what you're saying?"

He shook his head in agreement. I let go of his hand, looked around the room, and couldn't find anything, so I walked out to the desk and asked for something to write on. A nurse handed me a scrap tablet.

"Do you have a pencil I could use?"

"Sure," she answered and pulled one out of her pocket. "I need it back, though. We're constantly losing them around here. Okay?"

"No problem. I'll bring it right back."

I walked back into Dougie's room and handed him the pad and the pencil. He maneuvered it onto his swollen stomach. I knew he couldn't see what he was doing. I guided the hand that held the pencil toward the paper. He was so weak and trembling that I was sure he wouldn't be able to write anything. He surprised me. The handwriting looked like a child's scrawling numbers as he slowly formed something on the pad.

"Is that a one, Dougie? A one?"

He nodded yes and tried to scribble something else.

"What is that? A nine?"

He shook his head no as his hand fell back down onto the bed. His eyes closed, and his chest heaved.

"Do you want me to get the doctor?"

He moved his head from side to side, struggled to get his hand back to the pad, and tried to write again. This time it looked more like a nine.

"A nine. All I can see is a one and a nine."

He appeared to ignore me and scrawled a legible two. Then the pencil fell from his hand.

"One, nine, two? Is it an address?"

His top teeth all but bit his lower lip as he mumbled, "Four. One four two."

"Okay. One. Four. Two. Okay?"

He nodded yes again.

Dougie crooked his index finger and motioned me to him. I leaned down.

"Helena." He said the word slowly. "At the home."

When the doctor walked in and stood beside me, I felt a weird sense of relief.

"It must be the medication. He's not making much sense," I whispered. "Maybe I'd better try to come back later."

"There's some cops outside in the waiting room who are very anxious to talk to him. I'm going to hold them off until tomorrow." He edged around me, adjusted an IV that was dripping into Dougie's left arm. "We're going to take you into surgery a little early, Dougie. We'll take good care of you. A nurse will be in in a moment and give you some pre-op meds that will—"

Dougie raised his arm. His hand reached out toward me again.

"Two minutes. That's all I can give you with her, and then she has to leave." The doctor stepped back, making room for me to stand by the head of the bed. "I'll take you back out the way we came in unless you want to see those guys in the waiting room."

"You must have taken Perception 101 at med school. Thanks."

"I'll wait for you by the desk."

Dougie's eyes were open wider than they had been since I entered the room. "They're kicking me out," I said, "but I'll be back tomorrow. Dougie, do you know who did this to you?"

His eyes widened and he shook his head. With the pencil still in his hand, he drew something that looked like an upside-down hook and then tapped the lead of the pencil on the paper until he could no longer hold it.

"This is why they hurt you. Am I right?"

He continued to shake his head. Then it stopped, and he turned his eyes toward me.

"Helena. Ellen's there."

"Okay, Dougie."

A nurse came in with a syringe in her hand. "I'm afraid you're going to have to leave now."

"I'm on my way," I said, and looked up at her and then back to

Dougie. "I'll see you tomorrow. You're going to feel better. He's a good doc. Tomorrow, okay?"

He managed a weak smile and shook his head no. I was convinced the morphine had him out of it. I was getting more and more uncomfortable that I was trying to extract information from someone who could be a dying man.

Over the years I had never touched Dougie. Hadn't even shaken his hand. Now I leaned down and kissed him. "Take care, Mr. Cooper. We'll talk again."

Tears formed in the corners of his eyes and dropped down onto his cheeks. I turned and left the room. He wasn't going to make it. Shit. Mr. Cooper. I'd never even known his name, never even considered that he had one.

20

Sitting in Maggie's office, I was lost in my own thoughts, waiting for her to get off the phone. Dougie would be in surgery by now, or on his way. He knew he was going to die. I knew it, too. If mercy existed, he would go while under anesthetic. Douglas Cooper, local snitch and pervert, would simply fade away. His associates would clean out his apartment and divide the spoils, and someone else would occupy the premises by nightfall. In a year's time he would be the subject of one of those remember-when conversations that would come up less and less in his transient circle of friends.

I pulled the piece of paper he had scribbled on out of my jacket pocket and stared at it. One, four, two. If it wasn't an address, then what the hell was it? A locker number? Post office box? And the fish hook, upside down though it may be, sure as hell looked to me like a fish hook. I was convinced that when Dougie said that Ellen was in Helena, it was the drugs he was on and not fact, but I couldn't count anything out. It even tripped through my mind that Ellen wasn't the corpse in the motel, but that would be impossible. A lot had changed for the better in forensics, but even back then odds were they could make a positive identification. But what if?

"Phoebe?"

"Hmm?"

"Where the hell are you?"

"You worry me, Maggie," I answered as I put the paper down on the desk in front of her. "I'm right here, across from you. Or didn't you notice?"

"Sorry about staying on the phone. That was rude. But it's my trademark, so what the hell. Sorry about that."

"Take a look at this for me. Tell me what you think it is."

"It's a little early for quizzes. Where'd you get it?"

"From Dougie the Snitch."

"This isn't one of those stupid tricks where you see one thing and then you fold the paper and it looks like someone's butt, is it?"

"Would I?"

"In a minute. What is this, Phoebe, and who the hell is this Dougie?"

"A local off Montana Avenue. An old-timer."

"I guess his name says it all. Right?"

"Uh-huh. Someone decided to stomp him last night. I just left the hospital, Maggie. He's in tough shape. I doubt he'll make it through the day."

"Ya know, I heard something about that on the radio on the way to the office this morning." She turned the paper different ways as she looked at it. "This looks like a bunch of gibberish to me." Maggie handed the paper back. "By the way, Frank Chillman's service will be tomorrow at two. I took care of everything."

"Thanks, Maggie. I appreciate it. Oh, I ran into Gin. She looks good."

"How'd you like her new do?"

"Her hair? Looks good."

"That was my treat. I like 'em both, but what a handful. Both of them."

"You're telling me? I was in jail with them."

Maggie shook her head solemnly. "Now we need to get her into a job of some kind. She's one intelligent lady, a real computer genius. If we can polish off some of the rough edges, she'll definitely have something to offer."

"She seemed toned down to me. Hey . . . you're not looking for a little help around the office, are you? Didn't you mention that here recently?"

"Gin?"

When Maggie Mason puts the eye on you, you know you've been eyed. Only the ring of the telephone saved me.

"Hello?" Her eyes widened at the response on the other end.

"Robert," she said and then mouthed the word "Maitland" to me. "I'm not being formal, Robert, I just don't know what we have to talk about."

I sat up straight up in my chair. Maggie frowned as she listened.

"I'm answering my own phone because my secretary is out sick. Which, as I'm sure you've experienced, leaves me with my hands full. If you want to talk, you're going to have to let me put you on the speakerphone or call in a couple of days and make an appointment."

She smirked and then reached over and punched a button on the telephone base.

"Now, just what's on your mind, Robert?"

"Let's dispense with the Robert bullshit. If you're still pissed off about the scene your pal caused at the courthouse—" The sound of his voice filled the office.

"Excuse me? The scene *she* caused?"

"She's a flake. Why the hell you ever suggested her—"

"Don't fuck with me, Robert. You knew every damn thing there was to know about Phoebe before you suckered me in."

"You're acting paranoid, Margaret."

I did everything I could to keep from laughing. To call Margaret Mason anything but Maggie was asking for a verbal vasectomy without benefit of anesthetic. Her control surprised me.

"Why are you calling?"

"I've been in contact with Rosella Dahl. She wants to meet with Ms. Siegel. Apparently Ms. Siegel has been harassing Mrs. Dahl by leaving messages on her answering machine. It's become enough of a problem that she's considering filing a complaint."

I put my hands on the arms of the chair and lifted myself up. Maggie placed her index finger on her lips, picked up a pen, and started writing on a piece of paper.

"Are you willing to set up a meeting?" he continued.

I picked up the piece of paper and read it:

HAVE YOU BEEN HARASSING MRS. DAHL?

I shook my head no and held up one finger. She held up one finger and I shook my head yes.

"I'd have to talk with her first. What's the point here?"

"Mrs. Dahl does not want the pain of her daughter's death played out in public."

"Maybe she should be talking with you. It would seem you've brought more attention to Ellen Maitland than anyone."

He said nothing.

"Are you there?"

"She was my wife, for Christ's sake."

"Wouldn't it be sufficient to simply inform my client—"

"Your client?"

"Yes. My client. She's been publicly humiliated, slandered, I don't want to even think about the pain and suffering—"

"Knock it off, Maggie. Mrs. Dahl just wants to talk to her. In the presence of an attorney, of course."

"And you're that attorney."

"It makes sense."

"I'll get back to you."

"I'd like to set up a time."

"Don't push. I'll get back to you."

I grabbed a pencil from Maggie's desk and started writing on a piece of paper lying in front of her.

SET UP A TIME!

She shoved the paper away. I shoved it back.

"I'll be in touch." She waved me back. "I've got to run, Robert. I'll get hold of her."

She reached out and punched the button, cutting him off midsentence.

"Maggie, what the hell are you doing?"

"What, play into the son of a bitch's hand?"

"If it gets me to Rosella Dahl, I'll play."

"Like hell you will. He used me to get to you. Fuck him. He'll play by our rules. I've asked around about the reclusive Rosella Dahl. Real Iron Maiden. There isn't one person close to her that will give you anything but what a wonderful, charitable woman she is.

They sound like they all had the same microchips implanted. I find that curious. Don't you?"

"Damn it, Maggie, what if she changes her mind?"

"She won't. He wouldn't have called unless something was coming down. Have you found something? Anything that would have them running scared?"

"I don't know. There's a couple of names, and I'm working on a hunch that might turn out to be something, but until it's solid I can't see—"

"Watch your back, Phoebe. I've had some rotten feelings about this lately."

"Speaking of *watch*." I looked at mine. "Call him back. I've got an appointment at noon."

"Now?"

"Now. Set it this morning. Tell him we can be there in thirty minutes."

"I say we should let them dangle, but . . ."

I picked the phone up and handed it to her. I walked out of her office and into the reception area, poured myself a cup of coffee. When I walked back in, she was just hanging up the phone.

"Thirty minutes. I told him it would take you that long to get into town."

"What would I do without you?"

"You're on retainer, use me."

"I'm glad you said that, Maggie. I do need a favor."

"Am I up to it?"

"Make sure there are flowers for Frank Chillman's service."

"That's easy enough."

"This might not be. You don't know a few people that aren't doing anything around that time, do you?"

"Professional mourners? You're kidding."

"No, I'm not. Call the rescue mission, hire a few guys, and tell them they have to look like they belong at a funeral."

"Even if I could round them up, who says they're going to own suits?"

"They probably get enough suits down there to dress the Montana Bar Association. I want this to be nice, Maggie. It will mean something to his sister and her kids. Besides, I've got this note on my wall at home, it says 'It's never too late to be what you might have been.' Lurking somewhere in you is a Good Samaritan. Let her out."

"Well, I guess I could come back at you with 'Birds of a feather fly.' It makes just about as much sense, Phoebe."

"I'm dead serious about this, Maggie. Maybe I need to think more than three people will mourn Frank Chillman."

"And a sin eater? Should I round one of those up?"

"No. Let's keep it to the suits."

"And would you be wantin' a reception, ma'am?"

"Don't pull any Dublin Gulch on me, Maggie. And yeah, a little soiree afterward might be all right."

"I didn't crawl my way through law school to plan fake funerals."

"It would only be fake if Frank Chillman weren't dead. Do you want to ride with me, or are you taking your own car?"

"Ride in that truck? I don't think so. I'll meet you there. In twenty minutes. Bring your pepper spray. You might need it. And Phoebe?"

"Yeah?"

"Give a little thought to that job proposition."

"What?"

She followed me out of the office and toward the elevator.

"Jewel. You keep talking about how important the computer's becoming for you. Look what you'd be getting."

"Jewel?"

"Gin prefers her real name now. So what do you think?"

"Trouble. That's what I'd get, I think. I've had enough of that lately to take care of the next ten years."

I pushed the down button, waited for the door to open, and then stepped into the elevator. Maggie wasn't through. I leaned to the left as the door closed.

"We're not through talking about this, Phoebe," she said as she leaned to the right. "We're not through."

I stepped out onto the street. Downtown Billings was coming to life and trying, as it did six days a week, to pump some blood into its struggling economy. I walked to the corner of Twenty-seventh

Street and Second Avenue North, waited for the light to change, and crossed the street to where the truck was parked.

I pulled away from the curb just in time to hit the red light. I looked into the faces of the people who crossed in front of me and wondered if any of them would recognize the name Frank Chillman. Did any of them remember Ellen Maitland, or give a shit that Dougie the Snitch was dead or dying? But by some unexplainable quirk of fate they were linked and possessed an energy strong enough to pull the matriarchal Rosella Dahl out of her Gothic seclusion and summon me before her and her son-in-law. I was ready for them both.

21

Maggie and I had been sitting in Bob Maitland's mahogany-paneled office for a good ten minutes, waiting for Rosella Dahl to arrive. Maitland sat behind a desk large enough to seat a holiday dinner. The top was immaculate: none of the usual accoutrements of a person who *really* worked. Organization has always irked me. I don't trust impeccably put-together lives; no one should. It's a sure sign of a repressed personality, a nitpicky mind, and a detachment from all those flaws that make us feeling human beings.

He sat tapping his finger on the glass top as Maggie put the eye on him. Beyond the icy greetings when we were first ushered in, no one spoke. Periodically Maitland took the handkerchief from his suit jacket pocket and buffed the spot on the glass he was tapping his finger on. His hands were sweating. But then again, so were mine.

Some people walk into a room and take the space in a chair. When Maitland's office door opened and Rosella Dahl entered the room, her tall, slim presence filled the entire office and charged the very air around us. Maitland was up and out of his chair as if he'd been hot-wired. This was a woman of power.

"Rosella. Come in. Please."

He was at her side in seconds, helping her off with her fur coat. When he went to hang it on a freestanding rack, she grabbed it from him and folded it neatly over the back of the chair nearest her. Maitland blushed.

"Uh, Rosella, this is Ms. Mason and Ms. Siegel."

"I took who they are for granted, Robert, seeing how I asked for this meeting."

Maggie stood and reached out to shake Rosella's hand. Rosella turned from her without even an acknowledgment that she was in the room. Maitland, in the meantime, pulled a wing chair into position beside his desk. The dynamics of the seating was obvious: it was them and us. Not easily cowed, Maggie walked over to Maitland's desk and sat on the front edge.

"I sense some hostility here, Robert, and uh . . . I'm puzzled. What's this really about? All of us are aware that Ms. Siegel has not been harassing Mrs. Dahl." Maggie looked toward Rosella, who remained expressionless. "Isn't that correct, Mrs. Dahl?"

"Maggie—" Maitland attempted to interrupt.

"I'd like to talk with Ms. Siegel alone, Robert. Would you kindly escort *Maggie* into the waiting area while we—"

"Now wait a minute here. She doesn't talk to anyone without me present. You've made an accusation that you'd both better be prepared to stand behind or retract." Maggie stood and folded her arms across her chest.

"Well, Ms. Siegel, do you require the presence of your counsel to speak with me? I had hoped we could merely chat for a while. Perhaps enlighten each other."

"I don't see a problem with that." I looked at Maggie and Maitland and had to smile when I saw their mouths hanging open.

"That wouldn't be wise, Phoebe. You've been accused of—"

"It'll be fine. Wait for me. Okay?"

Maggie turned, gathered up her briefcase, and walked out into the waiting area. Maitland gave Rosella a pleading look. She glanced at him briefly and waved him away. He walked out the door and closed it, more gently than I would have expected, behind him. And there we were. One of us was the spider, and one of us was the fly. I just hadn't figured out which of us was which.

During the exodus Rosella had walked around Maitland's desk, steadying herself on the edge, and sat down in the chair behind it. We were sizing each other up, defining our territory. What we didn't have was a bush to lift our legs on.

"You're not what I expected." She opened her purse, took out a package of cigarettes, pulled one out, and lit up.

"I hear that a lot. I guess I could say the same thing about you."

And she wasn't. I watched as she stood and walked to the windowed wall that overlooked downtown. She was nearly six feet tall, with close-cropped brown hair that flashed hints of gray under the sunlight coming through the window. The dignity with which she carried herself, the diamond-studded pin in the shape of a leaf that rested on her dress, and the obviously expensive shirtwaist dress that accentuated her willow-thin figure did nothing to distract from the coarseness of her features. It wasn't that she was homely, but there was a rawness about her that even her enormous wealth couldn't conceal.

"Why are you pulling my daughter up out of her grave only to relive the ugliness of her death?" she said as she turned and faced me. "I don't understand it. Explain it to me, please."

"Bob Maitland approached me—"

"Robert approached you to find the man that murdered Ellen. The man that uncannily disappeared from the face of the earth. Nothing more. He informed me of what he was going to do."

"Your son-in-law—"

"Robert ceased to be my son-in-law the day Ellen was murdered, Ms. Siegel."

"But remained a part of all this." I looked around the opulent room.

"He's an integral part of the Dahl law firm, and has been for many years. But all of this has nothing to do with the fact that what you are doing is wrong. I was informed by Robert that you now consider yourself as representing Frank Chillman. May I ask why?"

"I'm not at liberty to share that with you."

"Are you afraid of breaching the confidentiality of a dead man?"

"Well—"

"Mr. Chillman was well known to me. It was this office he was caught breaking into. In his delusion, which obviously came from his depraved circumstances, he conjured up the idea that his sister's death and my daughter's death were somehow intertwined. All you need do is look back on the records, and there are many, of his troubled life. He was unstable and deserved—"

"—to have his brains blown out?" I was getting tired of the glaring affect of her voice.

She didn't reply verbally, but when she focused those steel gray eyes on me I was glad I couldn't hear the meaning behind the glare. "You're not afraid of me, are you, Ms. Siegel?"

"Should I be?"

"Perhaps. We had this dog when Ellen was young. Ellen was the apple of her father's eye, you realize, and when she asked for a dog, she got one. It was a mutt, a mongrel, and not much use. More important, it wasn't aware of its own limitations and insisted on chasing cars. Of course, that necessitated tying the dog up to protect it from its own foolishness. Do you need to be tied up, Ms. Siegel?"

"Are you threatening me, Mrs. Dahl?" I sure as hell wasn't going to end up the fly.

"Certainly not. There are, of course, people out there that could entangle your life, tie you up, theoretically speaking of course."

"I think that's already been tried."

"Are you referring to Robert's stupid display at the courthouse? That was an unfortunate incident for both of you. I was rather harsh with him on that matter. I believe he felt betrayed by your lack of faith in his intentions." She smiled at me, walked to a nearby book-case, took a small cloisonné bowl from one of the shelves, and put her cigarette out in it. "Sit down, Phoebe. It is Phoebe, isn't it?"

"Let's cut to the chase. You didn't ask to see me to share dog stories, so let's get to the point. That is, if there is one."

Rosella carried the bowl with her to the desk, set it down on the glass top, and situated herself in the chair. She winced as she settled down into it, closed her eyes for a moment, and seemed to brace herself.

"Are you all right?"

She looked at me with penetrating eyes and smiled. "I thought perhaps you would like to know more about my daughter."

"That's why I called you and left that *one* message on your machine. If either you or your . . . Mr. Maitland are committed to finding who killed her, I would think you'd want some dialogue on this."

"We know who killed her."

"Joey Marino? You're convinced of that?"

"You're not? I would think that the fact that he disappeared would be enough for you."

"There are many reasons people run, Mrs. Dahl."

"From the law? Any intelligent person would assume he was guilty."

"Maybe he was running from something or someone other than the law."

She just looked at me. "Do you have any theories regarding that?"

"What did you want to tell me about Ellen, Mrs. Dahl? I have another appointment in"—I looked at my watch—"forty minutes."

"I'd appreciate an answer. Do you have anything conclusive on that?"

"Mrs. Dahl, I'm a private investigator. Emphasis on *private*. I'm not bound by anything, legally or morally, to share any information with you at all. Now, if you want to talk about Ellen, I'll listen. It would help me tremendously. But like I said, I've got an appointment."

She pulled another cigarette out of the package and lit it. The pale blue smoke she exhaled curled out in front of her. She was thinking, studying me.

"My daughter was indulged throughout her life, and looking back, I suppose that could have contributed to her lack of success at being a woman and a wife. And although she was indulged, she was drawn like a moth to the flame to things far beneath her."

"Such as?"

"Infatuations, schoolgirl crushes, that kind of thing."

"Did she have a circle of friends that she ran around with?"

"Periodically. Always the wrong type. They never lasted long. Ellen was introverted, shy. She preferred books to just about anything else." She smiled and looked toward the window. "When Willard died, Ellen, both of us, were devastated. He had been the center of our lives. Our strength. Ellen sank deeper inside herself as time passed. It was bad enough that I sent her east to school, hoping that a new environment would help that curious melancholy she was trapped in."

"And did that help?"

"Ellen returned home in an even darker state than when she left. It was then that I considered having her committed to a private sanitarium. But as chance would have it, something wonderful happened in her life."

The thought of what she was about to say unnerved me.

"Robert came into the law firm and filled something in her that was nothing short of miraculous. They were married a short, although respectable, time later."

"But you said she was not very successful in her marriage? What did you mean by that?"

"As I told you, she was an indulged child. Spoiled rotten. The only real knowledge she had of men was through her father. Marriage brings its own challenges. Robert spent most of his time building a place for himself within the law firm. I do believe that it proved fatal. For you see, Phoebe, as shy as my daughter was, she was also . . . how can I say this? She was provocative. Even as a child she could become provocative to the point that at times it was embarrassing."

This wasn't the Ellen Maitland I envisioned. "What are you saying? That she was involved with someone because her husband was spending too much time at the office?"

That was a stretch, and she knew it from the look on my face.

"How else would you explain how my daughter ended up in a motel room on the south side? I believe she was lured there by a lover and dressed for the occasion."

"And that lover was Joey Marino."

"Yes."

"He was working construction, Mrs. Dahl, reroofing that motel."

"How convenient."

The door opened. Maitland walked in, followed by Maggie.

"Who the hell has been smoking in here?" He fanned the air with his hands. "My God."

He looked at me with vengeance. I shrugged and looked at Rosella. His shoulders slumped, and the look left his face.

"If I had known you were going to smoke in here, Rosella, I would have had someone go out and find you an ashtray."

"Oh, I did quite well without one."

"Without one?"

"Yes. I found this on the shelf. Hope you don't mind that I used it, Robert."

A visible tic pulled one side of his mouth up. "Of course not."

I stood and looked at Maggie. "I have an appointment I've got to be at. Ready?"

"I've *been* ready."

Rosella Dahl stood, too. "We'll talk again. I'm sure our goals are the same, Phoebe. Aren't you?"

"Why don't you give me a call?" I said as I pulled one of my business cards from my pocket and handed it to her. "That way there won't be any more misunderstandings."

She read it carefully. " 'Investigations with an attitude.' I like that."

Just as Maggie and I walked through the door, I turned. "What happened to the dog?"

"The dog?" Maggie asked and looked from one of us to the other.

"It was killed," Rosella Dahl said. "It came untied somehow and exceeded its limitations."

I pulled the door closed.

22

"*T*hat is one tough woman. Hell, I bet she uses a kick-start vibrator. What do you think?"

"Jesus, Maggie." I looked at her as she walked beside me toward the parking lot behind the Dahl building.

"You never should have agreed that I leave the room. You know that, don't you?"

"Like I had a choice. How did you keep Maitland occupied?"

"If I had had any ideas, they wouldn't have worked. He had his ear plastered on the speakerphone."

I stopped walking and turned toward her. "What?"

"Bob must have pushed the button on his speaker after she kicked us out. You've got to hand it to the little bastard. But did you see how Bob—"

"You're back to 'Bob'?" I started walking.

"It was a slip of the tongue. Now listen," she said and placed her hand on my shoulder. "Did you or did you not see how he was with her?"

"I saw how they were with each other."

"Oh come on, Phoebe. It put groveling at a new low."

"Don't be so sure of that, Maggie. By the way, where the hell was the receptionist through all this listening in?"

"Bob sent her over to the courthouse to 'pick up some papers.' "

"Before or after he tapped into the conversation?"

"Before. Here's my car. Do you have time to grab some lunch?"

"I do have an appointment, Maggie, or I would."

"You mean that wasn't some made-up—"

"No. I'm going to talk to Joey Marino's mother at noon, which gives me five minutes to get over there. And I've got to run someone else down after that."

"Phoebe, remember when I told you to watch your back?"

"The first or the fifth time?"

Maggie unlocked the door to her Suburban and climbed in.

"Why do you drive something you need a ladder to reach the seats of?" I asked.

"I love a challenge. Why do you drive something older than you are?"

"Good point."

"Call me later?"

"I'll try, but no promises. Please, Maggie, don't forget the flowers, and find some—"

"Mourners. How could I forget? It's a first in my illustrious career. It's why I became an attorney. It's—"

"Enough. What are friends for?" I pushed the door closed and waited for her to roll down the window.

"I think we need to renegotiate your retainer, Phoebe. Speaking of forget, don't *you* forget you're up against it, my friend. He plays hardball. I tried to tell you that. Think she'll call you?"

"She'll call. And no doubt Maitland will be in touch, and if he does, really feel him out. Make up to him."

"I can't believe you said that. No way." She started the car. "Not a chance. Fool me once? You know the rest. Hell, Phoebe. Do you think I'm a glutton for punishment or something? Friendship can only go so far."

"Just think about it, okay?"

"No. N-O. No way." She rolled the window up and backed out of the parking space.

She'd do it.

I pulled up next to a pay phone, leaned out, and dialed my home number. Kyle picked up at the other end.

"Hello?"

"It's a little after noon, time to get up."

"Shit. I feel like I just got to sleep. This couch sucks."

"You could have gone upstairs, you know."

"By myself? You've got to be kidding."

"Have I gotten any calls, Kyle?"

"Oh, yeah. Several," he said through a yawn. "They just don't talk back."

"Hang-ups?"

"Hang-ups. Wait a minute . . . some doctor called from the hospital about lunch. He said you have his number. Who is he?"

"He—uh, he was the doctor that was on when they brought Dougie in last night. Did he say anything about him?"

"No, but I called the office between a couple of your hang-ups. He didn't make it."

"Damn." I felt a knot form in my stomach. It wasn't as though Dougie and I were tight or anything, but the irony of having contact with him hours before someone else *really* had contact with him. . .

"They picked up some kids, two guys and a fifteen-year-old girl. They're pretty sure they were the ones that kicked the shit out of him."

"How sure?"

"The girl is talking her head off."

That made my paranoia about a Maitland involvement an endangered species. No matter. I had a few more.

"Are you going to be around when I get back?"

"I've got to go on shift at four. Will you be back before then?"

"I doubt it. Kyle?"

"Yeah?"

"Never mind. We'll talk later. I've got to go."

I hung up the phone, pulled onto Broadwater Avenue, and headed for Mrs. Marino's.

"I just wanted to thank you, Kyle. For holding me. Kissing me. I needed closeness from you right at that moment, only I didn't know it. I don't know how to ask for that," I said to no one, listening to my own words.

That feeling of vulnerability I hate covered me like an iron shroud as I cranked up the radio and caught the tail end of some song I didn't recognize. Dougie was dead, I'd gone one-on-one with the formidable Rosella; tomorrow, with fresh flowers and fake mourners, the earth would open up and swallow Frank Chillman into eternity, and I wasn't one fucking step closer to any answers.

I pulled up in front of Josephine Marino's house, turned off the truck, and sat there for a minute, wondering what the hell I was going to say. My money so far was on Maitland, and for some reason Rosella Dahl had wrapped him in a security blanket that, after seeing how they interacted, was probably damn suffocating at times.

The curtains on the front window parted, and I saw a woman looking out. They closed. I got out of the truck and walked up to the front door. Before I could push the doorbell, the door opened and I was face-to-face with an unsmiling Mrs. Marino.

"Miss Siegel?"

"Sorry I'm late. I got hung up on a previous appointment. Am I too late?"

"No. This will be fine. I kept some soup hot on the stove. You'll have some?"

"Sure." I really didn't think I had a choice. "That would be great. Feels like the temperature is going to drop again."

"So the weather report says. Below zero."

"I hadn't heard that, but you can sure feel it in the air."

"Are you from Billings, Miss Siegel?" I followed her from the front door into the brightest yellow kitchen I had seen. "Let me take your coat. You go ahead and sit."

I handed her my coat, pulled a chair out from the chrome dinette set, and sat down. "Yes, I am. And you? Are you originally from here?"

"Not in the beginning. I was born in New Jersey. My parents were from Italy, but I've been here since I was a little girl. It's home."

Her back was toward me as she ladled soup from the pot on the stove. There was a minute of uncomfortable silence as she stopped filling the bowls, placed both of her hands on the sides of the stove, and bowed her head.

"Are you all right, Mrs. Marino?"

She turned, walked to the table, and placed a steaming bowl of soup in front of me. She was an uncommonly beautiful woman who I guessed to be in her late sixties. Her chiseled features and dark complexion were framed by more white-streaked mahogany hair than I had ever seen on one head. She had tied it loosely at her neck, not bothering to tend the strands that hung in waves around her face.

"I'm fine," she said as she walked to a drawer, got out some silverware, and placed it beside the bowl. "It struck me, you know, that you were here, and that you were going to destroy what life my family has left, and I was feeding you."

"Mrs. Marino—"

She waved her hand in the air as she sat down across from me at the table. "No. Before we talk, I must ask you something."

"What do you need to know?"

She reached out and placed one of her hands over one of mine. She leaned close and looked directly into my eyes.

"Did you call here yesterday, pretending to be my son?"

"I—"

"After the call, and after I talked to Nick Spano, there wasn't much sleep for me last night. Nick said to me, 'Josephine, you can trust this woman. I give you my word.' So I pray a lot and it makes me feel better, but no sleep. So I say to myself, 'Josephine, you have known Nick your whole life. He would not lie to you, and if he says this woman will give me the truth, then she will.' Did you call my house?"

It was the softest verbal beating I'd ever had. I knew I had a dumb look on my face, and when she reached out with her other hand and placed it on my shoulder I wanted to throw myself on the floor at her knees and beg for forgiveness. For all I knew she was the Lady of Fatima incarnate, or at the least Saint Bernadette, and I was in deep spiritual shit. And I thought Irish mothers were good. I shook my head in disbelief.

"You didn't call?" she asked as tears teetered on the lower lids of her eyes. "It wasn't you, then?"

"No . . . I mean . . ."

"It was you?"

I said "Fuck," under my breath.

She leaned closer, raised her eyebrows, and looked at me quizzically. "What?"

I pulled my hand from under hers, sat up straight—which forced her to take her hand off my shoulder—and placed both of my hands palm down on the table.

"Mrs. Marino, I did call your house yesterday. It was me."

She crossed her arms across her chest and looked toward the ceiling and then back at me. "Thank you. Thank you for the truth."

"The reason I did that, Mrs. Marino, is because I don't believe your son is dead. Now it's your turn to be honest. Am I right?"

"Why is it important that you know that?"

"Because I also don't believe he killed Ellen Maitland."

She covered her face with her hands and sobbed. I reached out and tried to pat her on the shoulder. She reached up and grasped my wrist with so much strength the blood to my fingers was cut off.

"Mrs. Marino, could you please let go of my wrist? I can't move my fingers."

"I'm sorry. I'm so sorry," she said. "It's just such a relief to hear someone say that. Joey didn't kill her. He's a good boy."

"Then he isn't dead, is he?"

She stood and walked to the counter, picked up a towel, wiped her eyes, and turned to face me.

"Why is it important for you to know?"

"If Joey didn't, and I'm positive he did not, then whoever did is still out there. I have an idea, really a couple of ideas, about who could have killed Ellen. But I need to know why Joey ran."

"What do you know about my son, Miss Siegel?"

"Nothing. And I wish you'd call me Phoebe. I'd be more comfortable with that."

"My boy was a good boy. He had a steady girl, a good girl, and he always worked hard. He was young and he had some troubles with the police, but nothing like what happened."

"What kind of trouble with the police?"

"He bought that truck with his own money." She looked reflective as her mind trailed back. "His father had to sign for him to get it, but Joey made the payments. Gave me his check every week so that I could take it to the bank and put a little in savings, a little in cash, and the truck payment. He even wanted to pay rent, insisted on it. So I went along and took the money out of his check, but I added it to his savings account." She walked back over to the table and sat down. "You're not eating your soup. Do you want me to heat it up for you?"

"No, this is fine." I wanted her to keep talking, so I picked up the spoon and started eating. "This is delicious." And it was.

"Here, dip some bread. It's better that way." She pushed a sliced loaf on a breadboard toward me.

"What is this?" I asked as I continued to wolf down the soup.

"Pasta e fagiole. Joey's favorite. I thought it might be good luck if I made it today."

"It was definitely good luck for me. I appreciate it. You said Joey had a girl."

"Sherry." She smiled and nodded her head back and forth. "She'd show up on Saturdays when Joey would have to work and help me with bread. She said Joey was always talking about what a good cook I was and that she had to learn. He was just kidding her, of course, but she wanted to learn. They'd been steadies all through high school."

"Were they planning on getting married?"

"I think so. Joey didn't talk about it, but his brothers gave him a bad time about it. Just good fun, ruffling him at the dinner table."

"What happened the day Ellen Maitland was murdered?"

"Lord." She sighed and leaned back in her chair. "It was a nightmare. Joey, he came home from work and took a shower like he always did. We had all sat down for dinner, no one had even finished dishing up their plates, when the cops showed up. It was a crazy thing.

"At first they just wanted to talk to him. So my husband and I went with Joey into the living room and sat down. They said they knew he had left the job for two hours because Joey's boss had told them. He was a carpenter, you know, and, uh, they were putting a new roof on that place."

"Why was Joey away from the job?"

"I didn't know then, and I don't know now."

"Joey never told the cops?"

"Nope. He refused to. He said it was his personal business. I tried, and so did his dad, but he wouldn't talk about it. Then they wanted to look at the truck, and that's when they found the blood."

"Did he ever try to explain that?"

"Joey had a dog, some stray he found when it was a pup, they were pals, the two of them. That dog went everywhere with him. Rode in the back of the truck. When Joey left the job that day, he didn't take Bumper with him. That was the dog's name: Bumper. He asked a friend to keep an eye on him. When Joey got back to the job, old Bumper jumped up into the bed of the truck and went to sleep. Joey figured the dog must have walked through the motel room where all the blood was and then tracked it into the bed of the truck."

"And the blood turned out to be Ellen Maitland's."

"Yes. And then they arrested Joey."

"Didn't he get an attorney?"

"Oh, we tried. But no one wanted to go up against that Dahl name. We called lawyers all night. Even got some up out of bed. No one would help us."

"Then how did Joey get out of jail?"

She shook her head. "We got a call from a bail bondsman that said he had been instructed to write a surety note for Joey and he'd be bringing him home."

"That must have been one major bond. Murder? I'm surprised anyone set bond on that."

She shrugged. "Like he said, the bondsman brought him home. It was ten or so in the morning that he came home after being in jail all night. He was scared. Real scared." Her eyes teared again. "Something was different. We could see that."

"What do you mean different?" I finished the bowl of soup and pushed it away from me.

"Do you want more?" she asked and started to stand.

"No. I'm so full I'm going to have to logroll out of here as it is. That was delicious."

"Good. I've got some canning jars, and I will send the rest home with you." This time she made it to her feet, put my bowl in the sink. "I'll be right back."

She disappeared out a back door onto a closed-in porch. I could see her through the kitchen window as she pulled four quart jars down from a shelf and came back into the kitchen.

"You really don't have to do this. I mean, I live by myself—"

"I'll leave some headroom in the jars so that you can stick them in the freezer. It tastes even better with some age on it."

"This is really very nice of you. Thanks. Mrs. Marino, do you have any idea at all who would post that much money for your son?"

"No. But Joey knew."

"What do you mean?"

"He knew. A mother knows certain things, and my Joey? He knew."

"What happened that Joey left, and when did he leave?"

"We stayed up late that night. Joey, he wasn't saying much at all, just paced back and forth. Back and forth. I got up early the next morning and went to church to pray to the Blessed Mother. She'd never failed me. I was probably gone for two hours, maybe less. Father Shea was going to come to the house to speak to Joey later that day. But when I got home, Joey wasn't up, so I went to his room and he was gone. His bed hadn't been slept in."

"Then he just disappeared."

"Like that. We never stood a chance up against that kind of money. That kind of power. And I think Joey knew it."

"Mrs. Marino, is Joey alive? Do you know where he is?"

"I don't know if I should—"

"Look, with his help and with yours, maybe Joey would be able to come home."

"I never said he was alive." She capped all the jars and started wrapping them in towels. "You have to bring my towels back."

"I will. I know you never said he was alive, but just in case he is, wouldn't you like him to come home? Clear all this up?"

"Clear it up? Have you seen Mr. Maitland on the television? He wants my son back, all right."

"I have this friend. She's an attorney—"

"We don't, uh . . . I don't have that kind of money."

"That won't be a problem."

"But Mr. Maitland—"

"We can deal with that. Will you think about it? Do what you have to do today. If Joey is alive, and I'm saying if, I would like to speak with him. Give him my number." I handed her a business card. "Ask him to call me."

She double-sacked the quarts of soup and handed me the bag. "It's going to get very cold tonight. Keep a quart out and have it for supper."

"I'll do that."

"Here's your coat. I'll help."

I shifted the bag from arm to arm as she assisted me in putting it on. I liked her. "Thanks again. And I hope you call me tonight. Any time. I'll be waiting. And don't let the powers that be intimidate you, Mrs. Marino. They all have their Achilles' heel."

I opened the door and stepped out onto the porch. "Call me?"

"You know, my grandmother used to quote an old Italian proverb to me when she would come to visit. She said, 'Once the game is over, the pawn and the king go back in the same box.' "

"I think your grandmother was a very intelligent woman."

She was still standing on the porch as I pulled away from the curb.

23

There's a wind that gives birth to itself in the mountain peaks of Yellowstone Park. It strokes the snowpack like a sensitive lover, melting it in spring into the streams that eventually become the headwaters of the Yellowstone River. The wind then courses through Paradise Valley, gaining strength until it reaches Livingston, where it takes an abrupt right-hand turn toward Billings. On most windy days the local cowboys, drugstore and otherwise, pull their Stetsons down a little tighter, and anyone in a dress can do a respectable Marilyn Monroe imitation on any corner. No one complains.

But when it turns vicious, the wind can flip an eighteen-wheeler on its side and suck half a tank of gas in fifty miles if you're driving west into it. In summer it's a nuisance more than anything. But in the winter, the wind sculpts the snow into impassable drifts on I-90 and hides the road's black ice under an ever-moving veil of white. It can bring traffic to a halt and create windchill temperatures that have become legendary.

It also has voice: a mournful, haunting sound that the Irish know as a harbinger of death, or at the very least bad news. And since half of me was siphoned from the Irish gene pool, I have a love/hate thing with the wind. When it blows the pollution that sometimes hangs over Billings toward the Dakotas, I'm grateful. But most times it just ferociously blows, and sometimes it lives up to my Irish expectations.

I was crossing the Yellowstone River on my way to Blain's Mobile Home Court when the jock on the radio announced with great bravado that there were high-wind warnings out for the upper and lower Yellowstone Valley. I cringed and hoped like hell it wasn't an omen of the days to follow.

Initially I had wanted to track down the bondsman who Josephine Marino said had gotten her son out of jail. Only his answering machine was available. Joanne Mullins, however, was there in the flesh and agreed to meet with me midafternoon. Blain's covers a few acres south of the Yellowstone River on the road to the city landfill. It isn't exactly a high-rent district, or anyone's idea of country living, but it serves a purpose, supplying affordable housing in a marginally livable environment.

I dodged the potholes that had become craters and tried to find Joanne's trailer according to her directions. Finally I gave up and pulled up to the office, got out, and walked in. A friendly but harried woman at the desk looked up from her work.

"If you're selling something, you can take your ass back on out. There is no solicitation of any kind allowed out here. But if you're here to pay your rent," she said as she held out her hand, "I might consider tearing up your eviction notice. Who are you?"

"None of the above. Sorry."

"Hell, don't apologize, one of the above will be in sooner or later today. What can I do for you?"

"I'm trying to find Joanne Mullins's trailer."

"Why?"

"I've got an appointment with her."

"For what?"

"It's personal. If you've got a phone I can use, I'll call her and get directions again."

She looked at me skeptically before she handed me the receiver. I dug in my pocket and found the piece of paper I had written the phone number on and read it to her. Joanne picked up on the second ring. She was two streets and a right-hand turn away and would be standing on her porch.

I walked out of the office and felt the wind against my face. The clouds, swollen with weather, were low in the sky. It smelled like snow. I got into the truck and followed Joanne's new directions until I saw a woman standing on a porch, waving me down. As I pulled into the drive she walked over to the side of the truck.

"Sorry you got lost. This place is a maze."

"No problem," I said as I turned off the ignition and got out. "I'm Phoebe Siegel. Thanks for seeing me."

"Come on in. I've got a pot of coffee on. Do you believe this weather? It started off real nice this morning, and now I think we're in for it."

"I think you're right."

I followed her onto the porch and through the door into a cozy living room. It wasn't bad until something as big as Cujo rose up from the floor and growled. I stiffened and waited for the inevitable. The German shepherd jumped up on me and put a paw on each of my shoulders. We were standing eye to eye.

"Down, Sugar. Get down." Joanne reached over and grabbed the collar around the dog's neck. "This is a friend."

I moved nothing but my eyes and watched the dog as it reclaimed its spot on the rug.

"She's really a love, but very protective. A woman like me, living all alone, needs something these days."

"Jesus. You call her Sugar?"

"She really is sweet. I'm sorry that happened. I forget she's around sometimes. She gets owly when that damn wind blows like this."

"Don't we all."

"Not me. I like the wind. Makes me want to hunker down on the couch in front of the television with a good book. How do you take your coffee?"

"Black. Thanks."

"Sit down and I'll get you a cup. Do you smoke?"

"No. But I might start."

"I do. But I don't have to have one. If you don't smoke it probably bothers ya. Ya know, Ellen smoked. We used to practice down in her basement. I know a lot of people that have quit, but not me. I guess I'm just not ready."

"You grew up with Ellen?" I asked as she set the coffee down in front of me.

"I guess we were five years old or so. You know that castle she grew up in?"

"The Dahl's House?"

"Yeah. Mansion, whatever. It's big, huh?"

"That it is."

"Well, when we were little we used to peek at each other through the hedge. I lived down the block a ways with my mother. We had an apartment on the top floor. You probably know the place. That big white house that sits just up from Central High School?"

"There are a lot of big white houses just up from the school."

"It doesn't matter. Anyway, I used to walk back and forth in front of Ellen's house waiting for her to come out. One day she came out with her father and invited me in. I—I never had a better friend in my life. There isn't a day that goes by that I don't miss her."

Joanne Mullins wore a little too much makeup and was a little too thin to look healthy. Hints of brown roots gave away the bottle-blond hair that she wore short. She didn't look her age, but her eyes reflected a life that maybe hadn't been that kind.

"Are you married, Joanne?"

"Once. A long time ago. It didn't work out."

"Kids?"

"Nope. Couldn't swing that. Just wasn't in the cards. I've lived with a couple of guys since my divorce, but ya know how that goes. Besides, you're not here to talk about me, you want to talk about Ellen."

"Were you still involved in her life when she was murdered?"

"God, I'll never forget that day. As for your question—was I in her life? We tried. When she married that Maitland guy, a lot of things changed. He didn't approve of me."

"Why not?"

"Well, that's pretty damned obvious, isn't it?" she said and looked around the living room. "This is as good as it's gotten for me. I own this place, it's no rental. I'm proud of that. Hell, not many women can buy their own place off the tips and wages I make. It's old, but it's mine."

"I like it. You should be proud of yourself."

"Thanks for saying that. But let's get back to Ellen. I know damn well that old man of hers killed her."

"Why do you say that?"

"He was an abusive son of a bitch, that's why. He fucked, oops—" She covered her mouth with her hand. "Excuse my French—"

"It's not like I've never heard the word, Joanne."

"He fucked with her mind all the time. Ellen and me, ya know, we weren't all that popular through school. We were wallflowers. Her father used to keep a bouquet of real wallflowers in a vase in the house all the time. It was supposed to remind us of how pretty we were."

"Sounds like one of the good guys."

"He was. She'd told him one time that we were pretty much the brunt of everyone's jokes. Kids at school would dare guys to ask us out, and then they'd laugh like hell when we'd say yes. They'd look right at us and say, 'It was a joke, you dumb skags.' "

"That's pretty damn cruel."

"And at the dances? God. Ellen and me, we used to call ourselves the Wallpaper Ladies. We would spend the entire night up against the wall. It hurt all right, but we just stuck together. I probably wouldn't have survived if I'd been all alone, or I would have dropped out of school. But Ellen? God. She just was always there for me, and I was always there for her. She wrote poetry, you know. And she was good at it."

"No. I didn't know that. Joanne, why weren't you questioned by the police at the time of her death?"

"I don't think they knew that I existed, and her old man sure as hell wouldn't have said anything. And that dragon lady—"

"Ellen's mother?"

"Yeah. Well, let me tell you, she's the one that should have married Maitland. They could have destroyed each other instead of Ellen. Look, I know damn well he was the one that killed her. It wasn't that kid that disappeared that they tried to hang it on. No way."

"Joanne, is that a hunch, or is it something solid?"

"He told her she was worth more to him dead than alive. He threatened her with shit all the time. And he slapped her around, too."

"You know these things for a fact?"

"I'll tell you what, Ellen never, ever lied to me. Not once. There was about a year or so that I didn't hear from her. It started right after she got married, and I always thought she was really trying to make the best of things. Then all of a sudden she calls. Right out of the blue. I wasn't married yet, but I was living with the guy. You know, the one I'd marry?"

"I'm following you. Why did she contact you after being out of touch so long?"

"There's something you need to know about Ellen."

"And what's that?"

"She was pretty innocent all her life, even if . . ." Joanne paused and seemed to study my face.

"Even if . . ."

"A lot of times things happen, tough things, but you can still be innocent."

"Joanne, even if—what? Maybe I need to make myself clear here. Anything that you say to me is strictly confidential. It doesn't leave this room." I waved my hand in the air, which immediately brought the dog to its feet again with the inevitable growl.

"Sugar, lie down." Joanne snapped at the dog. Obeying, Sugar lay down but kept her ears at attention and focused her eyes on me. "She hates any sudden movement."

"That's good to know."

Joanne stood up and walked to the counter, where a purse was sitting. "If you don't mind, I think I'll have a cigarette." Her hands were visibly shaking.

"Do you understand the confidentiality thing, Joanne?"

"It's fine that you say it, but how do I know you mean it?" She lit the cigarette, turned back toward me, and leaned against the counter.

"I didn't know Ellen at all. I'd venture a guess that you probably knew her better than anyone. Someone murdered her, and I need to know who. There's a man out there who has been on the run since she died, and he's innocent. At least that's what I believe. So do you, Joanne. I need to know about Ellen so that I know where I'm going on this thing."

"Aren't you working for some dead guy?"

"Yes, I am. His name was Frank Chillman. His sister was killed at the same time Ellen was killed, and Frank always believed that the two murders were connected. Someone killed Frank because he believed that. They killed him because he knew something."

"So is someone going to come after me?" She looked startled, and I could have bitten my tongue off.

"That's not what I'm saying. Frank ruffled some feathers along the way. You've remained anonymous. If I thought you were in any danger, Joanne, I'd be the first to tell you."

She took long, rapid drags off her cigarette and stared at me. I could see her mind working through her eyes as she struggled with a decision.

"Come on. Don't you want to see Ellen's killer brought to justice?"

"I told you who I thought did it," she said in a whisper. "Maitland."

"Anything I tell you won't end up all over the papers if you get the dirt on Maitland?"

"I swear. And I'd raise my hand and swear, but Sugar would probably take it off."

She laughed, put her cigarette out, and immediately lit another one. She picked the ashtray up from the counter, brought it to the table, and sat down. "Hope this doesn't bother you."

"It's fine. Now, please . . ."

"Ellen had a baby."

"She what?"

"Ellen had a baby. A little girl."

"I don't understand. I've never heard anything—"

"That's because that old bitch told everyone that Ellen went away to school for a year, but she didn't."

"Wait a minute. I'm getting very confused here. Away to school? This wasn't a child she had with Maitland?"

Joanne rolled her eyes and chuckled. "No way. Maitland? That's another story altogether. This happened at the beginning of our junior year in high school."

"Did she send her to one of those unwed mothers' homes?"

"No. Rosella kept her in that house, away from everyone. And that's where Ellen had her baby."

I let out a long sigh and leaned back in my chair. "This is incredible." I was dumbfounded. Ellen Maitland had a child? I didn't know what to say. Joanne did.

"Not so incredible if you knew how Rosella was."

"Maybe you can tell me."

"Mean. Flat meaner than anyone I've ever known. But you couldn't even count on that all the time."

"Count on that?"

"Yeah. One time she went through Ellen's clothes and gave me a whole bunch of them. God, it was like Christmas. I thought it was a big breakthrough, like she decided to like me or something. Wouldn't you think the same thing?"

"Probably."

"Well, guess what? The very next day she comes up to Ellen and me and acts like I'm not there. She tells Ellen that she should never let me use her comb or hairbrush because I could have head lice."

"She said that in front of you?"

"Uh-huh. I wanted to cry. From then on, if I was wearing a coat, I had to hang it on the back porch. And there was only one chair I could sit in, a wooden chair in the dining room, and I couldn't drink out of their glasses."

"I'm sorry you experienced that, Joanne."

"It was nothing compared to what Ellen went through."

"Back to the baby. If not Maitland, who was the father?"

"Ellen didn't even know Maitland then. There was this kid, not a kid really, he was about three years older than we were, Waxy, that did all the yard work around their place. A handyman sort of thing. Ellen named him that. Waxy. He wore all this stuff on his hair to be hip, and Ellen used to tease him about it. It was just good-natured stuff, but I knew she had a crush on him. And he couldn't take his eyes off her when he was around there working."

"Is that—"

"Yeah. He didn't take advantage of her or nothing. She was more than willing, I guess, but neither of them thought about—well, you know."

"Ellen getting pregnant."

"It's the only time I didn't know what was going on in her life until after the fact. They did it, all right. You have to realize that after Ellen's dad died, there was no one around to love her. No one at all. That's how it happened."

"Did Maitland ever know about this?"

"If he did, Ellen never said anything to me. I kinda doubt it, though. And like I said, it was before Maitland."

"Where is this baby? Did she give it up for adoption?"

"She'd never talk about that. I just assumed she gave up the baby."

"Jesus Christ, Joanne. Are you sure about all of this?"

"As sure as I'm sitting here talking to you. Ellen, she told me the whole thing, but I gotta go back a bit. Then maybe you'll get the picture. When Ellen told me she was pregnant and that Waxy was the father, I really freaked out. And I was pissed off, too, because she hadn't told me she was doing anything to get that way. She said it happened only a couple of times. The day after Ellen told me all of this, I was supposed to go over to her house and pretend like we were going to a show. We had it all set up like I was picking her up for the movies. Then we were going to sneak my mom's car and drive down to Hardin and have Ellen see a doctor. Well, I showed up and Ellen was gone."

"What do you mean she was gone? She'd left without you?"

"I mean really *gone*. They had this housekeeper, and she was the one that answered the door. She said that Ellen had left on the plane that morning to go to St. Mary's Girls' School in Minnesota. They even put a little article in the social section of the newspaper the next week saying she had gone to St. Mary's."

"Did you believe that?"

"At the time? Sure. Why wouldn't I? I sobbed for days and days. My mother even tried to call Ellen's mom and find out how I could write to her, but boy did she get a cold shoulder."

"Then how did you find out she hadn't really left?"

"I didn't find out *where* she was, I didn't know that until Ellen told me. But I did find out where she *wasn't*. I went down to the library and found the number of that school and called. They never heard of her. It was the toughest thing I've ever gone through in my life, other than my divorce and being knocked around by a couple of guys. I felt like half of me had died. Ya know, it was seven months before I saw Ellen again. She just showed up at my house one day. Man, had she changed. There was no life in her anymore. When she told me about all of this, she told me without any emotion at all. I was the one that was crying. She just reached out and patted my hand and said it was all right. There should be a law, ya know, that people like Rosella Dahl couldn't have a kid and raise it no matter how much money they have. Ya know, in England they even have to have a license to breed dogs. That's what we need here."

"It really must have been hard on you guys."

"Have you ever had a friend you grew up with? One that just knew everything about you, and you about her?"

The question made me uncomfortable. "No. You said that Maitland was another story. What did you mean by that?"

"He was a mean man. I guess Ellen was so used to her mother being hard on her that it really wasn't much different for her when Maitland did the same thing."

"Let me rephrase that. When I asked if he was the father of her baby, you rolled your eyes. Why?"

"Ellen had been married four or five months when she called and wanted to meet for coffee. We used to drive out to Rockvale to the restaurant and just talk. But on this particular day she was really upset."

"Over what?"

"That was the first time she told me that he slapped her around, and the son of a bitch would punish her by not having sex with her. I guess he was into some kinky shit, and Ellen didn't want to do it. He kept telling her she wasn't much in bed, and then he'd physically push her out of bed with his feet."

I knew Maitland was a slug, but this took him to new lows. "Why didn't she get out right then? She could have had the marriage annulled or something."

"I asked her the same thing. She told me she wanted it to work. She said that when he was good to her, no one was better."

I took a deep breath. "Why didn't you go to the cops when she was killed?"

"I wanted to. I even went to a phone booth and called the cops once."

"Why the hell did you go to a phone booth?"

"I was married myself by then, and my old man, he wasn't real keen about me getting involved. He said if they wanted to talk to me, they'd call me. He was real uncomfortable about the whole thing. Said that it could only bring trouble down on us if I made any accusations about Maitland."

"And the cops never contacted you."

"No. How would they know I existed? Then they picked up that Italian kid, and my old man said to leave it alone."

"I'm surprised you let it go."

"My old man talked a lot with his hands. It makes a person listen real close."

"I'm sorry, I shouldn't have said that."

"Look, I've been carrying this around with me a long time. Maybe you can make things right, huh?"

"I'm trying. Uh, before I forget, what was Waxy's last name, Joanne?"

"Oh boy, Slade, something like that." She tapped her temple with her index finger. "Maybe it was Simmons or Sammons or . . . no, I know what it was. It was Waxy Slater. I don't know what his real given name was, but he's got a business here in town. He runs a bonding place. I always wanted to drop in and see him, but I never got around to it."

With everything else she had told me, there were few surprises left. What I didn't need was another player. "Shit."

"What's wrong?"

"Nothing. I'm just trying to keep track of things here." I caught myself with my elbows on the table, rubbing my own temples. "Let's go back to something. You said Ellen had the baby at home—"

"In the basement."

"The basement?"

"That's right. She had a hard time. She wasn't even seventeen yet, you know, and she was built real small. I guess they didn't want anyone off the street hearing her scream, so they took her downstairs."

"Who are *they*?" I asked.

"Rosella and some doctor and probably that housekeeper. Ellen went into labor a month early."

"I gave you my word, Joanne. I will never divulge anything you've told me. But know, for a fact, that I am going to get my hands on those medical records. What was the name of the doctor who delivered the baby?"

"She didn't tell me. At least, I don't think she did. It might have been the family doctor. But . . . ."

"But what?"

"It wouldn't make any difference if I knew his name."

"It would make it a helluva lot easier for me to dig up those records."

"I don't know why Ellen's baby has anything to do with Ellen's death. It was years earlier."

How do you tell someone that you'd use something as tragic, as sick as that, for leverage? As cold as it would come off, it was fact. You do what you've got to do. "Trust me on this one, Joanne."

"It was just a feeling. I wondered if they, you know, did something to the baby."

"What are you saying? And besides, there would still have to be records."

Joanne's face blanched white. "Rosella had, still has I guess, a lot of connections in this town. If there are no records, then that's because she wanted it that way. They could have sold it, killed it, anything."

I sat there, shocked. I cleared my throat. "Say that again."

Tears filled her eyes. She looked at me expectantly. I was so stunned I didn't know what to say to her. "Who are *they*?" I asked.

"I don't know if that's what happened for sure, but I do know that Ellen flat refused to talk about that baby."

I couldn't speak, but I didn't have to say anything. Joanne filled the silence. "She told me about being pregnant that first day she came to the house. She said she screamed and tried to make them take her to a hospital, but they wouldn't have any of that. I guess the doctor was a real son of a bitch. Wanted her to suffer, learn a lesson, that kind of shit."

"Who else knew about this? Did you tell anyone?"

"I talked to my mom about it once. She always liked Ellen. And when I told her, she was pretty upset."

"Would it be possible to talk to your mother?"

"My mother died ten years ago."

"Did Ellen ever bring it up again, Joanne?"

"No. And I didn't either."

Joanne looked toward the picture window of her trailer. "What'd I tell ya, look at that snow come down."

I turned. Sleet mixed with snow pelted the window. I watched as the mess slid down the glass and melted at the bottom. For the first time since I'd sat down I was aware of the wind and its plaintive voice.

We both stared outside. She said, "You just never know what that damn wind is going to blow in."

I knew.

24

The snow was coming down hard enough to put my windshield wipers to the test as I pulled onto South Billings Boulevard and turned left. The wipers etched a fan of visibility on the windshield that didn't solve the problem of the condensation on the inside of the glass as the '49 tried to generate enough heat to defrost. Billings was barely visible. I pulled into the parking lot of the Blue Basket, a quick-shop gas-o-mat, and parked by the pay phone mounted on the outside wall.

Pushing against the wind, I opened the door and got out. Life is not convenient: the phone book was gutted, and I didn't have any change. By the time I talked the guy behind the counter into breaking a twenty-dollar bill for me and borrowed his phone book to look up Slater's address, the truck had choked and shut down the engine. Only the headlights gave any hint that it was still alive. I opened the door, turned off the ignition and headlights, and tried to dial Slater's office. I was anticipating the answering machine and about ready to disconnect when he picked up.

"Slater here."

"Mr. Slater? Phoebe Siegel."

"Siegel?"

"Yes. I'd like to come down to your office and talk with you, if that's convenient."

"Siegel, huh?"

"That's what I said. Would this be a good—"

"The investigator?"

"Yes. Would this—"

"If you're calling about work, I do my own. Haven't had a jumper in over a year. Not bad odds."

"This isn't about work. It's about—"

"I was ready to close up shop for the day. The weather's turning bad, and like I said, I don't need—"

"I'm outside at a pay phone, Mr. Slater, and I can tell you first-hand that the weather is a real bitch right now. My nose hairs are freezing as we speak, and I probably have about two minutes before I won't be able to peel my hand off this receiver."

There was silence.

"Are you there?" I asked.

"What's this about?"

"I need to talk to you about Ellen Dahl. If not now, when?"

Again the silence before he finally answered. "Do you know where my office is?"

"I can find it. I'll be there in twenty minutes. Tha—"

The line went dead.

There's nothing like a warm reception on a cold day. It does wonders for the attitude.

Slater had a reputation. A good one. He was a loner who kept a low profile in town. As I pulled up in front of Clean-Eeze, a one-hour dry cleaners that catered to the downtown businesspeople, I looked up at the second-floor windows. The snowfall was getting heavier, but not so heavy that I couldn't see a large man looking down at me from one of the windows. It was Slater.

I'd run into him a few times at Sammy V's, a local pawnshop that specialized in collectibles. Chances were he wouldn't remember me, but I recalled some things that Sammy had told me once about Slater: He collected belt buckles with a passion, and he had a high-five-figure client who jumped bail a few years back. According to Sammy, Slater had taken over the business from his father and at one time had a corner on the bail-bonding business in Billings. Nothing can raze a bondsman quicker than a high-figure jumper.

I needed some middle ground with this guy. It's invasive to pry into people's lives, but necessary. I was going to jerk him back in time to memories he'd probably healed from and forgotten. I'd done work for practically all of the bondsmen in the state, but never Slater. Most of them were affable guys who could talk your leg off and loved to share their war stories with you. But not this guy. One of the edges that female PIs have is that they're female: easy to talk to and nonthreatening. A femme fatale I wasn't, but I could hold my own in any bullshit session. All I could do was hope Slater was into bullshit.

I pulled open a glass door with both the cleaner's name and Slater Bonding stenciled on it. An arrow directed me up a long, narrow flight of stairs. The muffled sound of hissing presses and the pungent odor of dry-cleaning fluids filled the stairwell. I was halfway up the stairs when the door at the top opened.

He was a hurt-your-hand-when-you-met-him kind of guy who almost filled the doorway. The closer I got to the top of the stairs, the more convinced I became that he wasn't going to move. It made me uneasy. I stopped three steps below him.

"Slater? Got a minute?"

"Yeah. Come on in," he said as he finally stepped aside.

I squeezed past him and walked into the office. There were no partitions, just a large open room that took up the entire second story. It was furnished in vintage Old West: buckskin-colored Naugahyde with phony wagon wheels cut in half to form the arms of the two couches and three or four chairs. There were four sets of oak stacking bookcases that I would have given my teeth for, jammed with books and magazines. Slater walked to one of the chairs and sat down.

"There's coffee over on that table if you're so inclined. It's from this morning, but I flipped the switch on when I saw you pull up out in front. If you don't mind it thick and black, help yourself. It'll be hot in a minute." He put his feet up on the coffee table in front of the couch, clasped his hands behind his head, and stared at me with ice-blue eyes.

There was just a hint left of what he must have been in his youth. As I had squeezed past him in the doorway, my head hadn't come up to his shoulder, so I put him at well over six feet. His hairline had crept farther back, but tight dark curls pressed against the side of his head. He was anybody, nothing extraordinary. Life had etched his forehead with deep grooves: either from frowning or from squinting against the sun. The lines didn't detract, they added to the raw good looks. What threw me was the lack of emotion on his face. I fought shifting in my chair.

"Nice belt buckle." The name Leonard, all in caps, inchwormed along the cab of a Kenworth eighteen-wheeler.

"Ya like this one, huh, Siegel?" he said as he twisted the buckle up toward his face and polished it with the cuff of this shirt. "I just found it last week down at Sammy V's. See what this says? Ten years' safety award. The guy must not have had a road wreck in ten years."

"Then your name isn't Leonard?"

His face twitched as he glared at me. "Hell, no, my name isn't Leonard. You people are all alike."

"Excuse me?"

"None of you appreciates an original American art form. That's what this little babies are. Nothin like 'em anywhere else in the world. I had one once that belonged to a bull rider from Longview, Texas. That one had a real history. This cowboy got his guts ground into that Texas soil, about a year after he won it, by a big white Brahma bull called Ghost Maker. Left a wife and two little ones. She fell on hard times and sold the damn thing down at Sammy's when she was passing through Billings on a Greyhound. Bet he didn't give her more than five or ten bucks for it. Guy's gone, family scattered to God knows where, but that buckle? It lives on."

"How the hell do you know all of this?"

"I don't. But it sure as hell sounds good, doesn't it? Had you going there for a minute, didn't I?" For the first time, he smiled.

"You definitely did," I answered sarcastically. Actually, I'd never look at belt buckles the same way again. "Waxy—" As soon as I said it, I knew I'd made a big mistake.

His forehead tightened, and the smile left. I could have handled that. It was the blaze that darkened his eyes that got my attention. His entire body stiffened as he raised his massive frame up from the couch.

"What the hell are you really here for? What gives you the right to walk in here and call me that?"

"It was a slip. I don't know your name, just Slater, and, uh . . ."

"You're talking bullshit. What's really on your mind?"

He towered above me. All I had to do was look into those eyes, and I could tell the guy was unstable, just barely holding it together. He was big enough to play make-a-wish with my body. There's an old saying that we are the masters of words we've never spoken and the slaves of the ones we have. I had definitely indentured myself. I reached into my mental bag of tricks and pulled out bluff.

"I'm sorry about that. It was a slip of the tongue. That name coming out of the past like that, and out of the mouth of a stranger, must cause you some real pain, Slater. I feel like a piece of shit, so could we start over? Let me put my cards on the table, okay?"

He seemed to relax a little, or at least in my wishful thinking he seemed to relax a little. But he said nothing. You could almost hear him thinking.

"I'm going to help myself to a cup of that coffee now," I said as I stood and walked toward the coffeepot.

That put my back to him: a kind of lopsided ploy that was supposed to say, "I trust you, and I know you won't hurt me." I heard him move and thought it was in my direction. The footsteps retreated. When I turned around, he was sitting on the couch. With the Styrofoam cup in my hand, I walked back to the chair I had been sitting in and sat down. Then things got scarier: The dark liquid in my cup wasn't moving. I tried to sip it.

"Good." I nodded and smiled at Slater. "Strong, but good."

"Let's get those cards out on the table." He continued to glare.

"Okay. Here they are. I was contacted a short while back by Bob Maitland." That got another reaction. Slater's eyes narrowed, but he said nothing. "He wanted me to find a man who was the main suspect in Ellen Maitland's murder." I waited for some confirmation that he knew what the hell I was talking about. I didn't get one. "Maitland and I had a parting of the ways. You probably saw that on the news."

"I don't watch television."

"Okay. It got a little nasty between us, and as it turned out, I couldn't work with him or for him. Then I got a call from this guy who was just recently paroled from Deer Lodge, Frank Chillman, and he said he had information that would tie the Maitland murder to his sister's murder. Her name was Rita Chillman. Frank ended up dead, and shortly after that someone took a shot at me. Being a rational woman, I sat up and took notice. There's something someone doesn't want me to find out. I've got it on reliable information that you knew Ellen, worked around her place when she was a kid. Is that true?"

He watched me a long time before he answered. I tried to choke down the diesel fuel he called coffee and watched him back.

"I did some stuff for her old lady."

"Did you get to know Ellen?"

"She was around sometimes when I was there. Sometimes she wasn't."

"So you didn't know her personally?"

"What the hell are you saying? That I did?"

"No. I'm just trying to find advocates for Ellen who could shed some light on this situation for me. From what I've heard, she was a good woman who came to a bad end, and that bad end came far too early in her life."

Something softened in his face. "Who told you that I knew her?"

"You know I can't tell you that, Slater. Can you help me out?"

He stood and walked toward the windows. "I can deal with it any other time, except when it snows. Then, all I can think about is how cold she must be. How lonely. I go down to the cemetery and try to get snow off her, but it keeps falling. She hated the snow. Said it covered up things so people couldn't see what was really there."

"Then you did know her?"

"Yeah, I knew her all right. She was, uh . . . well, she was perfect." His voice cracked.

"If you can just tell me a few things, put some things in perspective for me, maybe everyone can find some closure on this. There's a guy out there somewhere that would probably like to come home and resume his life."

"That Marino kid?"

"He's not a kid anymore."

"He didn't kill her," he said as he turned around and sat down behind his desk.

"Do you know that for a fact?"

"I just know it."

"Then maybe it's time for you to put *your* cards on the table. Do you know who killed Ellen?"

"She had all that luxury around her and didn't give a damn about any of it. That was the kind of person she was. When she died, it was like someone took a picture of her and stopped all that shit in its tracks. It couldn't hurt her anymore."

"What couldn't hurt her anymore, Slater?"

"Life."

"You were in love with her, weren't you?"

"In love?" He sneered. "Hell, I worshiped her. She wrote me this poem one time: 'We're a volume, a book for two. So much alike, we can't tell who is who.' "

"That's beautiful. Slater, do you know who killed her?"

He looked up at me. The sad and the reflective was gone; the dark had returned to his eyes. "Life killed her. It took her out of the pain and put her in a better place. If I were you, Siegel, I'd let the dead alone. No telling what could happen if you try to raise them up, pull them away from the peace."

"I can't do that. I—"

"Let her rest. Leave her to the peace she never knew. That's what's right." His brows were pulled down over his eyes. The imposing, scary Slater was back. His voice was low, barely above a whisper. "Now, get outta here. And don't come back, Siegel. You don't want to come back here. I got nothing to lose."

There are times when you just know how to react. I stood and placed the cup on the coffee table and walked to the door. I didn't bother to say good-bye; I doubt that he would have heard me. I pulled the door closed behind me and walked down the stairs, the odor from the cleaner's hanging in the stairwell.

I used my coat sleeve to brush the snow from the windshield. Before I got into the truck, I looked back up toward the windows. He was there. Watching. I got in, turned on the ignition, and reached for the choke.

25

When I pulled into the driveway, snow was sitting three inches high on the wires leading to my house. The wind had whipped the snow into cascading tiers of small drifts. If nothing else, the truck was one helluva drift buster. Stud was sitting in the window of my office, his breath appearing and disappearing on the glass as he watched me plug in the truck and walk up the stairs to the front door. I tapped on the window to acknowledge his presence, unlocked the door, and walked in. Stud bounded around the corner to greet me. I needed something warm and living in my life right then.

"Hey, Studley, ready to take your business outside?" I asked as I bent down and picked him up.

I carried his growling body to the back door and let him out. He disappeared into the meringue of whitecaps that covered the backyard.

I'd blown it with Slater with one slip. His mood swings, if that's what they were, were spooky. Then again, Ellen could have been the love of his life, that one person that steals a part of you that can never belong to anyone else. The brutality of her death must have created pain inside of him that, no matter how powerful or big he was, crippled him somehow. "Or . . ." I said out loud as I walked into my office.

Ellen's picture was still propped up on the computer monitor. I sat down and picked it up.

"Or . . . it was Slater who killed you, rescued the perfect you from an imperfect world. Come on, Ellen. Whose eyes did you look into during those last seconds before your death?"

When the phone rang, it scared the shit out of me. So much for channeling the beyond.

"Hello?"

"It's me."

"Kyle. Where are you?"

"Coming up on Burger King. Do you feel like eating something? I've got an hour to kill."

"I hate your choice of words."

"I've got an hour off. Is that better?"

"Much."

"I could pick up some chicken or whatever and bring it out, or we could meet somewhere."

"That sounds . . . wait a minute. How does a hot bowl of Italian soup sound?"

"You don't want to go out in this shit, do you?"

"I just got in. Seriously, doesn't that sound good? You can stop and pick up a loaf of fresh-baked bread from Buttrey's. That will be your contribution."

"Where, uh . . . are you planning to get the soup?"

"I made it. It's been in the freezer. All I have to do is pop it out and heat it up."

"I don't know, Phoebe. Doesn't chicken sound—"

"Safer?"

"You said it, I didn't."

"Take a risk. I'll start heating, and you just head your car this way."

"Christ. Let's hope I can finish the last half of my shift. I'll be there in thirty." He hung up.

It took less than ten minutes to grab the now-chilled soup out of the truck, empty it into a pan, let the cat back in, and change into something more suitable: I opted for clean sweatpants and an FBI Academy sweatshirt. Did I feel guilty? Only until those Italian seasonings filled my house with wonderful smells and my mouth with saliva. Besides, I'd tell the truth—eventually.

Two bowls and a loaf of bread later, Kyle leaned back in his chair and patted his stomach. "That was the best soup I've ever eaten. I'm impressed."

"I knew you would be."

"Why did you heat it up in a skillet, Phoebe?"

"I didn't have a pot big enough." I was improvising.

"Come on. This"—he tapped his spoon on the side of his empty bowl—"from someone who prefers fried bologna with her eggs rather than bacon?"

"Always the cop. All right. All right. Josephine Marino sent it home with me."

"Well, Josephine Marino is one helluva cook. Wait . . . Marino? Joey Marino's mother?"

"Yeah. I had quite a conversation with her earlier today. In fact, I've had several conversations today that have me drained."

"That good, huh?"

"Maybe. Or that bad. I don't know yet. Kyle?"

"What?"

"What's your take on a local bondsman named Slater?"

"John?"

"That's his name? John?"

"Yeah. He's been around a long time. His old man started the business, and John somehow fell into it when he got out of the service."

"How long ago was that?"

"Hell, I don't know. Why are you asking about Slater?"

"I'm curious. I met him today. He seemed to be a little to the left of the balance beam."

"He's been a little drifty as long as I've been around. There're a lot of stories, but—"

"Like what?"

"God. The only one I can think of offhand is how his mother split on his dad and him, and Slater raised himself. Guess he did odd jobs all over town. Then he enlisted, navy I think. I could be wrong on that."

"But no trouble as far as you know?"

"What kind of trouble are we talking about?"

"I heard he had a jumper that damn near broke him."

"Right. I do remember that. It was right around that time that his dad died. I think the insurance money from that is the only thing that kept him halfway solvent. You've got to give it to him, he hung in there. And I'll tell you something else, he's always gone a little further with some of his clients that he thinks have a chance at turning around. He's one of the good guys, Phoebe."

"Can you check him out for me?"

"Jesus. I told you I was staying away from this one. You're not trying to tie him into the Maitland thing, are you? That would be one helluva stretch."

I took the bowls off the table and carried them to the sink. "Maybe not that much of a stretch," I said under my breath.

"What?"

"Nothing. Have you got time for coffee?"

"I don't think so." He got up and walked toward me.

"Chicken." I leaned into him. "You were brave enough this morning to infect yourself through intimate contact. What, no guts after the sun goes down?"

"How do you feel, by the way?"

"I haven't had time to think about it." I snuggled up against his chest. "You tell me. How do I feel?"

"Good. Real good." He wrapped his arms around me. "I'd even go so far as to say too good. But I've got to go."

"To protect all those citizens that could give a shit if you're out there with your ass on the line."

"Whoa. Where did that come from?" Kyle held me at arm's length and looked down into my face. "Bad day?"

"Day, decade, whatever. I'm running around in circles. Losing my touch."

"I don't think so. You've just got to step back from it. Let me share a little native wisdom with you."

"Go for it."

"There was this Haida Indian woman. You've heard of the Haida?"

"No. I haven't."

"They're a West Coast tribe. Anyway she had this song, a song she sang when they sailed the ocean. The Haida even made it to Japan, you know."

"Is this going to be one of those life-changing fables that you're so good at?"

"Just listen. Anyway, you have to realize that this song got them all the way across the Pacific. Visualize her, Phoebe, probably sitting in the bow of the boat, looking up at all those stars floating in a pitch-black sky—her voice and the boat gliding through the water are the only sounds. She sings her song. It must have been weeks, maybe months, before they saw land."

"Am I missing something here, Kyle?"

"If this case has you stumped, maybe you haven't gone far enough."

"Jesus, Kyle. I've found someone who knew Ellen from the time she was five years old up until she was killed. What's left?"

"The very beginning, I guess."

"Okay, what's the punch line? Did they ever get back?"

"Of course. On the same direct route. Do you want to know how?"

"Probably not, but you'll tell me anyway, so shoot."

"She sang her song backward."

"Oh, that's good. I used to do a pretty mean Banana song—"

"Just think about it, okay? I've got to get out of here. If it happens that I don't have to hold over, how about I come by and give you a back rub?"

I followed him to the front door. "Let me propose this. If it happens that you don't have to hold over, why don't you come over and we'll *start* with a back rub?"

"There's a name for women like you. You know that, don't ya?" He pulled his coat on and opened the front door.

"I believe it starts with a *P*, right?"

"Uh-huh, and it ends in 'hoebe.' I'll only call if I can make it. If not tonight, how about breakfast?"

"Why not."

He leaned down and kissed me on my forehead. "You know what? You heated that soup up just the way I like it. There's hope for you yet."

"I'm not trying to get rid of you, I just wish you'd move one way or the other so I can close the door." The blast of cold air sent sprays of snow swirling across the floor.

"You're right. Later."

I closed the door, watched him through the window, and waited for him to get into his County Blazer. The dome light came on. I could see him talking on the two-way and writing something on his clipboard. His headlights captured the frenzied, swirling snow in the beams of light that widened as he backed out of the driveway. I turned out the porch light as he backed onto the road and headed toward town. A gust of wind erased his tire tracks, leaving no trace he had ever been there.

After locking the door, I started to pull down window shades. One of the drawbacks of an old house are the windows: When the wind blows, their frames and sills turn into mournful reed instruments that become orchestral nightmares. Combined with the howling of the eaves, the sounds bring forth all those things that go bump in the night.

It didn't help when the lights started flickering off and on. I looked out the back door window. The snowfall had disappeared into the moonless night, but I knew it was still coming down. A tired feeling settled over me and soaked through to my bones. At my feet, Stud walked a figure eight between my legs, purring like the kitten he wasn't.

"If the lights go out, that means the hot water tank goes out with it, so I'm going upstairs to soak in a tub of hot water while there still is some," I said as I leaned down and scratched the top of his head. "Wanna come? No? Then you make yourself useful and answer the phone when it rings."

Steam coated the bathroom mirror and glistened on the wainscoting. I pulled my hand through the water as the claw-foot tub filled. It's practically big enough and deep enough to float in. I continued to swish my hand back and forth as my thoughts went to the Haida woman and her song. Maybe Kyle was right. Maybe I had to follow the trail to the end, singing the song, my song, whatever the hell that was. Then I had to sing it in reverse to get back. There was one small problem. I didn't know the words.

I turned the faucets off, got into the tub, and settled down in the water. It was like slipping into silk. I pulled a towel off the rack above my head, folded it, and placed it under my neck. It couldn't get much better.

My thoughts became as fluid as the warmth that surrounded me. The water lapped up under my chin as I moved my arms slightly, allowing them to float freely on the surface. All was right with the world, and all that mattered was the moment.

I was gliding over the ocean. Stars hung like crystals against the ebony night. A song, someone singing, pulled me deep into relaxation. Words, undiscernible, pulsated through my mind. So this was what total relaxation was about. My first Zen bathtub experience: I was becoming one with the water. One with the—cat scream?

I bolted upright, grabbed the sides of the tub, and squinted. A mist hung heavy in the room, casting outlines and shapes in muted shades of gray. I heard nothing. Not a sound.

"Stud. Kitty, kitty." He didn't answer. But then again, he never did. "Here, kitty, kitty. Come on."

I chalked it up to my imagination. Just as I had settled back down into the water, the light flickered. I looked up toward it.

"Beat ya," I chided. "Go out. Stay on. I really don't care."

The room plunged into darkness. There's something primal about the dark. Maybe it's how vulnerable we feel in it. I never liked it as a kid, and I didn't like it now. I waited for the lights to kick back on. They didn't. The wind was howling through the eaves, and the woodwind section of the windows joined in. Gusts battered the sides of the house as I sat in the tub, hands gripping the sides, feeling suddenly very cold.

As my wind-fed orchestra moaned and groaned through the house, I stood up and climbed out of the tub. There was a chill, a definite draft coming from somewhere. I groped in the darkness for a towel. My hand sent something crashing as it grazed the back of the sink. I stepped back and felt a sharp stab in the bottom of my foot. Water dripped off me, making the floor slick. I struggled to keep my balance. Lifting up my foot, I ran my hand over it until I found a sliver of glass in my heel. It pulled out easily enough, but that wasn't what had my attention: The creak of a floorboard just outside the bathroom door pushed the adrenaline through my veins.

An odd thing happens when that fight-or-flight syndrome lets loose. It's a megarush of confidence and terror, and that split second when you're deciding which route you're going to take seems like an eternity. Time slows rapidly and then stops. I was in that split second. My chest tightened. Another squeak. There was no way to tell where the shards of glass were waiting, but the sound of it shattering would have led a deaf person to where I stood nude in the dark.

My hand probed more carefully. I felt the softness of the towel I had placed beside the sink, closed my hand around it, and pulled it toward me. Wrapping it around my dripping body, I tucked one end into the top and moved toward the toilet. I groped around on the floor until my hand found the plunger. It was all I had in the bathroom that could be used as a weapon. The hinge creaked as I put the toilet lid down and stepped up on it. If I couldn't see, then whoever was outside the door couldn't see either. I now had a two-and-a-half-foot stick and had added another two feet to my height. The best I could hope for was to find suction on the perp's face and suck it off. I figured the odds, thought better of it, and worked the rubber suction cup off the end of the plunger.

I pressed my back against the wall and waited. The split second ended as the door to the bathroom splintered under some great force. The wood tore and flew toward the tub in the dark. It didn't take much to figure out that someone had kicked the door in. There was a grunt and movement. A silhouette, black on blacker, moved toward me. I swung the plunger handle like a baseball bat and connected. The force staggered the massive form in front of me. I jumped past the form, leaped for the open doorway, and would've made it if it had not been for the hand that grabbed my ankle.

I turned on my back and started kicking. The sole of my foot battered the softness of someone's face. I drove my foot again and connected. And again. The grasp on my ankle weakened enough for me to pull loose. My feet were under me, and my hands were flat on the floor. I was out of the bathroom and into the hallway. It was either the bedroom or the stairs. I sprinted for the stairs. Something hit me in the back with such force that the air in my lungs burst out of my mouth. My knees buckled and crashed onto the floor, and then I was airborne. Hands reached under my arms, fingers dug into the sides of my breasts, and I flew against the wall, tossed with the ease of a rag doll. There was breathing and panting.

Slater stood over me, silhouetted by the lights from downstairs. He moved toward me and reached out again. I scooted back and made a vain attempt at kicking his legs out from under him. My towel was long gone, lost in the struggle. The floor felt cold against my butt. I didn't know if the water beneath me was sweat or if I had wet myself. He kept coming.

It was decision time. I didn't choose flight. I couldn't. With whatever strength I had left, I rolled to my right and stood. Springing off the wall, I threw myself at him, arms outstretched, and hit him full force in the chest as he stepped toward me. Off balance, Slater tipped backward and at the same time reached out and grabbed my wrist. He was falling toward the stairs, and he was taking me with him.

"You bitch." It came more as a growl than words.

I reached for the rail and held on as he teetered over the top step and then crashed full-length backward, twisted sideways, and dragged me down halfway. He let go of my wrist and continued to roll end over end until he hit the floor at the bottom with such force I could feel the vibration under me as I sprawled on the stairs. His scream was agonizing as he pulled himself on his side toward the open front door.

I crawled up the stairs and bolted for my bedroom. The 10mm was in my closet, hanging off a hook in a holster. I shoved the clip in, released the safety, and started back to the hall, my gun held stiff-armed straight out in front of me. He was on the porch, trying to stand upright, just before he fell again.

The sound of a vehicle starting, screeching from the drive, the flash of headlights, the burning pain on the sides of my breasts, the painful throbbing in my knees and back, the wind whipping snow through the front door, and the numbing cold came together in a sensory assault that threatened to shut my mind down. I don't remember my feet touching the stairs, but I was at the front door, slamming it closed. Locking it. I don't remember entering the living room or wrapping the afghan from the back of the couch around me. I don't remember dialing 911. But I do remember the feel of Stud as he nudged my head with his, and the feeling that his purring was somehow magnified one hundred decibels, and crystalline stars hung against a black sky that pulled me silently across the water, and that song, that mournful song floating somewhere just beyond my reach.

"This is Emergency. Do you need help? Hello? This is nine one one. Do you need assistance?"

26

Yellow, blue, and white shadow-danced through the windows and bounced from wall to wall in the living room. Stud, fascinated, turned his head rapidly from side to side and tried to keep up with the reflection of the light bars on the patrol cars parked in front of my house. The light show was mesmerizing. I sat on the couch, wrapped in the afghan, sipping coffee from a to-go cup.

"What is this?"

"Coffee. It's from my thermos. That's why you don't recognize the taste." Kyle grinned, reached out, and patted my back.

I winced. "God, don't do that. I think it's broken."

"We really should take you up to St. Vincent's and have you checked out, Phoebe. You look rough."

"I'll tell you what, if someone tried to polish the floor with your face, you'd look rough too."

"You're sure it was Slater?"

"Fuck." My mood was rapidly deteriorating. "I tried to tell you the guy was fucking crazy."

"No. You asked me what I knew about him, Phoebe."

"And did you tell me he was a damn homicidal maniac? Did you?"

"How the hell am I supposed to know that until something like this happens?"

Clint Beemer, a detective who had worked the Frank Chillman crime scene, walked into the living room and sat down in a chair across from where I was sitting. "We really should stop meeting like this."

"Is there a problem here? I mean, are you guys, any of you, taking this seriously? He tried to fucking kill me, for God's sake. What? Are you all freebasing Dippity Do on your off time or something? Jesus."

"Dippity Do, huh? What do ya think, Wolf? Maybe we should be looking at that."

"Could be," Kyle replied.

"See? See? That's what I'm talking about. That kind of shit really pisses me off."

"Calm down, Siegel. I'm just trying to lighten things up."

"Well, I'll tell you what. Lighten 'things,' as you call it, by picking the son of a bitch up. Why does that make sense to me?"

I knew my head was bobbing up and down, side to side, as I looked from Kyle to Beemer and back again. But what the hell, a little spastic display of irritation seemed to get the message across.

"One of the guys found where he jimmied the lock on the front door. The fool left the screwdriver he used on the porch. Was he wearing gloves?"

"How the hell do I know?"

"Well, you said you, uh, were caught without . . . you weren't wearing any . . ." Clint hemmed and hawed.

"I was nude. Naked. And I wasn't exactly taking an inventory of what he was wearing. Plus the fact that it was dark until we got out to the hallway."

"Then you could positively ID him?"

"It was Slater. S-L-A-T-E-R. I was in his office this afternoon. I know what he looks like."

"Damn." Clint rubbed the bridge of his nose with his fingers. "I've known that guy for a long time. I gotta tell ya—"

"I thought the same thing," Kyle interrupted. "If Phoebe says it was Slater, then that's who it was."

"You said you thought he was hurt," Clint continued. "Bad?"

"All I know is he crawled to the front porch, fell down the stairs, and somehow managed to get in his vehicle."

"There's a blood trail from the bathroom into the hall and down the stairs. Yours or his?"

"Both. I broke a glass in the bathroom and stepped on it. That was just before I swung the plunger."

"Let me see." Kyle reached down and grabbed my foot as I lifted it off the floor. "Not too bad."

"Plunger?" Clint looked astonished. "You used a plunger?"

"Well, I used the wooden part of the plunger, Clint. What the hell did you think I'd use, or should I have whipped him into submission with a towel?"

"I know you've been through one helluva time, Siegel, and I don't want this to be any rougher on you than it's already been. But . . . I have to ask you if there was any attempt on his part . . ."

I knew what was coming. "No. He did not try to sexually assault me. That wasn't what this was about."

There's a look a cop gets when he's about to walk into your mind through your eyes and ferret out what he needs. Not wanting to reveal anything, I reacted in the obvious way and looked away.

"Come on, Siegel, something's coming down here. I show up in the middle of nowhere and find you with a dead guy whose brains have been scrambled, then someone takes a shot—"

He stopped and looked at Kyle. Kyle stood and walked into the kitchen. My eyes tracked him as he left the room. Anything was better than getting into a stare-down with Clint.

He continued, "I get real irritated with you guys—"

"Guys?"

"Whatever. Like I said, first Chillman, then someone takes a shot at you, and now Slater turns out to be a hands-on kinda guy, busts in your door, and proceeds to—"

"I can't talk about it, Clint."

"That's just what I mean. What the fuck are we supposed to do? You're tying my hands. I need motive, and I know you know what the hell it is."

I stood and pulled the afghan tighter around me. "May I go up and get dressed now?"

"Siegel—"

"You pick up Slater and let him give you a motive. And—I want to be there when you ask him."

I turned away from him and walked toward the stairs I had so gracefully been dragged down. As I started up, I looked down the hall to the kitchen and saw Kyle on the phone. When he saw me, he turned away. Clint stepped up behind me.

"I think I can handle this alone, Beemer."

"All I wanted to ask, Siegel, is if you're going to be averse to giving a statement. I'll have Wolf drive you downtown."

"Are you going to be averse to checking the emergency rooms to see if he shows up at one of them?"

"I know how to do my job."

"You forget, Beemer, I know how to do your job, too."

The world looks different after someone invades your nest, your safe place. With the exception of once finding someone hanging from a cottonwood tree in my yard, I had considered my home inviolate. I had just had a crash course in vulnerability, and I didn't like it.

When the crime rate dropped across the country, Montana's doubled. I still remembered, as a kid, not locking the back door of our house, and my father was a cop. It seemed as if overnight we had Freemen holed up in the Bull Mountains north of Billings threatening shoot-outs, brutal murders cropping up in communities small enough not to have traffic lights, or maybe one at the most.

Drive-by shootings and carjackings were new to our vocabularies, but they were there. The Montana Militia made the national news and even did a stint in front of a congressional hearing on terrorism, and the parents of primary school kids were signing agreements stating that their children wouldn't bring weapons to school.

It was here and it was here to stay, whatever *it* was, and still we maintained a healthy dose of naïveté. Although it happened less and less, strangers stopped to help strangers stranded on the highways and byways. Young girls accepted rides from total strangers, and instead of getting a damn good chewing-out, they ended up in ravines, left for dead by some psycho. Old women accepted strangers into their homes to use the phone, and housewives still left their three-year-olds outside to play, unattended.

The cops knew all too well what was happening across the state. The citizens needed to wise up. I just had. Yeah, the world looked different all right, and for one reflective moment, I was more sad than I was pissed.

"Are you okay?" Kyle asked.

"No."

I looked out the passenger window of his patrol car. The night air shimmered. It was below zero, and no one was out on the streets except a lone, skinny dog that crossed the road in front of us. Kyle had stopped completely to allow it safe passage.

"Are you warm enough?"

"Sure."

"Phoebe, I damn near died when that call came over the radio with a 'respond to' and your address. I was way the hell out by Molt. It felt like it took two hours to get to you, but Beemer, no matter what an asshole you think he is, he was giving me a blow-by-blow all the way."

I couldn't even think about Beemer. "Did you get hold of my mother?"

"What I did was get in touch with Michael."

"Great."

"I didn't want her to have me, in uniform, standing at her front door. So I called Michael."

"It's okay. Don't listen to . . . I just feel beat up."

"You are."

I hated it, but I had to smile.

"He came down to the station and hung around while you were giving your statement. I told him I'd bring you over to your mother's."

"Did he say how she is?"

"Yeah. He did. Hell, she was married to a cop and had a son that was a cop, and God knows, she's got—"

"Me. Right?"

"You said it." He looked at me and smiled. "She's one tough lady, Phoebe. Her main concern was that you were all right. She wanted Michael to make sure that you stayed with her tonight. I'm sure she'll be real thrilled that you brought what's-his-name."

"Stud?" I looked behind me. Stud was sitting upright on the top of the backseat, looking out the back window. "I thought he was dead. Tonight, he goes where I go."

"I'm surprised Slater crawled out after tangling with your cat and you. What a lethal combination."

"Kyle?"

"Hmm?"

"It *was* Slater."

"For what it's worth, I haven't doubted you for one minute. It's just out of left field. Hell, he's been around for a long time. I know for a fact no one's doubting you. It's just that big *why* that's looming out there."

Kyle pulled up in front of my mother's and turned off the ignition. I looked toward the house. A faint glow filled the living room. The porch light was on. The walks were freshly shoveled. I felt Kyle's hand on my shoulder and turned toward him.

"Thanks, Kyle."

"For what?"

"For being born? How the hell do I know if you don't? For being there. Jesus."

He reached out and attempted to push my hair back from my face. "You've got to cool down, Phoebe. We'll pick the guy up."

"Am I being bitchy?"

"Let me put it this way. You've sharpened your teeth on anyone who's been within twenty feet of you tonight. We're not the enemy."

"That bad, huh?"

"That bad."

His hand continued to manipulate my hair back from my face. "Have I ever told you that I love your hair?"

"Want it? I'm already missing a chunk of it, anyway."

"I'm serious. I love your hair."

"You really know how to improve my mood," I said sarcastically. "Do you realize it was made by the same people that brought you Brillo Pads?"

"That's what I like about it. It's tough."

"What? That it could live on its own?"

"No. Because it's like you. It's wild and does its own thing, plays by its own rules. It's honest. Yeah. It's honest hair."

"Is this leading up to something?"

"Not what I wish it was. Come on, I'll walk you inside."

"I can find my way, Kyle. Come on, Stud, let's go see Gramma." I tapped my fingers on the top of the headrest. Stud jumped into the front seat. I picked him up and opened the door. "Ya know, this is Stud's first time in a real patrol car. He probably would have loved the siren and the lights going."

"Next time. Phoebe?"

"Yeah?" I had gotten out and had to lean down to see him.

"Why did Slater come after you?"

"Ask him."

Michael was sitting at the kitchen table. He said nothing when I entered the house. He looked scared. Concerned. Mom surprised me: She was calm. Within minutes, she had ushered me upstairs to my old room. The bed was turned down, the pillows fluffed. I put on one of her flannel nightgowns that she had placed on the bed and crawled in.

"We'll talk tomorrow, honey. I want you to get some rest."

"Mom? The front door was unlocked when I came in. Lock it."

She was quiet for a moment and then leaned down and kissed me. "Has the cat eaten?"

"Continually. He'll be fine." I had no sooner said that than Stud jumped up on the bed.

"Michael's staying over. So don't worry about anything."

"Easy for you to say," I teased. "He's got an in." She scowled. "Tell him thanks."

"Good night, dear." She walked to the door and flipped the light switch off.

When I heard her walking down the stairs, I reached over and turned on the night-light on the base of the lamp next to the bed. I'd had enough darkness for one night.

On the other side of sleep there are usually dreams. If I had any dreams that night, I couldn't remember them. And when someone's hand gently rocked me, whispered my name, and pulled me toward waking, I fought it: No one could find me in my sleep.

"Fee." The voice was gentle as it coaxed me. "Wake up. Come on."

I tried to throw the hand off. A stab of pain radiated to my back from my shoulder.

"Shit." I waited for the pain to subside and then rolled onto my back.

"I brought you a cup of coffee." Michael, sitting on the edge of the bed, smiled at me. "It's on the stand."

"God, is this some kind of penance, waking up to the good father?"

"It's a peace offering."

"For what?" I yawned and made a feeble attempt at stretching.

"For being so damn judgmental the other night. What happened to you was pretty sobering—well, first the shot and now this. I never want to lose you, Fee." He actually had tears in his eyes.

"Don't go soft on me, Michael. Besides, if you didn't have me, you'd have to pick on Kehly, and she couldn't take it. I'm a worthy opponent."

He rolled his eyes. "Make this easy on me."

"Never," I said as I reached for the coffee. "Now I want the truth. Why the room service?"

"Have you ever in your life taken anything at face value?"

"You mean people do that? Jeez." I smiled at him and took a sip of coffee.

"You're hopeless."

"Not hopeless, Michael. I'm your biggest challenge. Where's Mother?"

"Fixing breakfast. Kyle called right before I came up."

"And?"

"They've got that guy that attacked you in custody."

"No shit?" I felt as if someone had broken an ammonia capsule under my nose; I started to throw the covers back and get out of bed.

"No shit," he repeated and laughed. "Slow down. I told him you weren't even up yet. He said he'd be over in an hour."

"What time is it?"

"A little after six."

"Are you sure he said they had him in custody?"

"I asked him twice. They've got him, Phoebe."

"How's Mother?"

"She's been superb. I think we underestimate her."

"Michael, I'm sorry about the other night. Honest I am. It's just that—"

"Later. We'll get back to that when things quiet down."

I looked at him and said nothing.

"What?"

"When things quiet down? Fat chance."

"Why don't you jump in the bathtub and—"

"I'm off baths."

"That's what you said about showers after you saw *Psycho*. Your hygienic options are dwindling."

"There's always the car wash."

Michael stood. It was the first time I noticed he was wearing his collar. He was the best looking of the Siegels; he and Kehly had apparently dipped into a gene pocket that I didn't see.

"Come on down when you're dressed. If you hurry we can break some bread together." He looked at his watch. "I've got a Mass at nine, so get a move on."

"Michael, thanks for the coffee and the conversation."

"Anytime." He left.

By the time I had given my mother a modified blow-by-blow account of what happened, eaten a stack of pancakes, dripping with butter and chokecherry syrup, and consumed enough coffee to get a football team up and running, Michael had left to serve up the body and blood of Christ and Kyle had walked into the kitchen.

"Did she give you any trouble last night?" he asked my mother as she set a cup of coffee down in front of him.

"Not one ounce. How would you like some breakfast, Kyle? You look like you've had a long night."

"I'm fine, thanks. I grabbed something with a couple of the guys on my way over here."

"Coffee's over there, just help yourself if you want more." She turned toward me. "Phoebe, honey, I'm going to go upstairs and make up the beds. Will you be back over later?"

"Maybe, Mom. No promises."

"Yell up at me if you leave before I come back down."

"Will do."

Kyle watched her as she left the room and said nothing until her footsteps echoed through the hallway upstairs.

"What's up?" I asked. "Michael tells me you've got Slater."

"Yeah. We got a call about midnight from a doctor at the ER.

Slater came in, and the doc knew enough to call us. We had both ERs on notice and had his office and house staked out."

"Did he give anybody a problem?"

"None. When the doc finished with him, he was taken into custody. He's down at the station."

"Is he talking?"

"Yeah. He wants to see you."

"You've got to be kidding."

"No. I'm not. Which brings me to the next problem."

"Which is?"

"Where is the material, the stuff I don't know about, that Nick slipped you?"

"At the house. Why?" I leaned back in my chair. "Oh shit, it's in my office. Did anyone—"

"No. I went back out there after I dropped you off here and secured the front door." He reached into his jacket pocket and pulled out my keys. "Here. The last couple of guys were just wrapping it up when I got out there, so I waited until they were gone. It must be that Irish luck of yours."

"Why?"

"You've got all that Maitland shit spread out all over your desk. I went in there to use the phone, and there it was."

"Fuck."

"I don't know if Beemer saw or not. If he did, he didn't say anything to me."

"Was he in there?"

"How the hell do I know? But it's Nick's ass that's on the line here."

"Look, Kyle, most of that stuff is crap I got from Maitland . . ."

He held up his hand to silence me. "Yeah, well, our stuff is stamped, and it was right there, in plain sight. But there's more to it."

I breathed deeply and let the air out in an audible sigh through my pursed lips. "Am I going to like this?"

"A couple of city detectives heard about Slater and brought over Dougie's personal effects from the hospital. Seems he kept matchbook diaries. And on the inside cover of one of them, he wrote down

Slater's name, a time, and a partial telephone number. The date was the day he got jumped."

"Slater was the one that—"

"No. They've got the kids that rolled him. It's just one of those bizarre coincidences that it happened on the same day he supposedly had set up an appointment with Slater."

"You're sure about that?"

"I'm sure. What I want to do is get you back home and grab those files. I just don't know how the hell to get them to Nick."

"I do," I said. I stood and walked to the bottom of the stairs. "Mother!" I yelled. She came to the top of the rail. "Nick Spano is coming by for coffee this morning."

"Here?"

"Here. Are you going to be around?"

"Aren't I always? I haven't seen Nick in—"

"Well, you're going to see him real soon."

"What a nice surprise. Should I fix lunch?"

"Probably not. He'll be here in about an hour."

"That'll be nice, dear. You'll be here when he comes?"

"I'll be back. I won't be able to stay, but I'll duck in."

"Can I leave Stud here, or do you want me to take him home?"

"Well—"

"I pay well."

"Oh, go ahead and leave him. But he had best not use my furniture to sharpen his claws on, or worse. Wait—he won't do *worse,* will he?"

"No, Mother, he only *worses* in the privacy of his own home." I walked back into the kitchen.

"You call Nick, and tell him to be here in one hour, Kyle."

"I'd better do it from here. I don't want to use the radio in the car."

"You know, I don't get it. Why the rush on the Maitland files?" He was dialing the phone when he answered, his back toward me. "Sometime this morning they'll be charging Slater with Ellen Maitland's murder. It's in the works as we speak."

27

Slater's arrest and possible link to Ellen's murder was on every radio station. According to the news reports, Maitland was "overcome with emotion" when informed of the news. He was scheduled to speak to the press at ten A.M. in his office. I wanted to gag.

"You're not saying much," Kyle said. "Why?"

"I'm listening."

He reached over and turned off the radio. The static and intermittent conversation of the two-way filled the cab of the Blazer.

"There. Now, why so quiet?"

All I could do was shake my head.

"Come on. What's going on? Isn't this what you wanted, for Christ's sake?"

"What the fuck does that mean?" I said just as we pulled into my driveway. "What did I want, Kyle? You tell me. Just what the hell did I want?"

"Jesus. This takes 'wrong side of the bed' in a new direction." He got out and slammed the door.

Did I have a choice? No. I got out and slammed mine hard enough that the window slipped the rail and disappeared. Kyle walked around to my side, opened the door up, and tried to roll up the window. It just wasn't going to happen. He leaned up against the Blazer and just looked at me.

"Happy?"

"As a matter of fact, I feel much better. Thank you." I walked over and leaned against him. My breath was white on the air.

"Ready to talk?"

"Let's go inside. I'm half sick at my stomach over those files. Shit." I pulled back and started walking up the porch stairs.

"I nailed that door closed, Phoebe. We've got to go in the back. And about those files—"

"It could mean his pension, for God's sake. I don't think I could live with that."

"You won't have to. Is that what all of this is about? Those damn files?"

I opened the back door with my key and walked in. It didn't feel the same. It didn't feel safe. Kyle read my mind.

"He's in jail, Phoebe."

"I'm aware of that," I snapped.

"You're doing it again."

I walked through the kitchen and into my office. "Doing what?"

"Gnawing on my throat. This isn't just about the files, is it?"

I stopped shoving papers into the manila files. Ellen Maitland's picture was lying facedown on the desk. I turned it over and looked at her.

"Something's wrong, Kyle. Really wrong. It doesn't make sense that Slater would come after me unless he was somehow involved. But I've got this nagging voice in my head. Shit."

"What's this nagging voice saying?"

"I can't tell yet. I guess I'm not listening hard enough. There's just too damn much going on right now."

"The only thing going on, Phoebe, is that we need to get those files to Nick. No one else can get into that evidence room. So the worst that can happen is that he gets his butt chewed for not being there when he was supposed to be."

"Why does Slater want to talk to me?"

"I don't have the slightest idea. He refused to say anything beyond what he had up to that point until he talked to you. Got any clues?"

"No."

"You've got a choice. You don't have to do this."

"Yeah, I do. It just blows me away that he's going to be charged with Ellen's—"

"He was at the motel, Phoebe."

"What?" I leaned back in the chair. "How do you know that? There's nothing in any of this to even suggest . . ." I waved my hand over the files. "Where did that—"

"From the horse's mouth. She called him that morning."

"She who?"

Kyle walked to the chair across from the front of my desk and sat down. He stretched his legs out in front of him, removed the duck-billed Sheriff's Department cap from his head, and rubbed the bridge of his nose.

"She, Ellen Maitland."

"Ellen called him? There was no phone record of any calls she made that day from the motel or from her house."

"Probably from a phone booth, or someone's else's house. All I know is that according to Slater, she called him and wanted him to meet her there." He looked up and shook his head. "Hell, it's all there. The whacko attacked you, said he just wanted to scare you into backing off. I think he meant business. If he could take you out, then why the hell don't you think he could—"

"Don't ask," I said and put my hands in the air. "It's that voice. What can I tell ya?"

"The one you can't understand yet?" He stood and put his cap back on. "Grab that stuff and let's get out of here."

"Kyle?"

"What?"

"I'm sorry I was such a bitch, and I feel like shit over that window."

"It's on your side. Don't sweat it."

"I won't. I'm driving the truck back. Stay warm."

All hell had broken loose by the time we returned to my mother's. Reporters from both television stations and the *Gazette* were in the yard. We parked in the alley behind the house, I went in the back door, and Kyle walked around front to deal with the media. Mom had been calm, cool, and collected the night before. Nothing had changed. She was still in control, and God only knows control was her forte.

"Phoebe, honey, this phone has been ringing off the hook. How they knew you stayed here last night is beyond me. Detective Beemer has called four times, and those people out in front—I'm sure the neighbors are getting an eyeful. Why do they want to talk to you, honey?"

"Morbid curiosity, Mom."

"That Detective Beemer? He wants you to come in immediately."

"I know. But I'd like to see Nick first."

Nick was sitting at the kitchen table, and although he acted as if he was having the time of his life, the constant dabbing of the beads of sweat on his forehead with his handkerchief gave him away. He was as uptight as I was. Who the hell could have foreseen what had come down? Before I had a chance to speak, Kyle walked up behind me, took the files from me, and handed them to Nick.

"Would you mind dropping these off for me, Spano? I've got to go down to the shop and get my window put back on the track."

"It would make my day, Kyle. Anything to help." Nick looked at me, smiled, and asked, "Are you all right, Phoebe?"

"I'm fine. And yourself?"

"I've never been better. Your mom here is some cook. I gorged myself on those sweet rolls of hers." He patted his stomach. "Don't think I'll be doing any big meals for the rest of the day."

"Oh, come now, you barely ate two, and I had to bully you into those," my mother said as she wiped her hands on her apron and blushed.

Was this my mother? Twittering? I raised my eyebrows and looked at Kyle.

He looked away to hide the grin on his face.

"I was just going to ask if you'd like to come around Sunday for dinner. I'm sure Kyle could use a home-cooked meal—"

"And just how do you figure that?" I asked playfully.

Kyle raised his hand and said, "I can answer that question."

"Open your mouth and you're dead." I reached out, smacked him in the arm, and winced. Getting assaulted takes some of the fun out of being playful.

"I don't know about you, Nick, but I'm not turning her down."

"Well then, I guess I can't either. I'd like that, Margaret. I'd like that real fine." Nick stood, reached for the jacket hanging on the back of his chair, and pulled it on. "Do you need a ride, Phoebe?"

"I've got the truck. Meet you down there?"

"If you give me a head start." He looked straight into my eyes. Nick's voice had that edge that stressed he meant what he was saying.

"Half hour?" I asked.

The phone rang. "I'm not here, Mom, okay?"

She picked it up, said hello, and then mouthed the words "Clint Beemer." I reached for the phone.

"I'm on my way, Beemer."

"Let's hope so. This guy is close to the edge."

"Why does he want to talk to me?"

"You'll find out when you get here, Siegel. There is one thing I think you should know before you see him."

"And that is?"

"We got a search warrant for his place last night. We found a rifle."

"Gee, that's shocking. Who the hell would have a rifle in their house in this state?"

"Knock it off. I've had a long night, and I don't need more shit than I've already got on my plate."

I wanted to suggest he change his eating habits but resisted. Beemer sounded close to the edge himself.

"Along with the rifle we found a couple of boxes of Nosler custom loads."

"No way. Are you suggesting he's the one that shot at me?"

"I'm not suggesting. According to Slater, he was only trying to scare you. Said you moved the wrong way, or you wouldn't have been grazed. Also said that if he intended on planting one dead square in your head, he wouldn't have missed."

I said nothing.

"Siegel, are you there?"

"I'm here. I'm on my way down." I hung up.

"What was that about?" Nick asked.

"I can't give you that head start, Nick. Sorry."

I walked out the back door and left all three of them looking at one another.

They had already taken Slater to the Yellowstone County Detention Facility down on King Avenue: a small detail that Beemer had left out of the conversation. Locally known as YCDF, it was a relatively new building that when put before the voting public was supposed to take care of a bad jail situation for the long run. Now they couldn't even afford to staff all the space it had available.

Any cowboy worth his boots knew that raising hell in Billings was best done on a Saturday night, late. Chances are the jail would already be full. Not only was it keeping with tradition, but Billings's teens were cop-baiting on Twenty-fourth Street West by cruising and gathering like flies in K mart's parking lot. That gave the cowboys an edge. It was an ongoing problem.

By the time I drove uptown, found a parking space in the court-house lot, and found out that Slater wasn't even there, thirty minutes had elapsed. It was still snowing. The plows were out and had banked two, maybe three feet of weather alongside the roads. It was slow going.

I pulled off King Avenue, hit some ice on my way, slid into the parking lot, and kept sliding into a parking spot in front of the YCDF. Beemer, looking beat, was standing just outside the glass doors, having a cigarette. Most nights there were five cops on shift to split up the city. With a population of 87,000 within the city limits, the LEOs had it stacked against them the minute they hit the streets. The Sheriff's Department has jurisdiction not only in town but in the county as well; that ups the ante another 36,000 citizens. It takes its toll.

I walked over to where he was standing. "Jesus, Beemer—"

"I called back and you'd left. Ask your mother."

The dark crescents beneath his eyes spoke for the kind of night he'd had. I said nothing.

"If you're waiting for some kind of apology—" He threw what was left of his cigarette down to the ground and stepped on it. "Let's go in."

"What'd I say?"

"You, Siegel? You don't have to say a fuckin' thing."

They buzzed us through. I followed him down the hall.

"Where is he?"

Beemer stopped in front of a door and opened it. "Wait in here. I'll have them bring him in. He's got some tight-ass attorney that will be with him when you talk to him."

"I want to talk to him alone, Clint."

"Yeah? Well, I want a raise and ten more deputies. We don't always get what we want. Right? Have a seat." He walked into the room and pulled a chair out from a long gray table that was also anchored to the floor. "This is how it's going to be. You've got him until the doc gets here."

"What happened to him? You guys get a little rough?"

"I told you he was losing it."

"Seriously, what's wrong with him?"

"His light switch is flippin' on and off. They don't know if they can handle him, so they've got some shrink coming down to check him out. This place is packed. No room at the inn, as they say. They'd have one helluva time with Slater if he goes psycho on them. For all I know, you ran his sinuses into his brain when you plunged him." I watched his body shake as he laughed and walked out the door.

When the door closed I was alone. My mind struggled, trying to grapple with the thought of seeing Slater with nothing but a table between us. Five minutes passed like five hours. The door opened. He was shackled, hand and foot, and flanked by three deputies, including Beemer.

The blaze I'd seen in Slater's eyes was gone. The quiet madness remained there, rimmed with crimson. He didn't look as big, as powerful as he had felt to me earlier, but physically he still took up a lot of space. The soft sound of his feet shuffling across the floor scratched at my mind: I could hear the floorboard creak outside the bathroom door, see the darkness he had cast me into.

He didn't look at me as one of the deputies pulled out a chair and helped him sit down. Still, no one spoke. The deputy squatted down and hooked the chain of his leg cuffs to a bolt on the floor. Slater wasn't going anywhere. It didn't make me feel any better, but I was damned if I was going to let him know that.

"You okay, Siegel?" Beemer asked.

"Super. I thought I was supposed to talk with him by myself."

"Yeah, that's the deal we—"

"That wouldn't be wise." A voice erupted from somewhere.

A guy stepped from behind Beemer and straight out of the sixties. He was too young to remember the decade, but he knew the drill: hair pulled back in a ponytail, Lennon glasses, and an attitude. He had a gung-ho look that told me he also had a hard-on for Lady Justice. What he hadn't learned yet was that Lady J. was a tease.

Slater looked up at him. "I want to talk to her by myself, or I don't talk." His voice was subdued but commanding.

"I strongly advise you against that, Mr. Slater. As your legal representative—"

"As my legal representative, you do what I want. If you want to continue as my legal representative you'll get the hell out of this room."

Slater's voice rose steadily with each word and exploded at the end of the sentence. One deputy, standing behind him, moved forward and put his hands on Slater's shoulders.

"Settle down, man," the deputy said softly.

"It's okay, Dave." Slater looked over his shoulder at the officer. "I'm okay."

Slater's livelihood had come from people who found themselves clients of, as Gin and Tonic had called it, Hotel Yellowstone. He had been raised on the profits that his father made off writing bonds for the unwilling residents who had checked in. The buildings may have changed, but it was still a place where the bellhops wore guns and room service might be something you don't want.

I guess you could say he was in an allied field and probably had come to know these guys: joked with them, shared a certain part of their lives. I wondered if the deputies thought they knew Slater, trusted him, ever witnessed the violence I knew he was capable of.

There he was, bolted to the floor, cuffed at the wrist with three LEOs standing within feet of him, a table between us, and it still unnerved me. I could feel his hands on me, the voiceless, murderous intent in them as I fought him down the hall. Both of his eyes were black from my blow to the bridge of his nose. I wanted him marked, branded with a visible sign of what he had done to me. What I really wanted was to crawl over the table and tear his face off. The hell with sympathetic speculations.

"This is probably a bad idea," I said and got to my feet.

Slater stopped glaring at his attorney and looked startled. Beemer started to say something until Slater spoke up.

"No. Please." His voice wavered. "You've got to . . . I've got to make you understand." He looked at Beemer. "The deal was, I get to talk to her alone."

I looked at Beemer. It was one of those wordless conversations when two people become telepathic. It was my call. I shrugged and sat down.

"Behave yourself, Slater." Beemer motioned to the two deputies and the attorney. "We'll wait outside."

"This could jeopardize my client. Again—I am most strongly advising you against this." He looked at Slater.

Beemer, a good foot taller than the attorney, reached out and placed his hands at the back of the lawyer's neck and ushered him out of the room.

"We'll be right outside the door. You got that, Slater?"

He nodded. The door closed, and there we were. I didn't like the feeling. He leaned forward. I reacted immediately by leaning back in my chair.

"They're going to charge me with Ellen's murder." He was speaking barely above a whisper. I strained to hear him.

"What's on your mind, Slater? Want to talk about how you tried to shoot me?"

"That's a lie. I'm a damn good shot, Siegel. I don't miss."

"You didn't."

"All I wanted to do was scare ya enough to back ya off."

"What's your excuse for last night, Slater?"

"It got out of hand. I just wanted to talk to you."

"Talk to me? You broke into my fucking house. . . . Seems there was a slight language barrier."

"I don't like you, Siegel. I don't like what you do. Ya dig shit up about people that needs to be left alone. You hurt people. And what you think is the truth ain't nowhere near the truth."

"Then enlighten me. Just what is the truth? Did you kill Ellen, Slater?"

His eyes widened and filled with tears. His face visibly changed. Fell. I was looking at a tortured, rejected schoolboy. Slater hung his head and started to cry.

"Me? Kill Ellen? I tried to save her, for Christ's sake. I coulda saved her. Why didn't you leave her be? Just let her have some peace. Jesus. All she wanted was . . ."

He was loud enough that Beemer cracked the door and looked in. Slater didn't notice. Clint looked questioningly at me. I shook my head no.

"That fucking Chillman, man, he couldn't leave it alone either. Had to plow old ground. The dumb son of a bitch." Slater brought his hands up and smashed them down on the table.

Again Clint opened the door. This time he walked in.

"You better settle down, Slater, or I'm taking you out of here. You got that?"

He leaned down and got in Slater's face. Slater glared only for the length of time it took him to realize Beemer meant what he said. Again, it was the suddenly compliant schoolboy who sat across from me. Beemer left the room.

"Maybe I can make this easier for you, Slater. I have a hard time buying you killed Ellen."

For the first time, and for just an instant, a look of relief covered his face. "I didn't. I couldn't. But her old man did. As sure as I'm sitting here, he did it."

"You were at the motel. Why?"

"She called me for the first time in a long time the day before the motel thing. I'd heard from her on and off after she married Maitland. But then I didn't hear from her for a while. I knew she wasn't happy. There were problems. Maitland, well . . . he wasn't much of a husband to her. Made her feel real bad about herself. And hell, everybody in town knew he was fucking whoever he could get to his bed."

My mind snapped to Maggie. The guy was a walking disease time bomb.

"I'll tell you what kinda shit this guy is. I ran into him in a bar, about a year after they had gotten married, drunk on his ass. He didn't know me from nothing, but I knew him all right. He was talking all this shit about himself and what a power player he was. Then these two young women come in and he eyes them, ya know? And I say, 'I thought you were married?' He laughs and buys a couple of drinks to send over to their table, and says to me, 'You stand them on their heads and they all look alike.' That's what he was, right there in that statement. He's scum."

"Why did Ellen call *you* after so much time had passed?"

"She could trust me. Who else did she have? She was leavin' him. Said she was going to tell her mother that afternoon, and that Maitland already knew. Damn. She sounded so good, so full of herself. Told me she had looked at some apartments, and even a house or two."

God, it couldn't be this easy: Maitland killed her to keep her from leaving. "You're sure about this?"

"Yeah. I was sure."

"Did you two have something planned, Slater?"

"Neither of us said it, but we knew. That's how it was with us." He faded, lost in some dead memory.

"Slater?"

"It's just hard, ya know? I'm going down for it. It doesn't much matter anymore. What really gets me is Maitland. He played with her like a cat plays with a mouse, and then he killed her."

"Tell them the truth—"

"They have their own truth. I told 'em I was at the motel the day she died. That's all it took. I figured I'd better talk to you before . . ."

"Before what, Slater?"

He changed. He clenched his hands until his knuckles turned white. "You going to listen, or just flap your fucking mouth with a bunch of stupid questions?"

I held up a hand and backed off. Beemer was right. This guy was hanging his toes over the edge and teetering.

"What's the matter, Siegel?" He hissed the words through clenched teeth. "Are you like all those other pricks? You want *your* truth, not the real shit. Right?"

"Wrong." He was bolted to the floor. I wasn't. I stood and looked down at him. "Let's get something straight here. For all I know, this damn act is nothing more than you laying the foundation for copping some insanity defense. Well, I'm not buying it. And I sure as hell don't have to sit across from you and listen to this bullshit. You want to talk about Ellen? Fine. But this flip-flop back-and-forth crap doesn't pack it with me. You tried to kill me last night."

"I just—"

"I don't want to hear it, Slater. You shot at me. Did you take a shot at Frank Chillman?"

He looked shocked at the suggestion. "No."

"This is how it's going to be. Straight conversation, and then I'm out of here. It's your call."

He stared up at me and then toward the door and mumbled something.

"What was that? I couldn't understand—"

"I said we had a kid. Or is that something else you already knew about?"

I sat down and rested my head in my hands. "I knew, Slater."

"From who?"

"I can't tell you that. Do you want to talk about it?"

"I never knew. I swear to God, I never knew until that day at the motel."

"Was that the second time she called you?"

"Yeah. She was supposed to get back to me the night before. We had this . . . this plan, ya know? We were going to get together that night, have coffee."

"But she didn't call."

"No. I sat up and waited until I thought I was going crazy. I even drove past her house, looking up at those lighted windows. Hell. Thought I saw her in one, so I got out and stood by my car waiting for her to look out. But it never happened."

"You said she had already told Maitland. Did she tell you what his response was?"

For the first time Slater actually chuckled. "Oh yeah. He laughed at her. The son of a bitch. But it didn't throw her. She was out of there. There was no way I ever thought she'd leave, but that afternoon on the phone? I knew she would."

"The next day, that's when she called you again?"

"Yeah. Early in the morning. She sounded, I don't know . . . something was wrong. Bad wrong. It was strange."

"Strange how? Upset?"

"No. Quiet and then half laughing and crying at the same time. Then she got real calm and told me to meet her at the Bunk House."

"I tried to ask what the hell she'd be doing down at that place, but she backed me right off. Said if I asked too many questions she wouldn't see me. That wasn't like Ellen. She was gentle. Real gentle."

"She never said where she was even calling from?"

"Not a word. I asked that a lot because I would have gone to get her no matter where she was. She said she had something to take care of, had to talk to someone. I pushed her, kept asking her who she had to talk to, and she lost it, started sobbing. Finally she said she was going to talk to her mother."

"Hadn't she done that the day before?"

"I thought so. I could have had that wrong. She wanted me to park a block or so away from the motel. Said she'd watch for me. She was real definite about the time. Hell, I didn't know what was coming down by that time, so I just did what she said."

"The motel, Slater. What happened down there?"

"Christ, what a dump. There was a lot of construction going on. Guys crawling all over the roof, saws running, people hammering. It was a mess. There was this porch, ya know, that ran in front of the place. When I parked my car and walked over there, I came up on the end of the porch farthest from the office. Hell, I didn't want to go down there and ask for her, and then this door opens, and there she is." Slater looked up at me. "That day? The day she died?"

"Yeah?"

"I walked out of that motel a dead man."

Slater was bouncing from one thought to another. I could hear his teeth grinding together when he paused between sentences. There are times when you know it's better to just sit back and shut up.

I stood again, wanting some distance from him, and walked toward the door.

"Where're you going?"

"Just stretching. Keep talking. I'm listening, Slater."

"You're makin' me nervous."

The door opened as I started back to the table. Beemer walked in with the two detectives and another guy in a suit trailed by the attorney.

"Slater, this is Dr. Christiansen. He'd like to spend a little time with you." Beemer looked at me. "You'll have to step outside. This won't take long."

Slater glowered. "I'm not through yet."

"She'll be back," Beemer told him.

I walked out the door. When it closed behind me, I leaned against the wall and took a deep breath. I couldn't tell if he was tortured or just flat nuts. Either way, at some point he was going to lose it.

28

By the time Beemer and the doctor walked out of the interrogation room, I was almost asleep on my feet. Anything was better than the visions I had in my head of Ellen Maitland. Thanks to Slater, my body hurt, ached everywhere. But my pain would be temporary. Ellen? She had hurt a lifetime; the pain didn't go away until she was murdered. Maybe that's why there were no defense wounds. Had she welcomed death? And if so, what the hell could push someone to that point? What pain was left over stuck to Slater and was intense enough to cripple him. Intense enough to make him want to kill me just for coming in contact with Ellen's memory. He was protecting a dead woman.

Beemer turned his back to me and said something quietly to the doctor. Christiansen removed his glasses and started talking. I couldn't make out what they were saying, but the doctor looked grim. He turned and walked off in the opposite direction.

"Well?" I asked as I approached Beemer.

"The doc says he wants him transferred up to the Deaconess Psychiatric Center. He's making all the arrangements, and I've got to find a judge. He doesn't think it would be a good idea for you to go back in there."

"Jesus, Beemer. I told him I'd be back. You told him the same thing, for Christ's sake. I need fifteen more minutes. Thirty, max. Come on, Beemer."

He crossed his arms. "The guy is ready to really blow. Hell, he didn't make any sense to the doc, so what are you going to get?"

"He's all over the place, Beemer, but I'll piece it together. Twenty minutes?"

"He came after you, and I'm convinced he did Ellen Maitland. And about now I'm figuring we've got him on the Chillman thing also."

"It's not like he's going to jump over the table, Beemer. And I'll tell you something else."

"Do I have a choice?"

"No. You don't. Try this on: I don't think he killed Maitland."

"You're wrong, Siegel. He even told us what she was wearing. That was never released to the press. If it hadn't been that Nick Spano was nowhere to be found, I would have had the damned file. But from what I could dig up, he was dead-on."

"Beemer, you've got to let me back in there. It'll be low-key. I swear."

He looked down at the floor and scratched behind his right ear. I had him.

"All right. Fifteen minutes, and that's it. With a deputy."

"No deputy."

"You're not in a position to bargain this one."

"I need thirty."

"Shit." He stepped to the door and opened it. "Fifteen."

Slater didn't look up until I sat back down in the chair. Then he spoke.

"I figured they wouldn't let you back in here. That doctor thinks I'm crazy. He didn't say that, but I know he was thinking it. Wants me to get some rest at the hospital. Says I seem stressed. That god-damn attorney will love it."

"I'm sure he will."

"Do you think I'm nuts?"

"I think you're hurting. Nuts? I don't know, Slater."

He shook his head up and down and didn't take his eyes off my face.

"Slater, why did you leave the motel without her?"

"That was her idea. That's when it happened."

"What?"

"Ellen, she was wearing this coat, ya know. And she was made up."

"Made up how?"

"Makeup. Lots of it. Not like I'd ever seen her before. I never knew her to wear any. And that room, it was kinda dark and real small, but she kept walking from one end to the other. Back and forth. Back and forth, talking all kinds of shit. I just sat on the edge of the bed and watched her, tried to tell her everything would be okay."

"Why was she there, Slater?"

He ignored me, looked off into the distance, and continued.

"It was the baby, she said. Said that the baby kept haunting her."

"And you still didn't know that the baby she was talking about was yours."

"No. I thought maybe she had gotten pregnant from Maitland and miscarried. Lots of things were going through my mind. Lots of things."

"When did she finally tell you?"

"Over and over again, she kept saying she was trash and that nothing good would ever come into her life and that now she understood why. Then she got down on her knees in front of me and begged me to forgive her. Hell, I didn't know what I was supposed to forgive her for, and I didn't like her begging like that, so I kept trying to get her up. Her coat fell open. That was when I saw what she was wearing under it. Ellen looked like a . . . she . . . she was dressed like a whore. She tried to close her coat real quick, but I pulled it open. It didn't make any sense. No sense at all. That sleazy motel and her dressed that way. I didn't know what to think, what to say to her. I cried. Cried real hard. It was like she was someone else."

My mind tripped to the crime scene photos. "Did she try to explain to you why she was dressed that way?"

"No. She just pulled that coat back around herself and said I needed to know, to understand about the baby. And then she told me. Told me it was our baby."

"And you didn't know before then that she had gotten pregnant."

"No, I never even would have guessed it. I always thought she was too good for me. Being with her, even near her, was like a dream. When she left town—at least that's what I heard—I just thought she finally figured it out."

I glanced toward the door. Beemer was looking in through the glass. I shook my head no and held up five fingers. He looked disgusted, but he moved away from the glass.

"Slater, they're going to pull me out of here any minute."

Tears ran down his cheeks. His whole body relaxed, as if a great weight had been lifted from him.

"She was as cold as stone when she told me how she hadn't ever left, how she had our baby down in the basement, and that the doctor didn't do anything for her pain—"

"Slater—"

"She could of died, ya know? Just her mother and that butcher there to tend her."

"I need to know who that doctor was, Slater. Did she tell you his name?"

"She said he told her she'd remember the pain, that it was the price she had to pay for what she'd done. And all the time she begged *me* to forgive *her*." His hands were clenched again. "Then it changed. She changed. She wanted to go to Helena real bad. Said she wanted more than words and that she had to see for herself."

I thought of Dougie and how he said I'd find her in Helena. "Why Helena?"

"Every night through all those years, I played it over and over in my mind. The pain she must have gone through having that baby. How things could of been different had I known."

"Is that when you left, after she told you?"

"Yeah. But I was coming back. I had promised her I'd take her, but I had to gas the car up and get some money together. I wanted her to come with me right then, but she wouldn't. Said she'd get some rest while I was gone."

"Is it possible she was expecting anyone after you left?"

"No. She would have said."

"So you left her there."

"I did. I drove up on top of the rims and sat there for a while trying to figure things out. Understand what she had told me about our baby and all."

"How long were you gone?"

"Hour, hour and a half at most. Once I left the rims I drove down to town, gassed up, and picked up some money from the house and a few clothes. When I got down close to the Bunk House, there were cops everywhere. I parked a few blocks away and ran toward the motel. There was no way I was going to get close. No way. There were cops everywhere. I stood behind the line, and someone told me a woman had been murdered. I knew it was Ellen right off. Then I saw the cops in and out of that door."

"Why the hell didn't you say anything? Tell the cops you had been there, and that when you left, she was alive?"

"Why did I go up on those damn rims? Why didn't I force her to leave with me? I told you, I coulda saved her. Maybe in a way I killed her. Maybe—"

"Slater, what happened to the baby? Was the baby put up for adoption?"

He raised his head slowly. The fire was back in his eyes. A blaze of madness.

"The baby. They . . ." He seemed to have trouble forming the words. "The baby was born dead. They threw it in the furnace. They threw our baby straight into hell."

He put his hands under the table. A great roar tore from his mouth as he rose. I lunged out of my chair as the table ripped from the bolts that held it to the floor. Pandemonium broke out as he raised his hands above his head; the chain that had bound the cuffs together snapped. The room filled with deputies. I groped my way along the back wall to the door and out into the hall. I was running, stumbling through a maze of people, and stopped only when I hit a door that wouldn't move.

"Let me out of here!" I screamed. "Let me out!"

The grating sound of a buzzer slit the air. I pushed. The door moved. In seconds I was outside. I bent over, my hands on my thighs, panting. The frigid air dried my throat. I could still hear Slater. Someone touched a hand to my back.

"Are you all right? What the hell happened in there?" Beemer stood looking down at me.

"He didn't do it, Beemer. If the district attorney charges him, you'll all look like fools."

"We're going to look like fools if we don't. Now what the hell

set him off? There's six guys in there holding him down. Shit. I knew
I shouldn't have let you go back in there."

"You've got to listen to me—"

"He could have killed you last night, Siegel. Where the hell is all
this sympathy shit coming from?"

"Fuck you, Beemer. Do what you have to do. He did not kill
her."

"Whatever he's got wrong with him, Siegel, you've caught it."

I walked across the lot to the truck, got in, and started it up. With
any luck at all I had enough time to make it home and find something to wear to Frank Chillman's funeral. After my encounter with
Slater, that was the plausible next step in my day.

The moment I opened the door of Cooper's Funeral Home, I was
assaulted with the heaviness in the air: a lily of the valley odor that
I could equate with only one thing, and it wasn't rock gardens. I
caught myself not wanting to inhale, not wanting the scent of death
to slide in on my breath.

It wasn't that hard to find the chapel. All I had to do was follow
the organ music that was trumpeting Frank Chillman home. Maggie
was sitting in the back. I slid into the pew beside her.

"There's only one person in this room that is not supposed to be
breathing. Why the hell are you holding your breath?" she asked.

"I can't stand the smell."

"You'll like it even less when you see the bill."

Wrenching sobs rippled from the front of the chapel. It was hard
to tell which one of the twenty-five or so backs I was looking at had
lost control.

"Who's the weeper?"

"One of ours. Had I known he got this emotional I would have
gone with the out-of-work cabdriver. To think I got a law degree to
do this."

"It was a favor, Maggie. I owe you one."

"You got that right."

"Where's Becky and her kids?"

"In the family room off to the right of the coffin. She has some
friends, teachers I think, with her. The older couple might be her
parents."

"Good. How's she doing?" I strained but couldn't see through the darkened screen.

"I thought you were nuts for doing this, but it isn't a half bad idea. Not only is she a nice lady, she was very touched that so many people showed up for the funeral. Perhaps *amazed* would be a more appropriate word." Maggie patted me on the back.

"Oh my God, I almost forgot." She thumped her forehead with the tips of her fingers. "I heard they have a guy in custody for Bob's wife's murder. Is that true?"

"He—"

"I mean, call me stupid, but I have to tell you that I was one relieved woman. Now, that's not saying I would ever get involved with him on any level again, but I sure as hell feel better that I didn't bed a sociopath. So tell me."

"It's—"

"I heard he was a bail bondsman or something like that."

"Maggie?"

"Yes?" She leaned closer and bent her head toward me.

"If you'd let me get a word in—"

"Sorry. I get real nervous in these places."

"And I don't? Anyway, Slater—"

"That's his name? Slater?"

"Yeah. John Slater. He's got problems, Maggie."

"I'd call murder one a bit of a problem."

"He broke into my house last night and attacked me. If he could have, I think he would have killed me."

Our conversation up to that point had been whispered; now Maggie threw her hands up in the air and bellowed, "Jesus Christ!"

All the heads became faces as they turned and looked at us. Maggie's hands were suspended in midair. Her recovery was nothing short of brilliant: She clasped her hands together in prayer and started to lower them with great drama.

"Thank you, Jesus Christ, for bringing us all together in our sorrow." With that she brought her hands down to her lap and hung her head.

I exchanged the-poor-thing smiles with the spectators. As they all turned back around, the Weeper let loose with another round of sobbing wails. He was *too* good. For the first time in hours I felt like laughing.

"That was . . ." I strained the words through my teeth as I continued to smile. "What was that?"

"Would you mind repeating what you said about Slater? He attacked you? In your house?" Maggie kept her head bowed. "Jesus . . ."

"Do not do that again, Maggie, or I will get up and walk out of here. We'll talk about it later."

"If I'm good enough to handle your, uh . . . what should we call them? Let's keep it simple, your affairs. Then I'm sure as hell good enough—"

"It's a long story. Damn, Maggie, this is the first time I've seen you since yesterday."

"Phones, Phoebe. They've been around a long, long time."

"It was late. I ended up staying at my mom's—"

"Okay. Never mind. My God, were you hurt? Did he . . ." Maggie covered her mouth with her hand. "You weren't . . ."

"I'm stiff and I'm sore. Okay? And no, he didn't, I mean, I wasn't."

"Thank God for that." She leaned back in the pew and stared straight ahead.

"Could we get out of here for a minute?" I whispered.

"And do what?"

"Breathe some fresh air."

Maggie, shifting her weight from one foot to the other, listened intently as I related the highlights of the night before.

"Ya know, Maggie, the house even felt different when I walked into it today. Does that sound crazy?"

"Hell no, it doesn't sound crazy. It's a violation, for God's sake. If we're not safe in our homes, then where? You really need to learn how to carry your car keys defensively."

"I'm not in the habit of taking keys into the bathtub with me, Maggie."

"Never mind. I'm nervous. I don't know if I'm shaking from the cold or from what you're telling me. Are you sure they'll keep this guy locked up?"

"I'm sure."

"And naked? I couldn't take it naked."

"You could take it with your clothes on?" I had to smile.

"Look, I'm being serious. It must have been terrifying."

"I don't think I had time to think of how terrified I was."

"Jesus, even the thought of some enraged idiot's hands all over me gives me the creeps. I couldn't take it, ya know. I probably would have tried to drown myself in the bathtub."

"Gee, what an option. And to think it just never entered my mind."

"I hope they hang the bastard."

"I don't know, Maggie. There's something with him. He told me he died the day he walked out of that motel. It might sound a little crazy, but I'm not so sure he isn't right. They'll hold him at the Deaconess, try to stabilize him, and then this hotshot hippie attorney will ask for a psychological evaluation and get it—"

"Then they'll ship him down to Warm Springs for two months—" Maggie shook her head.

"Same old, same old."

"He's entitled to a defense, Phoebe."

"Shit. A few minutes ago you wanted him hung. I don't have a problem with him having a damn defense. What I have a problem with is this voice that keeps telling me he didn't kill her."

"Then who the hell did?" She raised both her hands in the air. "Never mind. Forget I asked that. Maitland, right?"

"I'm telling you, there's nothing left of this guy. He's just walking pain. And Maitland? All these years, like clockwork, resurrecting this whole thing. What a cocky—"

"You're obsessing, Phoebe, with nothing substantial to go on. The only thing you've shown me is what a prick he is."

"If I could tie him to Rita Chillman, really nail him on that one—"

"We should be going back in, don't you think? By the way, you look really great in that dress, nylons and all. I don't think I've ever . . . uh, seen your legs before."

"They're not mine. And speaking of legs, I've got to get these back to their rightful owner."

"Wait a minute, you're not staying?"

"I can't, Maggie. I need to stop by and see Joey Marino's mother. I'm sure she's heard about Slater's arrest by now. I can't leave her hanging."

"It's always something. I'll hang around long enough to pay everybody off, and then I've got obligations. Maybe not as important as yours—"

"Don't do this."

"Whether you want to hear it or not, I had some real identity issues yesterday while I was rounding up mourners for this gig."

"Here we go."

"There's a point to all of this."

"I'm feeling it, Maggie, and I don't know if I like it."

"I want you to hire Gin . . . uh, Jewel."

"Are you brain-skipping or something, Maggie? I'm up to my neck in shit as we speak, and—"

"My point exactly. You've put some real bucks out on both of them, and God only knows I pulled as many strings as I could. Tonie is more than likely not coming back. Jewel wants to stay, but part of her deferred sentencing included that she be gainfully employed after completing school."

"Maggie, I hear organ music. Could it be the services are starting?"

"I'm not some flunky. I'm your friend and half-assed attorney, and I'm not cut out for this supersleuth shit."

"Who got me involved with Maitland in the first place? Fuck."

"Do you realize we're having our first fight?"

"I don't have time for this, Maggie. Give me the bottom line."

"She needs a job. You need the help."

"Hell. Just until she finds another one. Is that clear?"

"When will you be home?"

"Today? You're talking about today?"

"Give me a time. I've got to get back to the mourners."

"Shit, I don't know. I've got—"

"Four?" She reached for the door and pulled it open.

Warm air flowed out and carried the nauseating sweet scent of death with it. I cringed and started walking toward the truck.

"Whatever," I yelled over my shoulder. "No guarantees I'll be there, dammit."

"You'll be there. Call me. Okay?"

I had a few choice things to call her all right, but I'd save that for another time.

I sat in the truck and let the engine warm up. There was no way it could have gotten more complicated: Frank Chillman was being offered up to God with Mourners "R" Us, Slater was probably doing the Thorazine shuffle at the psychiatric center, Maitland was fondling his ego and basking in the sweet glow of public absolution, and the key to all of it was hidden two hundred and fifty-four miles to the west, in Helena.

I added that up, throwing in the chaos that one reformed hooker could create in the midst of everything, the fact that my celibate priest brother was an oxymoron, and to top it off, that I'd seen my own mother twitter in the presence of Nick Spano. I could have sworn the Ides of March were a month early.

29

When Josephine Marino opened the door, I was looking into the face of a woman ten years younger than when I first met her. Tears streamed down her cheeks.

"It's you. I've called your house all morning. I just didn't know how to find you. He's coming home. He's really coming home. My Joey—praise the saints, he's really coming home." Her arms wrapped around me for a moment, then she stepped aside. "Come in. Come in."

"I guess this is the day you've been waiting for, Mrs. Marino."

"I've already been to Mass, and please, this is not a day to go back to formalities. Please, call me Josephine. I'm so nervous, I can't stop shaking."

She held her hands out in front of me to show me proof I'd already seen.

"I guess I don't have to ask you if you've heard the news."

"Sit down, Phoebe. Of course. I heard the news this morning while I was still in bed. I do that, you know, just lie in bed sometimes and listen to the early news. I was paralyzed. It was . . . it was like I was sleeping, still dreaming."

I sat down at the kitchen table. There was no way I couldn't get caught up in her joy. "Josephine, I'm really happy for you. When is Joey coming home?"

"Tomorrow morning around nine. He and Nona are driving to Cheyenne and getting on the plane there. My daughter, she's coming from Missoula, and my two sons who live here in town just left a little bit ago. We cried together, all of us. We—"

She sat down at the table, covered her face with her hands, and wept. Uncomfortable, I waited.

"I'm just so . . . I don't know, I just can't believe this has happened. I wouldn't believe it. I couldn't, until I saw on television that bail bondsman being charged. The phone"—she raised her hands above her head—"the phone started ringing off the hook. The newspaper people and the television people, my friends, the kids, they kept calling, and as soon as I hung up it would ring again."

"It's a wonderful day for you, for your whole family."

"If only my husband were here. He always believed this day would come. Never lost faith right up to the end of his life. He would have respected Mr. Maitland and what he's . . ."

I damn near fell off my chair. Maitland and respect didn't belong in the same sentence, hell, the same room. The real shock was that it came out of Josephine's mouth.

"What did you say? Your husband would have . . . The man hounded the cops for years trying to find your son. Why the hell would your husband—"

"It takes a big man to admit that he was wrong." She reached out and patted my hand. "When he called—"

"He called you?" I could hear my voice rise.

"He wanted to apologize for the misery my family has been through all this time. He cried. A powerful man like that, and he broke down."

At that point I knew the bastard had now become the hero, the big man.

"Josephine, there's something I need to talk to you about. Maitland—"

"I don't want to hear anything bad about Mr. Maitland, Phoebe. I told him you had been here once and were trying to help us and he told me that you and he had some kind of falling-out—"

"Falling-out. What else did he say?"

"Just how sorry he was, and that he wanted to make all the arrangements for Joey to come home, and that if I had children living at a distance, he would see that they got here also. That's a humble man that stands up and tries to make things right. He also said that he would like to be the first to talk to Joey, to make his apologies directly to him."

"I just bet he would." I mumbled under my breath.

"Pardon me?" Josephine leaned closer.

"I said I think he should. Apologize. Josephine, where has Joey been?"

"I guess it doesn't matter much now, does it?"

"No. I don't think so."

"He's been in Laramie, Wyoming, for the past twenty or so years. Before that, Los Angeles, Denver. That's where he met Nona, in Denver. Joey is married, has been for twenty years. I have three grandchildren. We did manage to get together a couple of times, but Joey was so nervous it made him sick. But the children, or Nona— Nona is Joey's wife—did I already say that?"

"Yes, you did. You were saying?"

"They have never seen the house Joey grew up in. His oldest girl is getting married in the spring . . . now, maybe . . ." She covered her face again with her hands and cried. "It's finally true. He's coming home."

"Josephine, I'm going to ask you a big favor. I want to talk to Joey in Laramie. Talk to him before he comes home. Will you give me his number?"

She looked at me curiously. "But why couldn't that wait until he got here?"

"If you could trust me on this . . . look, it's important to me. To tie up some loose ends. Come on, will you give me his number?"

"Well . . . I guess there wouldn't be any harm done."

She stood and walked to the cabinets, where she rummaged through a drawer and took out a pencil and notepad and wrote something on it.

"I'm afraid he's had more years with this name than his own." She handed me the paper.

"Jeff Carpita," I said as I read the name and number. "Does anyone else have this?"

"No. Not even my other kids. We could never take the chance. What I never told you was that we didn't know if Joey was dead or alive for over five years when he disappeared."

"He never contacted you?"

"Not once. Then one night, late, the phone rang. Never did we expect it to be Joey. It wasn't even really him. It was Nona. They had just gotten married."

"Why had he waited so long to get in touch, Josephine? He must have known you were—"

"Worried? He knew we were worried, all right." She chuckled. "It was one of those situations where I was so relieved to know he was alive, for God's sake, and then I wanted to smack him."

"I'm sure my mother would think the same thing."

"You know, the only thing he would ever say about not calling us for all that time was that it was safer for all of us in the beginning if he didn't. I never understood exactly what was behind that. We had to trust him. We knew how much he loved us, so I never questioned his reasons."

"I need one more favor, Josephine. I don't want you to tell anyone that I have Joey's number, and I don't want you to give it to anyone else. Can you agree to that?"

"I suppose so, but"—she shook her finger at me and smiled—"you have to remember that he's been called Jeff for a long time now. If you call him Joey, he'll know you talked to me or one of the family."

"Could I get you to call him and tell him I'm going to be calling?"

"I'll do that, but it will have to be from the church. He said to me this morning that it would be best if I still called him from the church."

"Tell him I'll call tonight around six, give or take a few minutes."

She looked at me with a worried expression. "There isn't still something that could go wrong, is there?"

I reached out and held her hand in mine. "No, Josephine. Don't worry about it."

"You're sure?"

"You bet I am. And now," I said as I stood, "I have to get going. I'm very happy for you. I'll be in touch."

She walked me through the house and to the front door. As I went down the steps, Josephine called to me.

"Phoebe?"

I turned to look at her.

"I have the funniest feeling there's something you're just not tell-ing me. If there is . . . I guess what I'm trying to say is that after all of this, I could handle it. No matter what it is. I'm tougher than I look."

"Your son is coming home. That's what you should be thinking about. And no, there isn't anything I haven't told you. By the way, thanks for the soup. It was wonderful."

"Do you need more? I have—"

"I'm going to take you up on that, Josephine, but not today. I'll be in touch. I promise."

It seemed to allay any doubts she had. A smile broke out on her face. I turned around and continued walking to the truck. With each step I felt a little sicker to my stomach. In the middle of her happi-ness, how the hell could I tell her that whoever helped Joey get out of town wouldn't want him coming back alive?

I pulled into my driveway and almost rear-ended a 1960 Chevy sta-tion wagon parked right in the middle. Next to it was a pickup truck with a camper on the pack. John Wolf, a Crow Indian from Pryor, and Jewel Baily were pulling boards from across my front door. I had worked a case for John, a relative of Kyle's, a year and a half back involving his son and the death of a guy by the name of Mon-day Brown, the same case that brought Gin and Tonie into my life.

"Hey, John," I said as I parked and got out. "This is a surprise. It's a little cold to be working outside today."

"Kyle called up this morning and told me you had some trouble out here. Said your door needed fixing." John kept working as he talked. "Sure chewed up the jamb popping that lock. Might have to replace it. What do you think about a deadbolt lock and a solid door?"

"A new door? No way. That door and the glass in it has been on this house for over a hundred years. It stays. Other than that, my safety is in your hands. Do what you think is best."

"White people," John said and grinned at me. "Never could fig-ure them out. Windows in their doors."

"I take it you've met Jewel?"

"Uh-huh."

"You're early," I said as I watched Jewel pull another piece of door frame from the house.

"Girl, you're late." She looked at me and smiled

I looked at my watch. She was right. "I didn't know you were a carpenter."

"It sure as hell beats sitting in my car freezing my ass off waiting for you. Moving around at least kept my blood from settin' up."

"Sorry about that. John, if you don't need her anymore—"

"Can't go much further until I make a run up to Eagle Hardware and get a couple of things. It won't take me too long."

"Can I put something against the door to keep it closed?"

"Go ahead. I'm just going to open it again to put up some new frame and the lock on."

"Here's your hammer, John, you little talker you." Jewel held it toward him.

John's mouth dropped open. He took the hammer from her and hurried down the stairs toward his truck.

"What the hell was that about?" I asked.

"Just teasing. He's seems like an okay guy, but the man never says a word. He just grunts a lot. I was loosening him up a little."

"John doesn't need loosening, Gin—Jesus, I mean Jewel, don't do things like that."

She patted me on the shoulder. "Don't worry about it, sweetie. We are going to have lots of time together for you to get used to the new me."

"Sweetie?" I'd never had a panic attack until that moment. "This is not, let me repeat, *not* a permanent situation. It's only until you find something else. Is that clear?"

"Uh-huh. Sure. Now let's get in out of this cold, and you can show me my new duties."

Once inside, I headed for the thermostat and turned it up to seventy-four.

"It's usually not this cold in here. You can hang your coat on that hall tree and put your boots down beside it. I don't know what the hell Maggie was thinking of. This is a one-person operation. One. I don't know what the hell you're going to do around here."

"Well, we'll just have to change that, won't we?" Jewel said as she hung her coat up and removed her boots. "Girl, this is about the biggest house I have *ever* seen. You live here by yourself?"

"Yes, I do, and that's how it's staying."

"Ooh. A little defensive, aren't we? I do understand that territorial instinct. In my former life, territory was everything."

"Let's not dwell on your former life."

She held her hands up in front of her and rubbed them together. "Let's get this show on the road. Where's my office?"

"Your office? I only have *my* office. Okay, let me show you where you'll have to set up and do God knows what. I had my office in here for a while," I said as I led her toward what had originally been a parlor. She followed me into the room. "My file cabinets are in here, and a desk, and a phone jack, although I don't think you'll be needing one. It's a mess, but it'll have to do for, uh . . . whatever it is you'll end up doing."

"I think this will work out just fine. It's a mess—" She looked at me and frowned. "But I can fix it up all right. Where do you work?"

"Over there, but—" I pointed across the entryway. She was out of the parlor and across the hall before I could finish telling her it was off limits. I followed her into my office.

"Nice setup. Modem?" She sat down behind the desk and turned on the computer.

"Yes. But—"

"We are in touch with the world. Do you realize just how computers impact our life? I mean—"

"Listen, Jewel. Why don't you just sit here and play for a while. I've got this call I have to make."

"Play? You're not one of those cybergeeks they talk about that just plays games on these, are you? Give me something to find. You got a server?"

"A what?"

"A server. Connection to the Internet."

She was looking damn sure of herself. "Of course I do."

"Right, we're in business, girl. What's your password, and what do you want me to find?" Jewel squirmed in her chair, meshed her fingers together, and cracked her knuckles.

"It's all automatic, the password thing."

"Okay, so give me something, anything."

"I don't have anything for you to find, Jewel."

"Oh, there must be something—"

I had to make that call to Joey Marino, and it had to be uninterrupted. "Okay. Let's see. Find out why anyone would go to Helena."

"Montana?"

"That's good. That's very good." It was getting scarier. "Hell yes, Montana."

"Why?"

"Oh, God. Isn't that what you're going to find out? For any reason, hell—look, I am going into the other room to make a call. A very important call. Do not bother me under any circumstances. Is that clear?"

"You got it, girlfriend."

Not only was I now in the middle of my second panic attack, I was pissed off that Maggie had bullied me into hiring Jewel in the first place. This wasn't going to work.

Mind-set is a strange thing. I expected a nineteen-year-old voice to pick up on the other end of the line. It was the only image I had of Joey Marino. When the deep, confident voice of a middle-aged man answered, I couldn't be sure of who it was.

"Do I have the right number for Joe . . . I mean, Jeff Carpita?"

"Who is this?"

"I asked first. Is this Jeff?"

He was silent for a few seconds. "Yeah."

"My name is Phoebe Siegel, and I'm a private investigator. Your mother, Josephine, said she'd tell you I'd be getting in touch with you."

"She called. What do you want, Siegel?"

There was no attempt on his part to hide his hostility. "We need to talk. A lot has happened in the last twenty-four hours. I'm sure you're aware of that."

"Oh yeah. I'm aware of it."

"Okay. If you're uncomfortable with this conversation maybe it would . . . Let's start over. I'm not the badass here. If you talked with your mother, she—"

"My mother trusts just about everybody. Me? Nobody."

"I understand that, Jeff. Your mother said you'd be coming home to Billings tomorrow. Is that still the plan?"

"You still haven't told me what you want. Just cut through the shit and lay it out or I'm off here."

"Okay. This is how I see it. Whoever engineered your exodus from Billings may be getting a little nervous about you coming back to town. We need to talk about that."

"What's your thing in all this?"

"My *thing* is—" What was my thing? "I have a good idea of who killed Ellen Dahl, and it wasn't you. I've felt that from the beginning."

"The beginning of what?"

"It's complicated. Are you willing to listen?"

"Hold on a minute."

He covered the phone for a minute and then came back on. "This better be good. I'm on a cellular, and it isn't cheap."

"Why don't you call me back, collect, and we'll use my dime. This may take a while."

"Let me put it this way. I'm about fifty miles out of Casper—"

"Casper? I thought—"

"You thought what? That I was stupid enough to buy into Maitland's free plane ride? I've been on a ride, over twenty-five years' worth—" The connection crackled with static. "Can you hear me?"

"Now I can. You were saying?"

"I didn't get dumber over the years. You think I don't know Maitland hired you?"

"It never happened. It fell apart long before any commitment was made on my part. You heard that from your mother, right?"

There was a hushed voice in the background, coaxing him, urging him to lighten up. "Your mom says this woman's trying to help. For crying out loud, back off a little."

"I can handle it, Nona." His voice was a whisper.

"Is your wife with you?" I asked.

"I don't think it's any of your business where my wife is, but yeah, she's with me."

His attitude was challenging my tact. I leaned back in my chair, got comfortable, and started giving him a condensed blow-by-blow, beginning with Maitland. He asked no questions. I didn't know if he was even still on the line when I finished.

"Are you there?"

"Yeah. We've got to check in somewhere for the night. I'll call you later."

"That's it? I'll call you later? Look—"

"What is it exactly you want from me, lady?"

"I want to know who got you out of town twenty-seven years ago, Jeff."

"I've got my own scores to settle on that one. You'll know soon enough."

"It would be a damned shame to find yourself in—"

"Trouble? You've got to be kidding." His laugh was cold. "What's your number? Write this down, Nona."

He repeated it as I gave it to him.

I had had this affinity with Joey Marino. After meeting his mother and hearing her say "my Joey" enough times, I created a profile of him in my mind: a good-looking, sweet-natured, wrongly accused, on-the-run, "God, I'm so glad you got involved, Fee-Bee" kind of guy. It wasn't happening.

"I strongly advise you to get back to me tonight. It would seem that you would want to avoid endangering your wife."

Again, he said nothing.

"What's she saying?" his wife asked from the background. "Dammit, what the hell is she saying?"

"Are you through?" His surliness was at an all-time high.

I'd had it. "Not quite. Just a couple more things. I'm betting you and I will get along just fine, Jeff, if—"

"Don't bet on it."

"I think it's possible if you leave the fucking attitude in Wyoming. And don't call me 'lady' again, fella, or you can hang your ass out there all by its lonesome. I don't need this shit, and whether you give

a damn or not, this hasn't been a real picnic for me. So get it together, or don't bother calling me back."

Static saturated the connection with a vengeance, and just in time.
Whatever he was saying was drowned out.

"I can't hear you, so I'm hanging up now." I hung up and leaned
back into the couch. I didn't like this guy. Even taking into consider-
ation all he'd been through, the years he had lost, I couldn't justify
his attitude. By his own account he had scores to settle, and depending on who those scores were with, it could prove to be lethal.

John had returned and hammered my mood into my dark side. By
the time he finished up and left, I was working on a bitch of a headache. The house was dead still. I stretched out on the couch, covered
my head with a pillow, and tried to make friends with the pain—a
trick my metaphysical sister had shared with me. When that didn't
work, I fucked the thought of friendship, got up and took a couple
of Tylenol, and went back to the couch. I'd forgotten Jewel was even
in the house until she shook me from an uneasy sleep.

"Didn't mean to scare you, honey." She sat down on the end of
the couch.

The tail end of the headache train was just pulling out of my
head, taking any chance of a good mood with it.

"God, I wish you'd stop calling me sweetie and honey and whatever the hell else comes into your mind." I sat up and glared at her.
"You scared the shit out of me."

"You aren't going to be one of those badass boss ladies, are you?
I mean—"

"I don't even want to be a boss, Jewel." I rolled my neck and
listened to the knots pop. "What's on your mind?"

"I just thought you might want the list of services in Helena."

"What services?"

Jewel stood, put one hand on her out-thrust hip, and scowled at
me. "The services you asked me to get," she said as she dropped
a pile of papers onto the coffee table. "I don't take no shit, *Ms.*
Siegel."

She was hurt and insulted.

"All right, all right. Sit down and tell me what you found."

Jewel had an infectious smile. I shook my head and started thumbing through the papers.

"What you're going to see there are mostly government, medical, historical sources. And there's some kinda ranch for meditation and that crap outside of town. Plus a hot springs west of town. Also a genetics testing lab, one hospital, jillions of doctors, shrinks, all that garbage, and several rehab sources and charities to help out folks who need it. I don't know what you're looking for—"

"I'm looking for something that Ellen Maitland would have gone to Helena for, something that supposedly was very important to her."

"Like what?"

"Like I don't know yet. All I've got is—" I hesitated.

"What? All you got is what?"

"How good are you at cryptic messages?"

She stared at me hard for a moment. "Cryptic? I don't do anything with dead people. No, sir. Nothing at all. I had an auntie who talked to the dead and all that shit and got herself in a real bind. Nope. Not me."

"Dead people? What the hell are you talking about?"

"Crypts. That's where they put 'em. Dead people, I mean."

I laughed out loud. "Cryptic doesn't mean dead, it's . . . a puzzle, a code. Something that needs to be translated."

"No dead people?"

"Not today."

"So tell me. What's this puzzle?"

I got up, retrieved the note from the office without looking at it, and handed it to Jewel. She grinned and handed it back.

"Guess I messed it up. I thought it was just some doodles you were making."

"What do you mean? Doodles." I looked down at the piece of paper. Where the upside-down hook had been, a lace-trimmed heart with an arrow going through it looked back at me. I wondered for a moment if it was even the same piece of paper, but the numerals were there, beside the heart. One-four-two.

"Did you do this?"

"Ten minutes pass, and I'm in trouble again. Shit."

"No, Jewel. You're not in trouble. Just show me what you did."
I drew an upside-down hook on the back side of the paper and
handed it to her. "Show me what you did. Exactly."

"Well, I was sitting in there in front of the computer, waiting for
a download of those services, and I was just thought-tripping
through my mind. Wondering how my sister and my mother were
doin' and hoping this job would work out . . ." She glanced sideways
at me.

"Just show me what you did. Please." I shoved the paper toward
her and handed her a pencil.

"I was just doing doodles, and I saw that funny line, so I just
drew another one like it, only the opposite way," she said as she
drew a mirror-image line from the bottom of the hook, curving and
connecting with the top into a perfect heart. "Like that. Then it
looked like it needed some decoration and stuff, and I did the rest."

"A fucking heart. Could be." I stared down at it. "Damn."

"I figured it was nothing important. I hope I didn't mess it up."

"One, four, two." I wrote the numbers down. "Four, two, one.
One, two, and four. Maybe it's an address of some kind."

"Maybe it's a date."

"Maybe, but what date?" I wrote two, one, and a four. I stared
at the numbers. "Four would be April. One would be January. Two
would be—son of a bitch. Two would be February, February four-
teenth—"

"That's, uh . . . that's—"

"That's Valentine's Day, my dear, Valentine's day. Dorothy Valentine." I lurched off the couch, grabbed Jewel by the hands, and
pulled her up. "Jewel, I owe you one. I owe you a big one."

Whatever had waited in Helena for Ellen, it started with Dorothy
Valentine. And if it started with her, then maybe, just maybe, it
ended with her too.

30

Jewel and I spent an hour going over the list she had compiled. Nothing fit. Nothing with a rational explanation as to why both Dorothy Valentine and Ellen were connected to Helena. If Dougie knew, it came from the streets, and the streets usually anointed just one keeper-of-the-secrets, and now that keeper was dead. What he knew died with him, and that left me with an empty space, a three-way stretch of nothing that bound a hooker, a madam, and a tragic young woman, who, through some quirk of fate, came from the wealthiest family in town.

Without putting on a coat, I walked out to the road and got the mail from the mailbox. I needed the cold to wake me up, clear my mind. The setting sun washed a Midas-gold sheen over the snow and shimmered it into a surreal landscape. I stood there, mail in hand, on the porch and watched as the gold faded to a faint purple and then to gray. In Montana, you learn early on that nothing separates you from the land. We live by the seasons and learn to read the air, taste it on the wind, and feel it in our bones. Chinook is an Indian word for "snow eater," and I caught myself praying for warm winds out of the southwest. I always take the doable stuff to God; the rest I handle myself.

I walked into the house, sat down at the kitchen table, and started opening the mail, most of which was junk. I saved the coupons from Domino's Pizza, put aside the utility bills, glanced at a handwritten envelope that had no return address, and pitched the rest. Stud decided it was time for dinner, pried open a cupboard, and started pulling cans out of it to get my attention. It did. That done, I went

back to the table, picked up the envelope, and opened it. There were
two sheets of paper. The first was handwritten.

Miss Siegel,
After we spoke I went through some old boxes and thought
you might need this. Ellen gave this to me about a year before
she died. It probably doesn't mean anything. It was written
while she was married to him. I don't know why she gave it to
me, but there's a name on the back. It just might be the doctor
you're looking for.

Joanne

The second sheet was a typewritten poem, signed by Ellen Maitland.

> WALLFLOWERS
> *I stand unnoticed against the wall,*
> *doomed to looking on,*
> *There I am, cradled in a porcelain vase*
> *Cloaked in sorrow's song.*
> *Alone in golden splendor*
> *Unprotected from the sun,*
> *Longing for attention's space,*
> *I wilt and life is done.*
> *If I but knew of passion's hand*
> *And fire in my soul,*
> *I would gladly wilt and fade away*
> *Just to know love . . . I'd let go.*
> *But here I stand, a Wallflower true*
> *Cloaked in loneliness that I scorn.*
> *And if I died tomorrow,*
> *Would not a lover mourn?*

It was signed Ellen. Whatever silver spoon Ellen had been born
with had tarnished enough that she was prone to writing morose
poetry. I turned the paper over. On the back was a single line: "Call
Doctor Sam in the a.m."

I walked into my office and pulled Ellen's picture out from the stack on my desk. There's a point you try not to cross with any client. It's not healthy or productive to get too involved. But there I was, looking into her face and wondering how the hell I wound up with two dead clients and still managed to cross that line. Marino was a wild card, and I had an uneasy feeling about the scores he had to settle. I had a couple of choices: wait around, ride it out, and hope he would call and spill his guts, or try my hand at a game of bluff with Dorothy Valentine before everything blew wide open. I never waited well, so the choice was made for me.

Just as I was considering calling Dorothy and telling her I was on my way, the telephone rang. I picked up the receiver.

"Hello?"

"Yes. Is this Mrs. Siegel?"

"Only if you're calling my mother. Who is this?"

"My name is Nona Carpita. Jeff's wife."

There was a God. "What can I do for you?"

"You're not a Mrs.?"

"Not today, and probably not tomorrow. My name is Phoebe."

"I've been sitting here arguing with myself as to whether I should call. Jeff would be furious."

"He didn't sound like that would be much of a stretch when I talked to him. Where is he?"

"He went out to get us something to eat, so I don't have much time. I feel like I need to explain him a little. He really isn't like you heard him on the phone. He's a gentle man, a good father and husband. It's just that—" Her voice sounded on the verge of tears. "It's just that he's so bitter. I mean he missed out on so much, Miss Siegel."

"I can imagine he did. But coming back to town like gangbusters isn't going to accomplish a whole hell of a lot for either of you. He could be in danger—"

"I know that. I tried to talk to him, but all those years, I mean we were virtually cut off from his family, and I don't have much of one."

"That's all understandable. What I'm offering is a buffer zone, protection of sorts. I'm making an assumption here, but Jeff is probably the only one that knows who got him out of town. That person could well be Ellen Maitland's murderer."

"But don't they have a man in custody?"

"They've got the wrong guy."

"That isn't what we—"

"Look, Nona, it's a long story. Ellen's murderer is still out there, and whoever that is, he knows Jeff is coming home. I really want you to listen carefully. If more than one person knew how Jeff made it out of Billings, it would give him a certain amount of protection for himself and for you."

"Two people do know," she said eagerly.

"What?"

"I know. When I first met Jeff, I was working in records at a Denver hospital. We dated for a long time and then lived together for a while. Jeff never talked much about himself. Always the mystery man," she said and chuckled. "Maybe that was what was so appealing to me, that shroud of who-is-this-guy. Ya know what I mean?"

No, I didn't know what she meant, so I didn't address it. "So he eventually told you?"

"It came to a point where the relationship got real serious. I wanted to get married, Jeff said he couldn't. It didn't make any sense. I knew he loved me, but I also knew he had been moving around working construction and getting paid under the table. You know, cash?"

"You never questioned that?"

"Not really. He didn't do drugs. He drank very little, and he was good to me. But when I wanted to get married I told him that I needed more, needed a commitment. I told him one of us had to move out. That's when he told me the whole story. It was unbelievable. In fact, I didn't believe it. Jeff made a call to his mother at the church one night, he knew when she'd be there, and she sent the newspaper articles. God, we've followed everything for so long it became obsessive."

"But you married him. Or did you?"

"Yeah. I did. But we had some hurdles. Jeff didn't have any identification, so to speak. I mean he had a driver's license he bought out in L.A. with the name Jeff Carpita on it. He got it through a guy he worked with. I guess this guy knew someone who knew someone, one of those things, and got it for him."

"It's a little hard to believe that he was never stopped for a traffic violation or something."

"If you know the level of paranoia he, I mean we, lived under. He wouldn't even spit on the sidewalk. Not Jeff."

"How'd you get around the marriage license and all of that?"

"We went to Vegas and got married. The real problem was when we came back to Colorado. He needed an identity. He already had a name. Working in records made it a whole lot easier than it would have been otherwise. One piece at a time, I started laying a paper trail. I handled acquisitions for forms and such, and when a rep came through trying to change us from one birth certificate outfit to his, I sweet-talked my way into a blank sample."

"What the hell is a blank sample?"

"Birth certificates are custom-made for hospitals, but when they give you blanks, they stamp a big For Sample Only across it. Talk about printing money? They're just as careful with a document like that. Anyway, I told the guy I needed it for a joke. Kinda you scratch my back and I'll change suppliers. I got one. That was the beginning. What I couldn't handle from work, we took our time on and piled everything piece by piece until we had it all. Joey Marino vanished forever, and Jeff Carpita was a well-documented man. It took over a year and a half, but we did it."

"That's about as astounding as his vanishing. Who helped him, Nona?"

"God, I just don't know if I should—"

"Then you're both going to have to take your chances. I've got things to do, so—"

"No. Wait. It was an attorney. An attorney that was friends with this woman's—"

"Ellen?"

"Yes. Her husband and this attorney were friends. His name is—"

"Look. Don't give it up unless you're comfortable with it. My world won't collapse, but yours might."

"Miss Siegel, can I ask you something?"

"Sure. Go ahead."

"Can anything, charges I mean, be brought against us for what we've done? The falsified records and all?"

"I guess my advice would be to get a good attorney. I happen to know one. I can set it up for you when you get here."

"Then something could happen. Oh, my God."

"There are a lot of circumstances involved, Nona. That would probably be in your favor."

"His name is Gordon. David Gordon."

"Gordon . . . Jesus Christ, you mean Judge Gordon?"

"Yes. Jeff has always said that he was protecting Maitland. He made every arrangement for Jeff. He drove him to Casper and put him on a plane for Los Angeles and handed him seven thousand dollars. That was a lot of money in those days."

"It's not small change today."

Dave Gordon. The same son of a bitch Becky Simon had overheard all those years ago at the slumber party, trashing her family. The good judge, for starters, would be an accessory after the fact. Throw in obstructing justice, tampering with witnesses, and soliciting the commission of a crime—hell, the list could go on and on. I knew that the statute of limitations was five years on most things, with the exception of murder, but it was sure as hell enough to bring him down. More important, Gordon had known Maitland was culpable, and he protected him. Why?

"Are you there?" Nona asked.

"Yeah. You're sure about the name? David Gordon?"

"Absolutely. We've lived with that name forever."

"Does Jeff have any proof that Gordon—"

"You bet he does. Gordon was smooth all right, but he made a bad error."

"Which was?"

"He was so shook up at the Casper airport that he forgot his briefcase. Walked right out and left it beside Jeff in the waiting area, so Jeff picked it up and took it on the plane with him."

"You've got his goddamn briefcase?"

"You bet we do. It's not new-lookin' like it was, it's been battered over the years, but we've got it. In fact, we have it with us."

"I was just going to ask you that. Is there anything in that to prove it belonged to Gordon?"

"All kinds of legal papers and things, all with his name, and some even have a signature. There're some bills and credit card receipts and an address book. Is that enough?"

"Oh, I think that will do. Listen, Nona. I don't know what Jeff has in mind, but—"

"Jeff, he's had this dream, ya know, of walking into Gordon's office and slamming that briefcase down right in front of him."

"That isn't the best idea. We're talking about a district judge here. Nona, I want you to tell Jeff you called me."

"Oh God, he's going to come unhinged," she wailed.

"Let him. Then talk some sense into him. I've got something I have to do tonight, and I don't know how long it will take. Are you guys driving on into Billings early tomorrow?"

"We plan to."

"You have to convince him that he is not to get in touch with anyone until we've talked. If he waits, I might be able to help this little dream of his become a reality, without his jeopardizing himself. Can you do that?"

"I'll try, but I can't guarantee anything."

"Give it your best, Nona. This is really critical. Why don't you call after you've talked to him and leave a message on my machine, all right?"

"I'll do what I can. God, he's so tense. But I will, I'll give it a shot."

"Good luck. I mean that. And for Christ's sake, don't let anything happen to that damn briefcase."

"I have to share one more thing with you. That is, if you have a minute."

"Why not? Go for it."

"When Jeff landed at the Los Angeles airport, he kept hearing his name over the loudspeakers. He knew it was Gordon. Jeff was sure he must have figured out who had the briefcase after it didn't show up anyplace else. Jeff never answered the page. He said that that was the only memory that made him smile. Up until he met me, that is."

"I'll tell you what. If he plays it right this time—"

"I know. I'll talk to him."

I hung up the phone and spun around in my chair. It was coming down, coming together. Now for Dorothy Valentine.

The exhaust from the cars in front of me hugged the ground under the unrelenting weight of the cold as I drove out Grand Avenue toward the Estates. There was just enough of a wind to send ribbons of snow snaking across the road, polishing it to the smoothness of an agate and making it treacherous. I slowed down when I started fishtailing on the ice.

The closer I got to the Estates, the more nervous I felt. Behind the grins and giggles and all that neon Lycra, there was something about Dorothy Valentine that was as tough as forged steel. She was a survivor, a predator. But I had experience on my side. I had learned from the best: my mother, Margaret Flannery Siegel. She made the grand inquisitors look like the Pillsbury Dough Boy. She had this way of letting you know that she already knew whatever it was she knew so that you knew she knew.

More than once, the Siegel kids, none of whom were pushovers, had fessed up under the calm, cool interrogations of Mother Siegel. She used the scantiest of hints, usually dredged from one of her I-have-a-feeling moments. I never knew it to fail. It wasn't a new concept. It had been used by law enforcement for years, but nothing would ever convince me that its origins weren't in motherhood.

I pulled into the parking lot of the Estates and parked away from the main entrance. I sat for a minute and tried to get my bearings. There had to be a way to Dorothy's place without using the main entrance. I decided to follow a path that wound east of the main building. It was well lit and slicker than hell, but I'd made the right choice. What I hadn't thought of was the locked wrought-iron gate that surrounded the independent living compound.

I checked for any visible signs of alarms and found none. The only security was the lock and a sign:

THESE GROUNDS ARE PATROLLED

That created another problem. If they had private security, I had no idea when they had last passed this way. My best bet was to go over the fence. I chose a spot a good way from the gate and hoisted myself up and over the wrought iron. I wound my way through until I came to a door that had a brass heart over the doorbell. It had to be her. There was music coming from inside that I recognized: one of my favorites, Etta James singing those Delta blues like no one else could. I pushed the bell, but no one came to the door. I pushed it again, this time with a little more urgency.

The music lowered. The door opened.

"Well, well, well. Now what do we have here?" She leaned out and looked up and down the walk. "Who let you in, or did you just take that on yourself? Let's see, I think they still call that trespassing."

"I want to talk to you, Dorothy, have that conversation you promised me."

"Well, I don't want to. So why don't you go right back the way you came, and I will spare you the humiliation of calling security."

She had obviously been drinking, and drinking obviously made her obstinate.

"Do I need to spell it out for you, honey, or should I just pick up the phone and dial?"

"I don't think so. Call if you want, but then I head straight to a reporter friend of mine that would love to know about you, Ellen Maitland, and Helena."

She flinched, looked shocked. She leaned against the doorjamb to steady herself. "What the hell are you trying to pull? Get the fuck out of here, you—"

"That's cool," I said and raised my hands. "You don't want to talk? Well, guess what, I know someone who wants to listen. To me." I turned and acted as though I was going to walk away. "You've got it. I'm outta here."

I took a step. Nothing. Then I took another, rolled my eyes toward the night sky, and started to believe I had used the wrong approach.

"Wait a minute here. Just hold on there."

I turned and looked at her. "Yes?" I was surprised at the calm cool tone of my voice.

"What are you really up to?"

"It's damned cold out here, and I don't have any intention of freezing my ass off while you play around. You don't want to talk to me? I'm okay with that." I turned again to walk away.

"Ah shit. Come on."

I turned back around and walked through the door as she stepped aside.

"This better be worth my time," she mumbled as she walked toward the couch and sat down.

Dorothy was a woman of habit. She flung her left arm over the back of the couch, put her feet up on the coffee table, and stared at me. I sat down in the same chair I had sat in that first time and felt just as rattled.

We said nothing for a minute and just stared at each other. I had my best poker face in place. She smiled.

"You're not trying to shake me down, little girl, are you? It's been tried before, you know. It didn't work then, just like it won't work now."

"I'm not into that, Dorothy. But I am into truth."

"Don't give me that shit. Everybody wants something from old Dot. Sometimes they get it, and sometimes they don't."

"You've got nothing I want."

"Then get to it. What's this all about?"

"I know about Ellen, Dorothy. I've been doing some digging since we last talked, and I've come up with some interesting information." I knew I was talking too much. It had to come from her. All I had to do was build enough paranoia with as few words as possible. Mother Siegel usually came in in under fifteen minutes. I glanced at my watch.

"Got an appointment?"

I had to make it work for me. "As a matter of fact, I do. I told this friend of mine that I'd meet him in thirty minutes."

"The reporter," she said sarcastically.

"Right."

"So what is this little something that you think you know?" This time *she* looked at *her* watch. "You've got five minutes."

"I don't need five minutes. Dougie the Snitch. Does that ring a bell?"

"You mean that grubby little man that—"

"I contacted Dougie the day before he died. I needed information that I thought was unobtainable. Damned if he didn't come up with it. After I speak with my friend—"

"The reporter." She was still smiling.

"He'll want you to confirm or deny. It's as simple as that."

"What the hell are you talking about?" She reached out and picked up a glass of something from the table and took a long drink. "Get to it."

"Dougie had a memory like nothing I've ever seen. This information came cheap: under fifty bucks. He told me that I'd find Ellen Dahl in Helena. He didn't say Maitland, he said Dahl." The truth was, I couldn't remember if he even used Ellen's last name, either of them. "But before I checked out Helena, I had to run down a local doctor that was involved with the whole dirty little thing."

"Sam, you son of a bitch," she said just above a whisper. She did a quick recovery and looked at me as if she wasn't sure if I heard her or not.

"Doc Sam was—"

"You talked to that old drunk? Hell."

"What can I say, Dorothy? You obviously know him much better than I do."

I was treading water and about to drown. There wasn't much else I could say. I was wondering how the hell she knew the same doctor whose name Ellen had written on the back of her poem. The hooker and the heiress didn't exactly run in the same circles.

"He damn well better not have implicated me in his schemes. What a cold asshole he was. I'm surprised he's still around, but I guess people say the same thing about me."

"Look, do you want to talk about it or not? A lot's coming down tomorrow. It's all going to hit the front pages and make life rough, real rough for a few people. Joey Marino is coming home."

She shifted almost imperceptibly on the couch. "Maitland know yet?"

"He knows. Talk to me, Dorothy, and maybe I can keep some people off your porch. You won't be telling me anything I don't already know. I just want to hear it from you and get the real truth."

A look of resignation spread over her face. "The real truth. Is there any such thing?"

I didn't answer. Now, nowhere close to Mother Siegel's time, it was time to sit back and listen.

"I got it good here, ya know? I invested in this place. Sunk a lot of money into it and figured I'd just sit back and take whatever time I've got left easy. Things just don't always work out the way you want them to."

Dorothy got up from the couch, walked into the kitchen, and returned with her glass replenished.

"Don't take it personal if I don't offer you something. I don't feel all that hospitable right now." This time she sipped out of the glass. "On second thought, take it personal. You want truth, right? Well, that's what you're going to get. So take it real personal, because I don't think I like you much."

Dorothy was a sloppy drunk.

"For years, no one knew. Just us." She held up her hand and counted four fingers with her thumb. "Four. I really didn't give a shit one way or the other. It wasn't like I had a reputation to worry about."

Again I had no idea of who or what the hell she was referring to, so I went for broke. "Maybe it was a secret that should never have been kept? Ever think about that?"

"A few times. Yeah . . ." She stood and walked to the stereo on the opposite side of the room and turned up the music. "You like Etta James? Like the blues?"

"Yes on both counts, but Etta's one of my favorites."

With eyes closed, she swayed back and forth as she sank into the throbbing beat. "Mine too. The blues make me happy, ya know?"

"Yeah. I do know. I feel the same way when I hear them."

"Even old Willard kinda got into them after a while."

"Old Willard? Not Willard Dahl?"

"Hell yes, that's who I mean." Her eyes opened. She looked at me suspiciously. "Who else?"

"I . . . uh, I just didn't have it pictured that way in my mind."

Dorothy walked back to the couch, sat down, and stared at me.

"I mean, the blues, it just didn't . . . what I mean is, from what I know of old Willard, he wasn't the typical type to get into the blues. You know—appreciate them?"

"Yeah. You might be right. Stodgy old goat that he was. But let me tell you, honey, he knew how to please a woman. Only problem was he liked talking more. That's what the relationship was all about mostly: talking. But Willard was good to me, and in a way good for me. I mean, look around you. Never in a million years did I think a trick would turn into all of this. When I was a kid . . ." She leaned her head back into the couch and closed her eyes. This time she hummed a few bars along with Etta. "Hell, who am I trying to bullshit? I was never a kid. But old Willard, he always called me his baby. Getting knocked up didn't even change all that."

I looked around the room. Knocked up? Where the hell was she going with all of this?

"Must have been a shock."

"Shock? Nah. Happens a lot in my line of work. It's easy to take care of. Willard, he was like this puffed-up virile son of a bitch. Had him walking real proud there for a time. He's the one that insisted on Doc Sam." She hummed a bar of blues.

I was floored. She was talking about herself.

"Me? I wanted to get it cut out. I didn't have time for a kid. I didn't want one, but Willard, oh no. He came up with this big elaborate scam. But what the hell, it worked out for everyone in the end. Like I said, look around. The girls and I used to sit around and laugh about him going home to an old horseface bitch. Man, was she a piece of work."

"Dorothy, I need to use your bathroom." I stood on shaky legs.

"Go ahead. Straight down the end of the hall and on your right."

I left her humming to herself and walked down the hall to the bathroom. I closed the door and locked it. I turned the cold water on low, splashed some onto my face, trying to get the shocked look off of it.

"My God," I said to myself as I patted my face dry with one of the towels that had been folded neatly beside the sink.

She had lied—or had she? I asked her if she knew Ellen Dahl Maitland, and her reply had been no. But Dorothy Valentine *did* know Ellen. She'd given birth to her and then handed her over to the man responsible: Willard Dahl.

I walked out of the bathroom and back into the soulful sounds of the blues. This time, they didn't make me happy.

31

The benevolent madam was a mother. It was hard to believe. I'd gotten far more than I'd bargained for, and I wasn't sure just where to go with it. When I walked back into her living room, she was standing staring out some sliding glass doors into the night. The music had changed. Now the low sultry voice of Cleo Laine floated through the room. At least she had great taste in music.

"I thought you were taking a lease out in there," she turned and said when I entered the room.

"Too much coffee. You know how that goes."

"Don't drink the stuff myself. I believe in this shit." She hoisted her glass in my direction. "Keeps the blood thin."

I sat back down. Dorothy walked, just a little too stiffly, back to the couch and took her familiar position.

"What did that little weasel Doc Sam have to say?"

"I really can't tell you that, Dorothy. Wish I could, but I can't." What else could I say? I didn't even know who the hell Dr. Sam was. It was time to walk into uncharted territory. "Why Helena?"

"It was close. I could keep in touch with my girls, and Willard could keep an eye on me. I lounged around for six months and let the good Sisters take care of me while Willard hustled himself up a wife and took care of everything else."

"So this Doc Sam, he set it up?"

"Hell, yes. And if he told you any different, then he's a lying SOB. I went to him to abort me, and he asked me if Willard knew what I was doing. They were friends, see? It was Doc that brought Willard around in the first place. Naturally me and him hit it right off."

"Then Willard wanted you to have the baby?"

"Hell yes, he wanted it. But not me. Saddled with a kid? Shit." There was a stone-hardness in her face that all the lifts and all the peels in the world couldn't cover.

"Then Rosella wasn't married to him for any length of time?" She was nothing more than a convenience: a stepping-stone to get what he wanted."

"Which was a child. His child."

"And a piece of me. I never led that man down any paths. For me it was a business proposition. For him it was something else. It was love." She laughed. "Can you believe that? Love. Hell, he was old enough to be my father."

"Why did you consider this a business proposition, Dorothy?"

"Look around you. He said he'd take care of me for life, and that he did. There was a fight for ya. It graveled her ass to know he had set me up. There was even a separate will. I thought she'd go nuts over that one. But ya know, when he died, I even missed the old fart."

"And when Ellen died? How did you feel, Dorothy?"

"She wasn't my problem. I didn't know the kid. Hell, it was a raw deal, but I'm not one of those sob sisters. Now Chili? That little girl had it coming. She tried to pull one over on me and learned her lesson the hard way. But let's get back to Doc."

"I'd like to know about Chili. What did you mean, she—"

She waved her hand in the air, silencing me. "Later. I want you to know what a lowlife Doc was. And you can't tell me he's changed much over the years. Right?"

"Right."

"Horny little bastard. He took care of my girls, you know, and made some damn good wages doing it. But Doc liked the perks best. A free piece of ass now and again kept my girls real healthy."

"What about Chili? What lesson did she learn the hard way?"

"Trying to shake down that ugly Rosella. Maitland and Chili had this thing going. She was a hot little number. Earned that name, Chili. Maitland promised her the moon, and I think he meant it. But she got greedy. Wanted that license in her hand. Wanted respectability. Now, I've seen some girls go to the other side and make good lives for themselves. But Chili? It wasn't in the cards."

"She went to Rosella? Why the hell would she do that?"

"I thought you knew all of this."

"We've got some blanks to fill in, Dorothy. Just some blanks. How do you know she really went to Rosella?"

"The little bitch told me. Ya see, Siegel, our little four-way secret became a five-way secret once Maitland came on the scene. Now, that was after Willard died. Little Bobby, that's what I called him. The only thing the fool ever stood up for was to take a leak. Spineless as they come, but he knew a hot property when he saw it."

"And that hot property was—"

"The kid."

"Her name was Ellen. E-L-L-E-N."

"What is your problem? She was my fucking kid, for Christ's sake. What the hell was she to you?"

"A human being. A young woman with her entire life and a future in front of her."

"What do you know? Maybe not as much as you think. She didn't have a damn life or future with Maitland. He liked it wild, honey. Real wild, and that straitlaced kid, uh . . . Ellen . . ." She pronounced it in two distinct syllables. "She and Rosella knew nothing about keeping a man. Odd, isn't it. Not even blood and had that twist in common."

"I guess I thought Maitland was a husband for hire. You're telling me he wasn't?"

"Hell, no. He worked in that law firm and got all that information, came across it somehow, and he used it like a noose around the old bag's neck. Besides, she never liked the kid anyway. Willard told me that."

"Ellen was close to her father, wasn't she?"

"He doted on her. Got her every damn thing she needed and wanted, and some besides. Funny though, I was never real sure who sired her in the first place."

The room was suffocating. The walls were closing in. "Willard Dahl wasn't even her damn father?"

"Don't get all bent out of joint. I wasn't exactly a Brownie Scout back then. Never pretended to be. Could have been anyone if I thought about it hard enough, but it also could have been Willard.

Hell, he believed he was her old man. That was the important thing. Right?"

"Jesus." I stood. I'd had enough. I walked to the door and opened it.

"Don't you go involving me in this. I had nothing to do with anybody's death. If I had known what was coming, I wouldn't have turned her out." Her words slurred.

"What are you talking about, Dorothy?"

"That morning, that day that someone murdered her. And don't get any ideas on it. It sure as hell wasn't me."

"You saw her?"

"She came to me all dressed up like something out of a dirty movie. Said Rosella had told her everything. Hell, I didn't know what to do with her. I told her to get lost. That's when she started acting real goofy, hysterical and all that. I had a couple of girls get her the hell out of there. Then she ended up dead."

"And you skipped town. Went to New Orleans."

"I didn't need the trouble. Nobody needs trouble like that. And who the hell are you to judge me? It's women like you that can't keep 'em at home. They all eventually come to us. Just like your old man, honey. Just like—"

I was across the room before I knew what I was doing. Dorothy shrank herself back into the couch. Eyes widened. My face was so close to hers, I could feel her booze-saturated breath sink into my pores.

"You are trash. A worthless, nothing piece of humanity. If you ever let my father's name pass over your lips I will personally rip them off and shove them down your throat. Have you got that?"

"You don't scare me."

I knew better. Her voice was shaking. "You should be scared, Dorothy, because I'm going to be thinking about you. And the more I think about you, the crazier I'm going to get. My father would have slit his throat before he touched something like you. You got that?" She didn't answer. If looks could kill, I would have been dead. "Don't fuck with me, Dorothy."

I don't remember feeling the cold on my face as I went back over the wrought iron. I didn't feel the wind whip the tears streaming down my cheeks into slivers of ice. And I don't remember ever wanting to hurt someone as bad as I wanted to hurt Dorothy Valentine.

I had driven from Shiloh to the corner of Grand and Rehberg before I realized I hadn't turned the heat on in the truck. It didn't matter. If water seeks its own level, then cold must do the same. It was hard to think of a human being coming into the world the way Ellen had: unwanted by her mother, unloved by her husband, and at the end, unmourned by her family. Rita Chillman had Maitland, for what that was worth, and a family that loved her. Frank, he had the same family and a rough road. But Ellen? Jesus.

I stopped for a red light. Kyle's Haida story was making sense. I had sung the song backward and navigated to the *real* beginning of Ellen's life, the one that started with Dorothy Valentine. But there was a big difference. The Haida found their way home. Ellen never did. I heard a horn honk behind me, looked into the rearview mirror, and saw someone waving me on. I looked up at the light. It was just turning red again. I waited for another green one, turned left, and pulled into the Cenex station. The pay phone was on the outside of the building. For once, the guts of the phone book were inside the cover. When I found the number I needed, I dropped a quarter in and dialed.

"Nick?"

"Yeah. Who is this?"

"It's me. Phoebe."

"What's up?"

"We've gotta talk, Nick."

"You want to come on over?"

"Sure."

"Where are you calling from, Phoebe?"

"Rehberg and Grand."

"I'm over on Lewis and Twenty-third Street. I'll put the porch light on."

He gave me the house number, and within minutes I was on his porch, ringing his doorbell.

"Hey, Phoebe, you didn't sound so good on the phone. What's going on? I've been trying to run you down all day."

"I know who did it, Nick. I know who killed Ellen. I just left

Dorothy Valentine's place. She was Ellen's mother, Nick. Dorothy Valentine was her mother."

"Hold on there a minute. Where the hell did you come up with that? Dot? Impossible."

"Not impossible. She told me herself."

"Damn. Was she drinking? Are you sure about all of this?"

"As sure as I'm sitting here."

"Wait a minute. You said you knew who killed Ellen. Dot? You're not trying to tell me that Dot killed her own kid, are you?"

"No, Nick. Not Dot."

"Then you got the goods on Maitland. Hot damn. I've waited a helluva long time to bring that son of a bitch to his knees. You done good, Phoebe." He smiled and patted me on the arm. "Your old man would be proud of his little girl."

"Nick, Joey Marino is on his way home. Dave Gordon is the one who got him out of town. *The* Dave Gordon."

"The judge? What the hell have you been doing all day to come up with this shit? He's a district judge."

"Marino, only that's not what he's being called anymore, it's Jeff Carpita, but scrap that for the moment. Joey has Gordon's briefcase."

"You're losing me, Phoebe."

"It's so screwed up and tangled, Nick, but that doesn't matter. He's coming into town tomorrow morning. I think he's an asshole, but what the hell, he's been on the run for a long time. He wants to settle his score with Gordon. I want it to be your collar."

"Phoebe, I'm in evidence, I'm not on the streets. I—"

"Do it for yourself and for my dad, Nick. You two are the only ones who hung in there. And there's something else I want you to do for me—"

"Slow down, for God's sake. You lost me all the way back at the beginning. What did you get on Maitland? It's going to have to be something damn hard, Phoebe. Damn hard."

"Dave Gordon believed Maitland murdered Ellen. That's why he got Marino out of town. There must have been some recessive gene of conscience left in him someplace. The dumb bastard thought he was doing the right thing for the wrong person and for the wrong reason. Personally, I think he was covering his own ass. Gordon and Maitland played it rough and loose with the women, and I think Gordon didn't want all of that to come out in the open. What do you think?"

"I think you need to slow down and give me some details."

"I don't have time, Nick. I—"

"You've got time. Let me make you a pot of coffee or get you a beer or—"

I stood. "I've got to go."

"Where?"

"Are you going to do those things for me, Nick? You know the Marinos. Joey will trust you more than he will me. I went the rounds with him on the phone today, and it didn't go well. He'll be at his mother's early in the morning. He's going to need an attorney, and I figured that Maggie Mason would be good for that."

I opened the door and stepped out onto the porch.

"Hey you, come back in here. You can't just dump this and run."

"You can handle it, Nick," I yelled as I walked to the truck. "And don't forget to show up early at Marino's. Okay?"

"Where are you going, dammit?"

"I've got an appointment with Ellen's killer."

I got into the truck, started it up again, and pulled away from the curb. I could hear Nick screaming my name as I drove away from his house into the frigid, still night.

32

L ewis Avenue in Billings is a residential street that takes a straight shot from the west end all the way downtown. Within ten minutes I was parked in front of Dahl's House. One faint light glowed through a drawn shade on a window on the side porch. I sat there and looked up at the towering structure that dwarfed the massive lot it rose from.

I got out, stood outside the hedge that surrounded the property, and stared at the hauntingly Gothic structure. Three stories, four walls of sandstone blocks, had imprisoned any chance of happiness for Ellen Maitland. And she was in there: mother, executioner, and murderer. I walked through the snow and up the stairs to the side porch. The moon was full overhead and flooded the area in an iridescent light. Even the air shimmered with cold.

There was a buzzer with a speaker just above it to the right of the door. I could not hear from within the house if the damn thing even worked, and then a voice came out of the speaker.

"Yes?"

"I'm here to see Rosella Dahl."

"And your name is?"

"Phoebe Siegel."

"Phoebe . . . what . . ."

I heard a click as if someone had cut me off. Just as I was about to push the buzzer again, the door opened and I stood there looking into Grace Driscoll's face. Grace had been my mother's church buddy for years and had known me my whole life.

"What are you doing here, Phoebe?" Her voice was low and scolding.

"I need to see Mrs. Dahl."

"Well, you can't, young lady, now you just go on and get out of here."

Grace started to close the door in my face. I put one hand up, pushed against the door, and walked past her into the house.

"Where is she?"

"She's in her apartment. Lord. What are you doing here?"

"Go tell her I'm here, Mrs. Driscoll."

"I certainly won't. It's late, and she's—"

"Sleeping?"

"She's very ill, and I won't disturb her."

"I'm not leaving."

"Then I'm just going to call your mother, Missy."

"Oh come on, Grace. Call my mother? That's a little ridiculous, don't you think? Just go tell Mrs. Dahl I'm here. She'll see me."

"I'm not going to do any such thing. Mrs. Dahl is critically ill."

"I saw her the other day, and she looked fine to me. What is it, a bad attack of gas?"

"You always thought you were funny, Phoebe, and just a little too smart for your britches around the edges. Mrs. Dahl is very ill. She has been for about a year now."

"With what?"

"I am not in a position to share that with you."

Grace looked behind her toward what looked like an entryway big enough to land a small plane in. For the first time, I noticed my surroundings. They were spectacular enough to take your breath away.

There was more polished wood and cloth wallpaper than I thought would fit in any house. But this wasn't just any house. The furnishings were elaborate, obviously imported, and just as obviously very expensive. To my left, two windowed doors led into a large glass-domed conservatory, full of lush and blooming tropical plants. And straight in front of me was a dining room right out of a European palace.

"So this is it." I wondered if I should genuflect.

"Now it's time for you to leave, my dear." Grace had changed her strategy and now sounded very solicitous.

"What's wrong with her, Grace?"

"If I tell you, will you please leave?"

I raised my eyebrows to give her at least that much hope.

"All right," she continued. "Mrs. Dahl is dying of cancer. She's been under a doctor's care for more than a year. She's close to the end, Phoebe. I cannot let you disturb her."

"She's dying tonight?"

"No, not tonight." Her voice rose and then dropped back to a whisper. "Soon. It could be at any time now. She is suffering more than anyone I've ever seen. Poor, poor woman. And she refuses pain medication. Now will you go?"

"Who is it, Grace?" Rosella Dahl's voice carried down the stairs.

"It's no one, Mrs. Dahl. Go on back to your room, and I'll bring some hot tea up for you."

"Is that Miss Siegel, by chance?"

I thought Grace's chin would bounce off the floor. "Why, yes. Yes, it is." Grace stared at me, confused.

"I've been expecting her, Grace. Bring her up, please. No, I'll come down. Come help me with my robe, and I'll take tea in the dining room."

"How did she know you were coming?" Grace asked me.

"I don't have the slightest idea. Has anyone called within the last thirty or forty minutes?"

"Yes. Someone did call. She answered the phone in her room before I could get it down here. Now, let me tell you something, young lady, you upset her in any way"—she shook her finger in my face—"and I will call nine one one and have you removed from these premises. And then I *will* call your mother."

"I hear ya loud and clear."

"Now, I'm going upstairs to help her. Follow me and sit at the table. Do not move."

I followed her and found myself sitting under a fringed chandelier made of bronze and stained glass. No matter which way I turned, the opulence was there. The furniture was heavy Empire, rich and polished to a high sheen. Wainscoting crawled all the way up to the elaborately carved ceiling. Small tiles embedded around the firebox gleamed like a thousand rubies. It was too much, too rich. That was the trade-off: Live a dead life surrounded by all of that.

I was so caught up picturing Ellen as a little girl, a teenager in that mausoleum, that I hadn't heard Rosella Dahl and Grace come down the stairs. I looked up and had to make sure that the woman I was looking at was Rosella. She was gaunt, with sunken eyes and only wisps of hair clinging to her head. There were no eyebrows above her eyes, and her skin looked waxen and dead.

"Don't be shocked, Miss Siegel. A little Lancôme and my wig, and I will look as presentable as I did the other day. I'm not in the mood for makeup, nor was I prepared for a guest."

Grace helped her sit down on a chair at the far end of the table.

"How did you know I was coming?"

"I received a call from Dorothy Valentine," she said and then reached out affectionately and patted Grace's arm. "You go on in the kitchen and bring a pot of tea. It can steep out here."

"I can stay if you want me—"

"I'll be fine. Now go ahead. It will help me sleep. Miss Siegel won't be here all that long, but I'm sure she'd appreciate some hot tea on a cold night."

"Nothing for me, Grace."

Rosella said nothing after Grace left the room. It was an uncomfortable situation. She looked bad enough to drop dead right in front of me.

"I didn't know you and Dorothy were such close friends," I said. "I'm surprised she called you."

"Oh, don't be. She was drunk and hysterical. She did tell me that you and she had quite a conversation."

"Yes, we did."

"What brings you to my house?"

"I know what you did, Mrs. Dahl. I know about everything. Is there anything you want to say to me before I go to the authorities?"

"I don't think anything needs to be said. Do you?"

"Why did you kill her? You beat her to death like a damn dog." What had been close to sympathy was now taking a U-turn back to rage and contempt.

"I don't remember saying that I did."

"And Chili?"

"She wasn't a very intelligent young woman, but then again her type never are. I knew about her all along. I guess some would say she had guts of a certain sort."

"She found out that Dorothy was Ellen's mother and tried to blackmail you into letting Maitland leave Ellen. Am I right?"

"No one kept Robert around. He could have left whenever he wanted to. You're wrong on that point."

"And Ellen? Could she have left?"

"Ellen was a freak of nature. A whore's spawn. Her life was destined to follow, how should I say it, a certain course?"

"And that course was to the Bunk House Motel."

"Ellen decided to leave Dahl's House. To leave her husband. That's not the way I was brought up. Marriage is a lifetime commitment, and—"

"And you didn't want the public humiliation of a divorce, which in turn would cause Maitland to spill his guts. But she didn't have to die."

"Ellen's life was over when it began. From the time she was a small child, she was always drawn to trash, just like her father. It was one of the nastier family traits. You see, Miss Siegel, I became Mrs. Willard Dahl with my eyes wide open. It was a compromise. I've had a very rich and rewarding life."

"You've got to be kidding me. Rich and rewarding? You fucking killed three—"

"I must ask you not to use that kind of crudeness to express yourself. I won't tolerate it. Not under my roof. As I was saying, Willard and I had an arrangement, a business deal. Take another look, Ms. Siegel. I raised his bastard child, played the role of wife and mistress of Dahl's House; I'd say it was a fair exchange."

"I don't buy it. I'm curious about something."

"Which is—"

"Mr. Dahl, didn't he realize how you felt about Ellen?"

"Willard? You must understand our relationship before I can answer that question."

"So fill me in."

"For years I lay in bed beside a man that smelled like the whore he had just come from. That was his obsession. When I couldn't stand it anymore, I moved into one of the other bedrooms. After that, between his obsession and his work, we talked very little. When we did, Ellen was not a priority."

Was she ever? The understatement disgusted me. "And Frank?

Why was it necessary to kill Frank Chillman? Everyone probably would have blown him off as some flake."

Rosella lifted the china cup to her lips and sipped from it. She lowered the cup just enough to watch me over the rim with emotionless eyes. It was incomprehensible to me that I was facing a human being this methodically cold.

"Frank was a fool. Bright, but a fool. Again, trash, and there's only one way to deal with it. You throw it out."

"You picked one hell of a night. I had a tough time getting out there, and I'm not—" I stopped midsentence and just shook my head.

"You can say it, Ms. Siegel. I'm dying. It's a curious condition, the state of dying. Once you accept the fact, a calm comes over you, a determination to experience it with the same dignity with which you lived. To ensure that, I had to come to terms with those things I could not accomplish and become more focused on the loose ends and how to tie them. I could not accept obstacles, including my health or the weather."

"That's how you saw Frank Chillman? As some loose end that needed tying up?"

"That's exactly how I saw him. If you'll think about it, being a loose end was better than the nothing that he was. Don't you think?"

I couldn't think.

She leveled a stare at me that could have moved the Rockies. Dying or not, the woman was powerful.

"You must realize, Miss Siegel, that you have no evidence against me. They have a man in custody that—"

"Loved Ellen. Probably the only person in the world that did, after your husband died. And Slater didn't kill anyone."

"They have their Mr. Slater. And according to Robert, that young Marino man is coming home."

"That young man is almost fifty years old. You really don't give a shit, do you?"

"I asked you not to use that—"

"I really don't give a damn what you want. You murdered these people in cold blood to serve your own purposes. To protect your own ass and solid reputation."

"Like I said, you have only your own speculation."

"I don't get it, Rosella. Why did Dorothy call you?"

Grace entered the room with a silver tea service and one cup. "Here ya go, Mrs. Dahl. You're sweating again, dear. Look at that forehead."

She took a tissue from her pocket and dabbed at the beads of sweat that stood out on Rosella's face. Rosella's breaths came deep and long. She was fighting pain. Determined not to let me see her vulnerability to it. Grace reached out for her; the look in Rosella's eyes stopped her cold.

"I think you've had enough. Let's put you back upstairs so you can rest," Grace said. "Are you sure you wouldn't like a shot?"

"I won't be long, my dear. Ms. Siegel and I will just be a moment."

Grace glared at me but left the room.

I looked into Rosella's face. She'd won. There wasn't a judge in the state who would incarcerate her, and she knew it. She was dying. And she was right, I didn't have one shred of evidence. But I knew, and she knew, and only time would tell if that would be enough for me. It was as if she reached into my thoughts and read my mind.

"Don't feel too badly. In a way justice has been served. I have become my own executioner."

I got to my feet and looked down at the frail, wasted woman whose body had laid an unmerciful siege to itself. All I could do was shake my head. I turned away and walked toward the door I had come in through, opened it, and walked out into the night.

Snow covered the hedge where Joanne and Ellen had peeked through to see each other over forty years ago. I crossed the grounds that Waxy Slater had tended, that put him close enough to Ellen to fall in love with her. I looked at the foundation of the house and saw the small basement window that looked in upon the darkness Ellen had shattered with her screams as her child had been torn from her to meet its own tragic fate.

I turned the collar up on my jacket and walked to the truck. This was a house of death, emotional and otherwise. I needed life. I wanted to be home, with Kyle lying beside me, feel each square inch of his bare skin upon mine. I looked toward the house once more before I pulled away. A curtain parted as someone looked out. It was a haunting sight; Ellen Maitland had viewed the world from those windows.

And when the day finally came that she found the courage to leave, she walked out those doors and did not return.

I would not return either.

Epilogue

"**I**'m not ready for this and I'm not going to do it." Mom struggled with both hands behind her back trying to unzip the dress she had just put on. "There's something . . . something obscene about this whole thing." Unnatural."

"It's the most natural thing in the world," Kehly said as she helped pull the dress up over our mother's head and placed it on the bed. "Now I want you to try this one on." Kehly took another dress from the hook on Mom's bedroom door and held it up in front of herself. "What do you think?"

"Yellow?" Mom asked.

"She'll look like a urine specimen if she wears—" I said as I leaned against the dresser.

"Shut up, Phoebe. She wants to look nice. Special. Don't you, Mom? Yellow is a wonderful color for her. She's more . . . uh, summer. Or is it spring? Damn, I can never keep those straight. Come on, slip this on."

"I don't want to slip it on, dear. I'm sure I have something in my closet that will do just fine."

"But this is my treat. Please cooperate, Mom. We only have a couple more to go."

Cara walked into the room carrying two cups of coffee with a can of pop tucked under each arm. "Okay, everybody. Take your order now before I lose my grip on this stuff. How's it going?"

"Just great. Kehly is determined to turn her into a lab test, and I think we should be talking about birth control." The room fell into dead silence. Cara and Kehly turned slowly and looked toward

Mother, who was staring at me. There was an audible gasp right before she grabbed her robe, burst into tears, and ran into the bathroom.

"God! You piss me off, Phoebe. You've got the tact of . . . of . . . You have no tact. That's the problem. Why the hell did you say that?"

"I just told you. I was—"

"I thought it was hysterical," Cara said and winked at me. "Now, would you both take your coffee and Coke respectively. I'll talk to her."

Cara walked to the bathroom door and tapped quietly before she went in.

"She's becoming quite a fixture around here, isn't she?" Kehly asked. "Is there something I should know?"

"Why don't you ask Cara?"

"Because I'm asking you." She raised the Coke to her lips and took a drink. "Are they fooling around?"

"Mom and Cara? Jeeze, Kehly—"

"You know damn well what I mean."

"Again, why don't you ask her?"

I walked to the bed and flopped down on it. Kehly followed suit.

"Isn't this a kick? I remember the two of us running in here to stand in front of that mirror. Now it's Mom," Kehly said.

We both looked at our reflections in the full-length mirror that hung on the closet door, and had for as long as I could remember.

"Have you ever been jealous that I was the pretty one?" She grinned at me maliciously.

"No."

"Not even a little tiny bit?"

"Not even a little tiny bit. You see, Kehly, looks fade, brains don't. Since I got the brains and"—I looked at her out of the corner of my eye—"never had to wear Super Odor Eaters in my shoes, I just figured I came out of the best end of the gene pool."

"Low blow," Kehly said and drew the words out in her lowest, most menacing voice. "Really a below-the-belt shot."

We both broke out laughing. It felt good.

"So what do you think of all this?"

"Mother going out on a D-A-T-E with Nick Spano?"

"Why are you spelling?"

"Whether you've noticed or not, she won't let anyone use that word in front of her. She insists she's only going out to dinner and then to a movie."

"Tonight's the night. Ya know I thought you'd be against this. I'm glad you're not. You've changed, Phoebe. I'm not sure how, but you have. I like it."

I looked back into the mirror and patted my face. "Nope. Just the same old me."

"Uh-uh, something has changed. My bet is it has something to do with that case you were working. Personally, I think getting shot would have to change you. Am I right? I am, aren't I? Your life flashed in front of you and—"

"Kehly, shut up for a minute and I'll tell you."

Kehly propped her chin on her hands and looked at me. I closed my eyes and took a deep breath.

"It's hard for me to talk about. It's so, I don't know . . . personal."

"I'm feeling good about this. We're about to really communicate. I swear, Phoebe, it stays right here, between you and me."

I sighed and took a deep breath. "Remember when I had that killer cold?"

"Sure. It was when Mom insisted that I drive her over to your place and then tried to talk me into cleaning your house."

"That's it. Well, something happened. Maybe it was because all my defenses were down, I don't know. Anyway, one night during The-Big-Sick I . . . I . . ." I covered my face with my hands.

This time Kehly reached out and held on to my wrist. "It's okay, Phoebe. Just say it."

I raised my hand and looked at her. "I accepted you know who," I rolled my eyes heavenward, "as my personal savior." I said the last four words as rapidly as I could and still be understood.

Her facial expression didn't change. "Excuse me?"

"It was the craziest thing. He looked so much like Elvis that—"

Kehly's expression still didn't change as she said, "I ask myself frequently why I hate you, Phoebe. Thank you for this; one more confirmation that I should hate you."

I turned onto my back and almost choked to death laughing. Finally, when she could contain herself no more, she broke loose and started flailing her hands at me. I fought back. Exhausted, we stopped and gasped for breath.

Mother emerged from the bathroom, her eyes swollen and red. Cara followed.

"Phoebe, dear? I'd like to talk to you alone, please."

Kehly leaned over and whispered, "This is one of those neener-neener moments that I live for. You are in big trouble."

"Get outta here," I said and pushed her off the bed.

"Want me to make some lunch?" Kehly asked Mom.

"Nothing for me, but if you and Cara want something, go on ahead and fix something."

They left. I felt ten years old.

"Phoebe, are you upset with me?"

"No. Why should I be?"

"I was shocked at your remark and—"

"Mom, it was a joke. Don't take it any other way."

"You're sure this doesn't have anything to do with Nick and me seeing, I mean Nick and me going . . . uh . . ."

"I like Nick, Mom. I like him a lot. I think it's great he's been coming around. I said something stupid thinking you'd get a laugh out of it. I didn't say it because I thought you and Nick would be—"

"Stop right there. That's just what I'm talking about," she said as she turned and shook her index finger at me. "Everyone had just better be getting their minds out of the gutter. The same thing happened when poor Eloise Fox started seeing old Mr. Abbott. The tongues sure started wagging on that one. They had those two . . . well, never mind. It was just awful."

"Mother . . ."

"Maybe I'm not ready for this."

"You're ready, Mom. Besides, I don't think anyone can start wagging over two old friends going out to dinner."

She brightened almost immediately. "Not really *that* old. You're right, though. Nick is a very dear friend, and to tell you the truth, it's almost like being with—" This time she looked away.

"Daddy? I thought the same thing when I had breakfast with Nick. This is a good thing for both of you. Come on, Mom, let's go downstairs."

Cara was just putting her sweater on when we walked into the kitchen. "I've got to go, so I guess I'll see everyone later. If you need me for anything, Maggie, just give a holler."

"I've got it all under control. See you later, then."

The back screen door slammed as Cara left. Then it opened and Cara stuck her head back around the jamb. "Hey, Phoebe. I was going to tell you they're having a big sale tomorrow down at the fairgrounds. It's all the stuff they salvaged from those houses down behind the War Bonnet Inn."

"Where behind the War Bonnet?"

"That eyesore tucked between I-90 and the hotel that the Chamber of Commerce constantly complained about. You know, there was two, maybe three blocks, some old houses and that motel that's been closed for years? The city finally bought it and trashed it, at least most of it. You might find something for your place. Wanna go?"

"I'll get back to you. I don't know what I've got tomorrow yet."

Cara shrugged and disappeared.

"I don't know how anyone can put something disgusting in their house that belonged to someone else. I mean, how do you know where it's been?" Kehly, ever dramatic, shivered.

"God, you're right," I said and feigned recoiling. "I don't want to even think about what someone used those old banisters for."

"I'm being serious here."

"I know you are. I've got to go, Mother. Need me later? A little support or chaperone?"

"You're impossible," Mother said as she put her hands on her hips and smiled. "Someone had to have switched you at the hospital."

"I've been saying that for years," Kehly chided. "But who listens?"

*   *   *

The sun was beating down on the windshield of the truck, my elbow resting on the open window as I pulled off Twenty-seventh Street South and drove around the War Bonnet until I came to road barriers the city had put up. I parked the truck and got out. The house where I had stopped for directions last winter was gone. Gone also were the shade trees that shielded the houses from the sun and their poverty from I-90. Tire marks half as wide as my truck scarred every inch of ground. I picked a rut and started walking toward where I hoped the Bunk House Motel would still be standing.

I'd dealt with the Ides in my usual fashion: by not dealing with them at all. One deft stroke of my hand rendered Mars impotent, unable to take a *Marchly* swipe at my life. I stopped doing March after it demanded an offering. That offering was the death of my brother Ben and my beloved aunt Zelda. It just seemed easier to rip the page off my calendar and let those memories sleep.

The winter we had just come out of was one of the coldest on record. In the bitterness of that cold, Frank Chillman had resurrected Ellen Maitland from her restless chamber and caught a lot of people's attention. There were no winners in the Maitland case, only casualties. Joey Marino lost twenty-seven years of his life and demanded ten minutes, only ten minutes, in front of District Judge Dave Gordon. And in that time he brought the good judge down, destroying a career Gordon had sold his soul for.

Joey had contacted me during the Ides and insisted that we meet for dinner at The Rex. I accepted. He turned out to be an okay guy. Some, not all, of his bitterness had softened, but he was still cautious. We stayed away from any heavy conversation during dinner, but afterward I couldn't resist probing him about the two hours he'd been absent from the Bunk House Motel the day Ellen died. All he would say is that his girlfriend needed the services of an out-of-town doctor.

"Hey! Where the hell do you think you're going, lady? You can't come through here!"

He was big and burly and had mastered the fine art of talking with a cigarette between his lips. He started walking toward me.

"Isn't this City property?" I asked.

He eyed me suspiciously. "Yeah. It's City property. But that don't make no difference. Turn it around and take it on out of here."

"It?"

"Your ass," he said as he towered over me. "Haul your ass on out of here."

I tucked my hands in the front pockets of my Levi's and looked through the roar of the heavy equipment toward the Bunk House Motel.

"Are you deaf?" he bellowed over the noise.

I looked toward him and said, "No. I hear you just fine. Are you stupid?"

He set his jaw, shifted his weight, and put his hands on his hips. "What the hell did you say?"

"It was a question. I asked you if you were stupid." I drew a question mark in the air with my index finger.

"Get the hell out of—"

"Talking to a woman these days and using derogatory words for parts of her anatomy can add up to trouble you may not want. I should warn you, I'm a few minutes away from feeling verbally abused and sexually offended. But let's not get into that yet," I said and smiled. "You need to watch your mouth and deal with that tendency of yours to slip into male territorial aggression."

"What the hell are you talking about?" He scratched his hard hat.

"You need it simpler? Try this on. I am a big girl. I can handle this, so stay the fuck out of *my* way. Did you get that?"

I left him standing there screaming. "You're just asking to end up a bow tie on that dozer if you don't watch your step! But it's your as—un, your problem, lady. I warned ya!"

I waved backward over my head to acknowledge I'd heard him and continued toward the motel. I stopped just before I got to the porch and looked around the site. It was the last place left except for the shack where the old guy, the caretaker, who'd slashed my truck tires that cold winter night, lived.

Just as I thought of him, he came around the shack carrying a single-size box spring to a battered Dodge truck and dumped it in the back. When he spotted me, he walked over.

"You got business here?" he asked casually.

"I don't know. I guess I do. I just wanted to take a last look."

"I know what you mean. Goddamn, this place was a money-maker. I used to do a little cleaning for the guy that ran it way back when. Then, after it happened—"

"It?"

"Hell, there was a real famous murder happened here, ya know. Some uptown broad got whacked and chopped up in little pieces. Carried her out in buckets, they did. Took place right over there in that end room." He pointed.

I watched him as he looked toward the room. It's tough to figure people: Sometimes the harsh realities of murder aren't enough for some memories. To hang on to them, they have to be embellished upon. All I had to do was look at the yawning, glassless window that even the narrow board nailed across it couldn't silence.

I'd tuned out the bulldozer's roar, so I was surprised when I turned and found it shut down. Four guys were walking toward a pickup truck; they piled in and pulled away. I checked my watch. It was exactly noon.

He was still working on his version of history. "Like I was telling ya, she was diced up and—"

I held my hand up to silence him. "Hey. That's okay, I don't need details." For me, the realities were enough.

"I best be getting outta here. My old place comes down this afternoon. Hell, there's a lot of memories being plowed under. Whole lot of people connected down here. Take that Slater guy—"

"Are you talking about John Slater?"

"That's him. The one that hugged that train up at Warm Springs. Well, he hung around down here at times. Just looking around like you're doing. Never said much, but this place had some kind of a draw for him. Don't know what. Maybe he knew her."

"Maybe he did." Slater. He'd been committed to the state mental hospital in Warm Springs for a ninety-day evaluation. He'd made it through ten, the day he stepped into the middle of the railroad track that ran through the grounds. No one could get to him in time.

"Like I said, memories won't be kept down."

"I hear you. Take care. Have you got somewhere to go?"

"Sure do. I got a room right on Montana Avenue. That town

noise is sure as hell going to be something to get used to. Know what I mean?"

"Well, good luck with it."

He looked at me oddly like he was shocked anyone would give a shit enough to ask. "Thanks. Thanks a lot. But you heed my words. They can tear this old place down and build their new shops. But those memories? They'll be here, right here." He kicked at the dirt with his shoe and walked off.

He was right. This *was* a place of memories. I walked to the last unit of the motel and stepped up. Bracing my hands on either side of the window, I looked in. Somewhere among the stench and the debris were Ellen's lifetime of memories. With the sun warming the air around me, my mind backtracked four months to the hard throes of winter.

On a night the wind howled through Billings, ripping trees limb from limb, scattering them broken but not quite dead upon the ground, Rosella Dahl died with only Grace Driscoll in attendance. Refusing, up to the end, any medication to ease her suffering, Rosella crucified herself on her pain and waited stoically for deliverance. Rosella had welcomed the cancer that ravaged her. In her own way, she embraced the very thing that devoured her and made it do her bidding, insisting that it give her something in return for what it was taking.

There was no reason for me to attend the funeral, but hundreds of others, from all over the state, did. I doubt I was missed. Robert Maitland turned it into a media event. And Grace, dear loyal Grace, succeeded in keeping alive the mystique surrounding Mrs. Dahl by sharing her at-the-very-end story with anyone who would listen. According to Grace, Rosella had lingered in a coma the last forty-eight hours of her life. Moments before her demise, however, she regained consciousness, smiled, reached out in front of her, and whispered, "I knew you'd come." The speculation as to just *who* came was the focus of many conversations. I had my own theories.

I hoped that someday I'd have the courage to tell my mother about Grace and the role she had played, one day long ago, in the basement of Dahl's House. But not now, the time just wasn't right. And someday, I hoped also that Frank's sister Becky would understand why I never went public with what I knew. Maybe by that time I would fully understand also.

Word got out, as it always does, that Rosella Dahl left Maitland two items in her will. The first, stated as a fulfillment of an earlier contractual agreement, was fifteen percent of the law firm. I wasn't surprised. If nothing else, Rosella kept her part of the pact. The second bequest was a material possession that had become her trademark, although I never saw it. It was an ebony walking stick with a brass eagle's head at the top. The stick ended up at auction with some furniture from Dahl's House. It didn't take any stretch of imagination to figure out why Maitland didn't want it.

I never kept up with Dorothy Valentine. I figured she'd probably continue to dress in neon colors and work the flaccid muscles of her geriatric charges. But the night would be her enemy as she sat and drank herself into oblivion under the mournful guidance of the blues.

The deep-throated growl of the bulldozer's engine heralded the return of the construction workers from their lunch. The sun felt good: It leached the smell of freshly turned soil from the gound. The dozer jerked and started forward. I didn't see the guy I had first encountered approach until he tapped me on the shoulder. I'd been thinking of Ellen's legacy and he startled me. I turned and looked into his shit-eating grin.

"Lady, now you really gotta get out of here. We start hitting this place and unless you want it to come down around your ears, haul it away."

"There's that *it* word again," I said as I walked away from the room where Ellen's memories ended.

He shrugged and walked away. A wall of orange moved toward me. I'd started to leave when something between the approaching bulldozer and the sagging porch caught my eye. I took a step forward to get a better look and there they were, pushing up through the debris-strewn soil. I dropped to my knees and blocked out the bellowing screams of warning from the dozer operator. The soil, soft and moist, gave way under my hands as I dug the golden clumps of Wallflowers from the earth. The roots loosened their grip as if they already knew there was a place for them on Ellen's grave.